CW01371985

AN OATH BETRAYED

MARK SEAMAN

The Book Guild Ltd

First published in Great Britain in 2024 by
The Book Guild Ltd
Unit E2 Airfield Business Park,
Harrison Road, Market Harborough,
Leicestershire. LE16 7UL
Tel: 0116 2792299
www.bookguild.co.uk
Email: info@bookguild.co.uk
X: @bookguild

Copyright © 2024 Mark Seaman

The right of Mark Seaman to be identified as the author of this
work has been asserted by them in accordance with the
Copyright, Design and Patents Act 1988.

All rights reserved. No part of this publication may be
reproduced, transmitted, or stored in a retrieval system, in any form or by any means,
without permission in writing from the publisher, nor be otherwise circulated in
any form of binding or cover other than that in which it is published and without
a similar condition being imposed on the subsequent purchaser.

This work is entirely fictitious and bears no resemblance to any persons living or dead.

Typeset in 11pt Minion Pro

Printed on FSC accredited paper
Printed and bound in Great Britain by 4edge Limited

ISBN 978 1835740 484

British Library Cataloguing in Publication Data.
A catalogue record for this book is available from the British Library.

For Lizzy, Joe, Lily and Dan.

Chapter One

I first met Karl when he moved in a few doors up the road from us in Canning Town. His father, Gustav, had worked as a docker in Hamburg but, following the strike there in 1896, he decided to seek new opportunities for himself and his family in London's rapidly expanding shipyards.

British ports were thriving around this time; witnessing a huge growth in both imported and exported goods, especially at our local dock, the Royal Victoria. There was plenty of work to be had, if you had the skills, strength, and experience required.

There had been earlier industrial action by dock workers in England over pay and conditions in 1889. At the time the national trade union for dockers and other affiliated groups were finding their feet and felt they'd garnered enough support to take on the paymasters of the day. With a growing membership, they were becoming increasingly militant in their actions against the previously all-powerful employers. Until then bosses had viewed their workforce as little more than paid lackeys, offering no formal employment rights, nor any reason to expect their demands for better wages and working conditions to be realised. This led to many of the dockers fearing the worst if the strike didn't succeed. But the union stuck fast and eventually the shipyard owners and associated authorities caved into the workers' demands. They agreed to pay what became known as the 'dockers' tanner', a penny increase in basic pay from five to six pence an hour. They also agreed to pay eight pence an hour for overtime.

The Victoria Dock was built in 1855 but changed its name to the Royal Victoria Dock in 1880. It was established alongside the River Thames in the London borough of Newham. This may have suited the authorities and dock owners, but did little to help the workforce, with the vast majority living some way from the dockyards themselves, at least in those early days. With little or no transport available to ferry workers to and from their place of work, a major housebuilding scheme was undertaken near to the port area itself. New settlements to house the dockers and their families were established locally in Hallsville, Woolwich, and Canning, which is where we lived. A lot of the building work was done on the cheap and, when complete, offered little more than slum conditions, with diseases such as cholera and smallpox running rife. Things improved slowly but because dock work was regarded, in the main, as casual, these settlements were never really awarded the attention they merited. Even so, the families who moved in did their best to make them home. And, whilst the powers that be may not have had much time for the residents of these communities, there was a definite feeling of camaraderie amongst the inhabitants themselves. Families made a point of looking out for each other and supporting one another as best they could.

That said, things were still tough in our house with Dad happy to show my sister Edith and I the back of his hand whenever the mood took him. Usually, this would be when he'd been drinking or rowing with Mum, both of which seemed to happen on a regular basis. Edith and I quickly learned to keep out of his way when he had a belly full of beer, or when the atmosphere became tense between him and Mum. However, things took a definite upward turn, certainly as far as I was concerned, once

Karl arrived. He and his parents, Gustav and Anna, moved in during the summer of 1898. They were immediately warm and welcoming, with Karl and I becoming the best of friends in no time.

Mum told me later their decision to move to England was also motivated by Anna losing a baby girl in childbirth around the time of the strike in Germany. This had served as an additional incentive for them to get away and start again. And, with both of them speaking good English, they decided London might provide the new beginning they were looking for. Anna also had distant family connections in England, although they lived in Yorkshire and only communicated by letter. The cost of travelling to visit each other would have been beyond them financially, certainly in those early days when simply surviving was challenge enough. Even so, having family already settled in the country helped in their decision-making when considering the move for themselves.

That said, life in Canning Town in 1898 was tough for everyone, whatever their hopes and expectations. Daily existence was pretty much hand to mouth. There was a lot of overcrowding, and little or no access to running water for the majority of residents. Toilets were built outside, offering less than efficient sanitary conditions for the two or more families forced to share them. Drainage was also a problem, and when toilets overflowed, as they often did, rats moved in, leaving even more filth and disease in their wake.

There were no designated green areas for us children to play in either, just the odd patch of wasteland. This meant we often met in the road outside our houses to kick a ball about or jump over a skipping rope. The roads themselves were often little more than dirt tracks and so by the time we arrived home we were usually covered from head to toe in mud or smelling to high heaven after falling into a pile of horse manure. As youngsters we never really viewed this as a problem. We were just happy to be outside, running around with our friends. If an accident happened or we fell headlong into a muddy puddle, or worse, then so be it. That said, you were rarely first choice for any team games if you were unlucky enough to fall victim to the ultimate street mess, dog muck. Falling into a pile of that assured you of being shunned by pretty much everyone. I can remember Edith and I getting the occasional clip round the ear from Mum for coming home with dog mess on our clothes. In the main though, she would just sigh and wash us down as best she could, reminding us not to say anything to Dad. We didn't need to be told that twice. We knew if he found out we really would be in trouble. If I'm honest, it was usually me who got dirty or fell into something smelly. Edith was always better behaved than me and tried to keep her clothes clean. Mainly she wore threadbare jumpers and shorts, the same as me, but she did have one dress, for Sunday best. I never understood why it was called that as we never went anywhere on a Sunday for her to wear it, or any other day come to that. We certainly never went to church. Dad said vicars were just a load of 'God-botherers'. He'd get quite animated about it. 'If there really is a God, then why doesn't he come down and give those bloody shipyard owners a kick up the arse and tell them to pay us poor buggers a decent wage.'

Church or not, Edith loved that dress. It was pale blue with yellow flowers on. She would sometimes put it on just to cheer herself up if she'd had a bad day, or if Dad had been shouting at us. 'I just want to feel pretty for a while,' she would say. 'Putting my dress on reminds me not everything in the world is dirty or horrid.' Mum must have understood what she meant as she was happy for her to wear it for a while, but always made her take it off again when Dad was around just in case it caused another argument. I didn't have anything special to wear, certainly not what you would call Sunday best, except for a grey shirt I would put on under my jumper, but even that had a rip in the collar. I always seemed to be tearing my clothes or getting them grubby.

This would result in me getting a lecture from Mum and yet another reminder to keep out of Dad's way.

'No point in upsetting your father, Harry,' she would say. 'He'll have had a tough day at work as it is, without learning you've put another hole in those trousers of yours.'

What she really meant was, if he did find out, it wouldn't be a simple clip round the ear I'd get but a proper beating, depending on how much he'd had to drink or how tough his shift had been. When I was very young, I used to think Dad was unhappy all the time and I would try to keep quiet or stay out of his way whenever he was at home. It was only as I got a bit older I learnt about his drinking and how his temper worsened whenever he had a skinful.

I was approaching my fifth birthday when I first saw him hit Mum, or at least first subjected it to memory. Up until then she'd managed to keep Edith and I out of the way when things got too bad. We'd been aware of them rowing on and off for a couple of years but were too young to fully comprehend what was happening. We knew we didn't like it though and would cover our ears or hide whenever they started yelling at each other. Edith might have been a year older than me, but it frightened her as well. We talked about Dad's moods and violent outbursts as we grew older, but at that age we were just trying to survive as best we could, and so not talking about it or hiding seemed the best thing to do. And, being too young to know any better, we just presumed all parents argued and shouted at each other. It was what grown-ups did. That said, when they were really going at one another, and Dad was laying into Mum, Edith and I would run to our bedroom and put our heads under a pillow to drown out the screams, our own as well as Mum's.

Whilst we learnt early on not to give Dad any encouragement to turn his attention towards us, it wasn't always possible to avoid his violent behaviour. I remember one particular occasion when Edith and I became the unwilling recipients of his aggression.

Edith had been at a friend's house while I'd been playing outside with Karl. I arrived home covered in mud, with a graze on my knee and a small cut on my arm after falling against a neighbour's wall.

Mum tutted and washed me down, reminding me, yet again, to be more careful the next time.

'Honestly, Harry, you've got more bruises on you than a boxer. The neighbours will think I've been giving you a beating at this rate. You're getting to be a big boy now, and big boys don't go falling about all the time and hurting themselves.'

'Sorry, Mum, but it was Karl, he knocked me over.' This wasn't entirely true, but it was easier to blame my friend than admit to being clumsy. Mum saw through that line of defence immediately.

'Well, I'm not sure I believe that. Karl doesn't strike me as the sort of boy to push his friends around. Are you sure you weren't just showing off and being silly?'

Rather than admit to the truth I stuck to my story. 'No, Mum, honest, it was Karl.' She looked at me knowingly. I felt my face colouring up. 'Although, it was an accident, he didn't mean to,' I added, hoping I'd modified my narrative enough to avoid further questioning.

'Just as I thought.' Ruffling my hair, she laughed. 'Honestly, you boys, what are you like.'

I felt safe with Mum and always enjoyed time alone with her. I'd never really considered it before, but now I was that bit older I was beginning to understand when Dad was around the atmosphere at home was different. Mum didn't joke with Edith and I so much, and there felt a pressure on the two of us to keep on his good side. If Dad was happy, then Mum was more relaxed as well.

This particular afternoon, Dad came home early but had still found time to visit the pub on his way. Mum was washing me down as the front door slammed shut. I felt her stiffen at the sound. A door being slammed in our house was never a good sign.

'That'll be your dad. Now remember, Harry, don't say anything about hurting yourself. We don't want to upset him.'

Mum rushed to wipe the last of the blood and mud from me as the sitting-room door swung open.

Still smiling at me, she spoke without turning. 'Hello, love, you're home early. Everything all right at work?'

'Bloody foreman sent me out. Said he had too many on shift, and the rest of the load wouldn't be ready to come off the ship till tomorrow. So that's me down on my hours again.' Running his coat-sleeve under his nose, Dad nodded in my direction. 'What's the matter with him?'

Mum pulled me into her. 'Nothing, he just came in a bit early himself. He'd got a bit mucky, so I was giving him a quick wash down, that's all.'

Shaking his head, he pointed to my arm. 'It doesn't look like nothing. The boy's got a cut on him. How did that happen?'

Sensing the potential for an argument, Mum tried to diffuse the situation by making light of my injury. 'He's fine, it's just a graze. He fell over playing that's all. You know what these lads are like. You're all right aren't you, Harry?'

I looked at her and smiled, equally aware of the tension in Dad's voice. 'Yes, I'm fine.' Raising my arm, I waved it in the air. 'See, it doesn't hurt.'

Stepping forward, Dad grabbed me by the shoulder. 'You look at me not your mother when I'm talking to you, do you hear?'

I could feel tears sting my eyes. 'Sorry, Dad, I didn't know you were talking to me. I thought you asked Mum what had happened.'

I felt a sharp slap to the back of my head. 'Don't answer me back either you little shit or you'll be sorry you did.'

Mum stood up, pushing me behind her. 'That's enough, Alf; Harry didn't mean anything wrong. He just fell over and gave himself a bit of a bump that's all. Like he said, no real harm done, he's fine.'

I looked on from behind Mum's legs as Dad raised his hand and took another step forward. 'Don't you tell me enough. Who do you think you are? This is my house, and you do as I say, all of you.'

I felt Mum rock backwards as his fist connected with her face. I screamed out in her defence.

'Dad, don't. Please don't hit Mum, she...' I felt another blow to my head.

'I've told you already, boy, don't answer me back.'

I looked at Mum, blood running from her nose. 'Please Alf, not in front of the lad.'

He threw another fist at Mum, catching her on the shoulder as she moved her head out of the way. Reaching out a hand, she pushed me to one side. 'Get yourself upstairs, Harry. Your dad's not feeling very well. He'll be all right soon. Go on now, get along.'

I rushed to the door with Dad's voice ringing in my ears.

'That's right, you run away you little sod, but I'll be up to sort you out when I've finished with your cow of a mother here.'

With tears streaming down my face and my heart thumping in my chest I ran upstairs as fast as I could. As I entered the bedroom, I could hear yelling and the crashing of furniture from below. Clambering onto the bed, I buried my head beneath a pillow. I'd heard Dad shouting at Mum in the past, even threatening to beat her on occasion, but this time it was different. I'd never seen him hit her so forcefully before. I was scared. We may not have gone to church but, in that moment, I was more than happy to give God a chance if he was real. 'Please God, don't let him hurt my mummy,' I whimpered, pulling the pillow tightly around my head.

I was nearly five years old, but that afternoon a small part of me grew from a young boy into a man. It was bad enough having my dad beat me; all children where we lived got a hiding occasionally, but when I saw him hit Mum that day, something changed in our relationship. I didn't understand what exactly, but, young as I was, I knew I had to try and protect her from it happening again. Sadly, it would happen again, many times in the years ahead, and for much of that period I would still be too young, physically, to do anything about it. I would shout at him, declaring Mum's innocence, for which I would also receive a whipping. When drink had a hold of my father there was no reasoning with him. Over the years to come I would learn to despise both him and the effects of alcohol in equal measure.

Chapter Two

I was around four when Karl moved to Canning Town. Although German was his native tongue, his parents had also encouraged him to learn English, prior to their move. His mother, Anna, had worked for an engineering company in Germany before Karl was born. They did quite a bit of business with other countries across Europe, including England. She had learnt to speak English for her work and had taught it to Karl's dad. Even in those early days of cross-border travel and relations, English was still an internationally recognised language. Having a basic understanding of it certainly helped encourage Karl's parents in their decision to move to London. Although he wasn't fluent in the early days of our relationship, Karl and I got on famously from the start, despite him being nearly a year older than me. Over the next few years we became inseparable, especially as Karl's English improved. His father, Gustav, or Gus as he became known locally, worked with my dad on the docks. In the early days the two of them got on okay, but over time their relationship cooled. This was mainly due to Dad's drinking, temper, and unreliability at work. Gustav was a big friendly man with a ready smile, especially for us children. I liked him immediately and wished my dad could have been as accepting of the mess we made, or of the dirt we brought into the house after we'd been playing outside.

'It's only a bit of mud, it will soon wash off. Let them be,' he would say with a laugh. 'Boys will be boys. There are worse things they could bring into the house than a bit of dirt.'

Anna was equally as accepting and kind, just like my mum. I think that's why the two of them got on so well. Karl and I would often find them talking together outside one of our houses when we came in at the end of the day.

They would laugh and point towards us. 'Here they come, look at the two of them. It's hard to tell them apart with all that muck on their faces.'

'You're right there, Anna. If I wash my one down and find it's Karl, I'll send him back to you, and you can do the same with Harry.'

The two of us would protest. 'Mum, you know it's me, I've got darker hair than Karl.'

'And Harry is uglier than me,' Karl would retort. This would set us off again, pushing one another playfully as our mothers attempted to separate us and take us inside.

'That's enough for today, you can play again tomorrow.'

'Okay Mum. Bye Karl, see you later.'

'Goodbye, Harry.'

Sometimes, if it wasn't too late, Anna would ask if I wanted to have tea with them so Karl and I could carry on playing for a while. I loved spending time at their house, it always felt friendly, warm, and welcoming. Even when Gustav came in from work there was laughter, not the tension experienced at ours when Dad arrived home. None of us could ever be sure what sort of a mood he would be in.

'Hello, Anna, I am home,' Gustav would shout as he closed the front door. Noticing Karl and I, he would wink at the two of us. 'I see we have adopted another boy into our family. Where did you find him?'

Karl's mum would enter from the scullery, laughing. 'You know very well it's Harry, stop teasing the boy. And before you ask, yes, he is staying for his tea. I told Florence it would be all right. She is teaching Edith to knit, and I was sure Harry would not be interested in that.'

Young as I was, I was fully aware of the kindness and consideration being shown to our family. Anna knew there was little to spare in our house, especially with Dad drinking most of our money away. She would often bring a pie, or half a cake round to ours, saying she had baked too much, and it would only go to waste. The tearful look of appreciation in Mum's eyes said all that Edith and I needed to know. Without Anna's generosity we might well have gone hungry that day, as would often be the case when Dad had been drinking.

'Thank you, Anna, that's very kind. But you shouldn't...'

Anna would smile and wave away Mum's protests. 'It is nothing, Florence, really. You are helping me out. Anyway, you would do the same for me, wouldn't you?'

Mum would smile and hug Anna. 'You're such a good friend to me.' Looking down at Edith and I, she would add, 'To all of us. Thank you.'

Karl's parents rarely talked about their time in Germany before moving to England. And when they did most of it passed over our heads. As children, Karl and I were too young to care, or show any real interest in the period before the two of us had met. Clearly though, from the little we did understand, it was obvious things had been difficult for them in Hamburg. Even with conditions at the docks here in London being tough, they still felt they would have a greater chance of making a better life for themselves in England. I didn't care what had brought them to Canning Town, I was just grateful they were here and that Karl and I were friends.

Gustav would usually knock for Dad when they were both working the same early shift. I soon learnt this was because it would give Mum a valid reason to wake Dad rather than let him stay in bed, which he would often do if he'd been drinking the night before. If he missed the start of a shift the supervisors would get somebody else to fill Dad's place and he would have no work that day. This would send him into a spiral of anger and frustration at how unfairly he was being treated, which, in turn, would see him head to The Blue Anchor to drown his sorrows. All of which meant we would be without a day's wages, along with the additional money he would spend at the pub.

Mum was embarrassed that Gustav and Anna were cognisant of Dad's drinking, and of the unreasonable behaviour he displayed towards his family at times. That said, she was equally grateful for their support. Also, for the fact they never gossiped to others in the street about what went on in our house, although it was highly unlikely most of our neighbours weren't already aware of how much Mum had to put up with.

She was a proud woman, but not too proud to accept help when it was offered, especially if it meant her children would be fed and clothed. And so, Mum was always grateful to hear that knock on the door first thing in the morning when Gustav called for Dad.

'Good morning, Florence,' he would say, doffing his cap in deference to her. 'Is Alf ready?'

Mum would smile, accepting Gustav's knowing wink as a sign of support and understanding that Dad probably wasn't even out of bed yet.

'I'll just get him. Come in for a minute,' she would reply, wiping her hands on her slightly stained pinafore. 'I'm sure he won't be long.' This was another ruse Mum had worked out with Gustav and Anna to avoid confrontation. If Gustav was in the house, it was less likely Dad would kick off at her for waking him.

Edith and I would stay in our beds, pulling the covers up around us as we listened to Dad cursing next door as he stumbled around the bedroom getting dressed. Mum would be downstairs again with Gustav making Dad a sandwich to take with him. That was presuming we had some bread in the house, which often we didn't. Even when there was little food to be had, Mum would always manage to conjure up something for Dad to take to work. Experience had taught her, if he was sent out without some form of sustenance for his lunch, she would be the one to suffer for it when he got home.

Gustav would smile knowingly as he watched Mum search desperately for something to give Dad to eat with his cup of tea. Again, she knew the consequences of sending him out on an empty stomach, even though the fault would be his, having spent the last of our money on drink.

'Don't worry, Florence,' he would say. 'Anna has made too many sandwiches for me this morning, Alf can have one of mine.'

As I grew and reflected on those early days, I reasoned Dad was probably a bit of a coward. He appeared quite happy to show Mum, Edith, and I the back of his hand, but rarely lost his temper with Gustav or the other men at the docks, unless he was drunk. Once he was full of alcohol anybody was fair game for his unreasonable and aggressive behaviour. He would also blame us for his shortcomings as a husband and father, with Mum receiving the brunt of those accusations and the resulting retribution.

Eventually, we would hear Dad stomp down the stairs into the sitting room.

'Apologies, Gus, I would have been ready earlier, but Flo forgot to wake me. Bloody women, eh? You think you've got them trained and they can't even do a simple thing like get you up in time for work.' Then he would look at Mum, adding sarcastically, 'You won't forget to ask for my money though, when I get home, will you?'

Mum would force a smile while Gustav looked to the floor in an effort not to respond. They both knew the truth; but equally, that it was easier to let the moment pass rather than inflame

Dad's ire. This would only ensure she would be in trouble yet again when he returned home later in the day.

Edith and I would wait until we heard the front door close before getting up to join Mum downstairs. Even if we were desperate for the toilet, we still wouldn't leave our room until Dad had gone; we'd learned that lesson early on, often to our cost. Incurring Dad's wrath first thing in the morning before his head had cleared was almost guaranteed to earn you a clout round the ear or, at the very least, a verbal battering with the promise of worse to come when he got back later in the day. If we simply couldn't wait, we'd take it in turns to use the pot under our bed while the other one looked the other way. Better this brief moment of embarrassment, than a sore ear or backside for the rest of the morning.

Life in Karl's house was noticeably different. Yes, money was tight, and Karl got into trouble with his parents like all of us kids did, but there was also love and laughter in that house, you could sense it in every room. Of course, Mum loved Edith and I, neither of us doubted that, but it was often more a form of protective love, designed to keep us safe from Dad and his violent outbursts. Any display of natural affection between us was kept for when he wasn't around. We rarely laughed openly in Dad's company or said the silly things that children often do in front of their parents. If we did, it would often be met with some form of criticism or reprisal depending on his mood at the time.

In Karl's house we were encouraged to be children and express ourselves. At home, when Dad was around, the total opposite was true.

'Can't you keep those bloody kids quiet, Flo, I'm trying to read the paper,' was a regular protest if Edith and I were playing anywhere near him. And when he'd been drinking, he often wouldn't bother consulting with Mum before yelling at the two of us or removing his broad leather belt and threatening to beat us with it.

'Shut up the two of you, or you'll get the benefit of this round your arses.'

Whilst he might hold back from physically admonishing Edith, in response to Mum's appeal that she was a girl, those same petitions for clemency on my behalf rarely met with success.

'He's a boy, Flo, and has to learn some home truths, even at his age. I don't want my son turning into some soft excuse for a man when he grows up, just because his mother says he shouldn't feel my belt across his backside when he's been up to no good.' Sometimes, when things threatened to get out of hand, I would run up the road to Karl's house.

Anna would usher me in, sensing all was not well at home. I would pretend everything was fine and that I'd simply come round to see my friend, but we both knew the truth. In later years I realised, witnessing a little boy shaking in front of her, fighting back his tears, told a very different story to the one I was purporting to be true. She was already aware of how bad things could get at our house from previous conversations she'd had with Mum. She had also noted the occasional telltale bruise on her arms or black eye. I'm sure she and Gustav would have volunteered to step in and take Dad to task over his violence towards us but, I'm equally certain, Mum would have begged them not to. She knew, had they done so, even greater reprisals would have been meted out against the three of us once they were no longer around.

'Come in, Harry,' she would say, her broad smile encouraging me to believe kindness still existed in the world, and that whilst in her home, I would be safe and cared for. 'Karl will be pleased to see you.' Then she would laugh, adding, 'Honestly, you two boys. I wonder sometimes what you did before you became friends; you are never apart.'

Hearing my voice, Karl would come bouncing into the hallway, a huge smile across his face. He would have no idea as to the real reason behind my visit of course, he was just happy to see me.

'Come up to my room, Harry, we can play with my marbles.'

I'd never seen marbles before Karl arrived. He'd brought them with him from Hamburg. They were already popular in Germany, having become a children's favourite from the day they were first introduced. It would be some time before they reached the same level of popularity in England. He had a large assortment of the tiny glass balls, all with different colours swirling around inside them.

Again, Anna would smile at the two of us. 'Go on then, off you go. But be careful not to leave them on the floor when you have finished playing. I nearly fell over the other day when I trod on one.'

'We promise, Mama.'

Scampering up the wooden stairs we would hear her calling after us, 'Don't run or you might have an accident.'

We would apologise before turning to each other and laughing as we cleared the last few steps in double time.

'I suppose you would both like some cake as well?'

I was always grateful when Karl answered yes, as I would often still be hungry, having not had as much to eat as I might have liked at home. Again, as I discovered in later years, the little food Mum was able to prepare for Edith and I often came at a cost to herself. She knew Dad would brook no excuse if there wasn't a hot meal ready for him when he arrived home, whatever time that might be. Even though most of his wages were spent on beer, he still expected his tea on the table when he got back. If there wasn't a full plate placed in front of him at the end of his shift, Mum knew all too well what the consequences would be. Daring to imply there wasn't enough money to pay for it would be viewed as direct criticism of him, and the resultant beating she would receive for speaking out was one she'd learnt not to encourage, no matter how well-founded her argument.

Whatever Mum could eke out from any money left was used to feed Edith and I, meaning she often went to bed on an empty stomach.

Unaware of the passing of time, Karl and I would play happily in his room for ages, feasting on cake and milk, until Anna came to say it was time for me to go. This usually meant Mum had called round to say things had calmed down at home, or that Dad had gone to The Blue Anchor, in which case I should come back and get ready for bed before he returned.

I was too young to feel ashamed of what went on in our house but was still aware I didn't like it. I couldn't understand why Edith and I weren't allowed just to be children, well-fed and happy as Karl appeared to be. We never blamed Mum for the way things were. Indeed, without her love and protection I'm not sure what Edith and I would have done. And, as time went on, the two of us lost virtually all respect we might have once held for Dad; even to the point of resenting the fact he was our father.

The two of us learnt, from an early age, how to survive, even if that meant lying or closing our eyes to some of the things we saw or were subjected to. The greatest pain for us was in watching Mum receive the full brunt of Dad's hostility, especially when attempting to defend the two of us. Witnessing her take a beating for some childish indiscretion we may have committed was often too much to bear. We would cry ourselves to sleep in the knowledge that Mum had stepped in, yet again, to accept some senseless and unwarranted aggression on our behalf.

Seeing Mum hurt was particularly hard for me as a boy. I felt I should step up and protect her in some way. I struggled at times not to lash out in her defence. However, I knew if I did, not only would Dad lay into me, but he would also make Mum pay an even harsher penalty for my childish attempts at interfering.

Things would ultimately take a darker and more sinister turn for the worse, with Dad eventually destroying any last hope of a normal family life between us. But for now, all we could do was try and survive, as best we could, his unmerited aggression and corresponding bouts of violence towards us.

Chapter Three

Whilst life at home was often dominated by the challenge of evading the consequences of Dad's unpredictable temper, much of the rest of the time was spent playing with Edith or teasing her. This was especially true as she began to grow and become more aware of herself as a young woman. In the main, we got on well. I think this was partly because of the built-in defence system we developed for each other whenever Dad was around. There were also occasions when Mum felt able to smile without fear and just enjoy spending time with the two of us. These fleeting moments of normality meant so much, and not just to Edith and I but to Mum as well. We held them dear in our hearts, acting as a shield against the harsher reality of life whenever Dad was in one of his moods.

For me personally though, the happiest memories of my childhood were of times spent with Karl. We hit it off from the day we met, even becoming blood brothers to validate the lifelong commitment we made to one another. In hindsight, I wonder if we viewed the concept of this vow as being more attractive than the physical act itself.

It was a sunny afternoon in the summer of 1903 when we made our pact. I was eight and Karl was about to celebrate his ninth birthday. We'd been playing football in the street. I was in goal and Karl had been taking penalties against me. The goalposts were made from our jumpers screwed into a ball and placed on the brown wooden window ledges between two houses. The goal itself was the brick wall dividing the houses behind me. All the houses in our street looked the same; fading red brickwork with equally tired-looking window frames, many of which were beginning to peel or rot. Getting the hired labour onto the docks to load or unload the ships had been the employers' first priority when the houses were originally built. There had been little prior thought or care given to any specific building regulations required for the safe erection of these properties, nor to their overall suitability for human habitation. Not that any of that bothered Karl and I as we prepared for our penalty shootout in the heat of that summer's day.

'Are you ready, Harry, I'm really going to hit this one hard,' Karl shouted as he ran up to strike the old leather ball his dad had given us. Gustav had played football in Germany for a while but didn't have the time anymore, and rather than have the ball gather dust under the stairs he'd given it to us boys to play with. We were thrilled to have it and, being a real football, were the envy of many of the other boys living in our street. Most ball games were played by kicking a tin can around or even an old piece of clothing that had been rolled up and tied together. Even if there was a ball available, it would usually be a small handball, not ideal for kicking around or taking penalties with. Karl and I carried that football with pride, rarely letting the other boys play with it unless we could be the team captains and choose those we wanted to play on our side. Another reason for not letting this spherical leather treasure out of our sight was that it had come with a stern warning from Karl's dad.

'Now listen you two, this is not a toy. It is a proper football and if it hits somebody it will hurt them. You must play with it carefully. And, whatever you do, do not kick it where there are little children or babies around. Do you understand?'

Grinning, we nodded enthusiastically. 'Yes Papa, we understand, don't we, Harry?'

'Yes, Mr Schmidt.'

I'm not sure either of us were considering this directive as Karl launched himself at the ball that afternoon; with me leaping to my left to save it. Trying to kick it as hard as possible meant Karl lost control of his aim, and with me failing to stop the shot, the ball crashed into the door of Mr and Mrs Porter's house. They lived just up the road from Karl. The brown wooden door rattled on its hinges as the ball connected with it. Karl and I looked at each other and smiled, mainly from the relief of it not hitting a window. As I moved to retrieve the ball, Mrs Porter opened her front door and glowered at the two of us.

'You two, I might have known. You're like two peas in a pod, both as bad as the other, banging on my front door like that. You nearly scared me half to death. I've a good mind to tell your mothers what you've done, then you won't be smiling will you?'

I was the first to speak, mainly because I knew if word of our footballing misdemeanours got back to Dad, it wouldn't just be a telling-off I'd be getting.

'We're really sorry, Mrs Porter. It was an accident, honest. We weren't aiming at your door, Karl just slipped, that's all. We didn't mean it. We won't do it again, please don't tell our mums.'

Most of the street knew about Dad's temper, including Mrs Porter. Although she was upset, she certainly wouldn't have wanted to see me get a beating for what had been a genuine accident.

With no real harm done, other than making her jump, she shook her head in mock derision and proffered a knowing grin.

'Go on then, be off with you. But if it happens again, I will say something. Thank goodness you're not brothers. Having one of you must be bad enough for your mothers, but two of you, well, I shudder to think about it, honest I do.'

It was Karl's turn to make good our apology. 'Thank you, Mrs Porter. Like Harry said, we are very sorry.'

Waving a fist playfully in our direction, she moved back inside and closed the front door.

'That was a bit of luck. She's all right is Mrs P. Let's go up the street a bit just in case. And next time don't try and knock my bloomin' head off when you kick the ball.'

Moving further up the road, we laid our ragged woollen goalposts against the wall of a house at the corner of our street. Being a side wall meant there was no front door to hit. And with the only window exposed to our scoring efforts being on the first floor, some fifteen feet or so off the ground, there was considerably less likelihood of another accident. As with the other window frames in our street this one was equally dilapidated and in need of varnishing or a fresh coat of paint. This was true for the front doors as well, but with little money available for nearly everyone who lived there, additional funding for decorating was a luxury few could afford. Encouraged by the reduced prospect of upsetting another of our neighbours we prepared to kick off.

'This is much better,' declared Karl. 'We should have come here before. I will go in goal this time, Harry. You can try to score against me.' Laughing, he added, 'I bet you won't though, I am a better goalie than you.'

We played happily for the next half an hour or so until Mum called out to the two of us as she made her way up the street.

'I was beginning to wonder where you boys were, you've been gone for ages. Karl, your mother says it's time for your tea. And I'll have you in as well, please, Harry. It looks like rain's on the way, and I don't want you out here getting wet.'

'Okay, Mum, but can we just finish our game? We've got two more penalties each to see who the winner is.'

Laughing, she turned back towards our house. 'All right, but don't be long, I know what you two are like.'

'Thanks, Mum, five minutes, honest.'

'I'll tell your mother, Karl. But remember, five minutes and no more.'

'Thank you, Mrs Thompson, I will make sure Harry is not late.'

Picking up the ball, I moved to Karl and punched him playfully on the arm. 'Flippin' cheek. You're the one who's always late, not me.'

The next few minutes were spent taking the deciding penalties. Thankfully, with me scoring the winner. We may have been young, but having the bragging rights over the other one meant a lot, even at our age.

'So, you're the better goalie than me, are you? I don't think so.'

Pushing me to one side as he grabbed the ball, Karl laughed. 'I will win next time; you see if I don't.'

As we walked home past Mrs Porter's house, Karl nodded towards her front door.

'You know what she said about us being like brothers? Well, we could be if you wanted.'

'Brothers? I don't understand. What do you mean?'

'We could become blood brothers. You know, we cut our hands and hold them together so our blood mixes. Then we would be brothers, in blood at least.'

I didn't much fancy the idea of cutting myself, whatever the prize. I'd got into trouble the last time I'd fallen over and grazed my knee, so the thought of wounding myself on purpose didn't sound like a good idea at all.

'I'm not sure about that, Karl. I mean I'm happy to be your best friend and all that but… cutting our hands! What would our mums say for starters, let alone our dads.

Mine would kill me; I can tell you that for nothing.'

Karl laughed again. 'You are such a coward, Harry. I don't mean a big cut, just a small one.'

Still unsure, I shook my head. 'I don't know. And like I said, my dad'll kill me if I go in bleeding and all.'

'Just tell him it was an accident. He can't kill you for having an accident.'

I shook my head again. 'You don't know him. When Dad loses his temper, nobody wants to be around, least of all me. I've told you what he's like. And I'm not a coward either.'

'You are if you are too scared to make a small cut on your finger.' He looked directly at me. 'Or maybe you don't want to be my brother.'

'That's not fair, it's just...'

Stopping outside his house, Karl interrupted. 'Come on, Harry, don't be such a baby, it's just one little cut. And afterwards we will be brothers forever, for the rest of our lives.'

I really liked the idea of Karl and I being brothers. After all, nobody could be any closer than the two of us were already. And, like he said, it would only be a small cut, not much more than a scratch really. What was the worst that could happen if Dad did find out? I'd get a beating. I'd already had more than my share of those over the past few years, so what would one more matter?'

I felt a grin spread across my face. 'Go on then, I'll do it.'

Karl's face lit up. 'Great. I know where my father keeps his penknife, I will bring it tomorrow and we can do it then.'

As he spoke, his mum opened the front door. 'There you are. Florence said you would be home a few minutes ago.'

Karl looked up and laughed. 'I know, Mama, and I'm sorry, it was Harry's fault. You know what he is like. I told him we should come home, but he said it would be all right and that we should keep playing.'

Taking his arm and pulling him towards her, she smiled. 'Karl Schmidt, don't tell such fibs. I am sure it would have been the other way around. Harry is a good boy and always does what his mother tells him, don't you, Harry?'

Grinning as she winked at me, I was happy to join in and enjoy Karl's discomfiture at her quip. 'Of course, Mrs Schmidt, I always do what Mum says.'

'You see, Karl. And how polite Harry is as well. Now come in and have your tea before Papa gets back from the dock; he will be home soon.'

Listening to her, I realised Dad should be arriving around the same time. I knew if I was late back it could mean trouble. Sometimes he wouldn't get home at the same time as Gustav, but that was usually because he'd stopped off at The Blue Anchor, as opposed to him having done any overtime. Edith and I knew if he'd had a few drinks and we weren't ready for bed when he came in, we really would be in for it. Mum would equally pay a price for not having his meal on the table and the two of us out of his way. I looked at Karl and his mum, the smile on my face fading as I spoke.

'I'd better go now as well, Mrs Schmidt, I don't want to…'

Fully cognisant of the reason for the hasty change in my demeanour she interjected. 'Of course, off you go, Harry. We will see you tomorrow no doubt.'

Turning to leave, I glanced affectionately at my friend. 'Bye Karl.'

Waving as I moved away, he grinned. 'Goodbye, my brother.'

I heard the front door close behind me as I moved down the street. Karl and I may have lived just a few doors apart but, for me, it often felt like we were from different worlds. I knew within the hour Karl's father would be home, and love and laughter would fill their house. The best I could hope for was that Dad might come in on time, sober and have had a good day at work. If that happened it might mean he would be more tolerant of Edith and I, and of Mum too, without finding the need to berate us for some undeclared reason, other than things weren't to his liking, which they often weren't when he'd been drinking.

As I ran up the alleyway by the side of our house I bumped into our next-door neighbour, Mrs Winter. She had been widowed a few months earlier when her husband had fallen off a ladder while repairing a leak on their roof. He'd worked at the docks as well but now, without his wages coming in, she was struggling to make ends meet. Mum always tried to help wherever she could but, with little to spare already in our house, there wasn't a lot we could do. Some of the other neighbours pitched in as well when funds allowed but again, with finances tight for pretty much everyone, the story was often the same for them. The rumour was she was going to move to Bristol to live with her son. He'd married a girl from the area and was working locally in one of the storehouses by the docks; something to do with importing tobacco I think Mum had said. Even though I didn't have a lot to do with her, I knew Mum liked Mrs Winter and so I tried to be polite whenever I spoke to her. She was a nice lady; kind to Edith and I, especially if she knew Dad had been drinking. Before her husband died, they would occasionally take us in and give us a cup of tea and a biscuit until things quietened down at home. Even now she was on her own she still kept an eye out for the two of us.

I wasn't thinking about that, or indeed anything apart from getting home before Dad as I hurtled round the corner at the top of the alleyway.

'Hello, Harry, where are you rushing off to?' she said with a laugh. 'Late for your tea, I expect.'

'Sorry, Mrs Winter,' I mumbled, extricating myself from her apron. 'Yes, Mum called me a few minutes ago and I've just run back from Karl's.'

Tousling my hair and patting me on the head, she laughed again. 'Well, you'd better get inside then. I don't want to be the one getting you into trouble by keeping you out.'

Smiling, whilst attempting to straighten my hair, I pulled away. 'Thanks, Mrs Winter, see you later.'

'Goodbye, Harry. Enjoy your tea and tell your mum I'll see her tomorrow.'

Grasping the handle on our back door, I waved my goodbyes. 'Will do.'

Running into the kitchen, I slipped on the newly polished red tiling and landed on my backside, much to the delight of Edith who was helping prepare the tea.

'Mum's told you about running in the house before, serves you right. I hope you're arse hurts.'

I was about to respond when Mum walked in from the sitting room.

'I heard that, Edith. We don't use language like that in this house, thank you very much.' Laughing, she looked down at me. 'What Edith meant to say was, I hope your bottom hurts, and that next time you'll remember not to run around like some demented animal, especially not on my nice clean floor.'

Grinning and rubbing myself down, I got to my feet. 'Thanks a lot, both of you. I could have really hurt myself then.'

'And if you had, maybe you'd have learnt the lesson to walk in the house, not run. Now wash your hands in the sink here, your tea's ready. I want you both fed before your dad comes in. He said he'd be early tonight, and I don't wany any arguments when he does get home, do you hear?'

'Yes, Mum.'

Surprisingly, Dad kept his word this particular evening and came in just as Edith and I were helping Mum clear away our tea things. The three of us froze momentarily on hearing the back door close, waiting for him to speak. Each of us knew those first few words would set the mood for the evening ahead.

'Evening, family. I hope you two have left something for me to eat,' he said, looking down at Edith and I, along with the empty plates in our hands.

We glanced towards Mum, noticing the obvious expression of relief on her face at hearing the agreeable tone in Dad's voice.

'Hello, love, nice to have you home early.' Allowing herself a smile as she wiped her hands down the front of her faded blue apron, she continued, 'There's plenty left for you, Alf. I wouldn't let you go hungry would I, not after a hard day's work?'

Acknowledging appreciation at the reference to his role as breadwinner for the family and head of the house, he nodded.

'No, you wouldn't, Flo, at least I hope not. A man's mood can turn a bit if he's left with an empty stomach, especially after a shift like I've put in today.'

And when he's had too much to drink, I thought, laying the plates I was holding on the wooden draining board next to the sink.

Turning to make my way back to the sitting room, I felt a slap to the back of my head.

'You're quiet, boy, cat got your tongue? You've usually got plenty to say for yourself.'

Rubbing my head, I turned and smiled. 'I'm fine, Dad, just a bit tired, that's all.'

Laughing, he looked down at me. 'Tired? What have you got to be tired about? It's the school holidays. Hardest thing you'll have done today will be playing with your mates I should think. I'd put money on you not helping your mum with any of the household chores.'

Pre-empting any desire on my part to answer back, Mum interjected. 'I've managed fine with Edith. Harry'd only get under our feet anyway; better he's out of the way. He's been playing football with Karl. Probably meant he's tired from all the running around they've been doing.' She looked at me, a sense of pleading in her eyes. 'That's what you meant, isn't it, Harry?'

Acknowledging Mum's appeal for harmony, I smiled and nodded tamely. 'Yes, that's right. I've just been running around with Karl.'

Rolling his shoulders in an effort to further assert his authority, Dad grinned. 'Wish I could kick a ball about with my mates all day, that'd be a bloody picnic compared to the work I've been doing. Just wait till you're a few years older, my lad, then you'll know what being tired really means. A full day unloading the cargo from those ships, that's what I've been doing. You do that for a while when you're grown and you'll look back on these days and think how lucky you were, having a kick-about with your mates. You youngsters don't know you're born.'

Sensing Dad's mood could change for the worse if this line of discussion continued, Mum jumped in again.

'I'm sure you're right, Alf. But, like you say, that's a few years off. A lesson for another day perhaps. Would you like a cuppa while I plate up your tea?'

Not suspecting her attempt to change the subject as anything more than genuine concern for his well-being, he looked at Mum and smiled.

'Thanks Flo, a cuppa sounds good.' Watching as she moved to put the kettle on, he turned to Edith.

'And what about you, girl, what have you been up to? Helping your mum, is that right?'

Struggling to respond, Edith looked to the floor. Like me, she knew that saying the wrong thing could see Dad's demeanour change in an instant. Equally, saying nothing was guaranteed to provoke him. Sensing Edith's reticence to answer, Mum interposed.

'We did some cleaning together, and we've been sewing as well, haven't we, love? I've been teaching her how to repair the holes and tears in your work shirts, and Harry's shorts.' Laughing, she added, 'Honestly, you two men get through your clothes in half the time us girls do. Isn't that right, Edith?'

Without looking up and moving her foot from side to side, Edith replied nervously. 'Yes, Mum.'

'The reason we get holes in our shirts and the like is because of the hard work we do in them.' Pausing, Dad looked at me and grinned. 'Well, the hard work some of us do. Others put holes in their clothes from rolling around on the ground playing football with their mates.'

With steam rising from the teapot as she poured in the boiling water from the kettle, Mum shook her head. 'That's as maybe, but either way, you'll both be grateful for the extra bit of life we ladies bring to them.'

Smiling at Edith, Dad laughed. 'I suppose that's true. Thank you, Edith, for helping your mum mend my shirt, or whatever else it was the two of you darned. At least you've done some proper work today, not like this one here, just kicking a ball about and saying he's tired.'

Desperate to bite back, but knowing the cost such a response would carry, I looked up and smiled. Thankfully, Dad registered this as acceptance of his intended jibe and decided not to push the matter further.

'You go through and sit yourself down, Alf, I'll bring your tea. Edith, Harry, you go up and get yourselves ready for bed, while I speak to your dad and get his supper served.'

Edith and I recognised this coded message as Mum's way of telling us to get out of the way while Dad was still in a good mood. If we started playing or teasing each other when he was eating his tea, his temperament could change for the worse in an instant. Additionally, if he'd had a tough day at work, he would complain about the pay and conditions he and the other men received, and what he would like to say or do to his bosses in response. When that happened, he would berate Edith and I for no apparent reason, other than to placate his desire to lash out at someone. Fortunately, on this occasion there were no violent outbursts. All remained quiet as he tucked into the supper Mum had prepared for him. He even came upstairs later to say goodnight to Edith and I without displaying any of the usual rancour and aggression we'd grown accustomed to whenever he'd had a tough day, or had been drinking which, thankfully, today he hadn't. A night of harmony in our house was cause for genuine celebration, and one Edith and I were happy to acknowledge as Dad left the room.

'Goodnight, Dad, sleep well. Hope work isn't so hard for you tomorrow.'

'I hope you're right, although I doubt it. Now, off to sleep the two of you and no noise. Your mum and I are planning an early night as well, and we don't want to be disturbed by either of you bleating on. Do you hear?'

'Yes, Dad.'

I looked at Edith, stifling my desire to giggle. We were both old enough to know what an 'early night' for the two of them meant, although not entirely sure of the physical mechanics involved. Even so, it was nice to hear them laughing together in the next room; that in itself was a rare event in our house, and one we were both grateful for. The two of us slept well that night.

Chapter Four

I woke early the next morning, my mind racing at the prospect of Karl and I becoming blood brothers. I was equally nervous about cutting myself but decided to push this part of the proceedings to the back of my mind, for now at least.

Dad had already left for work when Edith and I ventured downstairs for our breakfast. Being on school holidays meant we could both have a bit of a lie-in. It also allowed for us to keep out of Dad's way if he was on an early shift or running late because of the effects from the previous night's drinking. Thankfully, this wasn't the case today, and it was good to hear Mum humming happily to herself as we entered the scullery.

'Good morning you two. I was just about to send up a search party to find you. Did you get lost coming down the stairs?'

Edith jumped in before I could respond. 'Sorry if we're late, but the bed was lovely and warm and…'

Smiling, I interrupted. 'And we didn't want to disturb you and Dad after your *early night*.'

Mum laughed. 'That's enough of that from you, young Harry, although it was nice to have your father in such a good mood, I agree.' She took a deep breath and sighed. 'Let's just hope it lasts.'

Edith and I smiled at her. 'So do we. It's nice when he isn't angry all the time. I wish he'd stop drinking so much as well.'

Mum shook her head knowingly. 'I know, but your dad doesn't always have it easy at work. Sometimes he…'

Not ready to accept yet another excuse made on his behalf, I jumped in before she had time to finish her sentence. 'And sometimes he gets drunk and takes it out on us, and that's not fair either.'

'I know it isn't, Harry, and I'm sorry about that. All we can do is pray for more days like yesterday when he's in a better mood.' Reaching into her apron pocket she pulled out a few coppers. 'Look, your dad gave me some extra money before he left this morning. How about I buy some meat later and make a nice stew for your tea? Would you like that?'

Edith grinned. 'Yes please, Mum. Can we have dumplings as well?'

Laughing, mum nodded approvingly. 'Yes love, we can have dumplings. And if there's any suet left, I'll make a pudding as well. I think I've still got a little treacle in the cupboard, so you can have that on top. How does that sound?'

'Like a feast,' Edith replied. 'I wish Dad didn't drink so much as well. Then we could have dumplings every day.'

Mum laughed again. 'Well, maybe not every day. I think even you would get fed up with having dumplings every day.'

'Bet I wouldn't,' said Edith.

'Well, I would. But suet pudding and treacle does sound great. Thanks, Mum, you're the best.'

'And thank you, Harry, you're not bad yourself.' Shooing us into the sitting room, Mum slipped the money back into her apron. 'Now, go and sit down and I'll bring you some porridge and a cup of tea.'

Edith and I ate a lot of porridge, mainly for breakfast but also for our tea at times when money was short, as was often the case in our house. I didn't mind though, and it did fill you up, or 'stick to your ribs', as Mum would say. The only trouble with porridge was the oats we could afford were often quite rough, which meant Edith and I would leave a small pile of husks around the side of our bowls when we'd finished. That said, a big mug of tea helped wash it down and added to the feeling of having a full stomach. Edith and I knew Mum did her best to feed the two of us and were grateful for that. We were also aware there were times she would forgo her own breakfast so that we were able to eat. Even when the cupboard was bare because Dad had been laid off for a few days or had drunk away what little money there was, Mum would still find something to put in front of us. I remember one day when all we had in the house was a few spoons of brown sugar. Mum went next door to 'borrow' two slices of bread from Mrs Winter. She soaked the bread in hot water, gave me and Edith and sprinkled the brown sugar on top. Mum didn't eat at all that day and had Karl's parents not helped out by giving Edith and I bread and jam for our tea we would have gone to bed hungry as well.

Today though, there would be food in the house, and for once, we had Dad to thank for that. Instead of passing those few extra pennies to the barman at The Blue Anchor he'd given them to Mum, and because of that we would all eat well. The thought of stew, dumplings, and suet pudding with treacle to come made the day ahead a brighter prospect, even if it did include cutting myself with Karl's dad's penknife.

'Here you are, get that lot down you, that'll fill you up,' Mum said, placing two steaming bowls of porridge in front of us.

'You forgot to say, it will stick to our ribs,' Edith countered.

'I'll stick my hand to your bottom if there's any more cheek like that, young lady. Now eat up while I get your tea.'

I looked down at the thick gluey-like substance set before me and licked my lips. I was hungry and a full bowl of hot porridge looked just the job. Mum had put a spoon of brown sugar in the middle to add to its appeal. I mixed the sugar around the contents of my bowl, creating brown swirls across the top and adding a taste of sweetness to each mouthful.

The next few minutes were taken up with the two of us happily consuming our porridge and guzzling down our mugs of tea. The only noise to be heard was that of our spoons clinking against the sides of the bowls as we wolfed down their contents.

As we finished the last of our porridge, Mum joined us, a mug of tea in her hand. Taking a sip, she turned to Edith.

'If you'd like to help me make the beds, love, I thought we could go to the shops together afterwards and buy that bit of meat for our tea.' She smiled. 'There might even be a farthing or two left to buy some sweets; what do you say?'

Edith nodded enthusiastically. 'Yes please, Mum, I'd like that. Especially the bit about the sweets.'

'Well, I know you were hoping to play with Ruth today, but now she's poorly I thought it might be nice to spend some time together, just the two of us. I may not be as much fun as her, but I...'

Placing my spoon in the now empty bowl, I interrupted. 'What about me, I'd like some sweets as well.'

Mum turned, holding my gaze momentarily before speaking. 'Of course, Harry, I'm sorry, I should have thought. You can help Edith and I make the beds as well. Or, if you prefer, you can put the washing through the mangle and hang it out for me before we *all* go to buy the meat and sweets together.'

This wasn't the scenario I had imagined. 'But I'm going out with Karl, so I can't really help with the beds, or the washing. Couldn't I just have some sweets?'

Edith looked at me, frustration etched across her face. 'That's not fair. Why should you get any sweets? I'm the one helping Mum while you're off playing with stupid Karl.'

'Karl's not stupid, you are.'

Mum took a step forward, raising her hand to calm the situation before a proper spat ensued. 'Nobody's stupid, so let's not hear any more of that sort of talk from either of you. That said, Edith is right, Harry. It does seem a bit unfair that you should get a treat as well when she's the one helping me.'

'But, Mum, Karl and I have something special planned for today. It's really important and I can't let him down.'

'And what could be so important that you can't help your poor old mum with a few jobs around the house first?'

I looked down at the table. I couldn't tell her the truth as I was sure she would tell Anna, and that would mean an end to our plans to become blood brothers. And we certainly wouldn't be allowed anywhere near his dad's penknife if they knew what we intended to do with it.

'I can't say, it's a secret.'

'A secret eh? I'm not sure I like you having a secret that even your mum can't know about.'

Edith was enjoying my discomfiture. 'Yes, we shouldn't have secrets from Mum and Dad. So come on, what is this...'

Mum interrupted, anticipating my reply to Edith would be less than polite.

'All right, that's enough, let's not have an argument. And as for you, Harry, whatever it is you're doing with Karl it better not involve either of you getting into any trouble or upsetting your father. Do I make myself clear?'

'I nodded, recognising exactly what Dad's reaction would be if the two of us did get into trouble, or if he discovered we'd been engaged in joint bloodletting exercises with each other.

'Okay, Mum, I promise. We won't get into any trouble.'

'Good.' Turning to Edith again, she smiled. 'Now listen. Be honest, do you really want your brother hanging around with us all day? He'd only get under our feet and make a nuisance of himself. Whereas, if it was just the two of us, we could go to Mrs Jones's house as well and have a look at the wedding dress she's making for her daughter, Emma. She's getting married in a few weeks, and Ethel asked me just the other day if I'd like to see the dress. How does that sound?'

Edith's face lit up. 'Yes please, Mum, I'd love to see it. How romantic having a real wedding dress made just for you, I can't think of anything more exciting.'

I couldn't think of anything more boring and so kept my head down. A gesture Mum was quick to pick up on.

'Don't be shy, Harry,' she said with a twinkle in her eye. 'If you'd like to come with us, I'm sure Ethel wouldn't mind.'

I looked up, the sense of horror in my expression at the very suggestion I might like to be included obvious to both of them. 'No thank you. I'd rather have my head chopped off than look at some wedding dress.'

Laughing, Mum winked at Edith. 'Well, at least that's honest. It looks like it's just you and me then, love.'

'That's great, suits me fine.'

'I'll tell you what, Harry, as you're going to miss out on our special visit to Mrs Jones, Edith and I will still treat you to some sweets to make up for it, how does that sound?'

'Cor, yes please, Mum, you're the best.'

'Good, that's settled then. Now clear away your breakfast things both of you and I'll make a start on that washing, unless you did want to put it through the mangle for me, Harry?'

Shaking my head, I smiled. 'No, you're all right, Mum, you can do it. Is it okay if I go to Karl's after we've cleared away?'

'Go on then, I'm sure Edith and I can manage without you. But remember what I said about the two of you not getting into any trouble. If I find out you've been up to no good, it'll be me you'll answer to. I don't want you giving your dad any more reason to get angry.'

'Okay, Mum, I promise.'

After clearing the table with Edith, I sat down to put on my shoes. I only had one pair, and they were always scuffed from playing football with Karl. I'd also broken one of the laces recently; an accident that had earned me a slap round the ear from Dad. I'd replaced the lace with a length of string which served its purpose brilliantly and left me wondering what all the fuss had been about in the first place. Lots of children in our street had string holding up their shoes and boots. Some just ran around barefoot. Kicking a ball with nothing on your feet would hurt your toes, and so I considered myself lucky to have shoes. The fact that one was held in place with a black lace, while the other with a length of brown string appeared incidental, at least it did to me. Heading out the back door on my way to the alleyway, I passed Mum at the mangle. A strand of hair had fallen across her face as she battled to force Dad's shirt through the rollers, squeezing as much water as she could from the sodden garment.

'Bye, Mum, enjoy looking at that wedding dress. And don't forget my sweets.'

Pushing her hair back into place, she waved as I ran past her.

'Have fun, Harry. And no trouble, remember.'

'Yeah, I know. See you.'

Two minutes later I was stood outside Karl's front door, my heart racing from having run the hundred yards to his home; also, at the prospect of what the two of us were planning to do. Blood brothers. Even just the words sounded exciting, although I was still a little nervous about the prospect of physically cutting myself. But, if Karl could do it, then so could I.

Anna opened the door and smiled down at me. 'Good morning, Harry. I have just said to Karl I thought it might be you. How are you today?'

'I'm fine, thank you, Mrs Schmidt,' I answered, hopping from one foot to the other in anticipation of seeing my friend.

Acknowledging my obvious excitement at the prospect of spending another day with her son, she beckoned me in.

'Come on through to the front room, Karl is just getting his shoes.' Grinning at me she added, 'I think there may be a slice of toast left if you would like it? There's even a little jam to go with it as well.'

I knew from her generosity in the past, she was only too aware that sometimes Edith and I might be hungry or have missed a meal. Today was different, as I'd enjoyed a hot bowl of porridge only half an hour earlier. Even so, I was a growing lad and therefore unlikely to turn down the offer of more to eat.

'Cor, yes please, Mrs Schmidt, if that's okay?'

She laughed, pointing to the table as we entered the sitting room. 'You sit there while I get that piece of toast for you.'

I sat down and glanced around the room. Although our house was the same design as Karl's, the décor was entirely different. In our house, the few rooms that had originally been decorated now looked grubby, with paper peeling from the walls and the paintwork marked from being knocked. The rug in our sitting room was so threadbare you could see the wooden flooring beneath it in places, and its paisley-style pattern had all but faded beyond recognition. We had an old brown chenille-style tablecloth that was stained and torn in one corner. And, although we had four chairs around the dining table, one of them had a creaky leg that made it wobble when anyone sat on it. We had one armchair set near to the fireplace. It had a high back and was covered in a dark-green patterned material that was wearing thin on the edge of the armrests. This was Dad's, and woe betide you if he caught you sitting in it without his permission. Sometimes, especially in the winter, when he was at work, or in the pub, Mum would sit in it and invite Edith and I up on her lap. We would lie there, snuggling into her, happily watching the fire glow and crackle in front of us. We felt safe in her embrace. It was the one room in the house that benefited from any heat. Our bedroom always felt cold; even now in summer it could still feel chilly, unless we'd enjoyed particularly good weather. The outside wall faced north and so whenever the wind blew from that direction, Edith and I would hunker down beneath our thin blankets in an attempt to get warm. Thankfully, it had been hot for the past few days and so our room and beds felt cosy and inviting.

The two of us rarely moaned about how things were at home. We both knew there was little enough money already, even for the essentials, and that was before Mum dare think about treating us, or herself, to any extras such as new clothes or a sturdier pair of shoes. I think we all resented Dad spending what little money there was in the pub, although this was rarely discussed openly. Each of us had learned to accept this was how it was in our house. If you had at least some food inside your stomach and could manage to avoid Dad's belt connecting with your backside you were doing okay. That's certainly how it felt for Edith and I. Of course, we were aware Mum would have liked things to be different, but we also knew it wouldn't be fair or reasonable for the two of us to complain. After all, it wasn't her fault that we went without at times. The last thing she needed was her children making her feel guilty about things she wasn't responsible for or couldn't do anything about. We both knew she loved us and would do anything she could to make the two of us happy. For Edith and I that was enough to get us through the day, no matter how rough some of those days were at times.

Much of this occupied my thoughts as I sat waiting for my toast and pondering the very different appearance of Karl's front room to our own. The tablecloth was white, crisp, and clean, and none of the chairs wobbled or creaked as you sat on them. There were two easy chairs by the fireplace, each with a tartan-style blanket folded over the back to add extra support and comfort to the fortunate occupant. The fireplace was also clean and the tiles around the hearth highly polished. Again, I knew Mum spent a lot of time scrubbing the tiles surrounding our fireplace in an effort to clean them, but the added bonus of polish to bring out their shine was yet another luxury beyond her means.

I looked up at the pulley rail suspended from the ceiling used for airing clothes after washing and drying. Even here, though our pulley was the same in style and shape, the sight that greeted me was entirely different. Above me hung white blouses, brightly coloured shirts, and other garments, all appearing clean and fresh. At home, similar items of clothing would hang from our rail looking tired and worn, even though Mum would have done her best to get the sweat and grime from them. Again, not being able to afford additional soap or starch for her wash, she would boil our clothes and then rub them against the washboard in a further effort to get the dirt and stains from them. She would then rinse them before putting them through the mangle and hanging them up to dry. Some of my clothes had been through this process so many times they had developed holes simply through being pummelled and rubbed against the washboard. Poor Mum would then have to sit and darn them before I could wear them again. My reflections were suddenly interrupted by the appearance of a plate of toast and jam being placed in front of me.

'There you are, Harry. Would you like some tea as well?'

Cramming a piece of toast into my mouth I spluttered my reply. 'Yes please. That would be great.'

I loved tea, and the best thing about drinking it at Karl's house was it was always served with a full spoon of sugar. Often, at home, there wasn't enough sugar for both our porridge and tea. Porridge without any form of sweetener or sugary additive, such as a spoon of jam or syrup, would just go round and round in my mouth before I forced myself to swallow it. This was especially true if it had been made only with water because we had run out of milk to add. When this happened, it would also mean drinking black tea, and so the opportunity of a cup made with both milk and sugar was a treat not to be missed.

Karl entered the room as I was munching my way through the last of my toast and licking a bit of jam from my finger. Grinning at me, he drew an imaginary line across his palm.

'Hello, Harry. Are you ready for you-know-what?' Karl never questioned my eating at his house. Edith and I had come to terms with him knowing how bad things could be at home.

His parents had obviously explained the situation to him but without going into too much detail, certainly as far as Dad's drinking and violent temper was concerned. That said, I had shared a little of what Edith and I experienced at home, if only to get it off my chest and help release some of the personal angst and frustration I was feeling at the time. It was good having a friend who you could trust with your innermost fears, no matter how dark some of those concerns might be.

'Yes, I'm ready. At least I think I am.'

Karl laughed as his mum entered the room carrying a cup of hot sweet tea.

'I have made Harry some tea, Karl, there is another cup in the pot if you would like one?'

'Not for me, thank you. I am just going into Dad's shed for something.'

'What for? You know he is not keen on you going in there without him being with you.'

'Oh, it's all right, Mama, I put the football in there last night and Harry and I want to play with it again.'

Placing my tea on the table, Karl's mum smiled down at me. 'Honestly, you boys. Are there no other games you can play apart from football?'

Looking over his shoulder as he exited the room, Karl laughed. 'But we like playing football, don't we, Harry?'

Taking a sip of tea, I nodded my agreement. 'Yes, we do. Thank you for the tea, Mrs Schmidt, it's lovely.'

'You are welcome, Harry.' She ruffled my hair and called after Karl. 'Don't make any mess, Karl, I don't want your father telling me off for letting you go in there on your own.'

Sitting opposite me as I drank my tea, she smiled again. 'Karl's father is proud of his shed. He built it from wood he brought back from the docks. I don't go in there, but he likes it.'

'It looks great,' I replied, not really sure what to say about a shed. I actually thought it was a bit rickety. But as he'd made it from old wooden pallets he'd got from the docks and a few planks he'd picked up along the way I suppose he'd made a decent job of it.

Swallowing the last of my tea, I placed the cup back carefully in its saucer. 'Thanks again, Mrs Schmidt, that was lovely.'

'You are welcome, Harry, I am glad you enjoyed it. How is your mother?'

'She's fine. She and Edith are going to look at a wedding dress today. I can't remember why though.'

Looking across the table at me, she laughed. 'Are you not interested in wedding dresses then, Harry?'

'Not really, no.'

Not wanting to get further involved in a conversation about wedding dresses, I was pleased to hear the back door close and see Karl enter the room again. He held the football aloft.

'Got it. And before you say anything, Mama, I didn't touch anything else while I was in there.'

'That is good, thank you.'

Bouncing the ball in front of him, Karl nodded at me. 'Come on then, Harry, let's go.'

'Let Harry finish his tea and toast first, Karl, and please don't play with your football in the house.'

'Sorry, Mama.'

Getting up from my chair, I smiled. 'Oh, that's okay, Mrs Schmidt, I've finished now.'

'All right then, if you are sure. Off you go, and behave yourselves. I don't want the neighbours telling me you have been causing trouble.'

Tucking the ball under his arm, Karl turned on his heel and made for the scullery. 'We will be good, Mama, don't worry.'

Following after Karl, I turned briefly to face his mum. 'Thanks again for the toast and tea, Mrs Schmidt. See you soon.'

'As I said, Harry, you are welcome. Have fun both of you.'

'We will, bye.'

Closing the back door behind us we grinned at one another as we headed towards the alleyway.

'Your mum speaks really good English now, Karl.'

'Yes, Papa and I only speak English in the house now, except if he is explaining something particular to Mama. Then he might say it in German first so she can understand.'

Running behind him down the alley at the side of his house, I flicked the ball from under his arm. 'So where are we playing today? We'd better steer clear of Mrs Porter's house; we don't want her moaning to our mums.'

Karl stopped, his eyes flashing with excitement. 'We are not playing football, not yet anyway.'

'But you went into your dad's shed to get it, so what...'

Interrupting, he reached into his pocket. 'That was just so Mama wouldn't ask any more questions.' Taking a red penknife from his shorts he held it up for me to see. 'Papa keeps his penknife in there, so I had to pretend I wanted the football.'

A feeling of trepidation ran through me. 'Is that for... you know?'

'Well, I don't want to cut my hand on a stone. Papa keeps this knife really sharp so it will be easy to get a little blood from our hands.'

'Hands, I thought we were going to prick our fingers?'

Indicating his palm, he waved the knife at me. 'Yes, but if we cut here, we can hold our hands together so our blood will mix together better.'

I swallowed hard at the realisation this was actually going to happen.

'We will go near to the shipyard. There are more places to hide there, so nobody will see us.'

We wandered towards the docks, talking through our plans along the way. There were a lot of warehouses situated around that area. These were used to store cargo from the ships before it was moved on to its final destination. They were situated some way from the port itself so there was less chance of us being caught and getting into trouble. A warehouse was also a great place to practise our football skills. Other regular visitors to these huge stores were rats. It was an ideal place for them to nest and find food if any of the perishable goods from the ships were being held there, even for just a short period. Karl and I were used to having rats for company, as were most of the families living in and around the docklands. With little provision of adequate sewage or drainage facilities, residents would often find themselves battling an infestation of vermin, either in their home or in the immediate vicinity outside.

Even with rats for company, an empty or partly empty warehouse was still a great place to hang out. It meant having somewhere dry for the two of us to play if it started to rain. That said, we still had to keep an eye out for any dockers or security men who might be wandering around. They certainly wouldn't approve of two young lads kicking a football about in one of their storehouses, whatever the weather conditions. They also wouldn't have appreciated our method of entry. We would either force a window or jam part of a pallet under one of the doors at the entrance and squeeze our bodies through the small gap on the ground it facilitated. We'd been caught a couple of times in the past and duly chased away with the voice of authority ringing in our ears as we made a run for it.

'Clear off, you little buggers. Don't you know it's not safe to be playing in there.'

Their warnings about the potential dangers of getting into trouble or hurting ourselves may have been apposite, but at our age the threat of possible harm felt unlikely and entirely worth the risk involved. Like most youngsters we felt invincible. At least that's how we saw ourselves when measured against the cautionary advice from some grumpy docker who, we determined, was only looking to spoil our fun.

This time, our reason for seeking sanctuary in one of these

cavernous storage areas was different. Today, we wanted to avoid the gaze of anyone who might look to dissuade us from engaging in an act destined to take our relationship to an entirely new level. Today, we were to become blood brothers. A seal that would bind us together, forever. Surely, there could be no greater commitment demonstrated between two friends than this.

Taking cover behind several large pallets of stored materials, I attempted to hold on to that conviction as Karl pulled his father's penknife from his pocket.

Spitting on the blade and wiping a small amount of rust from it on his jumper, he turned to me and grinned. 'Are you ready, Harry? Would you like to go first?'

Doubt washed over me again. At this point, I was no longer sure I wanted to proceed with any of what we'd agreed, let alone go first. 'No, you're all right, I'll go after you.'

Laughing, he held the blade to his palm. 'I hope you are not going to be a coward, Harry, and change your mind. We must do this together.'

I felt my stomach knot as he drew the blade across his open hand, pressing down as he did so. 'I know, I just…' The words stuck in my throat as a trickle of blood oozed from Karl's palm and dripped onto the floor.

'Quickly, Harry, now you.'

Reaching nervously for the knife I smiled sheepishly at my friend. 'Are you sure this is a good idea? I mean we could just…'

Interrupting, Karl grabbed hold of the knife again. 'I'll do it for you. Hold out your hand before I bleed to death, and then you won't have a friend at all.' Shaking his head, he frowned playfully. 'I knew you would change your mind.'

Before I could answer he grabbed my right hand and forced the blade across the muscle at the base of my thumb. I watched as the blood ran across the inside of my hand.

Karl laughed again. 'You see, that wasn't so bad, was it? Now give me your hand and we will be true brothers, brothers in blood.'

Taking Karl's hand, I gripped it tightly; partly to staunch the flow of blood from my wound, and in relief that the deed was done. We sat there for a moment staring at our slightly bloodied hands clasped firmly together. Whilst I would have happily forgone the events of the past few seconds, I was equally aware of a deep sensation of joy and pride.

'Bloody hell, Karl, we've done it.'

Releasing his hand from mine, he smiled. 'Yes, we have. Now we are true blood brothers. We have a bond no one can break. No matter what happens in the future we are now joined together as one.' He looked at me excitedly. 'We should make an oath.'

Looking at my palm with blood smeared and congealing across it, I shook my head. 'An oath?'

'Yes, an oath. We must swear an allegiance to one another for our whole lives. This means looking out for each other and never telling the other one a lie or hurting them. We must never let anyone come between us, not even our parents. We are now joined together in blood, Harry, and that is a bond that can never be broken. Do you agree?'

I smiled, the smarting in my hand beginning to ease. 'Of course. But weren't we already best friends before cutting ourselves? I would never lie to you or want to hurt you anyway, you know that.'

Wiping his equally bloodied palm down the side of his shorts, Karl nodded authoritatively. 'Of course, we are friends and always will be. But now we are also brothers.' Raising his hand, he continued. 'And not *just* brothers, we are blood brothers. And that is a commitment for life.'

Sensing perhaps he was right and by exchanging blood we had indeed committed to a far deeper relationship than that of simply being friends, I nodded.

'Yeah, okay, an oath it is. Only we don't have to cut ourselves again do we? I mean...'

Laughing, Karl interrupted. 'No, don't worry, we don't have to cut ourselves again. Honestly, Harry, you are such a coward.'

'I'm not a coward, I just don't fancy being scarred for life with your dad's knife, thank you very much.'

Still laughing he nodded his agreement. 'Maybe you are right. I am sorry I said you were a coward. Perhaps you are just not very brave.'

I slapped him playfully on the arm. 'And perhaps I've also made a mistake in becoming your blood brother.'

'Okay, you win. You are not a coward, and we are both brave. Is that all right?'

'Yeah okay, I forgive you. After all, that's what a real brother would do. So come on then, what about this oath, what do we have to do?'

Biting his lip, Karl scratched his head. 'I don't really know; I have only just thought of the idea.'

'Why don't we just hold our hands together again and promise to do all the things you suggested?'

'Good idea, but we need to swear it to God as well. That way we cannot go back on our promise.'

Not being a great believer in God, I couldn't see any harm in what he was proposing, and so nodded my agreement. 'Go on then. You can say it though.'

Smiling and holding his hand aloft, he gestured for me to do the same. 'This is good, Harry, brothers forever, I like the sound of that.'

Taking his hand in mine and squeezing it, I concurred. 'Me too.'

'Maybe we should close our eyes while I speak, like a prayer.'

'I don't say a lot of prayers, and I don't think I've ever closed my eyes to say one. I mean if God really exists wouldn't he want me to talk to him directly and not with my eyes closed? If I talked to anyone else with my eyes shut they'd think I was being rude, or mad.'

Karl shook his head. 'Oh no, you mustn't say that, Harry. God is real, my mother told me. She is a great believer and says her prayers every day.'

'So do you pray as well?'

'Not really, but I like it when Mama does. It makes her feel safe she says, and that makes me feel safe as well.'

Still not sure praying would make any difference to our relationship, but equally not wanting to upset him, I nodded. 'Okay, I'll close my eyes then, if you really think it'll help.'

'I do.' Smiling and still gripping my hand, Karl closed his eyes.

I closed mine, partly, leaving my right eye open just enough to watch as he spoke.

'Dear God, Harry and I have cut our hands today and shared our blood to say we will be friends forever. We promise never to hurt or lie to each other and will always look out for one another, Amen.'

There followed a short silence, with Karl keeping his eyes closed as if expecting some form of heavenly confirmation that God was happy with what he'd heard. I glanced around the warehouse to check we were still alone, and that God hadn't made a surprise appearance to congratulate Karl on his prayer.

'Is that it?' I asked, still squinting just in case.

Karl opened his eyes and smiled. 'Yes, I think so. Except…'

'Except what?'

'I forgot to say the most important thing.' Closing his eyes once more and squeezing my hand, Karl began to pray again. 'I am sorry, God. I forgot to say that Harry and I will always protect each other from any danger, even if we die while doing so. Amen.'

I pulled my hand away. 'Die? Who's talking about dying?'

'True friends, real brothers, they would die for each other, wouldn't they? And we are better than just brothers, we are brothers in blood.' Slapping me on the shoulder and laughing, he continued. 'I will protect you, Harry, and give my life for you if I must. Are you saying you would not do the same for me?'

Not sure how to reply, I stuttered, 'Let's hope it never comes to that, at least the dying bit.'

'Of course, I agree. But we will still protect each other, yes?'

It was my turn to laugh. 'Yes, unless we get into trouble with our dads, then you're on your own. I've had plenty of beatings from mine already. And I don't fancy another one for something you've done, blood brothers or not.'

Still chuckling, Karl got to his feet. 'I am not sure you are taking our oath seriously, Harry. Anyway, we are brothers now.' Raising his hand again, he continued. 'Best friends forever, nothing can change that. Do you agree?'

That much I was prepared to commit to. 'Yes, I agree.'

'Good, then let us play football. And as my best friend you can be in goal and let me score many times against you.'

'But as my best friend, surely you want me to play well; so you'll only kick the ball gently so I can save it easily.'

Throwing the ball towards the wall and looking back over his shoulder as he ran after it, Karl shouted, 'We will see.'

I soon forgot the slight discomfort in my hand as we played happily together for the next hour. Eventually, hunger got the better of us and we decided to head home for something to eat.

'You can come back to my house for some food if you like, Harry.'

'Thanks, but I'd better go home. Mum said she'd leave me something. She's gone out with Edith. But we can play again later if you want?' I often felt guilty not asking Karl back to our house but knew there was little enough for us to eat already without bringing back another hungry mouth to feed. Mum wouldn't have told me off or said no, I knew that, but I was equally aware whatever she served Karl would have been taken from her own plate. Even when it was only Edith and I, there was still often not enough to go round and she would go without herself, despite our objections.

'I'm not hungry at the moment, I'll get something later,' she would say. We knew she was lying and that whatever was left would go to Dad. Mum feared his response to anything less than a full plate at the end of the day more than she did her own hunger pangs. Sometimes, Edith and I would pretend we'd had enough and leave a few scraps on the side of our plates for Mum to finish off.

I was sure anything left for me today would prove equally scant. The probability of Mum having left much more than a piece of bread and jam for me was highly unlikely. Of course, there was the promise of meat for tea later, along with the prospect of suet pudding and treacle, but that was hours away and I was hungry now.

'Please come back with me, Harry. Mama is making broth with sausage in, you will love it.'

A bowl of hot broth certainly sounded inviting, especially when compared to bread and jam. Even though I had eaten once at Karl's house already today, I accepted his offer. I reasoned if Mum had left me anything, she and Edith could have it when they got back.

'If you're sure?'

'Of course. Anyway, you are my brother now, so I have to look after you.'

I laughed. 'That may be true for you and me, but I'm not sure your mum would see it that way.'

'Maybe you are right, but she will still be happy to see you.'

Squeezing ourselves back through the gap by the warehouse door, we looked up as the sun beat down from a break in the clouds. Karl smiled. 'I am liking it when the sun is hot. Is that how you say it?'

I laughed. 'Sort of. I know what you mean anyway. Your English is really good as well now.'

Slapping me on the back, he grinned. 'Better than your German, that is for sure. Come on, I'll race you. Last one home has to give the other a piece of their sausage.'

Friendship was one thing, filling my stomach was another. I wasn't about to forgo even the slightest morsal of food if I could help it.

Knocking the ball from under Karl's arm, I started to run. 'Come on then, slowcoach. I'll tell your mum you said I can have all your sausage.'

Picking the ball up, he began to chase after me. 'You come back here, Harry Thompson. I will tell Mama you are not hungry, and you can watch me eat all the broth myself.'

Chapter Five

Lunch was every bit as delicious as Karl had said it would be. And I made sure to show my appreciation as I left for home with a full stomach and a contented smile on my face.

'Goodbye Mrs Schmidt and thanks again for the broth, it was lovely.'

'You are welcome, Harry. I am glad you enjoyed it. Say hello to your mother for me. Tell her I will see her tomorrow.'

'I will.' Turning to face my friend as I jumped from the doorstep to the pavement below, I held my hand aloft. 'It's a good job your mum was busy with the washing and didn't notice the cuts on our hands. I hope it's the same at our house, especially when Dad gets back. He won't be happy if he finds out what we've done.'

Laughing, Karl spat on his hand and rubbed it down the front of his jumper. 'He won't notice. Anyway, there is hardly anything to see. It just looks like a scratch. You can tell him you fell over and caught it on a stone.'

I stared at my hand. Karl's wound may have appeared as no more than a scratch, but mine looked very different. It was longer and deeper than his. If only I'd been brave enough to cut myself as Karl had first suggested. If I hadn't shown such concern that it might hurt, he wouldn't have grabbed my wrist and drawn the blade across my palm, resulting in the raised weal now plainly evident below my thumb.

Thrusting it into my pocket in the vain hope of hiding the scar from my parents, I nodded. 'I hope you're right. Anyway, I'll see you tomorrow.'

'Yes, and remember, we are now real brothers. We have shared our blood and taken an oath to be friends forever. Nothing can separate us.'

I laughed. 'What about when we die, we can't be friends then, can we?'

Karl's expression changed, becoming more reflective.

'When one of us dies, the other will still have their brother's blood running through his veins. This is a bond that can never be broken, in this life or the next.'

I wasn't sure about such deep theology or how it might work in reality, but I did know Karl was my dearest friend. And, as such, was equally happy to commit to the oath we'd made between us. Much as I was aware I was loved at home things were still never easy in our house. This rang particularly true when one of Dad's moods got the better of him, often for no good reason, other than he had a belly full of beer, or had been involved in some disagreement at work. Having someone who would never doubt me, or my intentions, sounded like the perfect relationship and, more importantly, one I could depend on when things got tough at home. I nodded my head and grinned. 'Okay brother, see you later.'

As I got to the alleyway by the side of our house, I noticed Dad halfway up the hill. Recognising it was still quite early in the day for him to be coming home I presumed he must have been laid off for some reason. I ran down the alley and into the house. Mum was sorting a load of washing in the scullery.

'Hello, Harry, what's the rush?' She laughed. 'Is there a fire?'

Catching my breath, I shook my head. 'Dad's coming up the road, Mum.'

Her face changed immediately, a look of apprehension and concern replacing her ready smile. Acknowledging, as I had, Dad arriving back at this time of the day rarely bode well for the rest of us, she responded accordingly.

'You go upstairs to your room with Edith while I tidy up here.' Quickly folding the washing into a pile, she continued, 'Hopefully, it won't be anything serious and I'll be able to bring the two of you down in a little while for your tea. I'm making that stew with the meat Edith and I bought earlier.' Attempting a smile, she added, 'And I didn't forget your sweets either. But let's see how your dad is before we get those out. We don't want to give him any reason to complain about wasting money, especially on sweets and the like.'

I didn't need telling twice that any extras to the family budget depended entirely on Dad's mood at the time. Either that or they had to be kept secret from him, at least until Mum could gauge his reaction to such apparent acts of financial profligacy.

'Of course. How was the wedding-dress thing?'

Folding the last of her washing, she forced a smile. 'It was lovely, although I'm sure you're not really any more interested than you were this morning. But thank you for asking. Now, go along and get yourself upstairs. I'll call you down when I've spoken to your dad.'

Turning to leave, I squeezed her hand. 'Love you, Mum.'

Recognising the concern in my voice, she nodded. 'Love you too, Harry. Off you go now.'

I'd just reached the top of the stairs when the back door slammed. Not a good sign. Entering the bedroom, I noticed Edith sitting nervously at the end of her bed.

'I saw him out of the window walking up the street. Why is he home so early?'

'I don't know. Mum said we should stay here until she's had a chance to talk to him and find out what's wrong.'

As I moved to close the door, the shouting from below began. Although slightly muffled by the distance between us and with the sitting-room door closed, Dad's mood was never in doubt.

'They sent two of us home, that's why I'm here at this time, you stupid cow. What did you think; that I'd come back early to spend a lazy afternoon with you and the kids?'

Continuing to rant, Dad's voice drowned out Mum's attempt to respond.

'Always the bleeding same. It's always George and me they release when there's not enough work. They never tell that German bugger up the road to go home. They always find enough work for him.'

Edith and I crept on to the landing and took a few steps down the stairs to hear better what Mum was saying in reply.

'But you always get so angry, Alf. Maybe if you didn't lose your temper as much, they might keep you on instead of Gustav and some of the others. I know it's not easy but...'

Mum's words were cut short, the sound of crashing furniture leaving little doubt as to the reason why.

'Don't you dare tell me about losing my temper. You'd lose your bloody temper if you were singled out every time to be laid off.'

We could hear the fear and trembling in Mum's voice as she replied, 'Please Alf, calm down. It isn't my fault, and it certainly isn't the children's. They're both upstairs, and us rowing like this scares them. Please, love...'

Her plea for reason was cut short again. This time, not by the noise of chairs being upturned but by the familiar sound of a physical blow being administered. Edith and I gripped each other in fear as Mum's cry reached our ears.

'Alf, no. Please stop it, I...'

'I'll give you fucking no. I get sent home from work by some shit of a foreman and all you can do is tell me to calm down.

That'll be another day on half pay and no food put on the table. What do you have to say about that, eh?'

The sound of Mum crying in pain as Dad hit her again was too much for us to bear. Young as we were, Edith and I ran downstairs to the sitting room in an attempt to protect her from further abuse. As we entered, she was sat cowering on the floor, blood trickling from her mouth. Crying, she looked across at the two of us.

'It's all right, you two, Dad's a bit upset. We've had an accident. I fell off the chair.'

Edith and I knew this wasn't true. We'd heard too many similar arguments in the past to know she was only trying to protect us. Dad's terse response confirmed our suspicions.

'Bugger off, you two, that's unless you want some of the same.' He swayed slightly as he spoke. It was obvious he'd paid a visit to the pub on his way back from the docks. I may have displayed a trace of cowardice earlier when not wanting to cut myself, but the sense of rage I felt towards my father at this moment provided me with a surge of courage I had never experienced before. Looking at Mum lying on the floor bleeding and scared was too much for me to accept. I ran over to Dad and kicked him as hard as I could in the leg.

'You leave her alone, you bully. Hit me if you're going to hit anyone. Only a coward hits a woman.'

Dad took a step back, surprised by my outburst. I clenched my fist as tightly as I could, forcing my nails deep into my palm and threw a punch hard into his stomach. As I did so the cut on my hand from earlier split open again. Almost immediately I felt the warm sensation of blood trickling down my wrist. Mum screamed in protest as Dad regained his balance, taking aim to strike me.

'Alf, stop it, Harry's bleeding.'

Her appeal fell on deaf ears as Dad brought his fist crashing down on the side of my head, causing me to trip against the upturned chair and go sprawling across the floor.

'Bleeding is he? He's bleeding good for nothing, I'll tell you that much, the little sod.' Still staggering slightly from the intake of alcohol and my kick to his shin, he reached to unbuckle his belt. 'Get up, boy. Who do you think you are, kicking me like that? You'll show me some respect if you want to keep living under this roof.'

I knew for certain I didn't want to live under the same roof as him. But, young as I was, someone had to protect Mum and Edith, and if not me then who?

Getting to my feet, I bit my lip, readying myself for the beating I was about to receive. I wiped the hair from my face with my wounded hand, leaving a trail of blood across my forehead.

Mum cried out again, 'Alf, please.'

Momentarily taken aback by the sight of blood on my face, he paused his advance towards me.

'Where's that coming from?'

I opened my still tightly clenched fist to reveal the cut to my palm; blood slowly oozing from it and running down my fingers.

Mum got to her knees and took my hand. 'What have you done, Harry, that's quite a cut?'

Without thinking, I blurted out what had happened. 'Karl and I did it. We used his dad's penknife. We were…'

Not waiting for me to finish, Mum interrupted. 'Why would you cut yourselves with a knife like that?'

'We took an oath to be friends forever. We did it to become blood brothers.'

Shaking his head as if trying to comprehend what he was hearing, Dad stepped forward. 'Blood brothers, what do you mean blood brothers? Cutting yourself with a knife. Are you stupid or what?'

Still angry that he'd hurt Mum, I responded without considering the consequences.

'A fat lot you care.' Pointing at her, I continued. 'Look what you've done to Mum. That blood on her face is because *you* hit her. You're nothing but a bully. I hate you, and I wish you were dead.'

Having remained silent up to this point, Edith chipped in. 'Me too. Why don't you just go away and leave us alone.'

Losing all sense of reason at being criticised by his children, Dad turned and reached for his belt again.

'And I hate you too, you little bleeders.' Grabbing at my arm, he continued. 'I'll teach you to talk to me like that.'

Mum threw herself forward to protect me, only to be greeted by another blow to the head which knocked her back to the floor. Edith ran to her, tears streaming down her cheeks.

'You leave my Mum alone. Like Harry said, you're nothing but a horrible bully.'

Edith and I had never got involved with an argument as serious as this between Mum and Dad before, reasoning we were too little and too scared to take him on. Also, we hoped if we kept quiet and didn't add to the tension, things might settle down quicker. This time was different though, we'd crossed a line, and I for one wasn't about to step down. I'd witnessed my father physically assault our mum and, in that moment, something within me had shifted. Young as I was, I determined he would never do it again, not without me saying or doing something to protect her. With this new resolve coursing through my veins, I stood resolute in front of Mum and Edith as I watched Dad pull his belt clear of his trousers. I knew what was coming, but acknowledged inwardly that any pain I was about to endure would be worth it if it kept the two of them safe.

'Come on then, hit me. You don't scare me anymore. You can beat me all you like; it won't make me respect you. Nothing you say or do will ever...' My words were cut short as the first blow from his belt met with my shoulder as I turned away to shield myself. Glancing at Mum and Edith I drew breath as I prepared myself for the next strike. I didn't have to wait long as the leather whipped hard across my thigh and legs. I'd felt the sting of Dad's belt before, but never as forcefully as this. Suddenly, a very real fear swept over me. Despite my earlier protestations to the contrary, I *was* scared. What if he didn't stop? What if he killed me? As another blow struck my body, I heard Mum scream.

'Stop it, Alf, that's enough. He's just a boy for God's sake. Please, I'm sorry I said anything. All of us are sorry if that's what you want to hear. Just stop hitting him.' Her voice shook as her pleas turned to sobs. 'Please, Alf, he's your son, he didn't mean anything. Can't you see he's frightened?'

Cowering as I waited for the sting of leather to meet with my trembling frame once more, I glanced towards my aggressor. He rocked backwards, reaching for the table to steady himself. Whether it was Mum's tearful appeal or the effects of the drink that caused him to pause his attack I wasn't sure, but I was grateful none the less.

'Let that be a lesson to you, you little bugger. If you ever speak to me like that again, you'll get worse, do you hear?'

Thankful the beating had stopped and fearful of incurring his wrath again, I conceded the victory to him, if indeed there was any victory to be had in a grown man thrashing a young boy to within an inch of his life.

With intense pain replacing the previous biting sting of Dad's belt, I turned to face him. Tears of hate as much as shock stung my eyes. I bit my lip again in an effort not to break down completely and let him see how much he'd hurt me. Everything inside of me wanted to scream out my loathing for him. But I knew any further expression of condemnation levelled against him would simply result in another beating, not only for me but, potentially, for Mum as well. Through gritted teeth, I apologised.

'I'm sorry, Dad, I shouldn't have said what I did.' I looked across to Edith who was sobbing into Mum's shoulder and hanging on tightly to her cardigan. She was equally stunned by what she had witnessed over the past few minutes. I knew the best way to protect the two of them now was to back down. If I continued to concede ground, hopefully Dad's anger might recede a little, at least enough to remove the immediate threat of any more violence being meted out to the three of us.

'Really Dad, I am sorry. It just made me angry when I saw you hit Mum. I was trying to protect her, and Edith.'

My apparent fulsome apology appeared to work, at least for now. Exhausted by the ferocity of his attack against me, Dad threaded his belt back through the loops on his trousers and slumped into his chair. Aware, perhaps, he may have gone too far, his gaze dropped to the floor. Without raising his head to acknowledge me, he mumbled a pathetic defence of his actions.

'Just don't interfere again when your mother and me are having words, I won't have it. It's none of your business what goes on between us. It's your fault I hit her anyway. You made me angry, speaking to me like that. I'm your father and you better not forget it.' Pausing, he threw a dismissive glance towards Edith. 'That goes for you an' all, you little cow. Both of you, just keep your noses out in future.'

Much as I wanted to contest every word he'd just uttered, I knew better and remained silent. I was learning quickly that having a reasoned conversation with Dad was never going to be easy. Even more so when he had a belly full of beer.

'Okay Dad.'

Whilst his anger towards us had abated a little, he was clearly still aggrieved about what had transpired at work. His body language made it clear he wasn't about to let that particular wound to his pride go without further analysis.

Nodding at Edith and I, he gesticulated towards the door.

'Go on, clear off upstairs the two of you while I speak to your mother.'

Recognising our reticence to leave her on her own with him again, she smiled, wiping a trace of blood from her lip as she did so.

'It'll be all right, your dad's calmed down now. We shouldn't have upset him.' Understanding she was also choosing the path to peace to avoid any additional confrontation, I tugged at Edith's arm as Mum continued, 'Go on, do as your dad says. It'll be all right now, won't it, Alf?'

Dad threw the three of us a non-committal look and grunted.

Getting to her feet and lifting the dining chair from the floor, Mum nodded. 'Honest, we'll be okay. Off you go.'

Edith kissed her on the cheek and took my hand as we headed for the door. I tried not to limp, having lost some of the sensation in my leg from the whipping I'd received.

'Are you all right, Harry?'

Fighting back tears of frustration and pain, I nodded. 'I'm fine, Mum.'

'Good boy. I'll call you both down when it's time to eat.'

Turning briefly as we exited the room, Edith and I forced a weak smile.

'Okay, Mum.'

Closing the door behind us, we sat on the bottom stair so we could hear their conversation. I prayed Dad wouldn't go into another rage. Determined as I was that he shouldn't hurt Mum again, I also didn't fancy another lashing from his belt, or worse. As we sat, listening in silence on the bare wooden step, it was clear Dad was still in combative mood.

'I told you, it's that bloody German's fault. He could have volunteered to go off shift. He's had plenty of work of late, they're never short of money. And now that boy of his has been cutting our Harry's hand in some stupid ritual.'

Trying to maintain the peace and protect Karl's family from Dad's growing annoyance with them, Mum struggled to reply.

'It's not really Gustav's fault, if you think about it, Alf. He didn't suggest you and George should be on short time. That was your foreman's decision, you should take it up with him. And as for Karl cutting Harry, I should think it was probably six of one and half a dozen of the other. You know what those two are like when they get together. Thick as thieves they are. They're just young boys, with no real harm done. His hand will soon heal. He'll have worse injuries than that before he's grown. Think what you were like as a lad. I bet you got into trouble with your mates now and then.'

'That's not the point, they shouldn't be playing around with knives in the first place. And where did they get it from anyway? The boy's father wasn't it, Harry said. I'm going round to have it out with him.'

'Alf, don't, please. He won't be home yet anyway, and there's been enough trouble for one day already. Wait till you've calmed down a bit. You know what can happen when you're in a mood like this. You really hurt Harry with that belt. He didn't deserve that. He was scared and trying to help me, that's all. He didn't mean anything when...'

With his mood darkening once more at Mum's attempt to placate him, Dad interrupted. 'Don't start all that again, woman. I won't have it, you speaking up for him like that. If he wants to be a man, then he'll have to learn to take a few knocks. Like you said, he'll get worse before he's finished.'

'But he's just a boy, he...'

Mum's words were drowned out by the sound of Dad's chair scraping the floor as he got to his feet. Edith and I stiffened as he spoke again. 'I mean it, Flo, that's enough. I won't have you say another word about it. He mouthed off to me and got a beating for his trouble and that's an end to it. Now get out of my way.'

'Alf, I've told you already, Gustav won't be home yet. You can go later when you've calmed down a bit. Look, sit back in your chair while I go and make us both a cup of tea and we can...'

Her renewed plea for reason was cut short as Dad's temper soared to the surface again.

'Don't bloody tell me what to do, woman, I've told you already. Not unless you want to feel the back of my hand again. I mean it, Flo, get out of my way.'

Realising Dad was about to exit the room, Edith and I bolted up the stairs as fast as our legs would carry us. My back and legs were still throbbing from the earlier beating they'd received but that didn't slow me down as we raced to our bedroom. I was more fearful of what might happen if he caught the two of us listening to their conversation than I was in worrying about any pain I might be experiencing. Entering the room, we ran over to the window as the front door slammed shut below.

'There'll be trouble now,' I said, pushing up the sash window and leaning out to get a better view of Dad marching up the road to Karl's house.

Edith poked her head out beside mine. 'Is there going to be a fight?'

'I wouldn't be surprised. Whatever happens, it won't be good news for you and me. Dad'll still be angry when he gets back.'

As we were talking Mum shouted up to us, 'Stay there, you two. I'm going after your dad; see if I can calm him down a bit.'

'Okay, Mum, be careful.' I looked at Edith. 'She's got a hope. I've never seen him so bad. I thought he was going to kill me. I still can't feel my left leg, it's all numb from his belt.'

Edith put her arm around my shoulder. 'I thought you were very brave.'

I grinned. 'Very stupid more like.'

Putting our heads out the window again, we watched as Mum followed Dad up the street. We could see Karl's house as it was less than a hundred yards away on a bend.

Edith leant further forward. 'I wonder what he's going to do?'

Stepping back into the bedroom, I shook my head. 'Just shout a lot I should think. Gustav won't be home for about an hour yet. Hopefully Dad'll have calmed down a bit by then. I hope so, I've had enough of him and his temper for one day.'

Pulling back from her vantage point, Edith commented ruefully, 'Don't suppose we'll get our sweets now either.'

'Doubt it. And I'm certainly not asking for them in front of him. He'll only go off on one about Mum wasting money and the like.' I turned to Edith, the look of disappointment on her face palpable as she tugged at a ringlet of hair. Like all siblings we had our disagreements from time to time but, in this moment, I felt an overwhelming sense of love for her. She looked frail and nervous standing beside me in her faded yellow knitted dress. A neighbour had passed it on after her own daughter had grown out of it. It was still a bit big for Edith, which only served to emphasise her fragile appearance. I put my arm around her and smiled. 'It'll be all right, sis. Mum'll give 'em to us when he's out of the way I should think. We can enjoy them better when he's not around.'

Nodding her acceptance at my suggestion, we craned our necks out of the window once more as Dad arrived at Karl's house. He banged his fist hard on the door. Mum arrived just as Anna answered it. We couldn't hear what she was saying but there was no mistaking Dad's voice as it boomed down the road.

'You tell that husband of yours to come and see me when he gets in, I've got a bone to pick with him.'

We watched as Mum moved towards Anna; the two of them exchanging a few words while Dad stood his ground.

'Come away, Flo. I've said what I came to say, this is between me and him.' Then, taking Mum by the arm and pulling her away, he pointed his finger accusingly at Anna. 'You make sure you tell him what I said. Bloody bosses' favourite, with that stupid smile of his. I'll give him something to smile about all right when I get hold of him.'

Squeezing my arm and with tears in her eyes, I felt Edith's body shudder. 'I hate it when he's been drinking. It always ends like this, with him getting angry and shouting at somebody, or lashing out at them.'

I nodded. 'And it's usually one of us he goes for, especially Mum. I don't know why she stays with him. I'd happily leave tomorrow.'

'Me too, but where would we go? And we haven't got any money either. It's bad enough now, it would be even worse if we left.'

Pulling ourselves back inside, I slid the window shut and looked across to Edith as she took a piece of rag from the sleeve of her dress and wiped her eyes. 'I hate him, Harry. I hate that he hits our mum, and that he beats you so hard.'

Any lingering discomfort I may have been experiencing from the earlier pasting I'd received paled into insignificance as I looked at my sister. That deep feeling of love I held for her swept over me once more, along with a very real desire to protect her and Mum from any future abuse from Dad. He'd already done his worst with me, so I had little to fear there, other than more of the same. And, if he did hit me again, it would be a cost I was more than willing to pay if it kept Mum and Edith safe.

'Don't worry, I won't let him hurt you, or Mum, I promise.'

I took Edith in my arms and hugged her. Any notion of the traditional spatting that went on between us evaporating as I felt her arms wrap tight round me. Our embrace of affectionate solidarity was suddenly shattered by the slamming of the front door, accompanied by the harsh growl of Dad's voice.

'Get down here, both of you.'

I felt Edith's body tremble in my arms as she reacted to Dad's demand for our presence. Releasing her, I rubbed her back.

'It'll be okay, I'll be with you.'

We smiled nervously at each other and moved slowly towards the stairs, our pace quickening at the sound of another order being barked from below.

'I won't tell you again. Get down those bloody stairs now.'

Whilst my earlier resolve to protect Mum and Edith from Dad's aggression remained intact, I equally saw no sense in antagonising him any more than necessary. Moving quickly to the stairs, I encouraged Edith to join me in stepping up our pace.

'Come on, we better do as he says. No point in setting him off again.'

As we entered the sitting room, Dad was pacing up and down like a caged animal seeking its escape.

'About bloody time an' all.' He stopped and stared at the two of us. Mum stood a pace behind out of his immediate line of sight, gesticulating for us not to upset him further.

'I'm off to the pub, while your mother feeds the two of you. When I get back, I expect you both to be in your beds. I don't want to have to look at either of you again today.' Pausing, he stroked his belt and looked directly at me. 'And I certainly don't want to see your face. You cheek me any more, lad, and you'll wish you'd never been born; have you got that?'

With all earlier attempts at bravery draining from me, I nodded acceptance of his terms.

'Yes, Dad.'

'Good.' He turned to Mum, his voice still harsh and with no sign of remorse for his earlier acts of aggression. 'I'll be a couple of hours. That'll be enough time for that German bugger to get home. By the time I've finished with him he'll be sorry, I can tell you.'

Mum, her lip red and swollen from Dad's earlier blow to her face, made another vain attempt at reason. 'Alf, there's been enough trouble for one day, can't you just leave it for now? Please. We all know you've had a tough time at work. But starting another lot of trouble with Gustav won't help the situation. Him and Anna have been good to us. They've helped us out a lot, especially recently, with money being tight and all. They're more like friends than…'

Interrupting her mid-sentence, Dad was in no mood to compromise. 'He's no friend of mine, just some German bloke I have to work with. We'll see what he's got to say for himself when I get back. No mate of mine would have let me get sent home early like that.' Turning for the door, he threw each of us a last withering glance. 'You're all as bad as each other. None of you understand what I have to put up with. If it wasn't for me and the money I bring in, you'd all be out on the street. And what sort of thanks do I get? Bugger all, that's what.'

Deep down, Mum may have loved Dad, but self-pity wasn't a trait she was willing to support, especially when fuelled by violent behaviour and alcohol.

'That's not fair, Alf. It's not our fault you got sent home early. And you going off to spend more of the little we do have at The Blue Anchor certainly isn't going to help feed any of us tomorrow, is it?'

Clenching his fist, Dad took a step towards her. 'I've told you more than once today, woman, don't you bloody speak to me like that, not unless you want some more of this.'

For the first time during one of his outbursts Mum didn't flinch. I sensed, having been subjected to yet another brutal assault earlier, and seeing me beaten so harshly, she had decided attack might be the best form of defence. I recognised, having made a similar commitment not to cower the next time he went on the rampage, how tough that might be for her to see through. None the less, Mum's bravery bolstered my own resolve. If she could do it, then so could I. I looked on with pride as she responded to his verbal attack, a note of strength in her voice as she spoke.

'That's your answer to everything when you've been drinking, shouting at us, or lashing out.' Pausing momentarily, she glanced reassuringly at Edith and I before continuing. 'We can't go on like this, Alf, living in fear of you and your moods. It's not fair on any of us. Things have got to change.'

Seemingly taken aback by her considered response, delivered without apparent fear of reprisal, Dad grunted and turned on his heel towards the back door.

'Yeah, well, we'll see about that. And don't forget I want those two out of my sight when I get back. I ain't gonna put up with any more cheek from either of them.'

And with that he was gone. We each stood in silence for a moment; a collective sigh of relief shared between us. Edith was the first to speak.

'I hate him, Mum, why can't we go and live with Aunty Ida and Uncle Walter in Brighton?'

Mum smiled. 'It's not that easy, love. We haven't got any money to get there for a start, and living with them is a lot different than going to see them for a few days by the seaside. They've only got a small house themselves. It's fine to sleep on their floor when we go for a visit, but we couldn't stay there all the time. Anyway, what would happen to your dad if we weren't here? He struggles enough when we are around, goodness knows what he'd be like if we left.'

Edith and I looked at each other, neither of us able to comprehend the motivation behind Mum making such a statement. How could she still care for Dad so deeply in a relationship as violent and one-sided as theirs? She did everything she could to make him happy, and all he did by way of thanks was to spend our money on drink and beat her mercilessly if she dared to question him or his behaviour.

'It's not fair the way he treats you, Mum, hitting you and the like. I agree with Edith, we should go and leave him to it.'

Ruffling my hair, she pulled the two of us into herself. 'Your dad's not all bad. When things are going well, and he hasn't been drinking he can be really nice. What about that time a couple of weeks back when we took a picnic and went to the fields for the day? He played with the two of you all afternoon.'

Edith looked unimpressed. 'Yes, until he decided to go to the pub on the way home. You said we could have fish and chips as a treat for our tea, but by the time he got back it was too late. He'd spent all the money on beer, so we went to bed hungry, and you two had another row. It always ends up the same with him. We either go hungry or there's a fight between the two of you.'

Hugging us, Mum did her best to remain positive.

'Well, you won't go hungry today. I've made that stew I promised. And before you ask, yes, I made dumplings as well. I didn't have time to make a suet pudding though. I won't be able to either now, I'm afraid, not with your dad wanting you in bed when he gets back. It'll take too long, and there's no point in upsetting him all over again. He won't be back until six or later I should think, but it'll still mean an early night for you two. I'm sorry about that, but you can play quietly in your bedroom for a while.'

Taking the initiative in trying to support her, I nudged Edith and winked. 'All right, Mum, if it stops Dad arguing again.'

Running her fingers through my hair again, she smiled. 'Thank you, Harry, and you, Edith, that's very grown-up of you both. And because you're being so good you can take the sweets I bought you upstairs as well. Only don't let your dad know, especially after you've cleaned your teeth, or we'll all be in trouble again. It won't hurt for one night. Now, come on, you can help lay the table while I get that stew served up. You both must be starving.'

The mood in our house was always lighter when Dad wasn't around, and with the added bonus of a proper meal being prepared Edith and I were happy to carry out our duties while Mum busied herself in the scullery.

The next hour was spent happily chatting with Mum and enjoying generous helpings of her delicious stew. She even provided a thick slice of fresh crusty bread to wipe the gravy from the side of our plates.

'Thanks, Mum, that was great,' I said, licking the last bit of gravy from my fingers.

'I'm pleased you enjoyed it. And there's still a nice big plateful left for your dad when he gets in.'

Turning on her chair, Edith looked at Mum. 'Do you think Karl's dad *will* come round? Dad said he had to, we heard him earlier.'

Mum shook her head. 'I hope not. I told Anna he shouldn't. We've had enough arguments in this house for one day. Hopefully, after a decent meal and a good night's sleep your dad will have calmed down. Tomorrow's another day, and fingers crossed he might get a full day's work which should make him feel better about himself as well.'

'And that'll mean a bit more money to buy food with.'

Laughing, Mum leant across the table to pick up our plates. 'You and your stomach, Harry Thompson. Honestly, I'd swear you've got hollow legs. You've just had a big helping of stew and you're already thinking about your next meal.'

Passing my plate, I grinned. 'That's not fair. Anyway, I wasn't thinking about my next meal, I was thinking about those sweets you said we could have.'

Rising from her seat, Mum laughed again. 'I might have known.'

Edith slid off her chair and walked towards the scullery. 'Can I help with the washing up?'

'Thank you, Edith, that would be kind. Harry, you can get some more coal in for the fire, although we probably won't need it. The washing dried outside earlier, so it won't need to go on the pulley. We don't want to waste coal if we don't need to, especially with the weather being warmer at the moment.'

Grateful to have escaped the washing up, I picked up the coal scuttle and made for the back door. 'Okay, Mum, won't be long.'

I decided to use the toilet while I was outside, not wanting to come back downstairs later when Dad got home. Edith and I had the pot under our bed for when we were desperate, but now we were getting older it was embarrassing listening to someone else pee in the same room, even though it was dark, and you couldn't see anything. We both felt the same but didn't know how to tell Mum and Dad without causing them further angst. A number of the houses locally had three bedrooms, but we only had two, and so Edith and I were forced to share. We both knew, as we continued to grow, one of us would eventually have to sleep downstairs in the front room. However, we also recognised this wasn't a topic for discussion in the immediate future, especially with Dad's violent behaviour and mood swings getting worse.

When I was younger, Mum or Dad would lift me up and place me on the toilet seat, but now I was older and taller I could manage myself. Age and height did nothing to improve the chilly and coarse feel of that rough wooden seat as it met with my backside though. It felt especially harsh this evening as I carefully positioned myself following the tanning I had received from Dad's belt. As I sat there doing my business, I turned to check there were no spiders hiding beneath the torn sheets of newspaper hanging from the piece of string nailed to the wall. I smiled inwardly, remembering one occasion when Edith had screamed for ages before anyone heard her pleas for help after a big spider had sited itself on the wall next to the paper. Terrified it was about to jump on to her, she sat rigid until Mum eventually heard her cries and came to the rescue. Whilst I wasn't particularly fearful of these eight-legged arthropods, I also wasn't overly enamoured by the prospect of a large one scuttling across the wall and dropping onto my leg as it emerged from its hiding place behind a torn sheet of paper.

'You took your time, Harry, did you forget where we keep the coal?' Mum enquired as I entered the scullery again.

'Been to the loo,' I replied, pushing my way past her with the loaded scuttle.

'Daydreaming more like. Anyway, let's get the two of you washed and ready for your bed. I know it's early, but we don't want any more trouble with your dad, do we? He'll be back soon I should think. He might like a drink, but he knows there's stew tonight and he won't want to miss out on that.'

'Or be too drunk to enjoy it.'

'Edith, that's no way to speak about your father.'

Placing the scuttle by the fire, I jumped to Edith's defence. 'Oh come on, Mum, how can you stick up for him after what he did earlier? Edith's right, it's not often he puts food before his drink.'

'That's as maybe, but he's still your dad.'

'Worst luck,' Edith countered, wiping a plate with Mum's frayed tea towel. 'Look at this,' she said, pointing to the ragged appearance of the towel. 'Everything in this house is either torn or got holes in. Mrs Jones's tea towels didn't have holes in when we went there earlier. They were nice and clean as well. And her clothes were clean. And I don't just mean her daughter's wedding dress. Did you see the dress she was wearing?' Turning to me, she continued. 'Bright green it was, Harry, and not a mark on it. I'd give anything to have a new dress like that.'

Mum's expression changed. Looking crestfallen and ashamed, she apologised. 'I'm sorry, Edith, truly I am. I wish you could have a new dress as well.' With tears filling her eyes, she turned to me. 'And you, Harry. I'd love you to have some new clothes too.' Attempting a smile, she continued. 'Look at those shorts of yours, they've got more patches in them than the original material.' Seeking to control her emotions, she paused and took a breath before continuing. 'I'm really sorry, both of you, but we just don't have any money to spend on new clothes at the moment.'

We both felt Mum's pain, understanding how upsetting it must be for her to send her children out in ill-fitting or hastily repaired clothing. Most of the families struggled to survive financially where we lived. Everyone found it hard to get by on the low wages paid by the shipyard owners, but most did the best they could on the little they had coming in. But poor Mum rarely had the chance to put even a penny or two away for new clothes, let alone shoes. Yes, Dad had been in a good mood the day before and given her what he had in his pocket, rather than spending it in the pub. That meant we ate well today, but what about tomorrow? Would there be anything left when he came back this evening? And if not, where would Mum find the money to feed us then? Knowing Dad, if he remembered the money he'd given her yesterday, he would probably demand it back to buy more drink. The fact she'd already spent it on food would only exacerbate his mood. Once fuelled by alcohol, Dad's desire for drink outweighed any reasoned argument proffered about the need to feed the family. He would argue Mum was spending too much on even the basics, choosing to forget that unless there was a hot meal on the table for him each evening, he would make her life hell. He would demand she account for every penny that found its way into her purse rather than across the bar at The Blue Anchor. Mum couldn't win. In his mind, she was either spending too much on us, or was incapable of organising the family finances correctly. Nothing could be further from the truth. Mum never gave a thought to her own well-being, or about treating herself to something nice occasionally. Her number one priority was always Edith and me. After that, it was Dad and how she could make him happy. Of course, he never saw that. Instead, he would berate her; placing the responsibility for all our ills at her door, when in reality the blame belonged squarely with him.

I understood Edith's sadness in seeing other young girls having a new dress to wear while she had to make do with hand-me-downs, or ones that had been altered to fit her. Even so, I still felt the need to defend Mum.

'It's not Mum's fault you can't have a new dress, or that our tea towels have got holes in them. She's not to blame for Dad spending all our money at the pub. She does the best she can.'

Embarrassed, Edith directed her frustration towards me. 'I know that. I wasn't saying it was her fault, I'm just…'

Interrupting, Mum moved to comfort Edith. 'I know what you meant, love, it's all right.'

Accepting her outburst had been unwarranted, Edith apologised. 'Sorry, Mum, I didn't mean anything.'

'Hush now, there's no need to apologise. Don't you worry any more about it.' Looking at the two of us, she smiled. 'I love you both very much. Don't ever think I don't. Now come on, let's get you washed and changed. I'm sorry you're having to go to your room so early, but we really don't want to upset your Dad anymore today. Hopefully, after he's had his tea, he'll be in a better mood, and we might all have an easier day tomorrow.'

The next half an hour saw Edith and I get ready for bed and make our way upstairs for an enforced early night. Mum was good to her word though and handed over a small bag of sweets as she tucked us in.

'This is our secret, remember. Not a word to your dad, or we'll all be in trouble.'

'I hope he's not too drunk when he comes back, Mum, he'd already had a skinful earlier.'

'Me too, son. Now listen both of you, whatever happens you're to stay up here, all right?'

'But what if he hits you again, we can't just…'

'Yes, you can,' she replied, waving away our protestations. 'Please, don't come down, it'll only make matters worse. I'm sure he'll be better once he's had his tea.' She smiled. 'Your dad always likes a stew, and with those dumplings in it, I'm sure he'll be fine.' Glancing back as she moved to exit, Mum blew us both a kiss. 'Enjoy your sweets and sleep well. Love you.'

Edith and I replied in unison. 'Love you too, Mum.'

We watched as she closed the door before clambering out of bed and opening our bag of sweets. Sitting opposite me on the floor, Edith sighed. 'I'm going to say a prayer that Mum will be okay.'

Shaking my head, I grinned. 'Good for you. Although I'm not sure God is that bothered about the likes of us. If he is, he has a funny way of showing it. Nothing good ever seems to happen in our house. Maybe you should pray that Dad has an accident and dies, that would be all right. Then we could go and live with Uncle Walter and Aunty Ida like you said earlier.'

'Harry, that's a terrible thing to say. I know he was horrible earlier, hitting you and Mum like he did, but you still shouldn't wish him dead. You shouldn't wish anybody dead.'

'Maybe not, but you weren't on the other end of his belt earlier. It really hurt.'

'Even so, to wish him dead.'

'Yeah, okay. Now hand over one of those sweets. What did you and Mum buy anyway?'

'Gobstoppers, 'cause they last longer.'

'Good thinking.'

Pausing to savour the moment, we both fixed our eyes on the delicious red balls of confection before cramming them into our mouths. Sucking hard on her sweet, Edith pointed to my hand and mumbled, 'Why did you and Karl cut yourselves? To be brothers, wasn't it? Seems silly to me. Why would you cut someone's hand if you want to be their brother?'

Removing the gobstopper from my mouth, I attempted to explain our earlier bloodletting ritual.

'Not brothers, silly, it's *blood brothers*. We cut our hands and held them together so our blood mixed up and now I have Karl's blood in my body and he has mine in his.'

Trying to control the sweet as it rolled around in her mouth, Edith replied, 'Sounds horrible to me. I don't like blood at the best of times. And I really don't like the thought of having someone else's blood inside me, yuk.'

'No, it's great. Our blood is joined together forever now. We took an oath to be best friends for always as well. It means we will never lie to each other, or hurt each other, or tell anyone else about what we do when we're together. It's like a secret agreement just between the two of us that can never be broken.'

'Still sounds silly to me.'

Sitting together happily sucking on our gobstoppers and exchanging childish stories in the safe haven of our bedroom, it was easy to forget the real reason for our being sent to bed so early. A few minutes later the atmosphere took on a darker hue with the sound of Dad's voice booming out from below.

'Those two in bed?'

Mum had obviously left the sitting-room door open when going back downstairs as we were able to hear their conversation. Her reply being delivered in a gentler and more obliging tone.

'Yes Alf, they're down for the night. Now sit yourself at the table while I get your stew and dumplings. I made them especially.'

Mum hadn't been wrong in hoping that a proper meal would have the desired effect on Dad's mood, as his response demonstrated.

'I'm ready for something to eat, girl, and that's a fact.'

Whilst he'd obviously been drinking again his tone appeared more tempered. Perhaps time away from the house had also given him the opportunity to reconsider his earlier aggression towards us. Whatever the reason, Edith and I breathed a sigh of relief.

'Sounds like he's calmed down a bit.'

'Let's hope so, Mum's been through enough today already.'

'And you, Harry, don't forget that belting he gave you earlier.'

Whilst the indignation at being beaten so harshly had diminished slightly, the discomfort from the stripes across my back and legs still lingered; certainly enough to remind me we both had some way to go in healing our relationship. This hadn't been the first time I'd felt the sting of Dad's belt, and I was sure it wouldn't be the last. Even so, I appreciated Edith's concern. In an effort to assuage her fears, I put on a brave face and smiled.

'Oh, I'm all right, it'd take a lot more than that to really hurt me.' We both knew I wasn't being entirely truthful but were happy to leave it there.

Finishing our sweets and climbing back into bed we heard Dad's voice again. Clearly, a generous helping of Mum's stew had facilitated the desired effect on both his stomach and his temperament.

'You make a good stew, Flo, I'll give you that.'

It appeared a second visit to The Blue Anchor had given him time to think, re-evaluate his mood and, more importantly, his good fortune in being married to Mum. If I was struggling to forgive his earlier display of violence, goodness knows how she must have been feeling. Her love for Dad obviously ran deep alongside, I suspected, her fear of him.

Just as Edith and I were beginning to think the evening might end on a more peaceful note, there was a loud knock on the front door. Rushing from our beds, the two of us looked out of the window to the street below. It was Gustav. Anna had obviously told him of Dad's earlier visit, along with his aggressive demand that he should come to our house as soon as he got home. From the insistent banging on our door, it was evident Dad's belligerent attitude demonstrated towards Karl's mum hadn't gone down well.

Edith and I slid open the window and popped our heads out to get a better view. We didn't have to wait long for things to kick off as Gustav continued hammering on the door.

'You come out here, Alf Thompson. I won't have you speaking to my wife like you did.'

We could hear Dad shouting below.

'It's that bloody German. Who does he think he is banging on our door like that?'

The front door flew wide as Dad launched himself into the street, standing toe to toe with Gustav.

'What the bloody hell do you think you're doing?'

'I could say the same to you. How dare you come to my house and threaten my wife.'

'I didn't threaten her. Anyway, it was you I was after.'

'Well, I am here now, so what do you want?'

'You watched me and George get laid off today, and you didn't say a word to the foreman. I can't afford not to be working.'

'I don't make the rules. I just work there, the same as you. What was I supposed to say, that he should send me home instead? Anyway, if you hadn't lost your temper, like you always do, he might have thought differently. You are your own worst enemy; you bring these things on yourself. You are not an easy man to like, or to work with.'

As the two of them squared up to one another, Mum moved in between them.

'Stop it, both of you. There's been enough shouting and fighting for one day. Gustav, I apologise for the way Alf spoke to Anna.' Turning to Dad, she continued. 'He's sorry as well, aren't you, Alf?'

Dad was in no mood to back down and pushed Mum to one side. 'I'm not sorry for anything, and I'm certainly not apologising to this fucking German, not when he…'

Before Dad could finish his sentence, Gustav's fist landed squarely on his nose.

'I won't be spoken to like that by you or anyone. And I won't stand by and watch a man push his wife around either.'

Mum made another attempt to ease the tension.

'Stop it, both of you. It's enough. Please, I…'

Her pleas for reason fell on deaf ears, certainly as far as Dad was concerned. Forcing her to one side again, he threw a punch at his opponent. Thankfully it missed. Edith and I looked on as he staggered forward, grasping at thin air, before falling to his knees onto the ground. Whilst the blow from Gustav's fist had clearly unbalanced him, an afternoon spent in The Blue Anchor had done nothing to improve his equilibrium either.

Gustav took a step back. 'I am sorry, Florence, you are right. I should not have hit him. But he is not an easy man to be with, and I won't have him shout at my Anna; not under any circumstances.'

Getting back to his feet and with blood dripping from his nose, Dad was not in the mood to make peace. He threw another punch, this time connecting with the side of Gustav's head, causing him to take a step back.

'You can apologise all you like to my wife, you German shit, but you won't get the better of me.' He swayed from side to side, waving his hands in the air like some demented boxer waiting for his adversary to strike. He didn't have to wait for long.

Rubbing the side of his head, Gustav turned to Mum. 'As I have said, I am sorry about all of this, Florence. I have tried to be reasonable with your husband, but now my patience has gone.' With that he landed another punch to Dad's face, this time knocking him to the ground. 'Now it is finished.' He looked down at Dad who was lying prostrate on the pavement, blood running from his mouth as well as his nose.

'I am going home now. You will not come to my house anymore, and you will never speak to my wife as you did earlier, ever again. Do I make myself clear?'

Mum knelt beside Dad to comfort him. Stunned by the second blow to his face, he nodded his understanding of what had been said, but was still in no mood to agree a truce.

'Yeah, go on then, fuck off home, but don't think you've heard the last of this, 'cause you ain't.'

Taking a deep breath, Gustav bent down and addressed Dad directly to his face. 'I hope for both our sakes you will reconsider what you have just said, Alf, because I don't want to argue with any of my neighbours. But, if you do decide to start another fight with me, let me make it very clear, I will hurt you again, and I will win. You should be ashamed of the way you behave, and of the way you treat your family.'

Mum was crying as she helped Dad to his feet. 'There won't be any more trouble, Gustav. I think we've all had enough arguing and fighting for one day. Please apologise to Anna for me.' Glancing briefly at Dad, she continued. 'For both of us.'

Shrugging her away, Dad moved to support himself against the wall. 'Don't you say sorry for me, you cow. I can speak for myself, and it certainly won't be to apologise to him or his bleedin' wife.'

Turning to leave, Gustav threw Dad an acerbic grin. 'Little men like you always think they are big when they have been drinking. And of course, you have been drinking, you are always drinking, that is what is so sad about you. It is the reason you are the first to be sent home when there isn't enough work for everyone. It is also the reason you complain about having no money. You spend what little you do have at the pub instead of giving it to Florence to buy food and clothes for your children. As I said, you should be ashamed of yourself.'

Mum moved to hold Dad back as he pushed himself away from the wall, clearly intending on renewing the fight.

'Get off me, Flo, or you'll get the same as him. I'm not letting some fucking German tell me what to do, or how to live.'

Stepping forward to protect Mum from Dad's flailing hands, Gustav spoke slowly and deliberately.

'I have heard that you have hit Florence before, but never witnessed it for myself. You will not hit her again. If you do, I will come and hit you much harder. I don't like men who hit their wives. Now go inside before you embarrass yourself and your family any further.'

By now there was a small crowd of neighbours standing around, having come outside to see what all the fuss was about. Everyone knew about Dad's drinking and his corresponding bad temper, but this did little to alleviate Mum's humiliation at having our personal troubles displayed so openly for all to see. She smiled apologetically and moved again to encourage Dad inside.

'Come on Alf, please, let's just go in now. Let's have no more trouble tonight, eh? I think we've all had enough.'

Clearly embarrassed himself and equally humiliated that his authority as a husband and as a man had been exposed, Dad stormed inside but not without delivering a withering riposte to all looking on, and to Gustav as he moved away.

'Seen all you want, have you? Go on, you can all piss off home now, the fun's over. And as for you, you German bastard, your day will come.'

Mum threw everyone another apologetic glance before moving into the house and closing the door behind her. Edith and I looked at each other as we moved away from the window, closing it quietly so as not to let on we'd also been witness to the events of the last few minutes.

'Flipping heck, sis, what did you make of that? That was quite a pasting Karl's dad gave him.'

'A good job too. I hope it hurt. I hate it when he drinks so much. He gets so angry.' I watched as tears filled her eyes, her voice cracking as she spoke. 'It scares me when I see him hit you and Mum; and now fighting with Mr Schmidt as well.' She looked at me wistfully. 'Sometimes, not often, when he hasn't been drinking, he can be all right. But, other times, like just now, or earlier with you and Mum, it makes me wish he wasn't our dad, and that he'd just go away and leave us alone.'

The chill of the evening air and unease from having observed the events of the past few minutes caused me to shiver as I climbed back into bed. Pulling the blanket up under my chin, I nodded my agreement.

'I know what you mean.'

As we sat, considering the potential of a life without Dad around, our thoughts were interrupted by the sound of his voice booming out from below.

'Who does he think he is, coming round here and shouting the odds like that. I'll knock his bloody head off next time, that's what. None of this would have happened if he'd have spoken up for me earlier. I was on his team. He could have said I was needed. It's all his bloody fault.'

Keen to hear what Mum would say in response and to make sure she would be okay, Edith and I climbed out of bed and made our way to the top of the stairs, slipping a blanket around our shoulders to keep warm.

We listened intently as Mum replied. Choosing her words carefully, it was obvious she didn't want to deny the truth of what had just happened, nor the reason behind it. Equally, she needed to be sensitive to Dad's wounded pride; also, of the potential for him to fly off the handle again should she get it wrong.

'Alf, love, it wasn't Gustav's fault you got sent home. Like I said earlier, it wasn't anybody's fault. It was just bad luck they chose you and George. Now, before you say anything else, let me look at that nose of yours, it's still bleeding a bit.'

'It's just a bit of blood, woman, don't fuss. There's worse happens at the docks every day.'

'That's as maybe, but I'm not married to the rest of the dockers, just you, so let me have a look at it.'

'If it hadn't been for that sodding German, I wouldn't have a bloody nose. Bastard.'

'And if you hadn't threatened him in the first place none of this would have happened at all. Now, hold still while I look at it.' There was a short pause before Mum spoke again. 'It looks all right, and your lip's stopped bleeding now as well.'

'That's right, blame me. I'm warning you, Flo…'

Interrupting, and with an air of assumed authority in her voice, Mum responded. 'Don't threaten me again, Alf, not tonight. There's been enough fighting in this house for one day.'

With the effects of his earlier intake of alcohol wearing off, coupled with a sore nose and a full stomach, Dad's rage was beginning to abate. He grunted. 'Well, like I say, it's that German you should be having a go at, not me.'

Sensing the change in Dad's demeanour, Mum's voice took on a more sympathetic tone as she replied, 'Please, love, just listen for a minute. I know Gustav was maybe in the wrong to speak about what goes on in our house like he did, but… well, he does have a point. You do drink a lot. And before you start, I'm not saying you shouldn't have a beer from time to time. I'm just asking you to think about the effect it has on you, and what that leads to sometimes, like earlier with you and Harry.'

'Now don't start on at me again about the boy, Flo. He lipped me and got what was coming to him. And as far as going to the pub is concerned; I like a drink and am entitled to a couple of pints after a day's work. I won't have you or anyone else tell me different.'

'I'm not saying you shouldn't have a drink with your mates occasionally but… take today, for instance. You get sent home early, which means less money coming in, and then you spend what little there is at the pub because you're angry.'

'I'm not having that, and anyway, you had enough money to buy meat for that stew, so things can't be that bad.'

'The reason I was able to make the stew was because you gave me a bit extra yesterday when you *hadn't* been drinking. But I bet you haven't got any money left in your pocket now, so there'll be nothing for tea tomorrow. Not unless I can get some credit from Ivy Miller at the corner shop. If she'll let me have a loaf on tick, I can boil up the bones left over from that bit of meat we had, along with a couple of spuds and make some sort of broth for us, but that'll be it.'

We weren't sure whether Mum had hit a nerve or that the blows from Karl's dad had finally knocked some sense into him, but Dad's reply took Edith and I by surprise. His voice measured and temperate as he spoke. 'I hear what you're saying, Flo, but it ain't easy, you know. Truth is I hate working on those bloody docks, but there ain't nothing else around, not for a bloke with my skills anyway.'

Recognising his frustration and perceived lack of purpose, Mum paused before responding, this time with genuine understanding and sensitivity in her voice. 'I know you're not happy working there, Alf, but it's the same for everyone. We all have it tough round here, and with not a lot of reward, but we do have each other. I just wish the three of us were enough for you, and you could find some happiness in that.'

Sensing he may have revealed too much about his personal demons, and not wanting to appear weak, Dad reverted to type.

'It don't help either when you start on at me for having a few drinks. And I certainly ain't gonna take any nonsense from that little bugger upstairs neither. He ain't old enough to tell me what to do, and I certainly ain't gonna have him jumping in when you and me are talking.'

Reacting to Dad's change in tone, Mum replied with equal determination. 'We weren't talking, Alf, we were arguing, like we always do. And… you hit me, so the lad stepped in to protect his mum. You should be proud of him for that, not take your belt to him.'

'And what about cutting himself with that Karl then, and then cheeking me for it? What's that all about then, little sod.'

'He's just a boy. It's the sort of stupid thing they do at that age. It's still no reason to beat him like you did.'

Edith leant across and whispered in my ear, 'See, even Mum says you were stupid to cut your hand.'

'What does she know about it? What do any of you know? Karl and I are mates forever now.'

'I know enough to agree with Mum, it was stupid.' She grinned. 'You're stupid.'

'I love you too,' I replied, poking her in the ribs.

The conversation downstairs continued. Thankfully, Dad was calmer again, although clearly still far from happy with Gustav.

'That's as maybe, but he still doesn't have the right to tell me what to do. And I'm certainly not having that bloody German sticking his oar in either.'

'Even when he's telling you not to beat your wife and son?'

There was a long silence as Edith and I held our breath waiting for Dad's response, praying it wouldn't be with more violence. After what seemed like an age, he spoke again.

'I don't like hitting you, Flo, nor the boy. I know I shouldn't, but when I get angry a red mist sort of comes down and I don't seem to be able to stop myself. I ain't ever hit Edith though. At least not like… you know.'

'Like you do Harry and me, is that what you're trying to say? It's all right to hit your wife and son but not your daughter. And why? Because she's a little girl? Harry's younger than she is, and there isn't much of me either come to that. But, according to you, the two of us are fair game though.'

Dad's mood switched again, and not for the good.

'Now don't start all that again. You may be a woman, but you've got a tongue on you as sharp as any bloke I know. I ain't going to sit here and listen to you bollocking me, do you hear?'

Recognising she may have hit a nerve, even though her point was apposite, Mum backed away from the potential for further aggression.

'I didn't mean to make you angry again, Alf. I was just pointing out that Harry and I are also pretty defenceless against you, especially when you've been drinking.'

'Yeah, well, I won't be drinking tomorrow will I, 'cause there ain't any money left. So you just better hope that shit of a foreman doesn't send me home early again or we won't be eating then either, or the day after, apart from that broth.'

'Then we'd better get to bed so you can be one of the first at the gate in the morning to get a full day's work in. And if Gustav says anything, just ignore him. You don't want to be getting into another fight. We really need you working and earning. I can't keep making ends meet when they're so frayed they don't even get close to reaching each other anymore.' There was another brief silence before Mum spoke again. 'I mean it, Alf, things have got to change, you've got to change.'

Edith and I jumped up as Dad replied, his chair scraping the bare wooden flooring as he got to his feet. 'I hear you, Flo, but I don't want to talk about it anymore, least ways not tonight.'

We raced to our bedroom, desperate to get there before Dad opened the door and found us at the top of the stairs.

Pulling the blanket over me as I clambered into bed, I called across to Edith, 'Night, sis.'

'Night.'

As I lay there thinking about all that had happened during the day, I ran my hand across the back of my legs. The weals from the beating I'd received were still raised, although the sting of pain that had accompanied them earlier had eased. I moved my fingers across to the cut on my palm and smiled. Whatever Dad said or did he couldn't take away what Karl and I had achieved together that day. We were now true brothers. I lay there, a broad grin stretching across my face as I thought about Karl's blood coursing through my veins and mine through his. I held my hands together as kindly sleep encouraged me towards its embrace.

Chapter Six

When you're young the cares of the world don't seem to matter so much. Even the occasional beating from Dad or going to bed on an empty stomach was viewed as just a part of life; a life which, in the main, I enjoyed, especially with Karl around. From pretty much the day we met until our mid-teens we were inseparable. Wherever one of us was, the other was sure not to be far behind. Even our parents began to think we were joined at the hip.

'Is there anything you boys don't do together?' Mum would ask. 'Apart from going to the toilet?'

'I've told you before, Mum, we're blood brothers. That's even closer than family.'

She would laugh and shake her head. 'I'm not quite sure how you come to that conclusion, Harry. There's more of your dad and my blood running through your veins than there is of Karl's.'

'Yes, but Karl and I chose to share our blood. I didn't have any choice about you and Dad.'

'Exactly my point. Without the two of us you wouldn't even be here.'

I knew she was kidding, no matter how much she teased me. Secretly, I think she and Anna quite liked the idea of the two of us being so close. It meant if there was any trouble, we would be there for each other to help raise the alarm.

Life wasn't easy for any of the families dependant on the docks for their livelihood in the early 1900s. This was especially true in our house. Even when Dad wasn't drinking there never seemed to be a lot of food around, nor the money to pay for it. After the dockers won the penny rise in their wages following the strike, it was hoped things might improve more generally; sadly, they didn't. There were some limited improvements to housing conditions towards the turn of the century, but proper sanitation and running water continued to remain an issue for most of those living in and around Canning Town at that time. And though there were schools, a proper education was still a long way off, as was the ability to attract decent teachers to the area. Despite the large amount of trade, money, and business the docks generated, along with huge profits for the shipyard owners themselves, there was little evidence of any of that profit being shared out amongst the dock workers and their families. As I grew older, I began to understand why Dad and some of the other men sought solace in the local pubs, rather than face the poverty that existed at home. It became a vicious circle with many of them drinking because they felt guilty in not being able to provide properly for their family. This, in turn, would mean their wives and children went barefoot and hungry because the little money earnt would end up behind a bar rather than spent on food and clothing.

There were a few exceptions of course, with Karl's dad being one of them. Perhaps, having faced similar hardship in Germany before arriving in England, Gustav had made the decision to put his family first and not spend his time drinking with the other men. He might join them occasionally and have a pint after his shift, but it was only ever one before heading home. Most of his wages would be handed over directly to Anna for paying bills and keeping the family clothed and fed. Men like Dad would tend to hand over what little was left *after* their drinking and gambling sessions. I think this was part of the reason why Dad resented Gustav at times. Not because he didn't drink or gamble as such, but rather because his own conscience was pricked each time he saw how much better off Gustav and Anna were. Sadly, this was a downward spiral Dad wasn't able to overcome. Perhaps, secretly, he didn't want to.

For the most part we children didn't know any different and simply accepted the life we had as being normal. Yes, we were aware of the shipyard owners and of the very different lifestyle their status and money afforded them, but we also knew this was a life we could never aspire to, and so just made the best of what we had. And when you're a child you tend not to ask the bigger questions in life, about fairness, social equality and so on. This was especially true for me and Karl. Although, I do think he became increasingly aware, as we grew, of the very different atmosphere and living conditions that existed in my house compared to his own. Even accepting those differences we were just happy to be in each other's company and let the rest of the world and its challenges pass us by. And so it continued until the summer of 1906 when the dynamic of our relationship changed forever.

Karl and I had been friends for almost eight years with hardly a cross word between us in all that time. And on the rare occasions we did disagree it would usually be over some trivial event such as whose turn it was to be in goal or which of us had come first in a race. Even after we became blood brothers, with Karl ribbing me about being a coward for not wanting to cut myself, I knew he was only joking. There was no malice intended. And so, when the dynamic of our relationship did alter, neither of us identified, at least initially, this particular event as being the catalyst for that change.

It had been a warm sunny day, with the two of us playing football in our road. We knew this wasn't the wisest place to kick a ball about and had been moved on numerous times by neighbours who were concerned one of us would eventually put the ball through their window. This particular day, it was Mrs White, who lived a couple of doors up from Karl, who was the first to read us the riot act.

'Listen, you boys, you've been told before about kicking that football around in the road. You'll knock something over or break a window, then you'll be in real trouble. Now go on, clear off the both of you before I fetch your mothers to sort you out.'

I was the first to respond. 'Sorry, Mrs White. We'll move somewhere else.'

Karl had never liked Mrs White or her husband. He said they were stuck-up and thought they were better than the other families in our road. She'd also just had a baby, their first, and was always telling us children to be quiet in case we woke it up. As if we cared. Babies just seem to cry or sleep whatever you did with them, as Karl was quick to remind her in his reply.

'We are all right here, Harry, and we won't be waking up her baby. That is if he's asleep anyway. He seems to cry most of the time.'

'You cheeky little sod. I'll go round and tell your mother what you said, Karl Schmidt, you see if I don't.'

'You can tell her what you like, she doesn't like you any more than I do.'

I'd never seen Karl like this. Normally, he would be happy to move on and let that be an end to it, but not today.

'Come on, Karl, we can play somewhere else.' I turned to Mrs White again. 'We are sorry, honest. Aren't we, Karl?'

'You might be, but I am not.'

I picked up the ball and tugged at Karl's arm, encouraging him to walk away as Mrs White's riposte rang in our ears.

'I heard that. You're as bad as your mother you are. Don't think you've heard the last of this, 'cause you haven't, either of you.'

Moving further up the road, I punched Karl playfully on the arm. 'What was all that about? What's she done to you to make you go off at her like that?' I laughed. 'Apart from telling us to bugger off whenever we play football near her house.'

'She had an argument with Mama last week. It was about her baby. Mama said she heard it crying in the backyard for a long time, and when she spoke to Mrs White about it and asked if the baby was all right, she got angry and told Mama to mind her own business. I think she thought Mama was telling her off for letting her baby cry for so long, but she wasn't. She was just concerned in case it wasn't well or there was a problem. Mama would never interfere or make trouble; she was just trying to be helpful. So that is why I said what I did to her.'

'Fair enough. But let's hope she doesn't say anything to our parents. We don't want to be the cause of another argument.' Reaching a piece of waste ground, I threw the ball down. 'Come on, let's play here.'

Karl shook his head. 'I don't want to play football anymore. Let's go to the docks and watch them unloading the ships.'

'Okay, but we better be careful. If we get caught we'll definitely be in trouble, whether Mrs White says anything or not.'

We'd watched the ships arrive and unload before. Children weren't allowed on the docks for safety reasons, but we'd found a couple of places where we could hide and watch proceedings without being spotted. Some of the ships that came in were massive and I used to wonder how they managed to stay afloat when fully loaded. As young boys, we were fascinated to think of these huge vessels sailing halfway round the world to bring whatever it was they were carrying to our port in London. We'd watch as men scurried up and down the gangplanks shouting at each other in different languages while cranes lifted large pallets loaded with supplies on and off the ships. It made us appreciate how hard our dads and the others worked for their money, and of the risks involved. Unloading cargo from a ship's hold could be quite dangerous if a pallet came loose and fell whilst being lowered to the ground. There had been numerous accidents in the past, with stories recounted of men being taken to hospital after being injured by a falling crate. Apparently, a docker had died as a result of his injuries during one particular incident. There were also times when crates were 'accidently' allowed to fall and spill open, especially if they contained food or sugar. Some of this bounty would quickly be squirreled away before the foreman or ship's owner arrived to assess the damage and potential loss. Later, once the bosses had retreated back to their offices, the contraband would be shared out amongst the men to help supplement their meagre income. Our family had been the recipient of a few of these windfalls in the past. Even Mum was happy not to ask too many questions when they arrived.

'Had a bit of an accident at work again today, Flo,' Dad would say, placing a package on the table. 'Bloody crate of sugar fell off its pallet. We cleared up what we could, but it seemed silly just to throw the rest away, so we split the leftovers between us.'

Mum would ask the obvious question but knew better than to push for too much detail in Dad's response. 'Did the foreman say it was okay?'

'Well, he didn't say no. But, then again, what he don't know won't hurt him, will it.'

Arriving at the dockyard, Karl and I forced aside a wooden panel on one of the fences and made our way towards a ship that had recently berthed ready for unloading. It had a steel hull and single chimney set halfway amidships, with steam and smoke billowing from it. There were thick ropes attached to the stern and bow to secure it against the quayside. Standing proud like some enormous Aladdin's cave, we watched as the men moved into position ready to receive whatever treasure was brought forth from the bowels of the vessel. The fact it had sailed from so far away only increased our sense of wonder. We looked on as cranes swung into action overhead, intrigued by the apparent efficiency of the whole process, yet equally aware of the potential risk to life and limb should anything go wrong.

'Just think, Karl, a few weeks ago that ship was in a different part of the world and now here it is in London. What must it be like to live in another country, like the West Indies, or America?'

'I do not know what the West Indies or America are like. But, remember I am from Germany, so I am already from another country.'

'Do you remember what it was like in Germany?'

'Not really. I was only young when we came here. But I know I like London because here I met you, and now we are friends.'

I laughed. 'Not just friends, blood brothers.'

We sat there for some time watching as the ship's cargo was unloaded, with heavy pallets of supplies being lowered to the ground from the towering cranes overhead.

'Do you think this is what we'll do when we're older? You know, work here, unloading ships?'

'Maybe, but I would rather do something different. We moved from Germany to have a better life, but my father still works on the docks, and so nothing has really changed.'

'What would you do instead?'

'I don't know, maybe go back to Germany, and see if things have improved. I like the idea of going home again; to my real home, even though I hardly remember anything about it. Papa says he enjoys living in England, but that we should never forget we are German, and that Hamburg will always be our real home.'

'You can't go back to Hamburg. If you do what will happen to us?'

Karl laughed. 'Maybe you could come to Germany with me and we could be friends there.'

'I'll have to think about that. Anyway, that's a long way off, we still have to finish school yet. I'll tell you where I wouldn't mind going though.'

'Where?'

'Home. I'm getting hungry, we've been here for ages.'

'Good idea. You can come back to my house if you want. Mama will make us something to eat.'

'Only if she says it's okay,' I replied, hoping it would be. Much as I enjoyed being at home with Mum and Edith, I also knew there was always more to eat at Karl's house.

'Come on then, let's go.'

We made our way back through the gap in the fence, carefully replacing the plank in its original position before heading for home.

As we arrived at the top of our road, we noticed Mrs White had placed her baby's pram outside the open front door, presumably in the hope the sunshine and fresh air might encourage the child to sleep.

Karl moved to cross the road. 'Come, I have an idea that will teach her a lesson after she was angry with us earlier.'

'What do you mean?'

'We can push the pram forward a little and tell her it is running away. She will be scared. But then we can stop it and she will thank us and tell our mothers we are good, and not make any trouble because we played football outside her house earlier. It is a good plan, yes?'

I wasn't so sure. 'Let's not. I'm sure she won't say anything to our mums about earlier. She said she will, but I bet she won't. She'll probably have forgotten all about it by now.'

It was too late. Karl was already by the pram and pushing aside the piece of wood under the wheel to stop it from moving. 'Here, I will push it forward a little and you shout for her to come.'

'Karl, I really think this is a bad idea. Let's…' My voice trailed away as Karl gave the pram a gentle shove forward.

Turning to me, he laughed. 'Go on, Harry, shout to her to come and I will stop the pram from running away. She will thank us, you will see.'

I moved to the front door which was open. Putting my head inside I yelled, 'Mrs White, quick, your pram is moving.'

I turned to look at Karl who was still smiling at me. 'Say it again.'

As I opened my mouth to shout again, the words stuck in my throat. Looking over Karl's shoulder I noticed the pram was now rolling at speed down the slope and away from us. 'Karl... the pram, it's moving too quickly. Go after it.'

Hearing the panic in my voice, Karl turned and lunged towards the runaway pram, slipping as he did so and falling to the ground.

I shouted again as loud as I could. 'Mrs White, your baby...'

Before I could finish, she was at the door. 'What are you yelling about?' Her voice froze. Looking beyond me, she watched as the pram gathered pace and bounced off the pavement into the road, making its way relentlessly towards the bottom of the hill. 'My baby,' she screamed, pushing past me, and chasing after the runaway carriage.

I moved to follow her, but my legs were rooted to the spot. I stood, gaping on in horror at the scene unfolding before me. Karl scrambled to his feet. 'Come, Harry, we must get the pram.'

I felt tears sting the back of my eyes. 'What have you done, Karl, what have you done?'

He began to race after Mrs White who was still chasing the runaway pram as it gathered speed down the hill. I stared at the two of them, still unable to move, as the full impact of what was happening gripped me. Several neighbours began to emerge from their houses to see what all the fuss was about in response to Mrs White's shrieks of terror. 'Somebody, help, please, stop my baby's pram.'

At the bottom of the hill I could see our milkman's horse and cart. The animal, a large brown-and-white dray with fluffy white skirts of hair around each of its hooves, stood patiently waiting for its owner, Mr Potter, to return from a delivery to one of the houses in our road. As the pram careered towards it, the horse panicked and reared up, its front legs rising high into the air, before crashing down onto the pram as it ran headlong into the animal. I'll never forget the scream from Mrs White that followed as the horse kicked away the remnants of the shattered pram in its desperation to be free.

'No... not my baby. Please God, not my baby, no!'

Mr Potter dropped the crate of milk he was carrying and moved to calm his still anxious horse. Taking hold of the strapping to the side of the animal's head, he patted it gently on the side of the neck.

'There Daisy, it's all right. There's a good girl.'

Daisy! What sort of name was that for an animal of such a size, and one that had just crushed a pram, along with the small life contained within it. Forcing my legs forward I began the descent towards the bottom of the hill. There was quite a crowd gathered by now around the tragic scene. Two women were attempting to hold Mrs White back from looking into the wreckage of her baby's pram.

'Come away, Joan, let Stan go first,' one of the women said as a burly man with his stomach pushing hard against his partly buttoned waistcoat moved towards the pram and knelt beside it.

Mrs White was utterly bereft, sobbing into one of the women's shoulders whilst gasping for breath at the same time.

'My baby, my baby,' she repeated over and over as the woman sought to comfort her.

As I arrived, so Mum came up behind me. 'What's going on, Harry?' Before I could answer she noticed the pram, immediately cognisant of what had happened.

Still gripping Mrs White tightly in her arms, the other woman nodded towards Stan. He looked up.

'He's gone, love. There's nothing to be done for him, bless him, he's gone.'

Mrs White screamed. 'No, he can't be.' Struggling free from the neighbour's protective embrace she rushed forward.

'Let me see him. He's my son, he…' Her voice was breaking as she slumped forward to her knees. The woman who had been comforting her knelt next to her, tears of sadness filling her eyes. 'Come away, Joan, there's nothing more you can do for him. Just get your breath back for a minute and…'

Her appeal was cut short as Mrs White lunged towards the pram. Taking in the full horror of the scene before her, she let out another scream. This time, even more heart-breaking than the first. 'No!' She fell to the ground, her body shaking violently with uncontrollable grief.

A man stepped forward from the crowd and, removing his jacket, handed it to Stan to place over the mangled wreckage and its precious contents. Although we couldn't see inside the pram, there were splashes of blood on the outer frame and on the ground immediately by the side of it.

'I'll get the police,' he said, nodding his approval at the respectful manner in which Stan had placed the jacket over what was left of the pram.

'I'll wait here, in case they want me to answer any questions about Daisy jumping up like that,' ventured Mr Potter as he continued to pat the horse's neck. It was clearly nervous and not relishing such a large crowd of people standing so close. 'There you go, girl, settle down now.'

I stood next to Karl shaking with incredulity as we viewed the execrable results of our actions. I hadn't wanted to be a part of Karl's plan in the first place but was equally culpable for what had happened and so was in no position to afford all the blame to him. I felt Mum's hand squeeze my arm.

'You two boys go up to the house. I'll be along in a minute after we've sorted Joan out.'

Mrs White, having recognised Mum's voice, raised her head from the ground.

'No, they're not going anywhere. It's because of them my boy is dead. They…'

Jumping to our defence, Mum interrupted. 'Hang on, Joan, what are you saying? That Harry and Karl had something to do with this? I don't believe it. They wouldn't...'

Not waiting for Mum to finish, Mrs White bit back. 'It was the two of them that shouted Billy's pram was running down the hill. They must have pushed it.'

Karl and I looked at each other as Mum responded with astonishment to Mrs White's accusation.

'That can't be true. They'd never do such a thing, would you, boys?' She looked at us with pleading in her eyes, seeking confirmation as to our innocence. I felt my legs wobble as I moved to speak.

'Mum, we...'

Shouting me down, Mrs White pointed a finger in our direction. 'I told them off earlier for playing football outside my house. And it's not the first time they've done it either. They gave me a load of cheek, especially him,' she said, pointing at Karl, who immediately sprang to our defence.

'That is not fair. Yes, it is true that we played football outside your house.' He turned to Mum. 'And it's also true that we were a bit rude when she told us off, and we are sorry for that. But we didn't touch the pram, did we, Harry?'

Before I could answer, Karl spoke again. 'We were walking past her house and noticed the pram was moving. I told Harry to shout and tell her, and he did.'

Mum interjected. 'But why didn't you stop the pram?'

Karl pointed to a fresh graze on his knee. 'I tried but I fell and hurt my leg as you can see. And then Harry shouted again, but by the time I had got to my feet the pram was running away and we couldn't catch it.'

Struggling to her feet, Mrs White moved towards us, her face a bright shade of crimson as she waved away Karl's claim of innocence. Her anger towards us was palpable. 'You bloody little liar. You've been nothing but trouble since you moved here. You come over from Germany and think you own the street.' She turned to me. 'And as for you, Harry Thompson, you're just as bad. Mind, it's no wonder, what with your father being a drunk. You're both as bad as each other. And… and now you've killed my Billy. Well, you won't get away with it, do you hear? You…'

Pulling Karl and I into her, Mum launched a passionate appeal on our behalf. 'That's not fair, Joan. You can't accuse the boys of hurting Billy like that. As for Alf, yes, he does drink; too much at times, but he's not a bad man. And Gustav and Anna have been good neighbours to us and…'

Mrs White turned, directing her rancour towards Mum. 'I'd expect you to stick up for them, seeing as your Harry spends so much time at their house. Mind, there's not much to choose between the two of you really. He either stays at home and gets a beating off his father or goes round to that little bugger's house and learns how to be a German liar.'

Mum, clearly hurt and embarrassed at having our dirty washing aired so publicly, yet equally aware of the overwhelming grief Mrs White was experiencing, responded with sensitivity.

'Joan, none of what you're saying is fair, but I know you're not thinking clearly, so I forgive you. I can't even begin to know how you must be feeling right now, but to accuse the boys of intentionally wanting to hurt Billy is just too much.'

One of the women who had been supporting Mrs White took her arm again. 'Joan, Flo's right, they might be a bit mischievous but… well, to say they'd push Billy's pram in front of Charlie's horse is a bit…'

Turning on the woman, Mrs White flew into a hysterical rage. 'Don't you dare stick up for them, the little sods. They knew exactly what they were doing and now… my Billy's dead. He never…' Her voice faded as emotion gripped her once more.

'Come on, love, let me take you home, there's nothing more to be done here, not until the police arrive.'

'No, I'll not leave my Billy here in the street.'

The lady put her arm around her and nodded towards Mum.

'All right Joan, if that's what you want. I'll stay here with you. Flo, probably best if you take the boys home for now. I'll tell the police they're with you if they want to talk to them.'

Mrs White looked at Karl and I, her eyes filled with tears of anguish, yet flashing loathing in equal measure.

'Talk to them? They should be arrested for killing my Billy that's what…' Grief overtook her once more as she buried her head in her hands.

I felt numb and unable to look at Karl; guilt racking my body as Mum pulled the two of us away.

'Come on, boys, there's nothing to be gained from you two being here. You can wait at our house, Karl, until your mother gets back.'

'Yes, Mrs Thompson. Thank you.'

As we moved away, I motioned towards Mrs White. 'I'm so sorry about Billy, we really didn't…'

Interjecting, she turned to face me again. 'I don't want your apology. I want you arrested for what you did, both of you.'

Mum pulled me away. 'Harry was just saying sorry, Joan. We all are. Nobody would wish what happened here on anyone, certainly not these two, I'm sure of that.' Motioning for Karl and I to move away, she spoke to the assembled crowd. 'You can tell the police the boys are at ours.' Gently ruffling my hair, she pushed Karl and I forward. 'Come on, both of you, let's go.'

As we trudged away, in silence, slowly back up the hill, I turned briefly to look at the scene below. The terrible sense of guilt and remorse at what Karl and I had done burning just as strong inside me now as it had moments before when attempting to apologise to Mrs White. I was determined to tell the truth whatever the cost to me personally.

'Mum, I…'

As if anticipating my intention to confess, Karl jumped in.

'It is very sad what has happened, Mrs Thompson, but we didn't do anything to the baby.' Before I could reply, he said, 'We wouldn't lie about such a terrible thing. I know you and my parents think Harry and I were silly to become blood brothers, but to us it is a bond we made.' Turning to look at me, he continued. 'No, it is more than that. To us it is an oath. It means we will always tell the truth and protect each other whatever happens. So when we say we didn't do anything to the baby or the pram, it is the truth. That is right, isn't it, Harry?'

Before I could answer, Mum responded. 'You're right, Karl, we didn't think much of the idea of you cutting yourselves in that silly ritual. But that aside, I'm sure neither of you would have dreamt intentionally of pushing that pram down the hill. I know Joan can be a bit outspoken at times, and that she's given you both a flea in the ear for playing football outside her house in the past. I've spoken to Harry about that before. But the thought of you deliberately causing that terrible accident is beyond imagination.' She looked at Karl and smiled as we arrived outside our house. 'And so, you don't need to swear on some oath the two of you have taken for me to accept what you're telling me as true. Not only do I believe you, Karl, when you say you had nothing to do with what happened, I would actually find it harder to believe you did.' Smiling again, she opened the door. 'Now, inside both of you while I make us a nice cup of tea. We've all had a nasty shock, and a hot drink should help settle our nerves.'

'Actually, is it all right if we go out the back for a minute, Mum? I could do with some more fresh air. I'm still feeling a bit wobbly.'

'All right, but just while I make the tea. I don't want the two of you wandering off again, especially if you're not feeling too good, Harry, and certainly not before your mother gets home, Karl. I'm sure the police will want to speak to you at some point as well. But don't worry about that, we'll be with you when they do.'

I felt a shudder of nerves run through me as I encouraged Karl towards the back door. 'Thanks Mum. We'll just be in the yard.'

Closing the door behind me I shoved Karl in the back. 'How could you lie like that? We did push the pram, or at least you did.'

Grinning back at me, he shook his head. 'Don't get so excited, Harry. Yes, we may have given it a gentle push, but we didn't mean for anyone to get hurt, we…'

'Hurt,' I blurted, struggling to contain myself. 'The baby's dead, and *we* killed him.'

Shaking his head again, Karl responded calmly. 'Yes, he is dead. But again, I say we didn't mean for that to happen. It was just meant to be a bit of fun to get our own back for her telling us off earlier.'

Still struggling with his casual attitude to what had happened I interrupted again. 'Fun… is that what it was? Well, it's not fun now, is it? We *need* to tell the truth.'

'Listen, what has happened has happened, and there is nothing we can do about it. If we say we did it on purpose it will only make our parents unhappy as well. They might even go to prison as we are only young. Or we might get sent away to a place for wicked children. And we are not wicked.' He could tell I wasn't convinced. 'Look, Harry, if we knew it would end like this, then of course we would not have done it. It was a very bad accident that we didn't choose to happen, but it *was* an accident.'

I hadn't considered the possibility of our parents being sent to prison, or that Karl and I might be sent away. The thought of that scared me, but I still couldn't reconcile myself to the suggestion we hadn't played an active part in Billy's death.

'But it's still not right to lie. We…'

Karl raised his hand. 'Is it a lie then to say it was an accident?'

'No. I mean, yes, it was an accident but…'

Raising his hand again, he continued. 'And, because it *was* an accident, we didn't mean for the baby to die, that is also the truth. We both know we did not intend to hurt the child. So, if we stick to what I have said already, that we shouted when we saw the pram moving and that I fell and hurt my knee when I tried to stop it from running away, then we will be telling the truth.'

'Yes, but we moved the wooden block from under the wheel, and that's what started the pram moving. But we're not saying that bit are we?'

'And what good would that do? Is it going to bring her baby back? No. Will it get us into more trouble and maybe see our parents go to jail, or the two of us locked away? Maybe, yes. But if we stick to what I have said then it will be over.'

I recognised the logic in what he was saying, but my conscience still wasn't prepared to make that leap and accept that to lie was better than telling the truth.

'I don't know, I still think…'

Karl, sensing my hesitation, interjected. 'And you need to remember, Harry, what I told your mother. We are blood brothers. That day when we cut ourselves, we promised to stick together and always put the other one first. Do you want to see me locked away?'

'Of course not, but…'

'Then there is no but.' He smiled. 'I do not wish to see you locked away either, my brother. Remember, we took an oath to support and protect each other, and that is what we are doing.'

'We also promised not to lie to each other.'

'We are not lying to each other, we are…'

It was my turn to interrupt. 'No, we're just lying to everybody else.'

'Not at all, we are protecting them.' He took a breath and smiled. 'As we have agreed, this has been a very bad thing that has happened, but it *was* still an accident. Nobody wanted the baby to get hurt, and we will only make it worse for everyone if we change our story now. Think how much more upset Mrs White will be if she thinks we did it on purpose. Believe me, Harry, we are better to stick with our story and let the healing begin for everyone. If not, we will only bring more hurt and sadness to our families, and to Mrs White.'

I still wasn't convinced. 'I don't know.'

Before I could continue Mum opened the door.

'Tea's ready, you two.'

Karl moved towards the scullery. 'Thank you, Mrs Thompson, we are coming.' As he passed by me he squeezed my arm. 'I am right, Harry, you will see. It will be better for everyone.'

Mum had placed three cups of tea on the table in the sitting room. I looked on as steam rose lazily from them, evaporating in mid-air, a bit like my objections to what Karl had proposed we say when questioned about earlier events. Whilst I had been brought up not to lie, I certainly didn't want to be locked up or see my parents sent to prison. Still struggling to appease my moral compass, I picked up a cup and, holding it in both hands, allowed the warmth radiating from it to soothe my troubled mind. Mum looked across the table and smiled.

'You boys have really been through it today. It must have been horrible seeing young Billy's pram run under the hooves of that horse.'

Not knowing how to respond, I was grateful Karl took the lead.

'Yes, it was a terrible thing to see. We were just coming home, and as we got near to Mrs White's house we saw the pram start to move a little. We ran towards it, and I told Harry to call for Mrs White, which he did. I tried to catch it but tripped on a small block of wood and fell over. By the time I got to my feet the pram was halfway down the hill and we could not stop it. The rest of the story you have heard.'

Mum leant across and stroked my hair. 'Are you all right, Harry, you're very quiet.'

Taking another drink from my cup, I nodded. 'Yes, I'm okay, just a bit shocked I think. It seems so sad her baby dying like that, and we were...'

Karl interjected, presumably concerned about what I might be intending to say. 'Yes, it is very sad. And like Harry was saying, we were there to see it but were not able to stop it from happening.'

Finishing her tea, Mum placed her cup back on the table. 'Well, I think you boys did very well under the circumstances. I'm only sorry Joan was so angry with you, accusing you of pushing the pram down the hill like that. As if.' Shaking her head, she continued. 'Mind, she probably wasn't thinking straight. If I'm honest, I'm not sure how I'd have reacted if that had been me. To see your baby killed like that, it doesn't bear thinking about. She must...' Mum's voice faded as tears filled her eyes.

Karl and I sat in silence while she regained her composure. Forcing a smile, she continued. 'Like I said, it must have been horrible for her. For all of you.'

'Will the police come to our house, Mum? You know, to talk to Karl and me?'

'I should think so, Harry, or we might have to go to the police station. They might want to talk to you together, or on your own.' She looked directly at Karl. 'Don't you worry, Karl; I'll explain to your mum what happened when she gets home.'

'Thank you, Mrs Thompson, that is kind of you. I must admit it all happened so quickly, and it is difficult to remember everything, if you know what I mean?'

I couldn't believe how calm Karl appeared, as if lying was something he did every day. He seemed to have no nerves as he spoke. 'We are only sorry we couldn't save the baby, aren't we, Harry?'

Much as I wanted to deny everything he was saying, I knew it was too late. We had agreed our course of action and what our story would be. I couldn't go back on that now, not without betraying our friendship and our allegiance to each other as blood brothers. I mumbled my agreement, keeping my eyes fixed to the floor. 'Yes.' I felt my cheeks burning. Surely Mum knew we weren't telling the truth. Perhaps she did have suspicions about our story but, if she did, she wouldn't have wanted to believe we could have done such a terrible thing, or that we might actually have been responsible for the death of baby Billy.

Chapter Seven

Over the next few weeks, the atmosphere changed in our road. Neighbours were more polite to one another and treated Mrs White's house as some form of shrine. People left flowers by the wall next to her front door, and there was always someone checking to see if she was all right or needed anything. Mum offered as well, as did Karl's mum. The two of them became closer as well following the accident. It was as if they were trying to build a mutually defensive wall around Karl and I, with some of the other neighbours not so ready to accept the two of us hadn't played some greater part in what had happened.

Things were different in our house as well, with Mum becoming noticeably more protective towards Edith and me. She would constantly check to see where we were going and what time we'd be back. Even Dad seemed to soften his attitude towards us, for a while at least. He no longer sought to blame the two of us so readily for his perceived bad luck or misfortune in life. He also stopped going to the pub so often, choosing rather to finish his shift and come straight home. It felt strange having him sit at the table with us for tea making idle conversation and not losing his temper. We were even able to share the occasional joke and laugh together, something we hadn't done in his company for as long as we could remember. Mum appeared a little lighter in her countenance as well, although she remained sad and downhearted whenever any mention of the White family was made. She said every parent in the street had been affected by Billy's death and were feeling equally protective towards their children.

Although I still felt guilty about what Karl and I had done, it was good not to have to be concerned about Dad's moods or temper for a while. I even allowed myself to imagine Billy's death as some form of blessing in disguise, with things so settled at home. Like most children, my thoughts were entirely selfish and focused only on what was happening in *my* life. I offered hardly a thought to the unspeakable grief and sadness being experienced just a few yards up the road.

Dad said Mr White would go to work in those first few weeks after Billy's death and not engage with a soul all day. It was as if he was in some sort of trance, unaware of the presence of those around him. Some days, he would finish his shift and walk away without even saying goodbye, no matter how much the other men tried to engage with him.

The police did call at our house briefly on the day of the accident, but after Mum said how shocked Karl and I were, they decided not to speak to us formally until a few days later. It was clear, at that point, they didn't view either of us as being directly involved or responsible for Billy's death. Even so, Karl arranged to meet with me the day before we spoke to the police to ensure our stories were fully aligned. He was aware I still didn't relish the idea of lying, especially not to the police.

'Why can't we just tell the truth? If we keep lying, we'll have to live with that for the rest of our lives.'

'And if we do tell the truth, we might spend the rest of our lives locked away.'

'But we're children. Children don't get locked up for life because of an accident.'

'Yes, it was an accident, but we did mean to give her a scare when we took the wedge from under the wheel and let it roll away. How do we explain that?'

I felt my heart battling with my conscience. Of course, I didn't want to go to jail, or wherever it was they sent child baby killers. Equally, I knew what we were planning to tell the police was wrong. How could Mr and Mrs White grieve properly if they never knew what had really happened to their son? And what would they say if they ever found out the truth in the years to come? Before I could argue the case for honesty again, Karl jumped in.

'I know it is terrible that her baby died, but what is there to be gained by you and I being locked away for something we didn't mean to happen? Mrs White will not only hate the two of us forever, but our parents as well. And what have they done to deserve that? The rest of the street will probably never speak to them again either. We might all have to move away and live somewhere else. Then what will our fathers do for work? And what will our mothers say when they have to explain that their sons are both locked up for killing a baby? You need to think about all of this when you speak to the police, Harry.'

I hadn't really considered Mum and Dad in any of this, or Edith. How would she feel in having a brother who was locked up for such a wicked crime? I could feel my opposition to Karl's argument diminishing by the second.

'So what exactly is it you're proposing we say to the police?'

'The truth, well, mostly, except for the bit about us moving the wedge from under the wheel.' He paused and thought for a moment. 'We will say what we have already told our parents. We had been playing football as we always do, and that as we were coming home we passed Mrs White's house and noticed the pram was moving a little. You shouted for her to come, and I went to stop it, but I fell and the pram gathered speed and ran down the hill. The rest of the story will be the same as everybody knows; that the pram reached the bottom of the hill and scared the horse. It jumped up and then came back down on the pram.' Smiling, he looked at me. 'That is not so far from the real truth, is it? And think again how much worse it will be for everyone, especially our families, if we tell it differently.'

'But we...' The words stuck in my throat as Karl spoke again.

'There can be no buts, Harry. We must think of our families first. Listen. Nothing we can say will bring Billy back, but we can save everyone else from a lot more sadness and pain if we tell our story as I have said.' He squeezed my arm. 'Come on, my blood brother, we must stick together. Neither of us would ever want to hurt a baby. It was just a terrible accident. And we don't want to ruin the rest of our lives over an accident we didn't mean to happen.'

Of course, I didn't want to admit what we'd done to the police. I already felt an overwhelming sense of guilt that we'd let things go this far. But now I was more concerned about the shame my family would face if the truth ever did come out. And so, with that uppermost in my mind, I reluctantly agreed to what Karl was suggesting. Even as I nodded my unwilling acquiescence to his proposal, my heart sank. Not only was I agreeing to lie to the police, but also to those who trusted and cared for me the most. And worse still, I was doing so in the full knowledge that I *had* been party to causing the death of an innocent baby.

My heart and mind were still in turmoil as I sat on the hard wooden chair in the police interview room with Mum by my side. She rubbed my hand reassuringly as we waited for the officer to arrive. I'd never been questioned by the police before. Come to that, I'd never been inside a police station before either. I looked around the room taking in the austere surroundings. The walls were a dull sort of grey and there was no covering on the floor, just bare wooden boards. There was a single window about halfway up one of the walls. It was open, for which I was grateful as a gentle breeze wafted through the room reminding me of the freedom that awaited us on the outside once this ordeal was over.

Hearing the door open, I jumped in my seat and turned instinctively to see who'd entered the room. I watched as a plump, jolly-looking policeman approached us. He patted me lightly on the head as he walked by. Pulling out a chair from the other side of the desk set between us, he sat down and smiled broadly. He had a dark-brown bushy moustache that stretched beyond his upper lip and out towards his equally fulsome sideboards. He was balding slightly, which made his thick facial hair appear even more pronounced. He wore a pair of round metal-rimmed glasses that sat halfway down his nose. I noticed his dark-blue uniform was crumpled slightly and the elbows on his jacket were shiny from constant wear and leaning on hard surfaces. Rubbing his moustache thoughtfully he coughed, as if to clear his throat.

'Good morning. Mrs Thompson and, Harry, isn't it?'

Squeezing my hand, Mum replied, 'That's right.'

Nodding, he continued. 'I'm Sergeant Harris. Thank you both for coming in and agreeing to answer a few questions.'

I was too nervous to reply, knowing whatever he was about to ask I was probably going to lie about in response. Thankfully, sensing my reticence to speak, Mum took the initiative again.

'Good morning, Sergeant. We're happy to help in any way we can, aren't we, Harry?'

I glanced down at my feet and nodded.

'Thank you.' Turning his gaze to me, he smiled again. 'You look a bit worried, Harry. There's nothing to be scared of, lad. Like I said, just a couple of questions to help us with, that's all.' I watched as he took a sheet of paper from a drawer in the desk and placed it in front of him. 'You'll be fine, son. And your mum's here to help if you get a bit tongue-tied. I know it can feel a bit daunting talking to a policeman, especially about something as difficult as this.' Taking a pencil from the breast pocket of his jacket, he laid it on the desk next to the piece of paper. 'Just for me to take a few notes,' he said, indicating the paper and pencil. Pausing and rubbing his hands together, he looked directly at me. 'Right then, we've spoken to your friend Karl, and he's told us what happened, or at least as best as he could remember. So now, I'd like to hear what you have to say about what went on. A terrible accident by all accounts, or so it seems.' He nodded as if gesturing for me to respond.

I looked at Mum, who squeezed my hand again before answering on my behalf.

'Yes, Sergeant, it's been an awful time for the boys. Such a terrible thing for the two of them to witness.'

Pursing his lips, he turned to Mum. 'I understand you want to protect young Harry, Mrs Thompson, but I'd like to hear what he has to say, if that's all right?'

Releasing my hand, Mum moved uncomfortably in her seat. 'Of course. I wasn't trying to…'

The sergeant smiled, waving away her protest. 'No need to apologise, I fully understand. I've got children myself, although not quite as young as Harry here. I'd probably do the same if I was in your shoes.' Stroking his chin, he turned to face me again. 'All right, lad, in your own time, tell me what happened.'

Shifting my bottom on the rigid wooden chair, I felt a bead of nervous perspiration run down the back of my shirt. Not sure where to begin, I responded with a question of my own.

'Where should I start?'

'At the beginning, son. You'd been playing football I understand? That's what your friend Karl said.'

Smiling weakly, I nodded. 'Yes, we're always playing football, it's what…'

On hearing Mum laugh, I stopped.

'Honestly, Sergeant, it's a wonder that ball hasn't fallen apart by now, the amount of kicking these two have given it over the past few years. They…' Realising she'd broken the thread of our conversation, she apologised. 'I'm sorry, I won't interrupt again, I promise. I'm just a bit nervous for Harry and… well, you know. Like you said, you've got children.'

The officer smiled. 'Quite. But as I also said, it's Harry I need to hear from now.' He looked at me again. 'You'd been playing football?'

Taking a deep breath, I continued. 'Yes, we'd been across to the bit of wasteland at the top of our road and were on our way home.' Noticing the sergeant writing on the sheet of paper in front of him I paused to allow him time to finish. He looked up.

'That's all right, son, you keep talking. I'll let you know if you're going too fast.' Gesturing towards me with the pencil, he nodded. 'You were on your way home?'

'We were talking about…' I paused again, remembering we'd been discussing the ships at the dockyard. I knew he wouldn't be impressed to hear we'd smuggled our way onto the docks. I also wasn't sure what Karl might have said about that part of our story. The sergeant put down the pencil and looked at me over the top of his glasses.

'This is going to be a long conversation, lad, if you keep stopping after every few words.'

Mum interjected. 'Harry's just a bit nervous, that's all. It's not every day you get interviewed by the police, especially not at his age.'

'I understand that. But he's not being accused of anything, so there's no need for him to be nervous. We just want to find out what actually happened that day. And Harry here, and his friend Karl, appear to be the only two witnesses to the tragic event, or at least the first part of it.' He looked at me again, shifting his glasses a little further up his nose. 'Now then, son, you were saying?'

Deciding Karl was unlikely to have mentioned our trip to the docks either, I stuck to the agreed line about us just having played football. My mind raced. I was already lying to a policeman, and I hadn't even got to the part about the pram yet. Taking a deep breath, I continued.

'We were talking about football as we got to the top of the road near to Mrs White's house, and we noticed the pram.'

'Was it moving at that point?' the sergeant interjected.

I stumbled in my response. I was now making things up as I went along, and just hoped my story would be in line with what Karl had said earlier.

'No, not that I remember. It was just there, sort of standing outside the house.' I could feel my resolve slipping. I hated lying and felt sure the two of them could tell.

Rolling the pencil between his fingers, the sergeant rocked his body backwards and forwards slightly. 'So when did you first notice it move?'

I glanced at Mum. She smiled. 'Go on, Harry, tell him. You're doing really well, isn't he, Sergeant?'

The officer blew out his cheeks. 'He would be if he moved along a bit.' Turning to me again, he continued. 'Listen lad, I understand this is not easy, but you do need to tell me exactly what happened, or at least as you remember it. If you keep stopping every five minutes we'll be here till Christmas. I'm not rushing you, just saying you don't need to pause after every sentence, not unless I ask you a question. Okay?'

I nodded. In the back of my mind a voice encouraged me to speed up as well. The quicker I told my story, the sooner all of this would be over.

'As we got near the pram it just started to move forward.'

Interrupting, the sergeant apologised. 'Sorry, Harry. After telling you to get on with it, it's me that's slowing you down now, but I do need to establish a couple of facts.' Rubbing his sideboards with the pencil, he continued. 'You say the pram started to move as you got near to it? You didn't touch it or knock it as you went past?'

I shook my head. 'No, it just started to roll.' Not thinking I sounded very convincing, I decided to embellish my account of what happened a little. 'We noticed the wooden block under the wheel wasn't... under the wheel, if that makes sense.'

Pausing, he took a notepad from his other breast pocket and turned the pages, eventually stopping about halfway through. He ran his finger down the page and grunted. 'That's pretty much what your friend Karl said. What drew your attention to the wooden block?'

My palms felt sticky as I held on to the sides of the chair. Another bead of sweat ran down my back.

'I don't know. We just noticed it wasn't under the wheel.'

'And when you saw the pram moving, why didn't you stop it from running away?'

It was Mum's turn to interrupt.

'What are you saying, Sergeant? It sounds as though you're suggesting Harry didn't try his best to help, that he was responsible in some way for what happened.'

'No, that's not what I'm saying at all. I'm simply asking why the boys didn't just grab hold of the pram to stop it rolling away. A perfectly reasonable question under the circumstances, I'm sure you'll agree?'

Mum nodded politely. She clearly didn't agree. I thought it best to keep going and avoid any further disagreement between the two of them.

'We did try to stop it, at least Karl did. He shouted for me to call Mrs White while he went for the pram. We were just a few feet away by this time. As he turned towards the pram he slipped. I don't know what happened exactly, but he fell over. I was too far away to get to it myself as I'd gone to the front door to call for Mrs White. It was slightly ajar, and I pushed it open, yelling for her to come.' I drew a breath. The worst was over, I'd told the lie. The rest of the story would be pretty much the truth. 'She came rushing out as Karl was getting to his feet, but by then it was too late, the pram was running down the hill really fast. It bumped off the pavement and into the road. Mrs White shouted and went after it. Karl ran after her and I followed behind, but there was nothing we could do to help by then and...' I hesitated as the full horror of what happened next flashed into my mind again. 'And then, it reached the bottom of the street, and the horse jumped up as the pram crashed into it.' Pausing, I stared down at the floor, not wanting either of them to see the tears of shame threatening to overwhelm me.

The sergeant cleared his throat. 'And we already have several witnesses to what happened next, so I won't need you to talk about that, at least not for now. But I must ask you one last question, son. And I need you to look directly at me when you answer, please.'

I wasn't sure what he was about to say but could tell from the expression on his face he was serious.

'Harry, are you certain you and Karl had nothing to do with that block coming loose from under the wheel of young Billy's pram? And remember, I'm expecting you to tell me the truth now.'

Much as I wanted to shout yes we had and admit my part in what the two of us had done, the greater fear of what might happen if I did held sway. I could also hear Karl's voice ringing in my ear, reminding me of the oath we'd taken to always be there for each other, no matter what the cost to ourselves. I couldn't let him down.

'No, we didn't.' Even at my age I knew, in those few words, I'd just condemned myself to a lifetime of guilt and shame but, hopefully, I'd also saved my family from a similar fate, or so it appeared to my young, addled brain.

I felt emotionally drained and looked across to Mum for support. Smiling, she came to my defence.

'I think that's enough for now, Sergeant.'

Placing the pencil gently on the desk in front of him, he nodded his agreement. 'Well done, Harry, thank you; that'll do for today. I think I've got enough information for now. If we need to speak to you or Karl again, we'll be in touch.' He smiled warmly at me. 'I know that won't have been easy for you, lad, reliving that horrible memory, but we do need to establish the facts. Your involvement may end here, but there are lots of other questions that need to be answered.' He turned to Mum. 'The poor milkman is struggling badly with all of this. Says he feels responsible, even though it appears to have been a genuine accident. He's finding it hard to do his round, what with everybody talking about what happened, and most of them avoiding going anywhere near his cart now. The children used to give the horse a bit of apple or carrot by all accounts, but not anymore. Their parents pull them away from going anywhere near it. It's like they think it's suddenly turned into some sort of wild animal. It just panicked, poor thing. I think we all would if something came crashing into us from nowhere like that.' Pausing, and with an expression of sadness etched across his face, he looked at Mum. 'And, as for Mr and Mrs White, I'm not sure they'll ever get over what happened, bless them.'

I could feel the weight of guilt pressing heavily on my shoulders as Mum spoke.

'There's a few of us who keep an eye out for the two of them as best we can, but she's certainly a changed woman, that's for sure.' Smiling weakly, she looked down at me. 'Anyway, probably best not to keep talking about it in front of Harry. I think he's been through enough for one day. Isn't that right, son?'

I nodded without raising my head, my face burning red with shame. I heard the sergeant's chair scrape across the bare wooden floor as he stood up.

'I agree. You take the boy home now and give him some dinner. What do you say, Harry, are you hungry?' He laughed. 'I was always ready for something to eat at your age.'

Getting to my feet, I felt the skin of my legs damp with

nervous perspiration as I peeled them from the seat. Without looking up, I mumbled my reply. 'I am a bit, yes.'

I felt Mum's arm move round my shoulder as she pulled me into her. 'Well, I'd better get you home then. We don't want the sergeant here thinking I starve you on top of everything else, do we?'

Moving to open the door, the officer laughed again. 'I wouldn't believe that for a minute. Your Harry looks as fit as a fiddle in my eyes.' Patting me on the head as we moved out of the room, he continued. 'Well done, lad. Like I said, that can't have been easy.'

As the three of us made our way to the front entrance, Mum and the sergeant continued their discussion.

'Have you spoken to Joan again? I should imagine she's still in denial about it all. She doesn't want to speak to any of us neighbours about what happened, not at the moment, that's for sure. As I said, we've tried to support her, but it's like she's shut down. Alf says her Bert just does his shift and goes straight home. It's like something has died inside of him, inside both of them.'

'Of course, we've spoken to the family and will continue to do so, but there's not a lot more they can tell us, at least not about the early part of what went on. That's why it's been so important to talk to Harry here, and his friend Karl. They're the ones who witnessed events from the start, so to speak.'

Stopping, Mum turned directly to address the sergeant. 'Joan swears the wooden block was under that wheel when she put the pram out the front. I didn't say anything earlier, but she did try and accuse the boys of pushing the pram down the hill, but I told her...'

I felt another shudder of remorse run through me as the sergeant interrupted.

'Like you said a minute ago, it's probably best not to keep discussing the detail in front of young Harry here. The boys have been through quite an ordeal already.' He puffed out his cheeks. 'What we do all have to remember is, she was in shock when this first happened, still is in many ways. I'm not sure we'll ever know the full answer to what went on that day. Of course, it must feel inconceivable to her, even to consider the possibility she might have failed the little one in any way, or that she may ultimately have been responsible for the accident itself. With that in mind, it's easy to imagine how she might look for someone else to blame. And, after telling the boys off for playing football outside her house earlier, it's not difficult to see why she might look to them as being responsible in some way. Maybe they were just in the wrong place at the wrong time, or not, depending on whose side you take.'

I lifted my head. 'We did say sorry for playing football outside her house. And she had told us off about doing it before, so we shouldn't really have been there.'

Ruffling my hair, the sergeant smiled down at me. 'You're right, lad, you shouldn't. But I was your age once and know how easy it is to get lost in a game of football. Just make sure you keep well away from any of the houses in future, and especially the Whites', do you hear?'

'Yes, Sergeant.'

Turning to Mum, he continued. 'The whole thing hinges on what happened with that piece of wood and how it came free. There's always the possibility, when she placed it under the wheel that perhaps she hadn't positioned it as securely as she thought. Then, if the baby moved it might have been enough to rock the pram a little and shift the wheel from its wooden brake. If that happened, it's not difficult to imagine the pram beginning to roll away as the boys have claimed. After all, it's hard to conceive of anybody intentionally pushing a pram with a baby in it down a hill just to see what would happen.'

Overwhelmed once more with guilt and shame, I tugged at Mum's arm.

'Can we go please, Mum; I don't want to talk about this anymore.'

'Of course, love, we shouldn't have carried on talking about it. As we agreed, you've been through enough already.'

On reaching the main entrance the sergeant opened the door.

'There you go, son, you're free again. Just remember what I said about playing football in future. Make sure you stay well away from your neighbours' houses. Doorways might make good goalposts, but people won't appreciate you kicking a ball against them.'

'I know, we won't.'

Mum shook the sergeant's hand. 'Thank you for being so understanding. I hope what Harry had to say has helped?'

'It has, and pretty much confirms what we've suspected all along; that the whole event was a tragic and terrible accident. Thank you again for coming in. Goodbye.'

'Goodbye.' I felt Mum prod my shoulder. 'Say goodbye to the sergeant, Harry.'

Without turning to face him I muttered my miserable response. 'Bye.'

I was still feeling uncomfortable about what Karl and I had agreed to; lying to our families and the police about what had really happened. Equally, the child in me wasn't overthinking or truly considering the pain we'd caused Mr and Mrs White, nor the life of emptiness we'd subjected them to. At this precise moment it just felt good to be out in the fresh air again, away from the confines of the police station. I was desperate to see Karl as well and compare notes about what we'd told the police. Then, we could finally move forward and put the events of the past couple of weeks behind us, or so I hoped.

When we arrived home, Edith was waiting for us.

'Oh, they haven't locked you up then,' she quipped, as Mum and I entered the front room.

'Edith, that's not very nice. Your brother has been very brave in talking to the police; it can't have been easy for him. You should be kind to him.'

'I would have been kind to him if they'd locked him up. I would have visited him in prison,' she said with a laugh.

I was eager to get away from Edith's teasing and see my friend. 'Can I go round to Karl's, Mum?'

'Not so fast, young man. You'll have something to eat first, and then you can go. And make sure you're back in time for your tea as well. Your dad will want to hear what happened, and I want you here to tell him about it.'

'Yes, Mum, I'll be back.'

We had a little bread in the house, so Mum made us each a dripping sandwich. I gobbled mine down in double-quick time as I was keen to be out as soon as possible.

'I've finished. Can I go now, please?'

Laughing, Mum shook her head. 'Honestly, you'll get indigestion eating your food like that. Go on then, off you go. But remember, back by five.'

'Okay, I promise.' Jumping from my chair I rushed to the back door, Mum's voice still ringing in my ears.

'I mean it, Harry, don't be late. I don't want your dad upset. Do you hear me?'

'Yes, Mum,' I shouted as the back door slammed shut behind me. Two minutes later I was standing outside Karl's house knocking on the door.

I hopped impatiently from side to side waiting for it to open. 'Come on, Karl,' I muttered to myself. 'I want to know how you got on with the police.'

As the door opened, I was greeted by the welcoming smile of Karl's mum. Wiping her hands down the clean white apron covering her dress, she laughed. 'I said it would be you. Karl is just putting his shoes on; he will be down in a moment.'

With that, I heard the clattering of feet running down the

stairs. 'I am here. Is it all right if we go out now, Mama?' Karl enquired, as he pushed past her to join me in the street.

Laughing again, she nodded. 'It looks as though you are already outside, Karl. Yes, you can play for a while, but don't get into any trouble, especially not after all that has happened. I think we would all like a quieter end to the day.' Turning to me she smiled. 'Would you like to have some tea with us later, Harry?'

Karl grabbed my arm. 'Yes, he would, wouldn't you?'

Wrestling my arm free from his grip, I shook my head. 'That's very kind of you, Mrs Schmidt, but I have to be home by five. Mum says Dad will be back around then and will want to hear about what happened at the police station.'

'Of course, I understand. I know Karl's father will also be interested in how things went as well. Maybe you can come another time?'

I nodded. 'Thank you, yes please.'

Karl tugged at my arm again. 'Come on then, let's go.'

'Remember, boys, stay out of trouble, and make sure you don't go anywhere near Mrs White's house. That poor lady has been through enough recently. She knows you've both been talking to the police, and we don't want any more unhappiness, at least not today. Do you hear?'

'Yes Mama, we hear you. We won't get into any trouble.' Casting each other a knowing glance, we waved our goodbyes and headed to the waste ground at the top of the road.

'How did it go with the police? Did you tell them what we agreed?' Karl enquired as we settled down behind the remnants of a wall that had collapsed some time ago and never been rebuilt.

'Yes, it went well, I think. I was nervous though. I felt he knew I wasn't telling the truth. I just wish we'd told him everything.'

'And what would have happened if we had? Mr and Mrs White would be angry with our families and never speak to them again. And our parents would be ashamed of what we had done also. We have talked about this before.' Leaning forward and taking my hand, Karl pointed to the scar on my palm. 'Remember, Harry, we are blood brothers now and that is a bond that cannot be broken. We must stick together, yes?'

I was torn. Yes, we'd taken an oath never to betray one another, but deep within, I also knew I had a greater responsibility to be honest with myself and the rest of my family. For all Dad's failings, with his drinking and violence towards us, I equally recognised the deeper shame I would be bringing into our home by continuing with this lie. This battle of wills would haunt me for years to come. For now though, as a child, the potential of maybe being sent to borstal or prison for what we had done, along with the prospect of never seeing my family again proved my greater fear. Reluctantly I nodded my guilty acceptance to what Karl was proposing.

We spent the next half an hour comparing notes about what we'd told the police sergeant and how understanding he had appeared to be about our involvement in what had happened.

'I thought he was a nice man. He certainly seemed to be on our side, not presuming us to be guilty of any more than being party to a terrible accident.'

Karl nodded. 'And that is what matters. If the police believe what we told them then everyone else will have to accept our story as well, even Mr and Mrs White. Of course, they will still maintain their suspicion that we might be lying, but she never liked us anyway, not since the first time we kicked our football against her door.'

I was concerned Karl was assuming because the police appeared to have accepted what we said as true, it therefore became the truth for everyone else, including the two of us.

'But we did lie. We didn't tell the whole story.'

Karl looked directly at me, his dark-brown eyes piercing deep into my psyche. 'Yes, we pushed the block from under the wheel of the pram, but we never intended to hurt the baby. That is the truth. And we told the policeman we could not stop the pram from running down the hill. That is also true. And how could we know the horse would jump up and crash down on to it?' He paused and shook his head. 'Maybe, if we could go back, perhaps we might not have chosen the path we did. But the pram could still have rolled away on another day when the block wasn't in place properly, and then what would you say?'

Although the events of what really happened that day still bothered me, I felt much of what Karl was suggesting to be equally true. On another day we might have done things differently. And, it *was* also a fact we hadn't intended any harm towards Billy. Taking a deep breath, I resolved to ignore the cries of guilt resonating in my mind and accept Karl's justification of what we'd done. It was a decision I would ultimately regret, and one that would affect the fabric of our relationship in the years to come.

Chapter Eight

The next couple of years passed without any other significant incidents involving Karl and me. And, with the events surrounding the death of baby Billy slowly fading into the background, life began to return to normality for the two of us and the rest of the dockyard community. Families continued to struggle to pay their bills and put food on the table, thanks, in the main, to the meagre wages paid by the shipyard owners. The same was true in our house with Dad making an unwelcome return to his regular visits to The Blue Anchor. These would often culminate in another violent outburst directed towards one or more of us if we happened to be in the wrong place at the wrong time or spoke out of turn. Edith and I had learned to keep out of the way whenever he looked likely to strike out, but things continued to be more difficult for Mum. She remained in the firing line, especially if she failed to provide him with a hot meal when he returned from work or the pub. Her excuse that he'd drunk most of the money away and there wasn't enough left to buy extra food held no sway with him, especially now Edith and I had left school and were earning as well.

As children, Karl and I had often fantasised about playing professional football after leaving school. However, when the day arrived, and with both of us accepting such dreams of sporting greatness were unlikely to be realised, we had to accept more mundane employment as apprentices to a trade. Karl began working with a local company that produced metalwork and parts for machinery. He'd always held an interest in mechanical design and so wasn't too disappointed at making the transition from schoolboy to full-time work. That said, some of his shifts began very early when the furnaces were fired up at the start of the day, so getting out of bed while it was still dark took some getting used to.

I also had some early starts after signing on as an apprentice bread and cake maker for a local baker. My earnings were little more than a pittance, but Mr Anderson, my boss, would often allow me to take home a cake or loaf that was misshapen or had been overcooked to help eke out my pay. Mum would cut away the burnt part and we would enjoy the taste of fresh bread, whatever shape it was. When you're hungry you don't worry too much about how your food is presented, you just want your stomach to feel full. Being older than me, Edith had left school a few months earlier and had begun work as a trainee seamstress. Again, the money wasn't great but Mum encouraged her to stick with it, reminding her, once qualified, she could work for one of the big factories or even set up on her own.

Whilst it was good to have additional funds coming into the house, it also encouraged Dad to feel he could spend even more of *his* wages at the pub. This meant, come the end of the week, there was little more for Mum to spend on food and other essentials than there had been when we'd depended on his money alone. Dad would never accept this argument whenever Mum attempted to raise it with him.

'Don't give me that. I still bring money into this house every week, the same as Edith and Harry. I don't know what you do with it all, Flo, really I don't.'

'The trouble is, Alf; you still spend most of *your* wages on gambling or in The Blue Anchor. Of course, the money Edith and Harry bring in helps, but it doesn't leave enough to pay all the bills and put a hot meal on the table for everyone at the end of the day. The two of them are growing fast; and now they're working they need more to eat to keep their energy levels up. The little they contribute hardly covers what you're spending on cards or beer.'

At this point in the discussion Mum's protestations would usually be met with a blow to the face or body, along with a terse denial of any responsibility on his behalf for the lack of funds coming through the door.

'The cost of a pint or two at the end of a hard day's work isn't going to break the bank, especially now those two are earning; and don't you tell me any different.'

Mum would often then receive another slap or punch to emphasise the point he was making. This was also intended to brook any further argument as to the opposite on our behalf.

As I progressed through my early teens, I would increasingly seek to defend Mum from these unwarranted attacks, but Dad was still a strong man and would easily overpower me. These incidents would upset Mum especially. She hated to see either of her children beaten, whatever the cause or circumstances.

Although these violent outbursts occurred on a fairly regular basis, we would all try to avoid referring to them for fear of provoking him further. Each of us learnt to accept that while Dad continued to spend his money at the pub, there was likely to be little left to buy extra food or clothing, unless Edith and I made up the difference. Although we both felt this to be unfair, we never said anything, preferring just to support Mum as best we could.

Eventually, the two of us reconciled ourselves to the fact we were better to go to bed hungry rather than being beaten for no good reason, other than Dad's drinking and temper had gotten the better of him yet again. As the two of us grew so did our realisation of just how difficult Mum's life had been for so many years. She loved Edith and I beyond measure, we knew that without doubt. And we would express our love for her in return whenever the opportunity arose. Sometimes it would be something as simple as Edith making her a daisy chain. She'd done that as a little girl, and even now she was older this simple act of affection still brought a smile to Mum's face. At other times the two of us would hold her in our arms, telling her over and again how precious she was to us. On one occasion she gave Edith and I a little of the money back that she'd saved from our contribution to the weekly budget and told us to treat ourselves to something. We gave it to my boss Mr Anderson and asked him to bake a special cake for her with icing on. We took it home and insisted she had the largest slice. Mum cried when we presented her with it. That memory stayed with Edith and I for a long time.

The love we shared for each other was never in question. What Edith and I could never quite understand was that she also loved Dad in equal measure, even if she clearly didn't like him very much at times. When we questioned her about this, her answer only served to confuse us all the more.

'A parent's love for their child is quite literally born from the heart,' she would say. 'But the love between a man and a woman evolves over time, it grows as the years go by. I know your dad can be difficult to live with, but he's not a bad man, and he does love us all very much, don't ever doubt that. He just struggles to show it at times. He drinks because he thinks he's failing by not being able to give us the life he would like us all to have. And much of the reason he can't afford to give us that life is because he drinks. It's a vicious circle, and one only he can resolve.'

Edith and I would look at each other and shrug our shoulders, failing to comprehend this unconditional love Mum apparently held for our father. We both agreed when we met the person we wanted to spend the rest of our lives with, it would be someone more like her than him, no matter how much she might try and convince us that deep down he really did love the two of us.

As for Karl and I, with our relationship back on track, and the fact that we were both adjusting to the new reality of having to get up and go to work each day, our dreams of escaping the dockyards and confines of Canning Town still occupied our thoughts in equal measure. Whilst Karl was not unhappy in his work as an apprentice engineer, he also began to show an interest in history and politics. I, on the other hand, was increasingly fascinated by the written word. I would dream of becoming an author, or perhaps a journalist for one of the national newspapers, even though I had no idea how to go about achieving this particular goal.

By 1910, Karl and I had been friends for almost twelve years and new interests were beginning to garner our attention. Girls began to appear on our horizon, but not to the detriment of our relationship, at least not at this stage. Whilst the terms of the oath we'd taken as young boys hadn't included the potential for girlfriends, it was clear to both of us whoever sought to win our hearts would also have to include befriending their blood brother as well. However, this seemingly unbreakable chord of unity was about to be tested in a way neither of us could have imagined.

It was a glorious summer's day with the two of us chatting together happily as we strolled by the river, looking on as the ships made their way to and from the docks. We'd both worked an early shift that morning and the cooling breeze rippling across the water made a welcome alternative to the heat and demands of our workplaces. We'd just reached the end of a path near to a footbridge when one of our neighbours, Mr Murray, came running towards us.

'Karl, you need to come home quickly, your mother needs you. There's been a terrible accident.'

Glancing at each other, we turned and began to run back along the footpath.

'What is it, what has happened?' Karl blurted out, trying to catch his breath as he gathered pace in his effort to get home.

'Your mother will tell you. You just need to get back,' Mr Murray replied, pausing to catch his breath.

'All right, thank you,' Karl countered as we ran ahead of him.

A few minutes later we arrived at Karl's house. The front door was open. As we entered, we heard a scream. It was Karl's mother, Anna. I'd never heard a scream like it before. It was a cry of anguish far beyond the physical. Something was terribly wrong, as we were about to discover. Entering the sitting room, we were met with the sight of Mum holding Anna in her arms. Her body, wracked in obvious distress, shook as sobs of genuine pain and suffering emitted from her.

Karl crossed to his mother and squeezed her arm. 'What is it, Mama? What has happened?'

Pulling herself away from Mum's embrace she fell into his arms. 'Oh, Karl, it is your father. My beautiful Gustav, he is dead.'

I stood in the doorway unable to speak as her words reverberated around the room.

Gripping his mother even tighter as his own legs threatened to buckle beneath him, Karl spoke again. 'Dead? Papa dead, but how? I don't understand.'

'There has been a terrible accident at the docks, I...' Her voice faded as unutterable misery overtook her once more.

Noticing Edith standing to one side, also on the brink of tears, I reached out to comfort her. Mum, still helping to support Anna, turned to me.

'Harry, take Edith home. I'll be back soon. There's nothing either of you can do here.'

Not wanting to leave my friend, I moved to protest. Anticipating my response, she spoke again.

'Please, Harry, do as I ask. Quickly now.'

Feeling tears of frustration and sadness for Karl sting the back of my eyes, I pulled Edith towards me.

'Come on, sis, let's go.' I turned to Karl who was still holding firm to his mum. 'I'll be at…'

Mum interrupted again. 'Just get yourself home, Harry, you can talk to Karl later.'

I nodded, grateful for her instruction, as I wasn't entirely sure what to say to my friend, in that moment, anyway.

'Yes, Mum.' I smiled weakly at my friend. 'See you, Karl.'

Without looking at me, he shook his head and buried it into his mother's chest.

With nothing I could say or do to help, I encouraged Edith towards the door, turning briefly as we left to witness, once more, the overwhelming scene of grief playing out before me. Mum and Anna were holding onto each other with Karl tucked between them, his arms wrapped around the two of them for support.

Closing the front door behind us, I tugged on Edith's arm.

'What happened? How could he be dead?'

'I'm not sure, Mum got here before me. Dad said there'd been an accident at the dock, and that Mr Schmidt had been killed. By the time I got here the two of them were crying. I couldn't make much sense of what they were saying. And then you and Karl arrived.'

'Was Dad there when it happened then?'

'I don't know, he just said Mr Schmidt was dead and Mum came straight round. Dad didn't speak to me, he just fell into his chair and stared into the fire.'

Arriving home, I noticed the door was ajar. Mum had obviously left it open after rushing round to Karl's house. Walking towards the sitting room, I heard two men talking. I recognised Dad's voice but not the other one. As Edith and I entered, Dad was sitting in his chair, with the other man stood in front of him. He was clearly not a docker; being dressed in a black suit, shirt, tie, and shiny black shoes. As soon as he saw us Dad got to his feet, appearing almost grateful for the interruption to their conversation.

'Hello, you two.' Forcing a smile, he turned to the man. 'These are my children, Edith and Harry.' Looking at the two of us again, he nodded. 'This is Mr Palmer, one of the dock managers. He's come to talk to me about what happened. I presume Edith and your mum have spoken to you, Harry?'

Feeling uncomfortable in front of Dad's boss, I mumbled my reply. 'Only that there'd been an accident, and Mr Schmidt was dead.'

Mr Palmer looked at me.

'That's right, son. And as your father was working on the same gang, I was asking him about what happened, or at least what he can remember.' Turning his attention back to Dad, he continued. 'There'll be a more formal enquiry in the days ahead, of course, Alf, you'd expect that. But it's always good to get things out in the open as soon as possible, while events are still fresh in the mind, so to speak.'

I noticed Dad grimace slightly. He was clearly uncomfortable being addressed by his manager in such a forthright way in front of his children.

'You two get yourselves up to your room while Mr Palmer and me finish talking. Did your mum say when she'd be back?'

'Not really,' Edith replied. 'She was with Mrs Schmidt and Karl when we left. They were crying.'

Mr Palmer took a neatly folded white handkerchief from his trouser pocket and patted his brow with it. I'd never seen a handkerchief in such pristine condition before. The ones we used were no more than small pieces of cloth and were rarely white. Mum usually made them from old shirts that were no longer fit for purpose.

'It certainly is a tragic story, lass. I'm sure we all feel for the family at this sad time.' Wiping the handkerchief across his mouth he smiled at the two of us and continued. 'Best do as your dad suggests, at least until your mum gets back. I won't be long. There's just a few more questions I'd like to ask before I leave.'

Tilting his head in the direction of the door, Dad cleared his throat. 'Go on then, off you go.'

Without formally acknowledging him, we left the room, closing the door gently behind us. Nudging Edith in the ribs, I held a finger to my mouth and encouraged her to sit beside me on the bottom stair.

'Keep quiet and we can hear what they're saying,' I whispered.

Nodding her understanding, we both sat and leant forward towards the door. Our vantage point was soon rewarded with Dad and Mr Palmer continuing their conversation.

'Nice children you have there.'

'They're not bad. Bit of a handful at times, especially now they're in their teens. Always hungry and growing out of their clothes every five minutes.'

'Times are hard for everyone these days, Alf.'

Edith leant across and whispered in my ear. 'Can't be that tough for him, not if you can afford to dress like that. His shoes looked brand new. You could see your face in them they were so shiny.'

'I know, I noticed that as well.'

Leaning forward again, we waited for the conversation to continue. Mr Palmer was the first to speak.

'As you were saying, before your children came in, the two of you were standing next to the loading bay as the pallet was lowered from the ship?'

'Yeah, and as it got nearer to the ground, Gustav walked towards it. A couple of the other lads shouted for him to stand clear until it was actually grounded, but he just carried on moving forward.'

'And?'

'And, when he was within a few feet of the pallet, the ropes jolted as if they'd jammed on something. There was a crack and the shipment slipped to one side. Some of the boxes broke free and fell to the ground. We all yelled at Gustav to get out of the way. He jumped to one side to avoid one of the boxes, but without realising it he'd moved directly under the pallet which swung free of the ropes and landed on top of him. It was really bad; we could see that. He had no chance.'

'And that's when you called for help, is that right?'

'Sort of. I shouted to the other lads to go and get the foreman while I went over to him, to see if there was anything I could do.'

'Gustav was under the pallet at this time?'

'Yes. It was on top of him, across his chest. There was still a couple of the boxes strapped to it as well. He was struggling for breath. It was a right mess.'

'Why didn't you try to get the load off him, or at least the boxes that were still tied to the pallet?'

'Because they were too heavy, and the others had gone to get the foreman.'

'Something *you* told them to do.'

There was a sudden change in Dad's tone. 'What are you saying? That I sent the others away so he would have to stay there, under all that weight?'

'I'm not saying anything, Alf. I'm just asking why your immediate reaction wasn't to see if you could get him free, or at least try to.'

'I did, but like said, I couldn't move all that stuff on my own.'

'Which is why I asked what made you send the others away instead of telling them to help Gustav first. It wasn't as if they hadn't seen or heard what had happened as well. They would have come straight over, as a few of them did, I understand? Not all of them ran to get the foreman, some stayed with you.'

'Yeah, and a couple of them did grab at the boxes, but they were in shock, we all were. We weren't thinking clearly. Anyway, it was obvious he wasn't going to make it, not with about a ton of wood and freight on top of him, nobody could have survived that.'

'Did he speak at all before he died?'

'Not really. I shouted that some of the others had gone to get help, but he just sort of gurgled and blood came out of his mouth. Like I said, it was obvious he was a goner.'

There was a slight pause in the conversation as Edith and I looked at each other. She shuddered.

'How awful. What a terrible way to die.'

'It sounds like he thinks Dad should have done more to try and save Gustav.'

'I don't see how, he...' Edith stopped as Mr Palmer began speaking again.

'I don't like to ask this, Alf, but... have you been drinking?'

'Drinking, are you serious? How can you ask that, I never drink on the job.'

There was another pause in the conversation. Edith and I held our breath as we waited for Mr Palmer's response. We knew how often Dad had gone to work the worse for wear after one of his drinking sessions.

'I think we both know that's not true, don't we, Alf? You've been sent home on more than one occasion for alcohol-related issues in the past.'

Dad's tone changed again; his response becoming more aggressive at being challenged about his drinking at work.

'Are you saying I was drunk earlier; that I'm responsible in some way for what happened, 'cause I'll tell you now I...'

Interrupting, Mr Palmer sought to stamp his authority on the conversation.

'As I said earlier, I'm not suggesting anything, not at this stage anyway. I'm just asking a question, that's all. And if you don't like hearing it from me, then God help you once the police begin their enquiries.'

'Police?'

'Yes, the police. A man has died on *our* property, remember. Crushed by a pallet of goods being unloaded on *our* docks.

They'll want answers to all the questions I'm asking, and a lot more besides, you can be sure of that.'

'And I'll tell them the same as I've told you. It was an accident, no more, no less. I didn't load that pallet. It's the ones on the ship that you and the police should be talking to, not me.'

'And they will, the same as I'm talking to you now. George Roper is already speaking with members of that shift right now. Hopefully, we'll get some more answers from them. My concern at the moment is to check that everything was done as quickly as possible to help Gustav once the pallet had come loose and fallen on him. Admittedly, he appears to have ignored the recognised safety procedures by moving towards the load before it was physically on the ground. That will have a definite effect on the outcome of our enquiries, and the police as well, no doubt. But we also have a responsibility to make sure everything was done on site to help him once the tragedy occurred.'

Dad's voice rose again. 'And it was. And if you don't believe me then that's your problem. And as for accusing me of being drunk on shift, and not doing what I could to help, well, you're wrong, and if you don't believe me, then you can piss off out of my house.'

'And using language like that won't help your case either. If it is discovered your work or response to what happened earlier *was* affected by alcohol, then you'll be for the high jump, I'll tell you that for nothing. It wouldn't be the first time you've arrived at the yard having had one too many the night before, we both know that. There have been times when you've been lucky to have kept your job at all. It's only because Gustav and some of the others have spoken up for you in the past, and that you *can* be a hard worker when you put your mind to it that has saved your hide on more than one occasion. Honest, Alf, you're your own worst enemy at times, you really are. Don't think for a minute your reputation for liking a drink and causing trouble hasn't gone before you, because it has. We both remember what happened during the strike.' He paused momentarily before continuing. 'But, I'm not here to talk about that, this is about Gustav Schmidt and getting to grips with what happened on the quayside earlier today. So for now, we'll leave it at that. I understand you're upset, we all are, and I don't think our continuing this discussion is going to help anybody, certainly not Gustav's wife and family. George Cranfield from the executive should be with her now. I'm going round to join him and offer my own condolences as soon as I leave here.'

There was another pause in the conversation. Dad was clearly taken aback by what his boss had said. Perhaps he recognised he had spoken out of turn or was still smarting from the remark about him being a troublemaker. Whatever the cause, he remained silent as Mr Palmer spoke again.

'I'll see myself out. You'll be hearing from me again, and of course, the police over the next few days. You won't be required to work for the rest of the week either. We'll let you know when we want you to return. In the meantime, do yourself a favour; keep away from the dock and stay away from the pub. Take these next couple of days to think about things and spend a bit of time with your family, something poor Gustav won't ever do again.'

Edith and I rushed upstairs to our room for fear of being seen as Mr Palmer left. On hearing the front door close we went to the window to watch as he made his way along the street to Karl's house. Moving back to the bed, we sat quietly in our room hoping Dad wouldn't call us down before Mum got back. It was bad enough knowing how upset he was about the conversation he'd just had with his boss without the two of us having to face his wrath as well. Fortunately, we didn't have to wait long for Mum's return, as a few minutes later we heard the front door open and close again. A familiar and very welcome voice drifted up the stairs.

'Hello, I'm back.'

Edith and I jumped up and ran downstairs. The sight that greeted us as we entered the sitting room wasn't one we were used to witnessing but were grateful for all the same. Dad was holding Mum in his arms. On hearing the door open, she turned to face us. She had clearly been crying, her eyes red and her cheeks flushed with emotion.

'What an awful thing to happen. Your poor dad having to see that. And as for Anna, well, all I could do was hold her while she broke her heart. Any words I might have wanted to say by way of comfort just felt inadequate. I don't know how she and Karl will ever get over this; I really don't.'

Smiling through her tears, she looked at me. 'You'll need to be a really good friend to Karl now, Harry. He'll need all the support he can get.'

Feeling my own eyes sting with tears as I thought about the pain Karl would be experiencing, I nodded. 'Yes, Mum.'

Taking Dad's hand and leading him to his chair, she continued. 'And as for your dad…' She paused to kiss him on the head as he sat down. 'He's had a terrible shock, so we'll need to look after him as well.'

Looking up, he shrugged his shoulders.

'I'm all right, Flo, don't fuss. Yeah, it's tough, but these things happen. It's not the first death I've witnessed on the dock, and it probably won't be the last.'

Mum stepped back, surprised by his reaction.

'I know that, Alf, but this is Gustav we're talking about. He and Anna are our friends. And Harry and Karl are more like brothers than…'

Dad interrupted. 'Anna might be your friend, but I'm not sure I ever really got on with her, or him, certainly not after all that trouble over the Whites' baby a few years back. I understand it's sad for her and the lad that he's gone, but *I'll* not miss him. Had an opinion on everything he did; always thought he knew best.'

'That's unfair. Gustav was a good man. He and Anna have been there for us on more than one occasion in the time we've known them. They've always been ready to help when we've needed it or been in trouble.'

'Help? Interfere more like.' Getting to his feet and standing directly in front of Mum, Dad shook his head. 'I've told you already, I can supply for this family, we don't need their charity.' He paused, nodding towards Edith and me. 'Especially now these two are working, we've been over that before. And don't think I don't know about the times they've fed our Harry when he's gone round to see their lad. How do you think that makes me feel, eh? I'm the master of this house, not bloody Gustav Schmidt.'

There was a stunned silence, with none of us knowing how to respond to such an unwarranted outburst. As ever, Mum attempted to calm the waters.

'That's not fair, Alf, and you know it. You're upset, I understand that. But suggesting that Anna and Gustav have been anything but kind to us is out of order, especially at a time like this. Poor Anna is breaking her heart. We need to be there for her and Karl in the days and weeks to come, not pointing an accusing finger at them.'

'You should tell that to Fred Palmer then. He's pointing the finger of suspicion at me all right.'

'What do you mean?'

'He's been round here suggesting I didn't do all I could to help when that pallet fell.'

Mum shook her head. 'I don't understand. You weren't responsible for it breaking loose, not according to what Mr Cranfield was saying. He explained what he'd heard had happened and said there'll be a formal enquiry at some point to establish the facts. But he never mentioned you being to blame?'

'Well that's not what Palmer said. He suggested when Gustav was hit by the pallet, I could have done more to get him out. Acted quicker, was how he put it.'

Recognising this to be a more detailed conversation the two of them needed to have, Mum turned to Edith and I, and smiled.

'This has been a horrid day for everyone, and we're all upset, but I do need to speak with your dad again for a few minutes. Why don't the two of you go back to your room while we talk. I'll call you down again for something to eat in a little while. How does that sound?'

Much as Edith and I wanted to hear the rest of their exchange, we recognised they weren't going to continue talking with the two of us in the room. It was also beginning to dawn on me the full extent of what had happened. My best friend had lost his father, and no matter how much time passed to ease that pain, things would never be the same for Karl again.

'Okay, Mum.' I tugged gently at Edith's sleeve. 'Come on, sis.'

Sensing my sadness, she slipped her hand into mine and squeezed it. I couldn't remember the last time we'd held hands, but I welcomed it for what it was, a loving gesture of comfort. As we moved towards the door Mum spoke again.

'Thank you both. We won't be long.'

Closing the door behind us, Edith rubbed my arm. 'Are you all right, Harry?'

I wasn't up to putting on a brave face. 'Not really.' Wiping a tear from my eye with the back of my hand, I continued. 'Poor Karl, and his mum. How horrible to lose your dad like that?'

'I know, it must be awful. Dad seemed pretty angry about it, didn't he? Like he said, he was never that keen on Mr Schmidt.'

Taking our customary seat on the bottom stair to overhear Mum and Dad's conversation, I nodded.

'He doesn't like anyone or anything that paints him in a bad light. If he...'

Edith interrupted. 'Shh, he's speaking.'

We leaned towards the door. Dad clearly wasn't happy.

'Bloody Palmer. He's got no right to accuse me of anything.

I didn't push him under that pallet, he walked under it himself. He knew the risks, same as the rest of us.'

'I don't think he was suggesting you did push him, Alf. They just need to be sure it *was* an accident, and that everything was done to help after the pallet had landed on Gustav.'

'Trouble is, most of the lads on shift knew I didn't have much time for him. Interfering know-it-all.'

'I've already said, that's not fair. Anna and Gustav have always been kind *and* generous towards us since they moved here, for all sorts of reasons. But if...'

Failing to placate Dad's inner rage, he shouted her down.

'Go on, say it. If I didn't drink as much, we wouldn't need their charity. Well, if you managed the money better, then maybe you wouldn't need to go begging to our neighbours for help either. God, woman, there's three of us working now, and there's the bit you get from your sewing and the like.'

Much as she loved Dad, Mum wasn't about to take the blame for his obvious failings. Certainly not at the cost of her relationship with those who'd proved themselves to be so much more than just good neighbours. Edith and I held our breath as she bit back, responding angrily to Dad's accusations.

'I'm sorry, Alf, but I won't have that. I try my hardest to make ends meet. Yes, we've had a few more knocks than most over the years, I'll give you that. But don't you dare say I don't do my best for you and the children, because I do. As for the two of them, I've told you already, they don't earn much more than a pittance between them as it is. And now they *are* working they need to have some decent clothes to wear. Harry can't turn up at the bakers in those old school trousers of his all patched up, or maybe you think he can? And Edith needs to look nice as a seamstress as well. She can't go dressed like a pauper. She's only ever had one nice dress in her life, and now she's growing into a young woman she needs to feel good about herself. Girls of a certain age need other things as well, undergarments and the like that you wouldn't understand, or even think about.'

Clearly frustrated by Dad's verbal assault, her voice cracked with emotion as she continued.

'I didn't eat for almost two days last week, because there was nothing left after you'd spent most of your earnings at the pub, again. And I can't be asking Edith and Harry for extra money they haven't got either. They both give me most of their wages as it is. But you still expect a hot meal on the table when you come in, whatever time of the day that might be. And I still have to find food for the two of them, especially now they're out at work for much of the day. Youngsters need to get the right sort of food inside them when they're growing. That is unless you want them having scurvy or worse. They don't deserve to starve because their father would rather drink than feed his family. It's *your* job to provide for this family, Alf, not theirs, so don't tell me...'

Mum's outpouring of righteous indignation was suddenly cut short as the crash of furniture erupted from the other side of the door.

'Don't you dare talk to me like that. I won't have it, you hear? I've told you before I'm the man in this house, and *I* make the rules. And if you don't like it, you can bugger off up the road to your friend Anna and live with her. She'll have room for you an' all now that he's dead.'

Edith and I looked at each other in disbelief at what we were hearing, but there was worse to come as Mum countered.

'Alf Thompson, you take that back. That's a terrible thing to say. All right, it's no secret you were never keen on Gustav, but to use his death to attack my relationship with poor Anna is unforgiveable. I...'

Mum's retort was silenced by the audible sound of a slap to her face. Edith and I jumped up and ran into the room to be greeted by the sight of Mum on her knees, blood trickling from her nose. Dad was stood over her like some raging madman about to strike again. Without thinking I shouted out in Mum's defence.

'You leave her alone, you bully. Why don't *you* bugger off and leave *us* alone? I hate you.'

Edith moved to Mum, placing her arms around her in an act of solidarity and comfort. Again, without considering the potential cost of my actions, I stepped between Mum and Dad to protect her from further blows. Dad's nostrils flared like some demented bull as he lunged forward, striking me about the head.

'Don't you tell me to bugger off, you little sod. You might be nearly as tall as me but you're nowhere near as strong.'

I staggered backwards as he lashed out again, spitting venom as his fist crashed into my cheek. 'Come on then, if you think you're big enough, hit me back, and you'll find out what a real beating feels like.'

Panic began to grip me as the realisation of what was happening began to take hold. I felt dizzy as the blows to my head took their toll. He was right, I was not as strong as him, but I couldn't back down, not without putting Mum and Edith back in the firing line. I shouted back at him, tears of anger, fear, and frustration overwhelming me.

'Go on then, hit me again if that makes you feel big, but you stay away from Mum.'

As I cowered, waiting for his fist to land, I heard Mum's voice from behind.

'That's enough, Alf, it's enough. He's still only a boy, leave him alone.'

'Only a boy is he? Well, he thinks he's enough of a man to swear at me. The little sod.'

I felt Mum's arm pull me back as she got to her feet and moved in front of me.

'If you've got to hit somebody then hit me again, not Harry.'

Dad drew back his hand to strike as Edith screamed.

'Stop it, Dad! Please, don't hit her anymore. Just stop it.'

I'm not sure what it was in Edith's cry that made the difference, but it worked. Dad stood for a moment, glaring at the three of us before smashing his, still clenched, fist into the table.

'Fuck it. Fuck all of you. I don't need this. As if I haven't been through enough already today; being told I should've done more to save that bloody German. Now, I have to take shit from my family as well.'

Time appeared to stand still. Only Edith's gentle and rhythmic sobs breaking the silence as each of us paused to draw breath. Eventually Mum spoke.

'Why don't you just go, Alf. Get out of the house for a while. You've done enough damage for one day.'

Fighting to contain his temper, Dad ran his hand across his forehead, pushing back the lock of hair that had fallen across his brow.

'Yeah, I'm going all right. I'm not staying here a minute longer to listen to this crap.' Grabbing his cap from the table, he moved to the door. Then, turning briefly, he spoke again, his voice no less strident. 'It's all that bloody German's fault.' Looking straight at Mum, he continued. 'You know what? I'm glad he's dead. And you can tell her I said that an' all. They should never have come here in the first place. There's plenty of local lads who'd have been grateful for the work he took off them.'

The three of us stood, struggling to believe what we were hearing. No matter how angry he might have been about what Mr Palmer had said, Dad's violence towards us had been completely unjustified, as was his verbal attack on Gustav and his family. A deep anger towards him settled in my chest as I watched him yank open the kitchen door and storm out of the room, slamming it shut behind him.

Lost for words, Edith and I stared at each other in silence as Mum attempted to defend Dad's outburst.

'Your father has had a terrible shock and…'

Edith interrupted, verbalising both our feelings perfectly. 'Don't, Mum. Please, don't try and defend him. You always stick up for him after there's been a row, or when he's hit you.' Glancing at me, she continued. 'We're not little children anymore. We know what he's like, and we hate it. I don't know why you stay with him. If you left, things couldn't get any worse. In fact, you'd be better off, as he wouldn't be hitting you.'

Wiping the blood from under her nose with the back of her hand, Mum forced a smile.

'You might be right, Edith, love, but, as I've said before, where would I go, especially with no money? And what about you two? You've both got jobs now and are beginning to make your way in life. You couldn't just leave and start again, it's not as easy as that.'

Pausing to catch her breath, she pursed her lips.

'Listen, I don't like it any more than you do when your dad loses his temper, but… he's still your dad, and I'm still his wife. And deep down, I still love him.'

It was my turn to interject. 'How can you say that, Mum, when he's just given you another beating? How can you love anyone who would do that?'

Mum shook her head as a tear formed in her eye. Pulling a chair from under the table, she sat down, indicating for the two of us to join her.

'Your dad wasn't always like this. A lot of the reason he drinks is because he thinks he's failing us as a family, and because he can't provide for us as he feels he should. It may not appear like that to the two of you, but you need to remember I've known him a lot longer than you.'

Pausing, she smiled at the two of us. I always felt reassured when Mum smiled. As a young boy it reminded me I was loved, and that no matter how bad a problem was, she would make it better. But now I was older I was able to see beyond the simple expression of love reflected in that smile. I knew it could also act as a precursor to a deeper or more challenging conversation shared between us, and so it proved on this particular occasion. Edith and I sat and watched as she placed her hands on the table, rubbing them together thoughtfully, considering how best to proceed. After a few moments she looked up and smiled again. The sun shone brightly through the window and encircled her head in a bright halo of light, providing her with an almost angelic appearance apart from the dried smear of blood beneath her nose. I felt a thread of trepidation run through me as I held her in my gaze. I wasn't sure what she was about to say, but sensed it was something she'd never shared before, at least not with Edith and I. Nervously, I moved my hand under the table, taking Edith's hand and squeezing it. She returned the gesture as we threw each other a glance of mutual understanding before turning to Mum.

'It's all right, Mum, you don't have to explain or say anymore. We understand, don't we, Harry?'

I nodded my agreement, even if not entirely sure what it was I was endorsing.

Separating her hands and placing them face down on the table, Mum leant back and breathed in deeply.

'Thank you, Edith, but I want… need to say this.' I watched as a tear ran down her cheek. 'You're both old enough now to know the truth about your dad and why he reacts as he does at times.' Holding the two of us in her gaze, she wiped away the tear with the back of her hand. 'Well, maybe not everything, but at least some of it.' She edged her chair a little closer to the table. 'When we first got married, he never seemed to get angry at all. And he hardly ever drank either. But… over the years he changed. I think a lot of it's because of the work he's been doing at the docks, certainly in recent years anyway.' Pausing, she looked wistfully into the distance for a moment before continuing.

'Your dad had real ambitions as a younger man. He wanted us to have our own shop when we first got together, selling fruit and vegetables. But, there never seemed to be enough money to get started, so he began working on the docks to get a regular income and help pay for us to get married. The idea was, we would try and save a little each week and put it towards getting our own shop at some point in the future. After a while though, our dreams began to fade. And once I became pregnant with you, Edith, your dad had to focus on the job he had to keep a roof over our head and put food on the table for his young family. That said, he didn't mind being a dock worker in those early days, despite the low pay and long hours. He hoped he might be spotted as someone with a bit of ambition and get promoted. But it soon became clear the shipyard owners weren't looking for bright young individuals who were looking to climb the ladder. They just wanted men, like your dad, to work as pack horses, loading and unloading the ships for as little as possible, while making as much money for themselves at the same time. That's why your dad was such a big supporter of the strike, when the dockers and shipyard workers fought to get their wages raised to sixpence an hour.

A man named Ben Tillett, who led the strike, saw potential in your dad as an activist for the cause. And it was due, in part, to the two of them and the other union members that they also won a little bit more for overtime as well. That whole period was tough for all the dockers and their families, with little or no money coming in, but we stuck together and won in the end. But, because your dad was so vocal and played a big part in leading the rebellion, he got singled out, along with one or two others, as a troublemaker. When the strike was over those same men were given the toughest shifts, working the longest hours as a form of undeclared punishment for upsetting the powers that be. Of course, the shipyard owners and their investors denied this, but everyone knew what was happening. And, short of calling for another strike, which would never have been agreed to, your dad and the rest of the men who'd been the main protagonists just had to get on with it. That's about the time he started drinking. It wasn't too bad at first. He'd just go for a pint on the way home to talk through his frustrations with the other men, but it quickly escalated. The others soon realised they weren't going to beat the system either, not without causing more problems for themselves and their families at the same time. They decided to settle for the increase in pay they'd won and keep their heads down, but not your dad.'

Struggling, Mum put her hand to her mouth as emotion threatened to overwhelm her once more. Edith and I sat in silence, waiting until she was ready to speak again.

'He's never been one for accepting his lot in life, your dad. That was one of the things that attracted me to him, when we first got together. He had all these dreams about setting up in business, declaring we'd have a big house and a nice garden to go with it.' She laughed. 'We were even going to have a car once the money really started to come in, but… it wasn't to be. And so, as one by one his dreams died, so did a bit of him. I look at your father sometimes and feel a deep sadness for him. I see a man crushed by the life he's been forced to live and the compromises he's had to make along the way. Of course, he loves us, but he's trapped by a sense of failure on so many levels. And because of that, he drinks to blot out those dark reflections of the man he might have been and of the life we might have had. So, when the drink takes hold, the three of us just serve to remind him, once again, of the responsibilities he feels unable to meet. And, instead of providing the comfort he so desperately needs, we become the unintended enemy, and so the downward spiral continues.'

'But that's not fair. It's not our fault he didn't open his own shop or couldn't afford a car.'

'I know, Harry, and so does your dad. In a way that's the real issue for him. He realises it's nobody's fault, it's just life. But when he's drinking his mind doesn't respond to that simple logic. Alcohol speaks a language of its own, and for your dad that translates into anger and frustration towards his lot in life. It's like he's two different people. There's the first, who loves his family and wants to care for them, and there's the second, who feels he can't. And so he finds it easier to drown that alter ego in a glass of beer.'

'I hate that other man.'

Mum smiled. 'So do I, Harry. Well, maybe not the man. I hate what the drink does to him, but I can't hate the man. Deep down, he's still your dad; still the man I love, and always will, I think. Although, there are times I struggle to remember that, like when he gets angry and violent, as he did earlier.'

Leaning forward, she stroked my hair. 'And even more so when he hits out at you, Harry. I'm so sorry that he…'

Sensing her distress, I interjected. 'Don't worry about me, Mum, I can look after myself.'

'That might be true, but fighting with your father is not something you should ever be doing. And, definitely not at your age.'

Whilst Mum's story about him had been unexpected, I don't think Edith and I were particularly surprised to have it confirmed the effect that alcohol had on Dad, whatever the reason.

Although Mum had said she couldn't hate Dad for his aggressive behaviour, I felt less forgiving about his hostility, especially when demonstrated against her. Young as I was, I recognised unwarranted violence against anyone, let alone the person you're meant to care for above all others, was unacceptable. I was also saddened by the fact he'd said he didn't care that Karl's dad was dead. I knew the two of them had never been particularly close, but to have such disregard for the life of another human being shocked me to the core. As I sat contemplating the rationale behind my thinking I realised, once evaluated, it was little different to that of Mum's. I too loved my father but, equally, hated the person he became when under the influence of drink. The one thing I did determine, he would never again hit my mother, not while I was around to protect her.

Chapter Nine

Try as she might, Mum could never alter Dad's mindset regarding Gustav's death. I think, following his outburst at Anna after Karl and I had been questioned by the police, along with the corresponding fight between the two of them, he had decided Gustav was the enemy, and always would be. He also resented the fact I spent so much time at Karl's house, often being fed there, and with Anna always looking to help Mum in any way she could. She, above everyone else knew how much we struggled to make ends meet, especially when Dad had been drinking.

The next couple of years also proved tough for Karl and me. I found it difficult to comfort my friend in his loss. Not having experienced a settled family existence myself, I struggled to come alongside him in any meaningful way. He also became aware Dad held a grudge against him and his mum; so rarely visited our home. Equally, I began to visit Karl's house less often as well. Mum and Anna maintained their friendship though, each supporting one another wherever they could. However, without Gustav's wages coming in, money became extremely tight for Karl and his mum. The small amount he brought in from his apprenticeship came nowhere near matching his dad's earnings. And, whilst Anna was an accomplished seamstress, the money she earned still fell some way short of what they needed to get by. Suddenly, it was Mum who was scraping a few extra coppers together to help them out. An almost complete reversal of the way things had been prior to Gustav's death. Edith and I were sworn to secrecy about this, even though it might be the two of us providing that little extra on occasion. We both knew, had Dad found out, he would have stopped this act of neighbourly charity in its tracks.

'I don't know why she doesn't just bugger off back to Germany,' he would say. 'Now that he's gone, there's nothing left for her here. Some other family could make better use of that house.'

Mum would argue to the contrary, but never to the extent where they would fall out over it. She knew if she sided too openly with Anna, Dad would forbid her from seeing her friend altogether.

Karl and I would still get together after work, mainly to play football in the street or on the wasteland nearby. But even here our passion for the game was beginning to wane. We were both in our mid-teens now and kicking a ball about pretending we were John Chalmers or Frederick Calvert, two of our favourite players from the Arsenal team of 1911-12, was less attractive than it had been a few years previously. In those earlier days the possibility of playing professional football had readily appealed to both of us, especially when weighed against the alternative of a life spent working in the shipyards.

Other differences in our relationship began to surface as well. We each began to take an interest in the changing face of politics. Not to the extent where either of us considered supporting any particular party or political ideology. It was more in how those who held positions of power and authority had the ability to influence the lives of others battling to survive at the other end of the social spectrum.

The political map was beginning to alter abroad as well. This was especially true in Germany where the Kaiser, Wilhelm II, was pushing forward with plans to turn the country into a world power, both economically and militarily. These changes were also beginning to influence Karl's thoughts and aspirations as a young German boy growing up in another country. He felt, following the death of his father, that perhaps his future and that of his mum's might better be realised in their homeland. I also think he resented the way Dad and some of the other dock workers had treated his father at the shipyard, along with their attitude towards his mum following Gustav's death. Anna already had family living near Hamburg so any adjustment back to life as a German resident would be less challenging for them both. It was hard to argue with that logic. Even so, I wasn't keen to lose my friend, although I recognised we were becoming noticeably less connected in our interests and plans for the future.

As time went on physical support for Anna and Karl continued to wane. Her circle of friends gradually diminished until only Mum remained as someone she could truly rely on. Others, like Dad, went further and began to promote the view that Gustav had considered himself a better worker than many of the other dockers. It was argued he had always been a favourite of the shipyard owners and managers, and given the more favourable shifts, or those offering overtime. The truth was very different. Gustav could always be relied on to turn up on time and complete the work demanded of him without recourse or complaint. Meanwhile, Dad and some of the others preferred to work the easier shifts, or those that afforded them more time in The Blue Anchor. And so, as often happens with the passing of time, rumour and conjecture begin to outweigh the facts. And without Gustav there to defend himself, fabrication increasingly became reality for some, resulting in Karl and his mum becoming progressively more ostracised by those in the dockyard community.

The other dividing factor that ultimately generated distance between Karl and I was when girls came on the scene. Being nearly a year younger, I wasn't as interested in the opposite sex as he was, at least not initially. But I soon caught up once their obvious physical attraction became more apparent. Karl had already had a couple of so-called 'girlfriends' before I entered the arena. Indeed, it was only when we both set our cap on one particular girl, Irene Burrows, that any sense of competition between us came to the fore.

Irene was the daughter of Ted and Betty Burrows. Ted owned an engineering company, making machine parts for the shipyard and other local businesses. There was talk for a while of Karl going to work for him, bearing in mind his interest in metalwork and engineering, but it never came to anything. Ted had done well for himself, and whilst the family never flaunted their money, there was clearly plenty of it to go around. They lived in a large, detached house on the outskirts of Canning Town next to a park. Irene was a single child. As a youngster she spent time with the other local girls, skipping rope or playing with dolls, none of which held any interest for us boys. But now, in our mid-teens, Irene offered a very different sort of appeal; one that Karl and I became aware of pretty much simultaneously.

The two of us were sitting on a wall at the end of our street one Saturday afternoon discussing the scoring abilities of a certain Arsenal player when Irene crossed the road and headed in our direction. She had just had her sixteenth birthday and appeared every inch the embodiment of a young man's dream as to what his ideal girlfriend might be like. We looked on in silence as she walked towards us, her highly patterned yellow dress swaying from side to side in tandem with her hips. Ringlets from her wavy blonde hair bounced carefree in the breeze as they hung loose by the side of her face. Aware of the attention she was garnering, she turned and smiled as she passed by.

'Hello, boys.'

'Hello, Irene,' we answered in unison, both feigning interest in being anything more than polite.

We watched as she strode confidently up the road and moved away. A sudden gust of wind caught the hem of her dress, lifting it a little higher than normal and exposing her leg just above the ankle.

'Not bad,' quipped Karl, interrupting his earlier flow about the football player.

'She's turning into quite a looker,' I responded, equally happy to be diverted from our previous conversation.

'I might ask her out.'

Nudging him playfully on the arm, I laughed. 'And where would you take her? You've got no money. She doesn't look like the sort of girl who'd be happy to settle for a walk down the docks to look at the ships.'

Pushing me back, he countered, 'Okay then, what would you do with her?'

'I know what I'd like to do with her.'

'Oh yes, that's likely. You've never even been out with a girl, not properly anyway. What makes you think the first one you ask out is going to let you put your arms round her, or kiss her?'

'I didn't mean it like that. Anyway, you're no great catch, are you? Apart from Enid Reynolds who you saw a couple of times before she went off with Tommy Peters, who have you been out with?

'Dorothy Brown.'

I laughed. 'You can't claim Dorothy Brown as a girlfriend. We played football with her brother a couple of times, and you had tea at their house that Sunday afternoon before walking her to her friend's house afterwards. And that was only because it was on the way back to yours. That's hardly going out with her, is it?'

'She let me kiss her on the cheek. And that's better than you've ever done.'

'That's because I've been saving myself for Irene.'

Jumping from the wall and grabbing me by the shoulders, Karl laughed. 'Well, I bet she hasn't been saving herself for you.'

'How do you know, she might.'

'Very well, we will have a wager on it. The first one she agrees to go out with is the winner, and the other has to give them a farthing.' Spitting on his palm he held out his hand. 'Agreed?'

Without thinking, I spat into my hand and clasped it to his. 'Agreed.' Immediately regretting my impulsive response, I sought to backtrack a little.

'Let's not rush into this though. She won't say yes to either of us if we push her.'

Withdrawing his hand, Karl poked me gently in the stomach. 'You are already a coward, Harry. Why do you not agree I am the winner before we start. Why not give me your farthing now. We both know I will win this bet anyway.'

Whether it was the impetuousness of youth, or the fact I really did like Irene, I reached for his hand again and shook it firmly.

'I'm not giving in that easily, so you get *your* money ready. Blood brothers or not, I bet Irene says yes to me instead of you.'

Karl laughed again. 'We will see.'

It was three days later I got my first real chance to speak to Irene. I could have gone to her house before but wasn't sure how her dad would react to some young lad knocking on his door asking to see his daughter. I was also worried he might send me packing before I'd even had the opportunity to talk to her.

On this particular day I'd been delivering something to a friend of Mum's and was heading home when I noticed Irene walking in my direction. She was wearing the same yellow dress that had caught my attention a few days earlier. I was grateful Mum had suggested I smarten myself up to run the errand for her. It helped me feel more confident about approaching Irene. As we drew nearer, I felt my heart leap in my chest. This was my chance, and I was determined not to blow it. I felt an inane grin settle on my face as we drew alongside each other.

'Hello, Irene.'

She pretended to act surprised. 'Oh, hello, Harry, I didn't notice you.'

I took this as a sign of encouragement. I knew full well she had seen me, having watched her check her hair and straighten her dress in anticipation that I might speak to her.

Attempting to control a nervous twitch that had suddenly developed under my left eye, I spoke again. 'I like your dress. I saw you in it the other day. Yellow is my favourite colour. It suits you.'

Her cheeks flushed red with embarrassment as she smiled. 'Thank you. I didn't know boys noticed things like that. I thought all you were interested in was football.' Nodding towards the wasteland across the road, she continued. 'I've seen you and Karl kicking a ball around over there in the past.'

'Yeah, but not so much these days.' Pushing my shoulders back in an attempt to increase my physical stature, I nodded. 'Perhaps we're growing up.'

Throwing her head back, she laughed as the breeze caught her hair and blew a ringlet across her face. 'I don't think boys ever really grow up. They might become men, but they'll always be little boys at heart.'

I didn't know whether to feel amused or wounded by her remark but chose the former.

'You might be right, but I still like your dress.'

A short, nervous silence followed as I waited for her response. It only lasted a few seconds but felt much longer. Eventually, after looking me up and down, as if considering my potential as a suitor, she nodded.

'And, as I said before, thank you.'

Gesturing towards the wasteland again, she continued. 'Where is your friend today?'

Not really wanting to talk about Karl, I sought to move the conversation on. 'I don't know, maybe I'll see him later. I've been running an errand for my mum. I was just on my way home when I saw you.'

Another short silence followed. I realised the onus was on me to say something more if I wanted our conversation to continue in any meaningful way but I wasn't sure what to talk about. Sensing my nervousness and not wanting to embarrass me further, Irene took the initiative.

'Well, it was nice to see you, Harry. I'd better go now.'

It was now or never. Swallowing hard, I cleared my throat. 'Would you like to see me again, Irene? You know, go out with me sometime.'

Stepping back, she smiled, her eyelashes fluttering as she feigned surprise at my proposal. 'I don't know, where would we go?'

'We could go for a walk.' I felt the palms of my hands wet with perspiration as I rubbed them nervously against the side of my trousers. 'What do you think?'

Considering my suggestion for a moment before responding, she shook her head. 'I'm not sure whether you're being honest with me, Harry, or cruel.'

Shocked by her remark, I scratched my head. 'I don't know what you mean. Why would I be cruel to you? I've asked if you would like to see me. Is that so awful?'

'No, it's not. But I think you might be teasing me. Your friend Karl asked me the same thing earlier this morning. I saw him at the end of your road as he was going to work. That's why I asked you where he was a few minutes ago. It sounds as though the two of you have agreed to ask me the same thing to make me look silly. I don't think I want to see either of you if this is the way you treat a girl.'

Suddenly, everything made sense. Karl had obviously made the first move to win our bet. The difference was, for me, I genuinely liked Irene and hadn't even considered our wager when asking to see her. I wasn't angry with Karl, but deep down

I felt it was more important to him to win the farthing than it was to spend time with Irene. Yes, he probably liked her, but his real desire was to see me lose our bet. I decided to come clean and be honest in the hope she might believe me.

'Please, let me explain before you make your mind up about my proposal.'

Staring directly at me, Irene considered whether to give me a second chance. The next few seconds took an eternity to pass before she finally replied. 'Well, it had better be good. And you better tell me the truth as well. I'm not going to be messed about by you two for a bit of fun.'

I sensed her frustration and immediately regretted that Karl and I had ever made our stupid wager. Even in these brief early exchanges, I realised I really did like Irene and wanted to get to know her better. Perhaps I *was* growing up after all. I gestured towards a low wall behind us.

'Let's sit down for a minute. And please don't jump to any conclusions until I've finished.' Touching her lightly on the arm, I smiled. 'I really do like you, Irene.'

Adjusting her dress, she sat beside me on the wall. I took this as a positive sign. At least she hadn't walked away before I'd had a chance to tell her my side of the story.

'Thank you. But as I said, this had better be good.'

I took a deep breath. I knew the next few minutes would decide whether I had any chance of gaining her affections. It could also affect my relationship with Karl.

'I'm sorry Karl spoke to you earlier; I had hoped to get to you first...'

Interrupting, Irene turned to face me, her demeanour anything but understanding.

'So, you *were* both wanting to tease me?'

'No, not at all.' I took another breath, exhaling slowly as I gathered my thoughts.

'You remember when we spoke the other day?'

'Yes.'

'Well, after you'd gone, we both said we liked you and wanted to ask you out, so we made a bet as to who you would say yes to. We…'

Jumping to her feet, Irene turned to face me; the look in her eyes telling me all I needed to know. 'You made a bet about me? What sort of girl do you think I am? Do you honestly think I would go out with any boy who thinks he can win me as part of a wager? And how much was this bet for, not that it matters? I'm just interested to know how much you think I'm worth.'

'A farthing, but that isn't the…'

Interrupting again, her face now red with rage, Irene shouted at me. 'A farthing! You think I'm only worth a farthing. Well, thank you very much. Let me tell you this, Harry Thompson, I wouldn't go out with you now, or your friend Karl if you paid me a hundred pounds. Do you hear me, not even for five hundred pounds.'

I noticed tears of anger and disappointment in her eyes as she turned to leave.

'Please, Irene. Please listen to me,' I pleaded, making a grab for her hand. 'I'm really sorry about what I just said. It wasn't meant to come out like that, even though it was what happened. Yes, maybe it was a bit of fun between us initially, but none of it was said to hurt you, or your feelings. We do both like you. I know Karl asked you first, but if you haven't already said yes to him then I hope you will at least give me a chance?'

Clearly upset, Irene snapped back at me. 'What, so you can win your farthing and have a good laugh at my expense? I don't think so. And just so you know I didn't say yes to Karl either. I told him I'd think about it. Well, now you can tell him from me I have thought about it, and the answer is the same for both of you, no. I wouldn't go out with either of you now if you were the only boys left in the world.'

Young as I was, I still felt a genuine affection for Irene and was desperate to heal the developing rift between us.

'I don't know what else to say, but I'm sorry. If you'll just give me a chance to make it up to you, I'll…' The words stuck in my throat as she pulled her hand free and turned to walk away.

'I meant what I said. You and Karl are just horrid, and you both deserve each other. Making bets about who can trick a girl into going out with them, and then asking to be forgiven when you get found out. Well, I won't forgive you, either of you, so don't waste your time asking me again. And if either of you do come near me, I'll tell my dad about your little bet, and we'll see what he has to say about it.'

And with that she was gone, her dress swinging in the breeze once more, but this time not from the seductive sway of her hips, but rather more stiffly as she moved determinedly away with no intention of turning back.

I sat, watching as she disappeared over the brow of the hill and, seemingly, out of my life forever. My first attempt at romance had failed even before it had begun. The blame, quite rightly, belonged with Karl and I and in the stupid wager we'd made. If only I hadn't agreed to it, I might still be talking to her now.

Berating myself for having been so stupid, I vowed to have it out with Karl the next time we spoke. This proved to be sooner than I'd imagined, following a knock at our back door around six thirty that same evening. We'd just finished our tea. This had been a meagre affair of dripping sandwiches followed by some leftover cold custard; all washed down with a cup of tea. Even with Edith and I contributing towards the household bills, there was still little left come the end of the week, especially with Dad continuing to spend most of his wages at the pub. I heard Mum open the door.

'Come in, Karl, Harry's just finishing his tea. You go on through, I'm sure he'll be pleased to see you.'

In truth, I was anything but. I was still upset about what had happened earlier with Irene. I was also determined to say my piece, and so wasn't entirely disappointed to see him walk into our sitting room.

'Hello, Harry, have you had a good day?' Not waiting for my reply, he continued. 'Shall we go out?'

I certainly didn't want to discuss Irene in front of Mum and Edith, and so agreed to his suggestion. 'Yes, okay.'

Running my finger around the edge of my bowl to garner the last of the custard that had stuck to the side, I moved from my chair and led the way to the scullery, carrying the empty bowl with me.

'Here you are, Mum. Karl and I are going out for a while, we won't be long.'

She nodded her approval, although I could tell from her expression, she wasn't entirely happy with me leaving.

'All right, Harry, but don't be late. We don't know what time your father will be home, and I don't want him worrying if you're not here.'

I knew she didn't really mind me being out, as I always came back before bedtime. Her primary concern would have been in having Dad arrive back from the pub the worse for drink and losing his temper because I wasn't there to greet him like some excited puppy along with Edith and her. Recognising this, I answered in the affirmative.

'All right, Mum, we won't go far. If I see Dad coming, I'll be straight back.'

'Thank you, son. Goodbye, Karl, give my best to your mother.'

'I will. Goodbye, Mrs Thompson.'

Closing the door behind us, Karl slapped me on the back. 'Listen, Harry, I have a story to tell you.'

Anticipating what was to come and still upset with how my earlier conversation with Irene had gone, I jumped in.

'I bet you have. And I have a story to tell you too,' I replied as we made our way down the alleyway to watch out for Dad. The road at the front was quieter at this time of the day, with most of the children having gone inside for their tea, or to get ready for bed. We sat down with our backs against the wall in front of the house next to ours.

'What is your story, Harry, you can go first.' He laughed. 'Although mine is very exciting and will mean you owe me some money.'

'I know, because you've spoken to Irene.'

Poking me in the ribs, he nodded. 'Yes, I have. And it sounds like you have as well, but you got there too late.'

'To win our bet maybe, but not to ask her to see me.'

Scratching his head, Karl laughed again. 'I do not understand, I thought the idea was to be the first to ask her out. That was our bet, wasn't it?'

'Yes, but I really did want to see her, and not just to win the bet.'

A look of confusion descended across his face. 'Now I am lost. I thought whoever asked her first and she would say yes, would be the winner. But now you say you want to see her, and not for our bet?'

'Look, I know we made that stupid wager, but the truth is I *do* like her, and really want to go out with her, but not...'

Scratching his head again, Karl interrupted. 'But I have already asked her out, this morning, and she has said she might go with me. Of course, I am not really interested in doing that, although she is very pretty, and it might be fun to see how far she would let me go with her.' Prodding my arm and grinning, he continued, 'If you know what I mean.'

Knowing exactly what he meant did nothing to temper my growing dislike at what he was suggesting. 'I know you've asked her out, she told me that when I spoke to her this afternoon. That's what...'

Chuckling, he interrupted again. 'Ah, so that is why you are upset. She told you no because she had already chosen to see me perhaps?'

'No, that's not it. And I don't care about the bet.'

'Then, I don't understand. If you don't mind losing the bet, what is upsetting you?'

'The fact that you don't really care about Irene, that's what. You are more interested in getting a farthing from me than you are about seeing her.'

'But we did not talk about caring for her, not in that way. We said we would both ask her out, and whoever she agreed to see first would win our bet.'

Realising I wasn't making myself clear, I drew a breath. 'Listen, and don't interrupt until I've finished, okay?'

'Okay.'

'I know we made our wager, and I recognise you spoke to Irene before me, I accept that. But what we hadn't thought through was that she might be hurt or suspicious about both of us asking her out at the same time.'

'Why would she be hurt by two boys asking to see her? If two girls asked to see me, I would be very happy.'

'I know you would, but Irene is different to you, and she *was* hurt. In fact, she became angry when I told her about our wager.'

'You told her?' A look on incredulity spread across his face. 'Why would you tell her that? To spoil my chances of winning perhaps?'

I felt a growing tension building within me. 'No, Karl, not to spoil your chances of winning. It's because I didn't want to hurt her, and I could see what we were doing wasn't very nice. I know we laughed about it when we first discussed the idea, but Irene is a nice girl and I suppose my conscience got the better of me, and so I told her the truth.'

'And so now she doesn't want to see either of us, is that what you're saying?'

'Yes. She said we should leave her alone.'

'I still don't understand why you told her about the bet?'

'Because I couldn't lie to her, even if you could.'

'Pushing me hard on the arm, Karl retorted. 'So, now you are saying you told her I was lying when I asked to see her?'

'No, that's not what I'm saying. I didn't say anything about you personally, other than we'd both made a bet about who could get her to go out with them first. She said we were as bad as each other and that she didn't want to have anything to do with either of us again, ever.'

Evidence of the growing friction between us demonstrated itself in Karl's response. 'I thought we were friends, Harry, but now I think you are more like your father. Because you couldn't get Irene to go with you, you tell her about our wager, and now she won't see me either.'

Growing irritation at Karl's wilful misunderstanding of what I was saying got the better of me.

'Oh piss off, Karl, you know that's not true. And what's my dad got to do with any of this?'

Equally frustrated and sensing a fracture in our relationship, Karl bit back.

'I have not said this before, Harry, because we have been friends and I thought you were different. But now I see you are selfish like your father, only thinking about yourself. Others have said he could have done more to help Papa when he was trapped, perhaps even saved his life, but he didn't. He was more worried about saving himself, or maybe he was too drunk to do anything.'

The brief but deafening silence between us that followed felt like a chasm of unmitigated proportion, and one that would be difficult to reconcile. I was the first to speak, my voice cracking with emotion.

'What are you saying? That my dad was responsible for your father's death? I can't believe you would think that.'

Without any display of remorse, Karl continued.

'Mama and I have always tried to believe your father did what he could to help Papa, even when others said he could have done more to save him. We never chose to fully believe those stories, even though we were aware your father didn't like him, especially after that fight outside your house. But now, hearing that you told Irene about our wager so she wouldn't want to see me shows me you are selfish just like him. You are not really my friend at all.'

I felt shocked and wounded by what I was hearing.

'I... I can't believe you're saying that. Yes, Dad drinks too much, but to think he wouldn't help, or that he would stand by and watch your father die... it just isn't true. And to say I would do anything like that to harm our friendship, well, I can't believe you would honestly think...'

Interrupting, Karl got to his feet.

'I don't want to talk to you anymore, Harry. I think you knew exactly what you were doing when you spoke with Irene, and I am angry with you for that. And yes, now I do think maybe your father didn't do as much as he could to save Papa. I think perhaps Mama is thinking the same thing too. She said to me the other day, she likes having your mother as a friend, but she finds it harder to speak with her since Papa died. There are so many people telling her about your father's dislike for him.'

Struggling to respond as a wave of righteous indignation rose inside me, I spoke in measured tones; aware our relationship was on the point of imploding.

'I'm not sure where all of this is coming from, and I'm truly sorry if you feel I've spoiled your chances with Irene; but as for Dad being responsible in any way for...'

Leaning towards me slightly, his face close to mine, Karl interjected.

'I will tell you something else as well. Mama was going to speak to your mother soon about this, but I will tell you anyway. We are going back to Germany.'

'Back to Germany! I don't understand. When? Why?'

'Because we are fed up with people saying things about my father, and our being German. When we first came to London we were welcomed as a family. But with everything that has happened since Papa died, and with people talking about what is going on in Germany with the Kaiser, Mama is feeling much less welcome here. And now with you betraying our friendship, I am feeling less welcome too.'

'I haven't betrayed our friendship, Karl; I wouldn't do that. All I did was tell Irene the truth about our bet because I didn't want her to be upset if she found out later after maybe going out with one of us.'

'And that person would have been me. That is what you didn't like or want, and I cannot forgive you for that.' Getting to his feet, he held up his hand to show where we'd cut ourselves. 'I may carry this scar on my hand to show the day we swore an oath of friendship to each other, but you have broken that bond now and so we are no longer blood brothers.'

Stunned by what I was hearing and with my earlier frustration dissipating, I made a final desperate attempt to heal the growing rift between us.

'Karl, you don't mean that. This is silly.' Standing to face him, I pointed to my own scar. 'I still want to be your blood brother *and* your friend.' I made a vain attempt to smile. 'Flipping heck, if we let a girl come between us at this early stage of a relationship what will it be like when one of us wants to get married?'

I could tell from his response he wasn't for turning.

'I wasn't the one who betrayed our confidence.' Shaking his head, he turned to walk away. 'I too am sorry our friendship has to end this way. But if we cannot trust each other to keep a secret, then the oath we took has no value. I must also think of Mama now, and how I support her when we return to Germany. After today I think this will be good for both of us.'

'Where will you stay?'

'Mama has a sister who lives near Hamburg, we have talked about that before. It is where we lived before coming to England. We will stay with her until Mama and I can find work. Then we will make a home for ourselves again.'

Not wanting to push him further and recognising the incident with Irene had probably acted as the catalyst for his greater tension and annoyance, I tempered my response.

'I'm sorry to hear that, Karl, I'll miss you. We've done so much together over the years. I hope there's still a chance for us to stay friends though?'

Staring at the ground rather than meeting my gaze he shrugged his shoulders. I sensed from his reply that perhaps he also regretted our parting in this way. That said, I also knew how stubborn Karl could be. Offering an apology for his earlier outburst was not in his nature. Ultimately though, he was right. I had broken the terms of the oath we'd taken, albeit not with any intention of harming our relationship.

'I do not think so. We will be leaving soon anyway. Goodbye, Harry.'

'Goodbye, Karl.'

As I stood watching him walk away, memories of our time together inhabited my thoughts. Yes, I would see him again before he returned to Germany, but whether we'd be able to resolve our issues and part as friends remained a question yet to be answered.

Chapter Ten

Karl and Anna left for Hamburg a few weeks later. The emotional divide between them and the local community becoming more evident as the time for their departure approached. Whilst Mum and I tried to remain supportive, many of the other families were more dismissive of them. Even more so with the growing national concern over Kaiser Wilhelm and the German authorities' outspoken ambitions to become some form of European or world superpower.

'Bloody Germans. The quicker those two bugger off back to where they came from the better,' was the cry from many of our neighbours. How quickly they'd forgotten what a positive influence Gustav had been, both at the docks and with the neighbouring community. Anna too had played her part in helping others where she could, especially when food or money had been in short supply. This was something Mum, Edith, and I could readily attest to.

In the days leading to their departure, Mum took Anna to one side, thanking her again for all she and Gustav had done. 'I know we've struggled a bit recently, but I'll never forget your kindness to us, and especially to our Harry when things were really tough.'

On the day they left, Mum and Anna shared a brief hug that was frowned upon by many of the neighbours. Most of them now living in almost total denial of the support and friendship Gustav and Anna had demonstrated towards them during their time in Canning Town. I thanked Anna again for her generosity towards me personally; and with Karl still struggling to speak to me, I asked her to tell him that I still considered him my dearest friend and hoped we would find a way to stay in touch. She promised she would and said she was also upset that he'd chosen to end our relationship in such a dramatic way.

'I don't know what happened between the two of you, Harry; Karl refuses to talk about it, but of course I will tell him what you have said. I hope one day he may change his mind and get in touch with you again. You boys have played such a big part in each other's lives over the past few years. I do hope your mother and I will remain friends also, even though things have been more difficult since Gustav's death.'

Making one last effort to heal the rift between us, I held out my hand as Karl and Anna climbed onto Mr Potter's milk cart. He'd agreed to take them to the station after his round, declaring them as, 'Nice enough folk who've had a rough time and deserve a bit better than we've shown them.' Other locals weren't so keen.

'Goodbye, Karl. I hope everything goes well for you in Hamburg. It would be lovely to hear from you if you ever feel like writing.'

Without making eye contact, he took my hand and shook it. 'Goodbye, Harry.'

Mum squeezed my arm to demonstrate her support, recognising my sense of loss.

I waved as the cart pulled away but garnered no response from Karl.

It was the late autumn of 1912. I was seventeen and had lost my best friend. I suddenly felt bereft and wondered for the first time, since meeting Karl, what the future might hold for me, apart from a life of baking bread with Mr Anderson. Up until a few months ago, I'd always assumed whatever adventures life held, they would be lived out in unison with Karl. As youngsters, we'd fantasised about the possibility of playing professional football but had long since given up on that particular dream. We'd also decided a life on the shipyards wouldn't be for us either. Although we had differing political and societal views, I'd always hoped we might end up working together in some way, perhaps even running a business of our own. Clearly, that would never happen now. For the first time in as long as I could remember, I felt alone, as if I'd lost a close family member. Of course, I still had Mum, Dad, and Edith around but, my best friend, the person I'd trusted beyond any other, had gone. Suddenly the world appeared just a little more daunting than it had a few weeks earlier. Little did I know my life and that of our whole family was about to change in a way none of us could ever have imagined.

I spent the next few weeks watching out for the postman, in the hope of receiving a letter from Karl, letting me know how he was getting on. I'd already written to him, wishing him well and asking how he was finding life back in Hamburg. Anna had passed her sister's address on to Mum before leaving so the two of them could stay in touch. Sadly, Karl's reply never arrived. And so, after a while, I began to accept our friendship was probably over for good. Indeed, with Christmas approaching, and the extra demands on my time at the bakers in preparing cakes, special breads, and pastries for the festive season, I found I was spending less and less time thinking about him. It wasn't that I'd forgotten Karl, or what great mates we'd been, it was just the pace of life. Equally, with him back in Germany and deciding not to reply to my letters, the way was clear for me to speak with Irene again, if and when the occasion arose.

It would be mid-December before the opportunity finally presented itself. I was walking home from work. The wind was blowing cold and there was snow in the air. Battling against the elements, and with my head down, I was unaware of somebody walking towards me from the other direction. Suddenly I noticed a pair of lady's shoes directly in front of me. Shuffling to a halt, I looked up and there she was; Irene. Wearing a thick grey winter coat with the collar turned up and a bright-blue scarf wrapped around her head, I struggled to recognise her. I had to look twice to make sure it really was her.

This was it, the moment I'd been praying for. Wiping a snowflake from my eye, I smiled. 'Hello, Irene. Cold, isn't it?'

'Probably got something to do with it being winter,' she replied. Even though it had been some months since we'd last spoken, I could tell the passage of time had done little to thaw her feelings towards me.

'Sounds as though you're still angry with me?'

Shaking her head and lifting a wisp of curly blonde hair from her face, she countered, 'Not really. In fact, I don't really think about you, or your friend Karl.'

'Karl's gone back to Germany.'

'I know, I heard. Good riddance too. It's a pity you didn't go with him.'

Even though I could tell she wasn't entirely happy to see me, I also recognised, with the wind picking up and the snow falling a little heavier, if she really didn't want to talk to me, she would have hurried away. Perhaps she did like me, or at least enough to listen to what I had to say. I had nothing to lose.

'Irene, I really am sorry about what happened between us before. I know Karl and I made that stupid bet, and I honestly wish we hadn't, or at least that I'd never told you about it. It was only because I didn't want to lie to you that I said anything in the first place.'

There was a pause in the conversation. She was obviously waiting to hear what I had to say next, while I was waiting for her to slap me or move away. As she did neither, I decided to keep talking while the momentum was with me.

'I really would still like to see you, Irene. Do you think you might be willing to give me a second chance?'

Stamping her feet to keep warm, she shook her head again.

'You certainly pick your times, Harry Thompson. First, you make a bet about me with your friend, and now you ask me out in the middle of a blizzard. I don't know what to say, really I don't.'

My heart leapt in my chest. At least she wasn't telling me no. Maybe, I *was* in with a chance.

'Well, just say yes and we can go from there. How does that sound?'

She drew a breath and smiled.

'How do you know I haven't got a boyfriend already?'

Clapping my hands together to keep the blood circulating, I shrugged my shoulders.

'I don't. Have you?'

'I might have.'

'Well, if you have, he's very lucky. And if you haven't, what about it? You know, giving me that second chance. You won't be sorry, I promise.'

'Where would you take me?'

I laughed. 'Out of this snow for starters.'

Grinning back, she nodded. 'Good answer.' Pausing, she smiled again. 'I like you too, Harry, I always have. But you really upset me making that bet with Karl.'

My heart leapt again; I could hardly believe what I was hearing. She liked me.

'I know, and as I said before, I really am sorry. But, if we had gone out together and you'd found out later about the bet, then you really would have told me where to go. I had to say something, even though it meant losing you. If you'd just…'

With the snow falling more heavily, Irene raised her hand to interrupt. 'If we stand here talking much longer, we'll turn into a couple of snowmen. Okay, I forgive you. And no, I haven't got a boyfriend.'

'Does that mean I can see you, take you out somewhere?'

Shaking the snow loose from her headscarf, she laughed.

'Yes, that would be nice. But not today as I'm really cold and want to get home.'

It may have been next to freezing but the warmth of her response took away any sense of chill in the air for me.

'That's great, really great. And like I say, you won't be sorry.'

Thrusting her hands into her coat pocket, she took a step towards me. 'I'm pleased you're happy, now can I go home before I lose all feeling in my fingers and toes?'

Moving to one side to let her pass, I touched her arm.

'Thank you, Irene. Shall I call at your house to arrange where we might go?'

'We have some of my mum's family coming to stay for Christmas so can we leave it until the New Year maybe?'

'Yes… if that's what you want.'

Sensing my disappointment at having to wait another few weeks before seeing her again, she smiled.

'I am happy to go out with you, Harry, but if we've gone this long without seeing each other, another few weeks won't make that much difference, will it?'

I was in no position to argue. 'You're right, I suppose not. I'll come over on the first Saturday after the New Year then, if that's okay, and you're not working? I'm off then because I said I'd work a bit over Christmas with all the extra orders Mr Anderson's got for Christmas cakes and the like.'

'I heard you were working there; do you like it?'

'It's all right, but it's not what I want to do forever. What about you? What are you doing?'

'I'm working at Campbell's factory, training to be a bookkeeper. I always liked numbers at school. My dad knows one of the managers and put in a word for me. I like it, although some of the more experienced workers treat me a bit like a skivvy, getting me to make their tea and so on. I suppose it's because I'm the youngest. But I'll show them, once I get the chance to prove how good I am.'

'Good for you. So, will that first Saturday be okay then?'

'Yes. Bookkeepers don't go in on the weekends, although I do go to church with my mum on a Sunday. I like the hymns. Well, some of them. You could come with us if you like?'

Religion had never played a big part in our family, and I wasn't sure what God would make of us anyway, what with all the rows we had and Dad's drinking and swearing.

'Maybe one day. Let's see how it goes, eh?'

Laughing, she made to move away. 'God'll get you in the end, Harry Thompson, he always does. I'll see you soon. Have a nice Christmas.'

I watched as she secured the scarf around her head and walked away. A broad grin spread across my face. I might not have been too sure about God, but I was more than happy to accept the Christmas angels were smiling down on me today. Peering through the ever-thickening snow as it swirled around and enveloped Irene in its icy grip, I called after her, 'Thanks again, Irene. Happy Christmas to you too. I really do like you. Bye.'

I just managed to make out a blurry wave of acknowledgement before she turned the corner and disappeared from view.

'Ruddy heck, Harry boy, you've only gone and done it. Irene Burrows has said she'll go out with you.' I patted myself on the arm in congratulations and turned for home. As I pulled the collar of my coat tight around my neck, snow fell from it and ran down the back of my shirt. I shivered as it melted, turning to water, and running between my shoulder blades. Even this unwelcome visitor to my winter garb couldn't remove the smile from my face. This was the best Christmas present ever.

With the prospect of Irene and I getting together early in the New Year, the pain of Karl's departure and breakdown in our relationship began to recede even more. Of course, I still missed him. As Mum had said, the two of us had been such a big part of each other's lives for so many years. But now life was moving on, for both of us. I had Irene to think about. In truth, I thought of little else over those interim weeks between our meeting again and the New Year.

Mum, Edith, and I decided, after everything that had happened over the previous twelve months, we would try to make this Christmas a time of genuine celebration in our house. We each squirreled away a few extra pennies here and there to enable us all to enjoy one or two additional treats on the big day itself. The prospect of a full roast dinner followed by Christmas pudding and thick yellow custard was enough to make my mouth water just thinking about it. We purposely didn't mention this 'Christmas pot' of savings to Dad. Not because we weren't intending to share the delicious extras with him. It was more, we didn't want him spending it on alcohol instead. In the end, he delivered a far more telling blow to our festive plans than any amount of illicit drinking could have done.

Edith and I hadn't long been in from work and were about to finalise our plans with Mum on how to spend the additional money we'd saved when Dad walked in. We were surprised to see him back so early; also, that he hadn't been drinking. Traditionally, he would spend the last couple of days before Christmas in The Blue Anchor. His argument being, 'If you can't enjoy a proper drink at Christmas then there's something wrong with the world.' Clearly, any sense of it being a time for spiritual reflection, or just spending time with the family had little to do with his idea of what the season should be about, other than looking at it through the bottom of a pint glass. Knowing this made it all the more surprising to see him home, early, and sober. The expression on his face as he entered the room was one of shock, even disbelief. Plainly, something was wrong.

'You're home early, love. Is everything all right?' Mum asked tentatively.

'They've signed me off, Flo, they've bloody sacked me.'

The three of us glanced at each other, hardly able to believe what we were hearing. We knew Dad wasn't the most popular worker at the docks, either with his colleagues or the management, but he'd always fulfilled his duties, at least when sober.

'What do you mean, they've sacked you? They can't do that, not just before Christmas.'

'They can and they have.' We looked on as Dad threw his jacket to one side and fell into his fireside chair. He sat, motionless, staring into the flames as they danced and flickered in front of him.

Getting up from her chair, Mum moved to comfort him, placing her hand lovingly on his shoulder.

'Tell us what happened, love. Maybe you've got it wrong.'

Pushing her hand away and looking up, he growled his indignant response. 'I haven't got it wrong; they've sacked me, and it's all that bloody German's fault. He pissed me off when he was alive, and he's still pissing me off now that he's dead.'

Mum looked across to Edith and I. 'Go and make your dad a cup of tea, you two, while I have a chat with him. He's obviously had a bit of a shock. A hot cup of sweet tea will help.'

Recognising the next few exchanges were going to be difficult, Edith and I rose without question and moved towards the scullery. We were desperate to know what Dad's reference to Gustav meant, but also wanted to give Mum the space she needed to speak with him. Closing the door behind us, we pressed our ears against it in the hope of being able to listen in to their conversation. Mum was the first to speak.

'Now what's all this about Gustav, and him being the reason for you losing your job?'

'Palmer came down to the yard a couple of hours ago and told me to report to his office; said he needed to speak to me but wouldn't say what about.'

'Fred Palmer you mean?'

'Yeah, it was him and George Roper who came round the day Gustav died.'

'Yes, I remember. So, what happened when you went to see him?'

'He said they'd had the results of the police enquiry into his death, and all the reports and interviews the shipping company had carried out as well.'

'And?'

'And, according to them, all the evidence suggested I could have done more to try and save him.'

A short silence followed before Mum spoke again. Edith and I craned our necks to get as close to the door as we could so as not to miss anything.

'I don't understand. I thought they'd done all of that at the time and found no one was to blame. A tragic accident everyone said.'

'And it was an accident. They're not saying that me or anyone else caused the pallet to fall on him, they're...'

Mum interrupted. 'Well, if they're still saying it was an accident then why have you been sacked? Why have they singled you out and not some of the others? There were plenty of other men working with you when it happened, have they been let go as well? And what about the police, what are they saying about all of this?' The pitch of Mum's voice rose as she verbalised her fears. 'Are you going to be arrested, Alf? What is it you're not telling me?'

Beginning to feel cornered, Dad sought to defend himself more assertively.

'Nothing woman, there's nothing I'm not telling you. And as for the police, they're still happy to treat it as an accident, which, as I've told you and everyone else a hundred times, it was.'

'Then why have you lost your job?'

'Because, like I told you earlier, Palmer and his cronies are saying I didn't act quick enough to try and help after the pallet fell on him. The police accept I didn't have anything to do with it coming loose, none of us did, it was just one of those things. He wasn't the first bloke to be killed on the dock in an accident like that and he won't be the last.'

'I still don't understand. If the police aren't going to charge anyone for what happened, then why are Fred Palmer and the other managers still pointing the finger at you?'

Edith and I didn't need to be so close to the door to hear Dad's reply; his voice and tone becoming louder and more aggressive.

'Because, maybe I *didn't* move as quickly as I could to help, all right? I never liked the man, even early on when they first got here, I wasn't that keen on him. I always felt he was critical of me. Not directly maybe, but times like when our Harry had been eating round there, or Anna had done something or other for you. He would mention it in passing, as if to say he was looking out for my family because I didn't.'

'Or maybe he was suggesting if you hadn't drunk so much there might have been a bit more coming into the house to pay for the things they were helping out with.'

'Don't start all that again, Flo, I won't have it. It's bad enough losing my job without you putting the knife in an' all.'

'I'm not putting the knife in, Alf, just telling the truth. And what did you mean by saying that maybe you *didn't* move as quickly as you could to help Gustav?'

'Exactly what I said. The pallet fell on him, and we all went over to see if he was all right. I got there first and could see straight away he was in bad shape. He mumbled something about not being able to breathe 'cause of the weight of the load on him, and I...'

Mum interrupted again, finishing Dad's sentence for him.

'And you called for help and tried to lift the pallet off him. At least that's what you told me and everyone else at the time.

Although, I seem to remember you said he had blood coming out of his mouth and hadn't been able to speak properly?'

'I'd forgotten that bit when they asked initially and didn't see any point in raising it later. It didn't stop him dying though, did it? Anyway, the thing is, I didn't try to get the load of him, at least not straight away. I shouted for the others to come over and help, and to tell the foreman what'd happened. Some of the other blokes said we should try and move the pallet off him, but I said we should wait until there were enough of us to do it properly. I said we didn't want any other accidents and that he was a goner already. And for all intents and purposes he was. I mean, there was nothing we could have done, not really.'

'But you're saying you didn't even try, even after Gustav said he couldn't breathe.'

'It was too late, woman. You weren't there, so you don't know what went on. It all happened so quick.'

Mum's tone became more measured as the impact of what Dad was telling her took hold.

'But, even so, you still didn't make any real attempt to lift the load off him, or to physically help him, at least not straight away; is that what you're saying?'

'I've already told you; he weren't gonna make it. And no, I didn't. It was an accident; everybody could see that.' There was a short but telling pause before Dad spoke again. 'But yeah, it was also an opportunity to get him out of our lives.'

Edith and I looked at each other in horror at what we were hearing. Mum's terse response was equally damning.

'That's a terrible thing to say, Alf, you should be ashamed of yourself.'

'The only thing I'm sorry about is that I mentioned any of this to Archie in the pub a couple of days ago. He's the one who told Roper.'

'I'm not surprised. Archie's always struck me as honest, and someone who knows when a quick drink after work means just that. One pint and then home, not the endless binges you go on.'

'Don't start on at me again, Flo, I'm not in the mood. And as far as Archie's concerned, he's proved a bit too honest, speaking to Roper like that. His interfering has cost me my job. Roper said he and the directors had decided to let me go in light of what they'd been told and taking into consideration my work record. Bloody cheek, I've always worked my shifts. That is when they've given them to me. How many times have I asked for more and they've said no. How am I supposed to support a family working like that?'

'You could have tried drinking less, then maybe they'd have been keener to have you around. You'd also have had more money to put into the family budget as well.'

'We've survived all right till now, haven't we? Anyway, they've both got jobs, so we'll be all right, at least until I can find something else.'

'If you think I'm going to ask Edith and Harry to contribute more than they do already, you'd better think again, Alf.'

His patience waning, Dad bit back.

'That's enough. Anyway, it's my wages that have kept them fed and clothed for God knows how long, so now it's their turn to put into the pot. None of this is my fault, remember.'

Mum's response was equally acerbic.

'Not your fault! It's all your fault. Your laziness and drinking have been the cause of all our woes across the years. But, because I loved you, I always hoped one day you might come to your senses and become the man I married again. A man with hopes and dreams to strive for, like you had when we first got together. A man who would do anything to provide for his family. But evidently my faith has been misplaced as clearly none of that was ever going to happen. And now, to make matters worse, you not only lose your job, but admit to allowing our neighbour and friend to die in agony when you could have done more to help as his life ebbed away in front of you. But you didn't. As ever, your first and only thought was for yourself. I'll...'

Mum's discourse was cut short by the sound of a blow to her body and the crashing of furniture as she fell to the floor. Edith and I rushed in to witness Dad standing over her, fists clenched, ready to strike again. I lunged at him.

'You get away from her, you bastard. You leave her alone.'

My attempt to shield Mum from further assault was met with equal contempt as Dad grabbed me by the throat and shook me.

'You little shit. You've been asking for this for a long time and now you're gonna get it. Think you're a man, do you? Well, let's see how much of a man you are.' With that he tightened his grip around my throat and, lifting me up, threw me bodily into a chair. The force of which took my breath away as I collapsed onto the floor next to Mum. Turning to Edith, he continued his rant. 'Do you want some as well?'

Edith stood, rigid with fear, tears streaming down her face as he moved towards her. Struggling to her feet, Mum screamed in her defence, 'Alf, that's enough. Do you hear me, it's enough! Don't you dare touch her. If you do, you'll have me to answer to.'

He turned to her again, spitting fury and rage.

'You, and what will you do? Fucking nothing, that's what. I'll kill you before you land a hand on me, you bitch.'

Holding my ribs, I got to my feet and swung a fist in Dad's direction, catching him squarely on the side of the face. Turning to me again, his body shuddered in response to the blow.

'Oh, so you want to take me on, do you? Well come on then, hit me again if you dare.'

Gripped by a consuming desire to protect Mum and Edith from further assault I swung at him again; missing completely but placing myself within range of his own fist which crashed into my face. I staggered backwards. Then, with righteous indignation and adrenaline coursing through my body, I brushed aside the acute feeling of pain in my jaw and hit out at him again, this time my tightly clenched fist meeting full-on with the side of his head. He fell backwards into his chair. Whether in shock at the ferocity of my punch or the need to catch his breath, he sat motionless for a moment staring straight at me. I knew what would happen if I let him get to his feet again. Pre-empting his response, I landed another punch of my own, this time straight into his face. Blood instantly spouted from his nose and lip as my fist met with their intended target. I stood over him, a lifetime of anger and frustration at the way he'd treated us across the years getting the better of me. I threw another punch into his now bloodied face. Suddenly, I was no longer scared of this man who had bullied and dominated my childhood years through fear and violence. I was the man of the house now and it was my responsibility to protect Mum and Edith from this drunken excuse of a husband and father. I hit him again, my hand red with the stain of blood from his face and from my knuckles meeting with his teeth, tearing the flesh from them. I was beyond caring what happened to me; this was my moment of revenge for all we'd suffered under his cruel and brutal reign for so long.

Years of pent-up frustration and anger exploded into his face and body from my flailing hands. I hit him again and again until somewhere in the back of my mind I heard a voice screaming at me to stop. It was Mum. She threw her hands around me in an effort to halt my mindless assault on this man who, until a few minutes earlier, had held a very different profile and position in my life, but who I now viewed as little more than a violent drunk and abuser of those I loved and cared for the most.

'Stop it, Harry, please. This house has seen enough violence already without you using your fists as well.'

The desperate pleading in her voice and tears running down her cheeks stopped me in my tracks.

Exhausted, both physically and mentally, I stood back. 'Sorry, Mum, but he had it coming after everything he's done to you. I hate him.' Staring down at my father's bloodied face I repeated myself; the tone of my voice expressing the utter contempt I held for him.

'Do you hear me? I hate you and everything about you. You drink all our money away and then blame Mum because she struggles to make ends meet with the pittance you give her. And now you tell us you could have done more to save Karl's dad, but you didn't, and are pleased that he's dead. Why don't you just bugger off back to the pub or, better still, just leave and never come back.'

I felt Mum's hand on my shoulder. 'Stop it, Harry, that's enough.'

I turned to face her. 'Sorry, Mum, but it's the truth, we both know that.' I glanced across to Edith who was also crying. 'We all know it.'

Wiping the blood from his nose and face with the sleeve of his jacket, Dad struggled to his feet. Fearing the worst, I clenched my fists again in preparedness for any retaliation he might attempt. Instead, he just stood there, swaying slightly from the surprise and ferocity of my attack, choosing to respond verbally rather than with his fists. It was obvious when he spoke I'd hurt more than just his pride and was to be taken more seriously as an adversary in the future.

'You throw a good punch, boy; I'll give you that. But that's the last time you'll get the better of me. I'm still your father and the one who decides what goes on in this house, not you. The next time you raise a fist to me, you'd better be ready to face the consequences. And if anybody's gonna leave this house, it'll be you.'

Recognising something significant had changed in the dynamic of our relationship, Mum came to my defence. Her voice trembled slightly as she spoke.

'Harry's not going anywhere, Alf. And if you don't like it then, as he says, you can leave. I don't ever want to see the two of you fighting like that again. That said, the lad stood up for me, and I'm proud of him for that.'

She paused, smiling briefly at Edith and I before speaking again. This time there was steel and determination in her delivery, motivated by years of disappointment and unhappiness. As a younger woman, she'd given her heart to Dad, but he'd failed her time and again. And now, with that original bond of love and trust between them finally broken, she knew things would never be the same again.

'I haven't been proud of you for a long time, Alf. I'm not sure I even truly love you anymore. I thought I did, but after today…' Tears began to run down her face once more. 'I've put up with your drinking and bullying for years, always hoping things would change, but they haven't. You're not the man I married anymore. I've tried to hang on to the hopes and dreams we shared together in those early days, but now… now, I realise they're nothing more than a distant memory, never to be fulfilled.'

Dad took a step forward. 'How can you say that, any of it. You know the bad luck I've had, especially over the past few years. It's not been easy, girl, you know that better than most, certainly better than these two.'

Mum's controlled response to Dad's appeal for understanding left him in no doubt as to her determination not to be swayed.

'Yes, you've had a few knocks, but the man I married would have taken them in his stride and started again, not felt sorry for himself, and sought succour from a bottle. I can't remember the last time we had a proper conversation between us. At least not one where I could offer an opinion without the threat of getting a slap or a punch for my trouble. I've been frightened to say anything for fear of you hitting me or taking it out on Harry and Edith. They've witnessed things over the years that no child should have to see, and I can't defend you or your unreasonable behaviour anymore, Alf. I'm tired of your bullying and worrying about what sort of mood you'll be in when you come in from the pub.' Glancing at Edith and I, she continued. 'Edith and Harry aren't small children anymore, they can see for themselves the effect drink has on you... on all of us. I've had enough, and so have they.' Wiping away her tears with the back of her hand, she took my arm and squeezed it. 'And I won't watch you and Harry trading blows anymore either. It's your responsibility to care for this family, not his to protect us from you.'

Not choosing to recognise the truth in what he was hearing, Dad demonstrated yet again the validity of what Mum was saying as he spat out his verbal riposte.

'So what are you saying, that I should leave? That's likely.' Shaking his head and looking straight at me, he continued. 'Like I said, he's the one who can clear off.' He turned to Mum, anger writ large across his face. 'This is my house and I say what goes on in it, do you hear? And if you don't like it, you can go an' all. In fact, you can all piss off for all I care. I don't need any of you.' He paused, fixing his gaze on Mum. 'I never thought *you'd* turn against me, Flo. But if you'd rather take their side in all of this after all we've been through together then... then, I'm better off without you, without all of you.'

Recognising this wasn't a time to speak, but wanting to demonstrate our support for her, Edith and I moved to stand either side of Mum. She took our hands and squeezed them in recognition of our solidarity with her.

'No, Alf, if that's what you truly think, then it's you that must leave. If you don't, I'll contact the police and tell them what it's been like living with you these past few months. I'll tell them about your drinking and the times that you've hit me. I'll also tell them what you said about not helping Gustav, and that you're happy he died.'

Surprised by the calmness and authority in her voice, Dad pulled back from his verbal onslaught to collect his thoughts. We squeezed each other's hands again, waiting for his response. The three of us recognised, whatever he said, a Rubicon had been crossed and there was no turning back for either of them. Rubbing the bloodied stubble on his chin, Dad shook his head from side to side.

'You need to think carefully about what you're saying, Flo... you know, about speaking to the Old Bill. Do you really want them involved? What about the neighbours? What will they think? If she knew about Gustav, why didn't she speak up before? That's what they'll all be saying. You'll be tarred with the same brush.' He nodded towards me. 'And as for me beating up on him; well, after today, I could most likely claim self-defence.'

Mum stepped forward, emboldened by the bravery she'd already demonstrated in speaking out. She was determined not to succumb to any more of Dad's threats.

'You can do and say what you like, Alf, but I want you gone. I'm not prepared to listen to any more of your self-serving whinging about how the world has failed you, and that it's always somebody else's fault when things go wrong. And as for the neighbours, they know all about your drinking and bullying. If anything, I should think they'd give Harry a pat on the back for standing up to you like he did, protecting his mother and sister. Watching the two of you fighting like that broke my heart, but it also made me realise I couldn't do this anymore. Getting drunk and taking your frustration out on me is bad enough; but today you come home sober and still find a reason to fight. And not only with me, but with our son.'

Taking a step towards him, she placed a hand lightly on his arm. Her tone now more measured, but no less determined in its delivery.

'Alf, you need to accept it's over, we both do. I just can't take it anymore, and I certainly can't stand by and watch you and Harry tear each other to pieces again.'

Finally accepting the truth in what he was being told, and without alcohol to cloud his judgement, he reached for Mum's hand. His expression shifting from anger to one of defeat. For the first time in as long as I could remember I felt sorry for my father. Taking a deep and reflective breath, his voice cracked with emotion as he replied.

'I'm sorry, Flo, I really am.' He nodded in my direction. 'And you as well, lad.'

I forced a smile, not really knowing how to respond as I waited for Mum to speak again.

'Thank you for that, but it doesn't make any difference to what I've just said. We need to part, Alf, we can't go on living like this. *I* can't go on living like this. You need to leave. Maybe not today, but soon.'

'So that's it, you're kicking me out of my own house?'

'Like I said, I need some time and space to think, we both do. Please don't make this any harder than it already is. Just agree to leave.'

Edith and I looked at each other. The seismic proportion of the exchange we were witnessing not yet fully registering with us, although we both recognised life would never be the same again, for any of us.

Christmas came and went in our house, with little in the way of celebration. The one thing I held on to during the so-called festive period was the promise of seeing Irene again in the New Year. But, as for life at home during those intervening weeks, each day brought a new set of challenges. Edith and I both felt as though we were walking on eggshells at times. There were long silences between Mum and Dad as the two of them came to terms with the reality of the decision they'd made to part, and with him preparing to move out. Perversely, although he continued to go to the pub, Dad rarely came home the worse for drink following the fight we'd had. Whether this was in the hope of Mum relenting in her demand that he move out we weren't sure. Sadly, and despite his best efforts at change, there was still the occasional flash of unjustified rage demonstrated towards us. Unfortunately for him, these occurrences only served to remind

Mum yet again that she'd made the right decision in asking him to leave.

Dad finally moved out towards the middle of January, almost a month after Mum had asked him to go. He found lodgings with another shipyard worker, Willie Cooper, who had recently split with his own family. Willie was one of Dad's regular drinking pals. Whilst Mum had concerns about the two of them living together, she also determined Dad's well-being would no longer be her responsibility once he left.

Willie's wife, Mary, had left after similar drunken abuse following his failure to deal with the loss of their baby through tuberculosis. Willie was quite a bit younger than Dad and had only been married a few years prior to Mary leaving. Like Mum, she loved her husband, but equally couldn't countenance his drinking and unreasonable behaviour no matter the circumstances. Willie adored Mary, but the unwarranted feeling of personal guilt over their loss, and inability to support her when she needed it the most led him to finding solace in the bars of the local hostelries, the same as Dad. Mum and Mary had spoken together of their mutual sorrow at the weakness displayed by their men at a time when it was their strength and support they both needed. Mary had moved away a few weeks earlier, having decided to return to her parents' home in Bromley, a few miles south of Canning Town.

It felt strange coming home from work the day Dad left. I'd said goodbye the night before as I was on the early shift at the bakery the next morning and would be gone by the time he got up. I just shook his hand and wished him well.

Gripping mine in what appeared an act of genuine affection and remorse, he smiled.

'Take care, son. Look after your mother for me. Remember you're the man of the house now. I'll see you again no doubt. Hopefully soon.'

Whilst Edith and I both felt a degree of sadness in seeing him leave, we also knew things couldn't continue as they had, especially not for Mum. And so it proved when we walked through the door the next day following his departure. Any initial sorrow we might have felt about him going was quickly replaced by a sense of lightness and freedom; something none of us had truly felt for years. Of course, we tempered these feelings of release for Mum's sake. She put on a brave face, but we knew she was hurting. Dad may have failed her in the years they'd been together, but they'd also shared moments of genuine happiness and affection during that time as well, certainly in the early days. Edith and I were testimony to that. Over the next few weeks each of us sought to support one another as best we could. Not only did things change at home but in the wider context as well. The next two years would prove like no other, for any of us.

Chapter Eleven

Shortly after Dad left, I began to see Irene on a regular basis. Following early conversations between the two of us, she had talked to her parents about the reason for Dad's departure and of the events leading up to it. This, in turn, had raised concerns for them that I might have inherited some of my father's less than appealing traits. I think Irene may have also related the earlier tale about Karl and I competing for her affections. This would have raised similar suspicions as to my intentions regarding their daughter's happiness and well-being. Fortunately, these fears were assuaged once they got to know me, and I soon became a welcome visitor to their home. In the end, I think they began to pity me having had such a seemingly dysfunctional upbringing, although it never really felt like that for Edith and I at the time. I think most youngsters adapt to the circumstances of their childhood, no matter how challenging or chaotic they might be. If there's love on offer you grasp it with both hands, and if the potential for violence threatens, you learn to keep your head down and stay out of the way. Both scenarios proved true for the two of us when Dad was around. Now though, with him gone and Mum released from the ever-present fear of violence being meted out against her, our days were filled with love and laughter. Irene witnessed much of this change for herself whenever she visited and, likewise, soon became a much loved member of our family.

'It's lovely having you here, Irene,' Mum would say. 'You make Harry happy, and that makes me happy as well.'

Edith got on well with Irene too. She said it was like having a sister to confide in. In fact, there were times when the two of them would take sides and gang up on me, especially if Irene and I had differing opinions about something. That said, these would always be playful exchanges with no malice intended, just affectionate teasing.

I always enjoyed spending time at Irene's house, although I was extremely nervous during my first couple of visits. But once I'd proved myself and my intentions towards her, I was received with open arms.

Irene had already been to our house a couple of times before I was formally invited back to hers. Her parents wanted to meet for themselves this young man who they'd heard varying reports about. They wanted to make up their own minds as to his suitability for their daughter.

I remember the first time I visited. I think we were all unsure what to expect or how to respond to one another. That said, they couldn't have been more hospitable, despite any misgivings they might have held about me.

'Irene's friends are always welcome here,' her dad said, shaking my hand firmly.

Her mum was equally as effusive as she ushered me into their sitting room. 'Come in, Harry, it's lovely to meet you. Irene has told us all about you.'

'Not all about him, Mum,' Irene said with a laugh. 'Only the good bits.'

I looked around, overwhelmed by the size and splendour of the room. It was three times as large as our sitting room, decorated from floor to ceiling with thick red-and-gold-striped wallpaper. There were large paintings on each wall, mainly of landscapes, including one of the park and adjoining space next to their house. Over the fireplace hung a huge mirror with a gold carved surround. The fire itself was blazing brightly and there was a pile of logs set by its side to ensure the steady flow of heat was maintained. My feet sank into the thick green carpet as I was ushered towards a pair of red velvet settees set opposite each other in front of the fire. I smiled inwardly, reflecting how different our sitting room was with its heavily scratched dining table, shabby brown chenille covering and chairs, along with Dad's battered armchair. Our floor covering was equally depleted, consisting of no more than a threadbare rug laid on top of bare wooden floorboards. The same dark-brown patterned wallpaper we had inherited from the previous resident still hung on the walls. The only difference being now, the paper was peeling away in lengthy strips from its original setting. Life in the Burrows household appeared very different.

Patting a seat beside her on one of the settees, Irene smiled. 'Sit next to me, Harry.'

'That's it, you two sit there and talk to each other while Ted and I get some tea,' her mum replied.

Grinning at me, Irene's dad nodded in his wife's direction. 'See that, Harry? She's got me under her thumb. You be careful our Irene doesn't work the same magic on you, lad.'

'Dad, stop it. You'll embarrass Harry,' Irene retorted, with her mum adding weight to her appeal.

'Irene's right, Ted, don't embarrass the boy. He's only been here five minutes.'

Winking in my direction as he turned to leave, he chuckled. 'Sorry if I've embarrassed you, Harry. As you can probably tell, my wife wears the trousers in this house. I was just trying to make you aware of how men are treated around here, that's all.'

Opening the door, Irene's mum called out to him again. 'Ted Burrows, you get yourself out here immediately before I really do start on you.'

Dropping his head forward like a guilty puppy, he moved towards the door, laughing as he went. 'Coming, Betty, my love.' Glancing back at me as he left the room he chortled. 'See what I mean?'

I liked him and thought immediately how different a similar exchange would have been handled at home with Dad around. He would have responded without humour had Mum dared to speak to him like that in front of company, no matter how light-hearted her remark, or intention. I turned to face Irene.

'Your mum's really nice, and your dad's funny. I like them.'

'Dad's always like that anytime I bring someone home, especially a boy. He likes to tease them, and me.'

'So I'm not the first boy you've invited home?'

Pursing her lips, she blushed. 'I didn't mean it to sound like that, but yes, I've had other boyfriends.'

Panicking that I'd upset her, or might be perceived as sounding jealous, I blurted out my response. 'Of course, why shouldn't you? I didn't mean anything by it, I was just saying… well, you know.'

Seeking to reassure me, Irene took my hand.

'I know what you meant. It's all right, really it is.' Squeezing my hand, she continued. 'Yes, I've had other boyfriends but I'm here with you now, and that makes me happy. You make me happy. Is that okay?'

I nodded. 'Yes. And you make me happy too.'

'Good, that's settled then.' She laughed. 'It's like your mum said, we make each other happy.'

Glancing around the room, I exhaled. 'Your parents have a lovely house, not at all like mine.'

Leaping to my defence, she shook her head. 'Don't say that, there's nothing wrong with your house.' Smiling in recognition of the fact there was actually a world of difference between our two homes she continued. 'All right, maybe our house is a bit bigger than yours but…'

'A bit!'

'Okay, our house is a lot bigger than yours, but it's not the size of the house that matters, it's the people who live there that count. And your mum is lovely and so is Edith. I really like her.'

'I know. I can tell from the way the two of you tease me.'

'Well, there you are then.' Withdrawing her hand, she turned and looked directly at me. 'Can I ask you something, Harry? You don't have to answer if you don't want to.'

Not quite sure where this was leading but not wanting to upset her, I smiled. 'You can ask me anything you like.'

'You seem different to when I first met you with Karl, more relaxed.' She laughed. 'Maybe that's the effect I've had on you?'

'Of course it is.'

Accepting my compliment with a grin, she paused before pushing me again for a more considered answer.

'Thank you for saying that, but I'm serious. It felt as though you needed to prove yourself when we first met. I liked you even then of course, but now… oh, I don't know, you just appear easier going, more confident, if that makes sense?'

I really liked Irene, and the fact she could read me even after just a few weeks of knowing each other accentuated my feelings towards her. She was right of course; I had felt under pressure when we first met. Partly to beat Karl in winning her affections, but also because of the ongoing tensions at home. I knew in those early days there was no way I could have taken her back to meet Dad. You could never tell what sort of mood he might be in, or if he would be sober. This meant inviting anybody back to our house, especially someone as special as Irene, was never going to be on the cards. Looking at her sitting opposite me; her smile warm and encouraging, made me realise I needed to be honest with her. And not just as our relationship progressed but about the things of the past as well. That said, I also remembered my first attempt at being truthful with her, when confessing the bet Karl and I had made about who could get her to go out with them first. Although that was now in the past, it still served as a reminder for me to think carefully about any future revelations I might consider making.

'You're right, I do feel more relaxed these days. And whilst a lot of that *is* to do with you and how you make me feel, it isn't the whole reason.' I took a breath before revealing more of my emotional journey to her. Being honest with someone is hard enough at times, especially if what you are about to disclose has a darker side to it. But to go further and allow your inner self and deepest feelings to be exposed; to make yourself truly vulnerable to another person is a step many of us rarely take, no matter how long or intense the relationship. Although gripped by a natural reticence to take this next step, I also recognised if Irene and I were going to have any kind of future together I needed to tell her the truth behind my change in demeanour. Rubbing my hands together, I exhaled slowly.

'I've told you about the bet Karl and I made about asking you out?' She nodded. I could tell from her expression she wasn't keen to revisit that particular wound. I was equally determined not to put my foot in it again and hurt her. 'Well, the truth is, I really liked you even then. I was worried if you found out about our wager without my being honest from the start I would have even less chance of getting you to say yes to seeing me.' I paused, knowing the next part of our conversation would be the most challenging.

'The real reason I was different before Christmas, was because of how things were at home. I...'

Irene raised a finger to my lips. 'You don't have to say any of this, Harry, it's all right. I know your father has left, and that can't have been easy for you, or Edith, and especially not for your mum.'

Taking her hand in mine, I smiled. 'Thank you. But that's only part of the story. Please let me finish.' Nodding, she drew an imaginary zip across her mouth. I leant forward and kissed her lightly on the cheek.

'I really do like you, Irene.' Returning my kiss, she gestured for me to continue.

'You're right, Dad leaving did have a big impact on life in our house, but not in the way you're thinking, at least not entirely. Him going was actually a relief, certainly for me and Edith, and I think Mum as well, although there'll always be things about him she misses.' I paused again. 'Yes, you're aware that things were tough at home, but what you don't know is just how bad it could get at times.' I drew another breath. 'Dad wasn't just a drinker; he could be violent as well. And when he'd been drinking and was in a mood none of us were safe. When Edith and I were younger we would hear Mum and Dad arguing, and I mean really arguing, until Dad would lose it altogether and start to hit her. When we were very little, Edith and I were too scared to do anything for fear we might get a beating as well. We would just stay in our bedroom crying and hugging each other until things settled down. Later, as we got older, we would shout at him to stop when things got too bad, but that usually meant he would take his belt to me after he'd finished with Mum.'

Pausing again, I looked at Irene as tears began to fill her eyes. 'Oh, Harry, I'm so sorry. I had no idea things were so awful.'

I reached for her hand again. 'It's all right, he's gone now. But, strangely enough, when we do see him these days, he really makes the effort to behave himself, or at least when he's with us anyway. He still drinks though.'

'It can't have been easy though when he left, certainly for your mum, no matter how bad things had been?'

'She was sad at losing her husband of course, but not the man he'd become. Like I said before, it was more a sense of relief, especially after that day just before Christmas when he was sacked from his job. He came home early in a bad mood. Thankfully though he hadn't been drinking at that point.'

'Why was he sacked? I don't think you told me that.'

'Apparently, someone told the shipyard owners he hadn't been as quick as he could in getting help for Karl's dad when the pallet fell on him. Whether that's true or not, I'm not sure, but it wasn't a secret that he didn't like Gustav. Dad wasn't the most reliable worker either, especially if he'd been drinking. If I'm honest, I think his boss had been looking for an excuse to get rid of him for some time. Perhaps that accident provided the opportunity they'd been looking for. Anyway, as I said, he came home early and in a foul mood. He and Mum got into an argument, and he lashed out at her. Edith and I were there and shouted for him to stop, but I knew he was too angry to listen to reason, so I stepped in and, to my shame, exchanged blows with him. We had a terrible fight. I just kept hitting him. It was as though the previous seventeen years of putting up with his abuse just bubbled up to the surface and took me over the edge.'

I felt tears sting the back of my eyes as I recalled that defining moment in our relationship. Glancing at Irene, I smiled ruefully. 'I'm not proud of what I did, but I know if I hadn't hit him he wouldn't have stopped and would maybe have killed one of us. I was beyond caring about myself; I had to protect Edith and Mum, especially Mum. She'd been through so much over the years protecting the two of us. We'd both lost count of the times she'd made an excuse for him or lied about how she'd got a black eye or split lip. I just couldn't stand by and see her get beaten again. I knew it was him or me and I just...'

Emotionally drained from recounting the events of that terrible day, my voice faltered and faded. Irene kissed me softly on the brow, allowing a moment's silence between us as I regathered my equilibrium. Before either of us could speak again, the door opened and we were greeted by the shared laughter of Irene's parents. Ted was the first to speak.

'If we'd stayed in that kitchen much longer they'd have thought the two of us had moved out.'

'I just said to give them a few minutes to themselves, that's all.'

'And if we'd have given them any longer to themselves we'd have had to boil the kettle again as this tea would have gone cold before they'd had a chance to drink it.' Placing a silver tray, overflowing with highly decorated teacups, saucers, plates, and a large fruit cake, onto a polished coffee table in front of the fire, Ted laughed. 'I'm right, aren't I, Harry? I bet you're desperate for a cup of tea and a slice of cake.'

Not sure how best to respond and still feeling the emotion of my earlier exchange with Irene, I smiled politely.

'Always happy to drink a cup of tea, Mr Burrows, thank you.'

Noticing the slightly strained expression on our faces, Irene's mum jumped in.

'That's quite enough from you, Ted. Leave the boy alone.' Turning to Irene, she continued. 'Is everything all right, dear?'

Squeezing my hand again to reassure me, Irene smiled. 'Yes, everything is fine, thanks, Mum. Harry was just telling me something a bit sad, but nothing for you and Dad to worry about, before you ask.'

Clearly interested to know what our secret might be, but choosing instead to respect her daughter's wishes, she smiled politely at the two of us.

'Well, so long as it's nothing your father and I have said, that's the important thing.'

Oblivious to his wife's sensitivity and to the notion that anything might be wrong, Ted spoke up again, waving a long cake knife in my direction as he did so.

'A large slice for you is it, Harry?' Laughing, he gestured towards his wife. 'Better say yes, lad, or she'll be offended. Made this cake especially she did when our Irene said you were coming.'

Seeking to defend herself, Irene's mum playfully chided him. 'I did not make it especially. I always make a cake at the weekend.'

'True, but usually it's a sponge one with jam, not a fruit cake.'

'Stop it, Ted, or you'll make Harry feel uncomfortable. I've told you before.'

It had been a long time since I'd witnessed genuine light-hearted banter between husband and wife. Things would have taken a far darker turn in our house had this been an exchange between Mum and Dad. Not that she could have afforded to make a fruit cake as large as this anyway. Certainly not on the money Dad brought into the house when Edith and I were younger. Appreciating the shared humour between the two of them and with my mouth salivating at the thought of sinking my teeth into the delicious-looking fare set before me, I nodded fervently.

'That would be great, thank you, Mr Burrows, and you, Mrs Burrows. If that's not being greedy?'

'Not at all, lad, and a wise choice. My Betty makes a top fruit cake, even if it is only when we have special guests.' Turning to his wife and nodding, he continued. 'Only joking.'

Pouring the tea from a matching floral teapot into a cup, she grinned, accepting his apology and compliment in the same breath. 'I know, and just as well for you I do.' Turning to hand me the tea, she smiled. 'Help yourself to milk and sugar, Harry. I always think it's best to suggest that. After all, you know how you like it, don't you? I'd probably put in too much milk. I like mine milky. So does Irene, don't you, love?'

Raising her eyebrows at her mother's obvious attempt to change the conversation, she laughed.

'Yes, Mum, I like it milky, but I'm sure Harry's not interested in that particular fact about me.'

Noticing the glint of encouragement in her dad's eye, I smiled. 'I'm interested in everything about you, Irene, milky tea and all.'

Handing me a generous slice of cake along with a small fork to tackle it, Ted chuckled. 'Good lad.' Cutting another, slightly smaller, slice and handing it to Irene, he tilted his head in my direction. 'I like this one, Irene. You better hang on to him. I can see we're going to get on.'

Blushing, Irene shook her head. 'Dad, what a thing to say. You'll embarrass Harry.'

Winking at me again, he smiled. 'I'm not so sure. I think the lad's got a bit more about him than to be embarrassed by my feeble jokes. Isn't that right, Harry?'

I could tell by the tone in his voice he trusted my feelings towards Irene, even at this formative stage in our relationship. After just a few dates together I was already hoping it might develop into something more serious. And to have that recognised so early on by her father served as a real encouragement to my hopes for our future relationship together.

And so it was in the months ahead that Irene and I established a deep affection for one another. I became a regular visitor to her home and on each occasion was greeted more effusively than the time before. Ted and Betty, as they insisted I call them after a few weeks of Irene and I seeing each other, came across to meet Mum and Edith once our relationship began to develop more seriously. Mum was desperately embarrassed when I first suggested they come, even though Irene had already visited on a few occasions. She never once commented on the difference between our houses and lifestyles, other than to say she felt equally at home with Mum and Edith as I did with her parents. Mum wasn't so sure.

'Oh, Harry, I don't know about that. I mean, what will they think when they see this place? I've seen for myself how big their house is and how successful Irene's father has become, what with having his own business and all. They've obviously got plenty of money and can afford nice things. You've told me how beautifully their house is decorated, and with all that expensive furniture. They even have a matching tea-set, you said. And what have we got to offer? No two cups are the same. And we've only got five altogether. With them here, that'd be six of us. What am I supposed to do, pretend I'm not thirsty so they don't know we can't afford enough cups for us all to have a drink?'

I took her in my arms and hugged her.

'It's you they're coming to see, Mum, not your cups and saucers. And they'll love you, just as Edith and I do.'

I stepped back and smiled. 'Anyway, Edna and Frank next door have got a full tea service. Her mum left it to them when she died, remember? I'm sure they'll be happy to lend it to us. And if I can't get Mr Anderson to let me have one of his biggest cakes on the cheap, then I'll just have to leave and find work somewhere else.'

Mum laughed. 'You will not, Harry Thompson, that's a good job you've got there, and Mr Anderson has already done this family proud since you've been working for him. There isn't a week goes by that he doesn't send you home with a loaf or a bun or two. I don't know how we'd manage without him sometimes, especially now your dad's not around. Not that he ever contributed much.'

'Come on, Mum, it'll be fine, I promise. They're not at all stuck-up. They're just normal like us.' I grinned and shook my head. 'Well, maybe not quite like us.'

'Now see what you've done by saying that. You've made me all nervous again.'

I continued to encourage her that all would be well over the next couple of weeks until the day arrived for the Burrows' visit. Thankfully, Edna agreed to let Mum borrow her tea-set, so that was one thing less for her to worry about. And Mr Anderson came up trumps as well, generously supplying the biggest selection of tea buns and individual cakes I'd ever seen.

'Here you go, lad, if this doesn't impress them, nothing will. I just hope they'll have the right effect when you pop the question?'

'Pop the question? What do you mean?'

'I thought this big visit was so you could ask the lass to marry you, or have I got that wrong?'

Laughing, I shook my head. 'I think it's a bit early for that yet. We've only been going out for a few months.'

'A few months! I'd asked my missus to marry me and put her in the family way after a few months of us going out together.' Smiling, he added, 'That's to say, she agreed, and we were wed in those few months *before* she got pregnant. But, even so, it all happened in less than a year. If you like the lass, Harry, then you don't want to lose her, not with the world the way it is today. Not with that grandson of Victoria's shouting his mouth off about making Germany the greatest nation in the world. I don't trust him. Anyway, like I say, if you think the lass is the one for you, you better ask her quick, before someone else does. The good ones always get snapped up first.'

'I'll bear that in mind, Mr Anderson. And thanks again for the cakes.'

As I wandered home with the late summer afternoon sun shining down from a clear blue sky, I thought about what Mr Anderson had said. Maybe I should ask Irene to marry me. After all, I did love her, and she'd told me on more than one occasion that she felt the same way about me. So why hadn't I asked her? By the time I got home my mind was made up. I would pose the question when she came for tea with her parents the following afternoon. Or better still, I would surprise her by asking in front of our families. That way, she couldn't say no, or at least that was what I hoped.

Mum spent the next morning cleaning through the house, preparing for the royal visit of the Burrows family. At least that was what you'd think from the way she fussed. That said, I was really proud of her for going to so much trouble, even though I knew how nervous she was. Yes, she loved our house and the home she'd created for us within it, despite Dad's best efforts to the contrary at times. But this was different, at least for her. There's nothing wrong with wanting to have your home decorated well and to have nice things around you. Most families who worked around the dockyards aspired to that. The truth was, however, few ever realised those ambitions, having to settle for what they could afford. And on the wages paid by shipyard owners at the time this proved to be relatively little.

Being a close-knit community, we each accepted our lot in life and got on with it. Most families decided having regular work and a roof over their head was still reason to be grateful. We may not have had as much as some, but with love in our hearts for our families we felt every bit as rich as the bosses who lived in their big houses on the other side of town. That said, maintaining that sense of belonging is a lot easier to do without the well-heeled parents of your son's girlfriend coming for afternoon tea. A point Mum made again moments before they arrived.

'Irene's a lovely girl, Harry, but why couldn't you have fallen for Ada round the corner at number 32? She's always liked you.'

'She might do, but I'm not keen on her, never have been.' Laughing, I added, 'I'm sorry, Mum, but Irene's the girl for me, and always will be.'

Before she could challenge me further, Edith rushed in.

'They're here. I've just seen their car stop outside our house.'

Mum turned to me. 'Are you sure I look all right in this dress, Harry? Not that I've got another to wear, not for visitors anyway. Irene's mum will be dressed beautifully, I know she will.'

I smiled. 'You look great, Mum, honest. And your hair looks lovely as well. Edith has done a really good job in helping you with it. You look really pretty.'

Shaking her head, she smiled. 'Thank you, Harry. I just don't want to let you down.'

I watched as she brushed her hands down the front of her slightly faded blue-and-white dress.

'You've never let me down, Mum, never.'

Glancing at the table, she pursed her lips. 'Thank you. Now, what about this table? Are you sure it's laid out all right?'

'It looks great, Mum, stop worrying.'

Edna had not only lent Mum her tea service but her prized white linen tablecloth as well. With the cups, saucers, and matching plates laid out next to the selection of freshly prepared sandwiches and cakes, the table resembled a feast set for a king, let alone afternoon tea with my girlfriend and her family.

Opening the front door, I ushered Irene and her parents inside. As I did so, I noticed a number of children crowding around Mr Burrows' shiny black Ford motor car.

'We don't get many cars in our road. Your visit will be the talk of the street for the next week or so.'

'I'm still getting used to it myself, Harry. I had it delivered from the factory in Manchester a couple of weeks ago. It can travel up to forty miles an hour apparently.' Laughing, he added, 'Although I can't see me driving it at that speed. I can't imagine anybody wanting to go that fast; it'd frighten the life out of me.'

Entering the sitting room and sensing Mum's anxiety, Betty immediately sought to put her at ease.

'What a wonderful spread, Florence. You really shouldn't have gone to so much trouble. And what a lovely tea-set, such bright colours.'

Accepting the compliment, rather than explaining the truth regarding ownership of the tea service, Mum smiled. 'Thank you, Betty, it's lovely to meet you both at last. And to see you again, Irene. But it's always nice to have you here, you know that.'

I looked on as Irene's parents took in their surroundings. She had obviously prepared them as their words never wavered from complimentary as they registered the peeling wallpaper, threadbare rug, and dilapidated furniture that filled the room.

'These houses are actually a lot bigger on the inside than they first appear,' Betty said, attempting to maintain her positivity.

'If you talk to the neighbours, I think you'll find we'd all like a bit more space. But it's home, and that's what's important.'

'Quite right, Florence. And a home is what you make it. And, knowing your Harry as we do now, yours is obviously a happy one.'

Mum, Edith, and I glanced at each other; a wry grin appearing on each of our faces. Mercifully, Betty had never visited when Dad had been around, or she might have commented differently.

The next hour passed without event, as Irene and her parents tucked into Mum's sandwiches and the generous supply of buns and cakes supplied by Mr Anderson. I made a mental note to thank him again when I was next at the bakery.

As we sat, letting our stomachs settle and enjoying another cup of tea, I decided now was the time to make my announcement. Coughing lightly to clear my throat, I stood up.

'Mr and Mrs Burrows, and you, of course, Irene, I have a question to ask.' Already feeling I could have phrased my opening address better, I began to doubt myself. Perhaps the idea of proposing marriage in front of our families before speaking to Irene separately wasn't such a good idea after all. It was too late to change my mind now though, much as I might have liked to, with Ted pre-empting my intentions.

Laughing, he turned to Betty. 'There you are, I told you it wasn't just afternoon tea we'd been invited for.'

Leaning forward, Betty nudged him in the ribs. 'That's enough, Ted, let the lad speak.' Smiling up at me, she continued. 'Ignore him, Harry. You ask your question, whatever it is.'

I looked at Irene, her expression a mix of hopeful expectation and embarrassment. Mum and Edith stared at me intently, unsure of what I was about to say next, but equally confident in their shared suspicions of my intentions. I took a deep breath.

I smiled at Irene. 'I thought this was a good idea up until a few minutes ago, but now I'm not so sure. Not in what I want to ask, but more whether this is the right time and place. You see...'

Laughing again, Ted interrupted. 'Come on, Harry, lad, just ask her. We all know what the question is, but if you don't spit it out soon she'll have...'

It was Betty's turn to interrupt. 'Ted, I've told you already, leave him alone.' Nodding as if to reassure me, she smiled again. 'I'm sorry, Harry, I should have left him at home. Now what was it you wanted to say?'

I watched as Irene, avoiding my gaze, shifted uncomfortably in her chair. It was now or never.

'Irene, you know how I feel about you; we've talked about that before. But what I want to ask is... if you'll marry me?' Turning to her parents, my mouth feeling dry and my tongue sticking nervously to the roof of my mouth, I continued. 'I probably should have asked you first, Mr Burrows, but I thought if I asked Irene in front of you then it would...'

Clearly enjoying my discomfiture, he interjected. 'Kill two birds with one stone, is that what you were going to say, son?'

Feeling a bead of sweat run down my back and regretting I had ever started this conversation, I shook my head. 'No, that's not it all. I just wanted to get it right, but it seems I've done the exact opposite.' I looked at Irene. 'I'm sorry if I've made a mess of this. All I'm trying to say is, I love you and would be honoured if you'd consider being my wife?'

Turning to his daughter, Ted nodded in my direction. 'What do you say then, Irene? I know what I'd say, but...'

Striking him playfully on the arm, Betty frowned. 'Well, he *wasn't* asking you, so there's no need for you to say anything more, thank you very much. You've already embarrassed Harry enough without starting on our Irene as well.' Shaking her head, she smiled. 'I apologise for your father, sweetheart, but we both know what he's like.' Glancing at Mum and Edith, she continued. 'And I apologise to you, Florence, and to you as well, Edith. My husband has a strange sense of humour at times, and not one that portrays him in the best of lights. Unfortunately, this is one of those occasions.'

Praying the floor would open up and swallow me whole I looked at Irene, searching for any sense of encouragement or support in her eyes. She smiled lovingly towards me.

'Don't worry, Mum. And yes, I do know what Dad's like. And yes again, I would like to marry you, Harry, if you're serious?'

I felt my body shiver with relief. 'Never more so.'

Mum and Betty beamed at each other, with Mum being the first to speak. 'That's wonderful, how exciting. Congratulations, both of you.' Rising from her chair, she continued. 'How about another cup of tea so we can propose a toast to the two of them? I'm just sorry I haven't got anything stronger to offer everyone.'

Also getting to his feet, Ted moved to encourage Mum. 'A cup of tea would be lovely, Florence. There'll be plenty of opportunities to raise a glass or two in the days ahead.' Smiling broadly, he offered me his hand. 'As for you, Harry, I know I've teased you a bit, son, but I couldn't be more pleased to have you join our family.' Leaning towards Mum, he touched her lightly on the arm. 'And for us to become a part of your family too, Florence. You've got a good lad here; you should be proud of him. I know we are, and in the way he cares for our Irene.'

Taking a faded handkerchief from her pocket and raising it to her eye, Mum nodded her agreement. 'Thank you, Ted. And yes, I am proud of him, very proud.' She turned to Irene, a tear of emotion running down her cheek. 'And thank you, Irene. I've only known you for these past few months, but every time we've met, I've seen how happy you make my Harry, so again, thank you for that. And welcome to our family.'

Edith laughed. 'I'll second that. It'll be great having a sister to confide in, and especially one that'll help sort my brother out.'

Hugging Irene briefly, Mum turned towards the scullery. 'I'll make that tea. Help yourself to another cake, Ted. I saw you eyeing up that iced bun.'

Betty rose to join Mum. 'I'll give you a hand, Florence.'

Taking her arm, Mum smiled. 'Call me Flo, everyone else does.'

I watched as they left the room, chatting animatedly together. Although not entirely sure just how much our lives were about to change, I knew beyond doubt things would never be the same again, for any of us. I looked at Irene, my heart swelling with love and pride for her. Suddenly, the years of struggling to survive because of Dad's drinking and violence seemed a dim and distant memory. For the first time in as long as I could remember, I felt positive about my place in the world and of my future in it.

Chapter Twelve

Following my proposal, Irene and I became officially engaged in the autumn of 1913. The next thing to do was to set a date for the wedding itself. Ted and Betty may have agreed for me to marry their daughter, but they weren't going to let her go that easily. They wanted the wedding itself to be a 'day to remember' for everyone. After much deliberation, it was decided the two of us would be wed the following summer. The exact date to be confirmed, but Saturday August 15th was the day chosen to work towards. Little did we realise just how different the world would look in those few short months to come.

One of the more positive outcomes of Irene and I getting engaged was that Mum and Dad started speaking again, and on friendlier terms than they'd done for some time. Dad began to visit more regularly as well, often staying for a bit of tea, although Mum still insisted he leave again afterwards. She still wasn't sure about taking him back on any permanent basis; and certainly not while he continued to drink. She remained resolute on that point, no matter how hard he tried to convince her that he'd changed.

'Honest, Flo, things are different now, I'm different now.'

'I'm sorry, Alf, but I've heard all your promises about change before. I'm not saying the door is closed forever, not like I did when you first left. But, until you've stopped drinking, and I mean really stopped, I'm not going to put myself or the children at risk again.'

'They're hardly children anymore. Harry's practically a married man. He'll be moving out to a place of his own soon.'

'And that's even more reason for me to say no, at least for now. Without Harry here to protect me and Edith, I'm still scared of what might happen if you came in one night in a bad temper and with a belly full of beer.'

I always made sure I was around when Dad came home, just in case. But to be fair, over those next few months, in the run-up to Christmas, he never once came home the worse for wear. He might have had a drink or two, but not enough to affect his mood or start an argument. It was as if he knew he was on trial, certainly with Mum. If he truly wanted to get back together with her, he had to prove himself, and not just for a few weeks or months, but for as long as it took.

I remember the first time I introduced him to Irene. It was a short while after the two of us had got engaged. Dad had come home for his Sunday tea, and I'd agreed to bring Irene over to say hello. With all the stories she'd heard about him, she was understandably as anxious about meeting Dad as I was about him meeting her. The last thing I wanted was for my fiancée to witness a fight between her prospective husband and father-in-law.

'Are you sure this is a good idea, Harry? I don't want to let you down or make your father angry.'

'You'll be fine, don't worry. You won't let me down. And I won't let him say or do anything to upset you either, I promise.'

'That's what I'm worried about, causing an argument between the two of you.'

On the day itself, Dad couldn't have been better behaved, or more polite. He'd even had a shave and put on a clean shirt, albeit with the collar slightly frayed. He kept his jacket on, and waistcoat buttoned up as well. Mum and I could hardly believe how considerate he was the whole time he was in the house, and with no trace of alcohol about him either. Maybe he really had changed?

I think we were all nervous, not knowing what to expect, or even hope for from the meeting. But, much as we'd had our differences in the past, he was still my dad and I wanted him to meet the woman I intended to spend the rest of my life with, and for the two of them to get on.

Irene looked especially pretty that day, wearing a bright-red dress with a blue-and-yellow paisley design. She wore matching red shoes, and her curly blonde hair was tied up and back to highlight her face, emphasising her high cheekbones and natural beauty.

'You look fantastic, Irene, you really do.'

'Just so long as your dad thinks the same. I'm really quite nervous about meeting him.'

'Don't be. He'll think you're wonderful too, just like I do.'

Irene squeezed my hand as we entered the sitting room. 'Just don't leave me on my own with him, Harry, I won't know what to say.'

'Of course I won't. Anyway, you'll have Mum and Edith there as well, so there's no chance of you being completely on your own with him.' Pinching her bottom, I laughed. 'Although, you're probably safer in being alone with him than you are with me.'

Dad jumped to his feet as we entered the room, extending his hand towards Irene and proffering a welcoming smile.

'Hello, you must be Irene. I'm Harry's dad, Alf. It's nice to meet you.'

Not having known what to expect and taken aback a little by his courteous greeting, Irene smiled and shook his hand.

'It's nice to meet you too, Mr Thompson. I've heard a lot about you.' Immediately regretting her choice of words, she bit her lip before speaking again. 'What I mean is...'

Sensing her embarrassment, Dad laughed. 'That's all right, love, I know what you meant. I do have a bit of a chequered past as far as this family's concerned.' He smiled at Mum. 'But hopefully we're getting ourselves sorted. Isn't that right, Flo?'

'Hopefully Alf, yes.' Placing her arm through Irene's, Mum led her to a chair by the table. 'Now you sit here with Harry and his dad while Edith and I put the kettle on.'

The three of us exchanged pleasantries until Mum returned, carrying a tray of tea and a Victoria sponge she'd made earlier. Thankfully, the rest of the afternoon passed by without incident until it was time for me to take Irene home. Mum had already made it clear to Dad that when Irene and I left he would also be expected to leave. He had argued for leniency, but Mum was adamant. If he wanted to meet Irene in our home and begin rebuilding proper family relations between us, then he had to agree to her conditions. Recognising this wasn't the time or place to revisit this particular element of the contract between them, he honoured his part of the agreement as soon as I said we were ready to leave.

'I think I'd better be getting Irene home now, Mum. Thanks for the tea and cake.'

Irene concurred. 'Yes, thank you, Mrs Thompson, it was lovely.'

'You're welcome, Irene, love. And I do wish you'd call me Florence. Mrs Thompson seems a little formal now, what with you being part of the family. Well, almost.'

Irene laughed. 'Maybe once we're married. Mum says the same to Harry, but he still calls her Mrs Burrows.' Turning to Dad and offering her hand, she smiled. 'Nice to meet you, Mr Thompson. I hope it won't be too long before I see you again.'

'You too, love. Our Harry's definitely picked a winner in you.' Getting to his feet, he continued. 'And I don't want to outstay my welcome either. I better be going an' all.'

Mum nodded her approval. 'Thanks Alf. I'll see you to the door while these three say their goodbyes.'

'All right.' He leant across to Edith and squeezed her arm. 'Bye love. Look after your mum for me.'

Edith still struggled to trust Dad completely but, like me, was grateful at his efforts to change, and so was also willing to give him the same second chance as Mum was affording him. 'Okay Dad, I will. Bye.'

The three of us watched as they left the room. Irene was the first to speak.

'He seemed okay. Although I suppose it must be tough for all of you after everything that's gone on in the past?'

Edith shook her head. 'I'm still not sure. Some of what happened when he lived here before is still too raw for me. But, I get that we need to try, if only for Mum's sake.'

'I agree, sis, but you can't fault him this afternoon. He was definitely on his best behaviour; I'll give him that.'

As we were talking Mum re-entered the room.

'He's gone. Thank you all for that. Alf really was impressed with you, Irene.' Kissing her on the cheek, she added, 'As we all were. You're a real blessing to us, and especially to our Harry.'

Edith laughed. 'Forget Harry. I'm just pleased to have a new girlfriend to talk to.'

Moving to stand next to Edith, Irene nodded. 'I agree. Boys are all right for a while, but us girls need to stick together.'

'In that case, Edith, you can walk Irene home. I'll be quite happy to stay here and finish Mum's cake.'

Laughing, Irene shook her head. 'Normally, I'd agree with that idea, but as it'll be dark soon I think you'd better take me, Harry. It might not be safe for Edith to walk back on her own.'

Mum and Edith said their goodbyes as Irene and I headed for the door.

'Goodbye, Edith, and you, Mrs Thompson. Thank you again for a lovely afternoon.'

'Goodbye, Irene, love, come and see us again soon.'

Opening the door and standing aside as Irene moved past

me, I smiled at Mum. 'Thanks again, Mum. I'm pleased Dad behaved himself as well. It was good to see the two of you together again, if you know what I mean?'

'I do. See you when you get back, son, we can talk some more then.'

As I closed the door behind us, Irene took my hand.

'I really enjoyed myself this afternoon. I hope it wasn't too difficult having your dad there?'

'I must admit I was a bit worried what he might be like. But to be fair, he did himself proud.' I laughed. 'Seeing him with a clean shirt and tie on was definitely a first. I can't remember the last time I saw him look so smart. Mind, he looked like he was ready to burst with that waistcoat buttoned up the whole time though. Mum must have really laid down the law about him being on his best behaviour. Although, to be fair, he has been a lot better of late whenever he's been round. I ran into one of his former mates from the shipyard the other day and he said Dad wasn't drinking as much as he used to. He said he wasn't losing his temper as much either and that he was just nicer to be with. It's good some of his old workmates have kept in touch, it'll help boost his confidence. Hopefully, he might find some other work soon as well, that would be good. Maybe he really is trying to change. I hope so, for Mum's sake at least. These past few months have been really tough for her, but if it means she gets Dad back as the man she first married then it'll have been worth it, for both of them. She still loves him. I think he knows that. Perhaps that's why he's trying so hard this time. Maybe he realises how close he came to losing her altogether.'

Releasing my hand, Irene slipped her arm through mine. 'I hope we never fall out like that. I hope we'll always be happy and never argue.'

Turning towards her, I laughed. 'So long as you do as I tell you, we should be fine.'

'Idiot. If anything, it should be the other way round.'

I laughed again. 'You're probably right. Anyway, what would be the point in me disagreeing with you, you'd only sulk until you got your own way. I've got a sister remember; I know how a girl's mind works.'

'Thank you very much. I can see Edith was right now. We girls *do* need to stick together.'

'See what I mean? What chance does a man have?'

As Christmas approached so the plans for our wedding moved on apace, with August 15th becoming the confirmed date for the ceremony. Although we weren't actually getting married until the following summer there appeared to be an ever-lengthening list of things to organise. Irene's parents were determined to give their daughter a day to remember, no matter what the cost. Mum felt embarrassed as the endless list of items to be paid for kept rising by the day. Bridesmaids' dresses, outfits for the ladies, suits for the men, a venue for the reception, wedding invitations, food, and drink; it felt never-ending. Even I began to feel nervous about the size of the event being planned. It appeared to get bigger and more extravagant with each passing day. I'm not sure I'd truly thought about the wedding day itself when I first asked Irene to marry me. I certainly hadn't imagined it would be anything like the occasion Irene's parents were envisaging. To be fair, I think even Irene began to have second thoughts about some of what her parents were planning, and the money it was going to cost. Of course, she was looking forward to being a bride, but the whole occasion appeared to be growing out of all proportion.

With differing thoughts and opinions being verbalised on all sides, it was decided to hold a crisis meeting for everyone to air their concerns. Mum had voiced her worries again about how much money was being spent and of her inability to contribute. Irene's dad had already made it clear he wanted to hold dear to the tradition of the father of the bride paying for the wedding itself; adding it was his pleasure, and that he and Betty only wanted the best for their daughter. However, it was clear that my side of the family, including myself, felt the whole event had grown to such a size that the simple family affair Irene and I had initially hoped for had gone by the wayside. Thankfully, Irene was fully supportive of my concerns and in total agreement that everything should be honed down, in both size and cost. The two of us experienced a couple of challenging conversations with her parents over this, but eventually they conceded Irene should have the wedding *she* wanted and that they would scale back accordingly.

Christmas arrived and plans for the wedding took a back seat for a few days whilst we all enjoyed the more traditional yuletide festivities. It was hoped this would be a very different Christmas to the previous year when Mum had given Dad his marching orders. Irene and I spent the early part of Christmas Day with her parents, before visiting Mum and Edith later to exchange presents. We then arranged to spend the early part of Boxing Day at Mum's again, before returning to her parents for a party in the evening. However, when Boxing Day arrived it quickly turned from a day of intended family celebrations to one of unmitigated horror, matched only by the atrocious weather. Heavy rain had been falling all morning and showed no sign of abating.

Irene and I hadn't long arrived at Mum's and were drying off by the fire in the sitting room chatting to Edith when there was a knock at the front door. Mum entered from the scullery, wiping her hands on a tea towel as she moved past the three of us.

'I'll go. You get Irene and Edith a drink, Harry. There's some homemade lemonade by the sink.'

'No, you do that, Mum, I'll answer the door. We're not expecting anyone are we?'

Smiling, she turned back towards the scullery. 'Not that I know of. Unless it's your dad. He said he might pop round later to say hello and maybe have a bit of tea. If it is him, he's early.'

Wondering why anyone, including Dad, would venture out on such a wet and windy day I moved to open the front door. There in front of me stood Willie Cooper. I'd only met him a couple of times since Dad had moved in with him, but had found him to have a cheerful disposition, at least in company, so was surprised to notice a look of sadness in his expression. He wasn't wearing any proper covering against the elements either and was soaked from head to toe.

'Hello, Willie, come in, you'll catch your death out there in this weather. How's Dad? Is everything okay?'

He stepped in and wiped his face; a pool of water gathering on the floor around him as I closed the front door.

'Is your Mum here, Harry?'

'Yes, she's in the scullery getting a drink for Irene and Edith. Come on through and join us. Happy Christmas by the way.'

Removing his cap he looked at me again, his gaze unresponsive to my greeting.

'No, I won't come in, thanks. It's about your dad. Maybe you could get your mum?'

Not sure of the message he was bringing but fearing it wasn't good news, I nodded.

'Okay, you stay here. I'll get her for you.'

As I entered the sitting room Mum was handing Irene and Edith their drinks. I thought how happy she looked with her family around her and hoped whatever it was Willie was about to say wasn't going to upset her. Mum had endured years of misery and struggle and deserved these days of new-found purpose and happiness in her life. With concern over Dad's drinking and violence seemingly a thing of the past she was a changed woman. Now when he came to visit it was on her terms, with the two of them making genuine attempts to rebuild their relationship on all levels. She actually looked forward to him coming to the house and spending time with her again. They'd even gone out together a couple of times recently. Nothing special, just a walk and an opportunity to talk again as husband and wife as they had in the days before Dad's moods and drinking had so badly damaged their relationship. Mum had even suggested if he continued to drink less that she might consider having Dad back home again on a permanent basis. They both still loved each other, and he'd even begun to put the smile back on her face that she'd worn so readily in their early days together. It was good to see her happy again and enjoying life once more. Little did I know the next few minutes would rip that sense of well-being from her forever.

She smiled as I approached her. 'Who was at the door, love? Not your dad obviously. Nor Father Christmas I presume, with a present he forgot to deliver yesterday? I thought we all did really well. That scarf your mum and dad bought me, Irene, was beautiful.'

'It's Willie, Willie Cooper. Says he wants to speak to you. I invited him in, but he said he'd wait by the front door. He's soaking wet. It's still chucking it down out there.'

'Willie Cooper, I wonder what he wants?' Her expression becoming more sombre, Mum reached for my arm as she walked towards the door. 'Come with me, son, would you? Just in case it's not good news. I know I'm probably being silly but, well…'

Interjecting, I glanced towards Irene and Edith and winked. 'That's fine, Mum, of course. Won't be a minute, you two.'

Willie was still standing by the front door as Mum greeted him.

'Hello, Willie, lad. Look at you, you're wet through, come on into the sitting room, the fire's going, it's nice and warm in there.'

'Wiping a hand under his dripping nose he forced a weak smile. 'No, you're all right, Flo. I… I've got some bad news for you.'

'Bad news, what's that then? Don't tell me Alf's fallen off the wagon and got himself legless again.' Laughing unconvincingly, she continued. 'What's he done then, sent you round to make excuses for him, is that it? He still hasn't had his Christmas present yet.'

A sense of foreboding filled the room as Willie struggled to reply.

'Alf won't be coming, Flo, he... he's dead. Alf's dead.'

I felt Mum's fingernails dig into my arm. 'What do you mean, dead? He said he might come for his tea later; he can't be dead.'

I eased Mum on to a chair as her body tremored and tears began to flow. If ever she needed me, it was now, and I was determined not to let her down even though I could feel my own body shaking.

'What happened, Willie? How did he die? Where is he?'

I knew he couldn't answer all the questions I was firing at him, not immediately, but I couldn't stop them from forming in my head.

'We had a couple of pints together last night, early on. Not any more, honest. He talked about coming here and wanting to stay sober, for you, Flo.'

'So what happened then? If it wasn't drink, what was it?'

'We both had a sandwich for our supper last night about half eight. Using up a bit of bread and some meat we had left over from a few days ago. I said I thought the meat might be off, but Alf said it should be all right. You know what it's like when you've had a beer or two, you don't always think straight. Anyway, an hour or so later we both had pains in our stomachs. I said it must have been the meat, so we went to bed, hoping to sleep it off. But when I went in to wake him this morning, he was dead on the floor by his bed. I went next door to John Taylor, he's a copper, and told him. He came round and said it looked like Alf had been sick and choked on his own vomit. He arranged for a doctor to come round. He said he thought that was what had probably happened an' all. It'll have been that dodgy meat. I nearly threw up myself. Still got a bit of a bad gut now. Anyway, the doctor's going to have Alf's body taken to the hospital morgue so they can try and find out exactly what happened.'

Pausing to wipe the drips of rain from his brow, Willie looked at Mum. She was sat, head in hands, weeping openly.

'I'm sorry, Flo, really I am. I told John I'd come round and speak to you. He said some other copper would come round to speak to you and all, probably later today.' He shrugged his shoulders.

I leant across and rubbed Mum's back. I could feel tears sting my eyes as I nodded at Willie.

'Thanks for coming round, it can't have been easy, especially not in this weather. We'll wait to hear from the police then, is that what you're saying?'

'Yeah. John or someone else'll be round later, that's what he said.'

'Are you sure you don't want to come through and dry off for a bit before you go?'

'No, that's all right, Harry, I'd better be off. I can't get any wetter than I am already. I really am sorry, Flo. Alf was a lovely man, despite his liking a drink. He adored you and the kids. He pretty much told me that every day, and how he was hoping you might have him back if… well, you know.'

Sensing this line of conversation would only add to Mum's grief, I interjected. 'Thanks Willie, that means a lot. I think we should give Mum a bit of space now if that's okay. Give her a chance to come to terms with what you've said. I'll need to tell Edith and Irene as well. They're in the other room.'

Putting his cap back on, Willie nodded his understanding.

'Yeah, of course. Let me know if I can do anything. You look after yourself, Flo.' Offering me his hand, Willie reached for the door. 'Bye, Harry.'

I watched for a moment as he walked away. My body shivered as I absorbed the full impact of what he'd said. My father was dead, and life would never be the same for any of us again, especially Mum. I turned to face her; my emotions torn as I considered the future. None of us would ever need fear the prospect of Dad drinking too much again or of becoming the unwilling victim of his violent behaviour. Equally, the agony of losing him in such tragic circumstances was a pain that would long outlive any concern we might carry regarding our safety or well-being had he lived. I knelt in front of Mum, taking her head in my hands and brushing the tear-soaked hair from her face.

'I'm so sorry, Mum, truly I am. I know it wasn't easy at times when he was here, but he was still the man you loved, and our dad.'

Smiling at me poignantly through her tears, she nodded.

'Thank you, Harry. You really have become the man of the house in this past year. I'm so proud of you, son, and of Irene. I'm just sorry your dad won't…' Her words faltered as the rawness of the moment overwhelmed her once more.

'That's all right, Mum, you don't need to say any more. Edith and I love you so much, the same as Irene. She's really taken you into her heart these past few months. Come on through to the sitting room and I'll tell the two of them what Willie said. We'll get you a cup of tea as well. Then you can sit by the fire and drink it while we decide what to do next.'

Reaching for my hand, she rose to her feet.

'I just can't believe he's gone, not when he was trying so hard to get himself sorted. I think we were both hoping this time he could stay off the drink and find his way home again, hopefully for good.' Brushing away her tears, she smiled through pursed lips. 'I loved him so much, son. Despite everything, all the drinking and the fighting, I still loved him, if that doesn't sound silly.'

'It doesn't sound silly at all, Mum. To be honest, I'd begun to like him again as well. It can't have been easy for him to take on board just how far from us all he'd grown. And then, to accept that and apologise, knowing he'd have to start all over again to win your love and confidence back won't have been easy either, especially for someone as tough as Dad. Perhaps it was that same dogged determination that was helping him turn the corner. Whatever it was, I'm grateful he made that choice and was working his way back to you; to all of us.' Rubbing her arm, I encouraged her towards the door. 'Come on, let's get you that cup of tea.'

The next few minutes were amongst the worst of my life. Seeing Edith and Irene's reaction as I told them about Dad was almost unbearable to watch. They fell into each other's arms and wept openly. It was an act of true sisterhood, but one neither of them had envisaged nor wanted, at least not under these circumstances. I was so proud of them and the way they supported Mum over the next few hours, especially when John Taylor and another police officer arrived to tell us formally that Dad was dead. Having them there to help comfort Mum as the two men relayed the detail of what had happened was as much of a blessing to me as it was to her. John was the first to speak. He'd promised Willie he would make it his business to talk to Mum personally once the doctor had ascertained for himself the circumstances surrounding Dad's death.

'I'm so sorry to be the bearer of such bad news, Mrs Thompson, especially with it being Christmas, but I did promise Willie I'd come round once the doctor had been. There will be a proper autopsy of course, but the doctor said it does look like a terrible accident with Mr Thompson having choked on his own vomit due to some sort of food poisoning. It was most likely caused by the piece of meat the two of them had eaten earlier in the evening. Willie hasn't been right since eating it either. It's likely that, as your husband had been drinking, he was probably in a deeper sleep than usual and hadn't been able to wake up sufficiently to realise he was going to be so violently sick.'

I looked on as Mum sat listening intently to what was being said, hoping beyond hope that what she was hearing might not be true. I watched as the girls stroked her shoulders in an act of loving condolence as John continued.

'Like I say, there will be a formal autopsy, but the doctor's pretty sure that's what happened. It certainly doesn't look as though there was any foul play involved. Of course, I understand that whatever the circumstances, the final result will still offer little comfort to you.'

Irene and Edith dropped to their knees and placed their arms around Mum as the full reality of what she'd been told finally took hold. Dad was dead and wouldn't be coming home again. Not for Christmas, not ever. The next few minutes were difficult for all of us as John and the other policeman explained more about the autopsy and how it would be the New Year before any final conclusions could be recorded. It meant Dad's body couldn't be released to us for burial either because of the autopsy and the time of year. I was glad the girls were there to console Mum as I took note of what the police were saying. Clearly, she was beyond absorbing that sort of detail. And, difficult though it was for me as well, I also recognised the need to be strong for Mum, not only today but in the weeks and months ahead. How all of this would affect Irene and I and our wedding plans only time would tell. For now, our attention had to be focused on Mum and getting her through this terrible episode in her life, in all our lives. As we sat listening to the police officers recount the circumstances of my father's death, I realised 1914 was set to be a very different year from the one we had been planning. Just how different was still to be revealed.

Chapter Thirteen

Christmas and the New Year came and went in a blur for all of us following the news regarding Dad's death. Irene's parents were entirely sympathetic with our suggestion that, depending on how Mum was, we might need to review the date for our wedding. She, however, was having none of it.

'Your dad was thrilled to know you and Irene were getting wed. He was looking forward to it, the same as the rest of us. And so, the wedding will go ahead as planned, and that's an end to it. We could all do with some happiness in this family after the past few years. And I for one am looking forward to having Irene as part of that family. She's brought so much love into our house already, and the thought of becoming a grandma once you both decide to have children of your own just fills me with joy. So, like I say, this marriage goes ahead, even if I have to drag the two of you down the aisle myself.'

Irene's parents were equally as enthusiastic, and with Betty just as keen as Mum to become a granny.

Irene and I laughed, partly from relief that the wedding was to proceed, but equally, because our mothers were already planning the next generation of our respective families before we'd even tied the knot.

'Hang on you two, we're not even married yet and you're already talking about having grandchildren.'

Irene's dad agreed. 'Don't listen to them. You take as long as you like in having a family. I feel old enough as it is without having a little one coming along and calling me Grandad!' It was good to hear laughter again after the events of recent weeks.

Dad's funeral was eventually held in late January. And although it brought back the pain of losing him, Mum managed to find some form of solace in his passing.

'I miss your dad desperately, Harry, but I'm not sure he would ever truly have been able to stop drinking, not completely. He had a love affair with alcohol that rivalled his feelings towards us at times. And when he'd been in The Blue Anchor and was in one of his moods, no amount of love or goodwill on my... our, behalf, could win out against the beer and whatever else he'd been consuming. Even though he'd made a fantastic effort to beat the booze in those last few months of his life, he still needed a couple of pints just to give him the courage to face us, or even to have a normal conversation. I don't doubt for a minute he loved the three of us, and in his own way would have done anything for us, at least when he was sober but, when he'd had a drink, the real love of his life took over. And none of us could fight against that, let alone win. The really sad thing for me is, I think in the end he recognised that for himself as well.'

Hearing Mum talk like that was upsetting yet reassuring in equal measure. Of course, Edith and I felt for her as she struggled to come to terms with the loss of the man she had loved for so many years. But we also took comfort in knowing that, despite that loss, her love for him had not diminished; rather it had grown and found its solace in the knowledge he was now at peace. He no longer had to battle the demons that threatened to take him away from us and destroy his family altogether. In a way she was free to love him again as she had done when they were first married, before alcohol had taken its callous hold on him and threatened to tear their relationship apart.

Towards the end of February plans for our wedding were seemingly back on track. Mum, Edith, and Betty were investing in new ideas regarding colours and material for the bridesmaids' dresses and outfits for the mother of the bride and for Mum. Edith was excited at being asked to be Irene's maid of honour. This was a form of senior bridesmaid, recently returned to favour a couple of years earlier when Ivy Gordon-Lennox had been appointed maid of honour to Queen Alexandra.

'If it's good enough for the royal family, then it's good enough for our daughter,' Betty had argued, much to Ted's chagrin. He wasn't opposed to the idea of Edith taking on the role, rather the additional cost of the associated apparel to go with it.

'I thought we'd agreed to cut back a bit on this wedding,' he argued. 'Irene and Harry said they didn't want a big do, and now we've got a maid of honour added to the list!'

'I suppose you'd have Edith walk down the aisle behind our Irene in her work clothes then would you?' retorted Betty.

'That's not what I'm saying, woman, you know that. All I meant was…'

'All you meant was, how can I save some money. I know you, Ted Burrows. Irene and Harry may have pulled back a bit on the wedding we… I, would have liked for them, but that doesn't mean she can't have the best in what they do decide on.'

Winking at me, Ted countered, 'I don't know why you don't just go the whole hog and see if Westminster Cathedral is available and move the wedding there. After all, the royals seem to like it, and you've already decided what's good enough for them is good enough for our two. Surely, nothing else will do?'

'Now you're just being silly, although…'

'Don't even think about it.' Winking at me again, he continued. 'Help me out here, Harry. You don't want all that palaver, do you, son?'

'It's not about what I want, it's Irene's day. I'll settle for whatever she and her mum decide on.'

'Now you're being as daft as they are. Can you imagine, bloody Westminster Cathedral? I think you've all gone mad, honest I do.'

I laughed. 'I was joking. I don't...'

Irene stepped forward, a look of disdain on her face as she interrupted my flow. 'For all the talk about this being *my* big day, I don't hear anybody asking me what I want.'

Ted smiled. 'I'm almost scared to ask but, go on then. What is it you'd like?'

'Thank you, Dad. What *I'd* like is the wedding we've already planned; except I agree with Mum and think having Edith as maid of honour would be lovely. That's what *I* want. All the rest you can sort out between yourselves.'

Discussions for the big day continued over the next few weeks until unrest from afar threatened to disrupt our plans altogether. Tensions across the Balkan region of Europe had been rising for some time but were now beginning to gain momentum. These concerns were heightened with several alliances being formed between various European territories who were feeling under threat because of the collective instability in countries such as Bosnia, Serbia, and Herzegovina. The long-established Ottoman Empire seemed to be destabilising and causing political and military uncertainty across large stretches of the European continent.

Although the date for the wedding was still fixed for August 15th, awareness of events unfolding across the channel were beginning to cause some limited concern about the final preparations for our planned celebrations.

By the middle of June, with less than two months to go before our big day, the increasing instability across Europe was threatening more than just our wedding. Rumblings of growing political unrest began to jeopardise the increasingly fragile peace between certain countries and their leaders. Then, on Sunday June 28th, in a brutal act of political protest, a Serbian nationalist, Gavrilo Princip, lit the blue touchpaper that would ignite the fuse leading to the start of war in early August. Princip assassinated Archduke Franz Ferdinand, the heir to the Austro-Hungarian Empire, and his wife Sophie. He shot them dead in Sarajevo in a vain attempt to end the Austro-Hungarian rule over Bosnia and Herzegovina.

The assassination of Ferdinand saw Austria-Hungary blame Serbia for the attack. Although viewing Princip's murderous action as the trigger to inflict an equally violent response against Serbian nationalism, there was also awareness of the support Serbia had from Russia towards its cause. This meant waiting until Germany agreed to back Austria-Hungary before announcing any official hostilities against Serbia. Once they had received that tacit agreement of support, they were able to declare war on Serbia and its allies. They did this in the full knowledge it could also involve France and Great Britain, both allies of Russia at the time. And so it was, through the initial act of one man's warped ideology that the world was set on course for war, along with the loss of millions of lives over the next four years.

Almost immediately the cry went up from the British government for young men to join the armed forces. They would play their part in protecting, not only their loved ones, but also their country as well.

It was a call that resonated with me, and one I felt unable to ignore. I loved Irene so much and knew from the moment we became husband and wife my role in life would be to protect her from any threat of harm, whether through war in Europe or closer to home. With Dad no longer around, I also felt the weight of responsibility to look out for Mum and Edith as well. Their safety and security were equally important to me. It was an obligation I felt honour bound to fulfil.

My thoughts also turned to Karl. Although we were no longer in regular contact, I still thought about him and how close we had been in our formative years. I wondered how the advent of war between our two countries would affect him and, more especially, our relationship. Although we hadn't spoken for some time, I still held a special place for him in my affections and wondered if he felt the same way about me. I remembered how, following his father's death, Karl's attitude towards life in England had changed. He no longer viewed it as his adopted home; rather as some form of pariah state that had failed him and his family on a variety of levels. I wondered if this declaration of war would further validate his animosity towards me and all things English, or if he would also recall those halcyon days of fun and laughter we shared together growing up. Whatever his feelings towards me now, it was highly unlikely we would ever meet again, or have the opportunity to revisit old childhood memories. My attention for now had to be focused on protecting Irene and our respective families.

This formed much of the reasoning behind my wanting to sign on. Not that I wanted to go to war as such, more it was something I felt was the right thing to do. I think in part, it may have been driven by a desire to discover more about myself as well, or perhaps to prove myself to Irene. I wasn't sure, but the need to do my bit felt very real and I couldn't ignore it.

I decided to wait until after we were married before informing Irene about my intentions. This was partly driven by fear she might not agree to marry me if I told her before. Also, until war had been officially declared, there wasn't a physical conflict for me to be party to anyway. That all changed on August 1st when Germany declared war on Russia. Three days later they announced hostilities against France and invaded Belgium. Britain sent an immediate ultimatum for Germany to withdraw, which it rejected. The following day, August 4th, Britain declared war on Germany, just eleven days before Irene and I were due to be wed. Everyone agreed the war shouldn't interrupt our plans, although it raised obvious concerns.

The service itself went without a hitch. We were also blessed with good weather to accompany our equally sunny celebrations. Whilst Irene had maintained she wanted a smaller family affair, something her father had readily agreed to; it was still at a level my side of the family could only have dreamt of, had it not been for the financial generosity exhibited by her parents. For all Ted had been happy to try and save a bit of money in the initial planning, there was little evidence of any cutbacks in spending on the day itself. The church was crammed full of flowers, mainly yellow and red roses, particular favourites of Irene's. To save any financial embarrassment on our part, Ted had also insisted on paying for Edith and Mum's outfits, despite her protestations about his continuing benevolence.

'It's not a case of being benevolent, Florence, it's more to do with being practical. Obviously, with Edith being maid of honour, she'll need to be dressed the same as the bridesmaids, so it'll be easier just to order their outfits together. And Betty says she wants the two of you to complement our Edith's dress, whatever that means. So again, it'll be more cost-effective to have your fittings done at the same time. She says, that'll mean there's no chance of the two of you clashing.' Raising his eyes to the heavens, he shook his head and grinned. 'Clashing. I give up, honest I do. We men will all be wearing the same colour and style of morning suit, so I don't understand what all the fuss is about over a few frocks.'

In reality, Ted understood fully how much this day meant to Betty, Mum, and most of all, Irene. Mum, Edith and I recognised and appreciated his true motives in choosing to meet the entire cost of the wedding. He knew if Mum didn't have to worry about her outfit she could fully engage in the planning and preparation for the big day as an equal member of the ladies' team, rather than as a struggling onlooker. I thanked him numerous times for his generosity, and on each occasion was greeted with the same gentle but dismissive response.

'There's no need to thank me, Harry, it's my duty and my pleasure. If anything, it's me who should be thanking you. I've never seen our Irene so happy, and that's all down to you, lad. From the day she first started going out with you, all she's talked about is Harry this and Harry that. So, you just let me pay for this wedding and then it's over to you to keep that smile on her face. That seems like a fair exchange to me. What do you say?'

'Absolutely, Mr Burrows, that's more than fair.'

'That's settled then. And as we're about to become related, I think it's time you called me Ted.'

'If you're sure Mr... I mean, Ted.'

'I am, lad.' Winking, he added, 'And despite my joking about it before, the truth is I won't be opposed to be being called Grandad either when the time comes. I'll be proud as punch when it happens. I know our Betty can't wait to be a grandmother either.'

Encouraged but also slightly embarrassed, I spluttered my response.

'We haven't really talked about having children yet, Ted, but I'm sure we will in time.'

As well as paying for the wedding, Ted and Betty also proffered a welcome proposal about where Irene and I might choose to live once we were married. Additionally, they gifted us a surprise honeymoon treat as well. Ted raised the subject at one of the many family gatherings held to resolve the list of outstanding details yet to be agreed before our August 15th deadline.

'Irene, your mother and I have been talking and would like to make a suggestion for you and Harry to consider.'

Irene smiled. 'You can suggest what you like, Dad, but after Harry and I are married, he'll be the one you'll have to talk to. He'll be the head of *our* house.'

I grinned. 'If only that were true. Your dad's told me how bossy you were growing up. And I've discovered for myself how headstrong you can be when the mood takes you, in the time we've been together as well.'

Ted threw back his head and laughed. 'Well, if you've learned that lesson already, Harry, lad, I'm just grateful you still want to marry her. She's just like her mother.'

Shaking her head in derision, Betty responded to her husband's jibe. 'That's quite enough of that sort of talk, thank you very much, Ted Burrows. We just have a deal more common sense than you men, and that's all there is to it.'

Still laughing, Ted slapped me on the arm. 'See what I mean? You've got another fifty years or more of this ahead of you, son. It's still not too late to back out.'

Leaning across the settee, I squeezed Irene's arm. 'That's all right, Ted, but thanks for the offer. I think I'll take my chances. Anyway, I'm pretty good at doing what I'm told.'

Laughing, Irene addressed her dad. 'See, I've got him trained already.'

Stroking the greying beard on his chin, he nodded. 'A lost cause already. I thought you had more about you, lad, really I did.'

Moving forward in her chair and straightening her dress, Betty interrupted. 'That's enough, thank you, Ted. Irene and Harry will work out their differences for themselves. Just get on with telling them about the cottage.'

'Cottage! What cottage?'

Turning to face us, Ted nodded. 'It's something your mother and I were discussing and have been meaning to speak to the two of you about.' Scratching at his beard, he continued. 'You know that bit of land behind our factory that we've not developed yet?'

Irene nodded.

'Well, there's a small cottage at the end of it. You might have seen it? Anyway, our engineering foreman, Charlie Barrett and his wife Helen have been living there. But she's just given birth to twins so they're looking to move somewhere with two bedrooms, being the cottage only has one. So, your mother and I wondered if it might be somewhere you and Harry might like to think about? You know, to begin your married life together. I know we've talked about you staying here, or even at your house, Harry, just to start with, until you found somewhere of your own. But, well, I know if I was you, lad, I'd prefer to close my own front door at night rather than creep around in someone else's house trying to keep quiet, if you get my drift.'

Sitting upright, Betty interjected. 'Whether he gets your drift or not, Ted, that's quite enough of that sort of talk, thank you very much.' Turning to me and shaking her head, she continued. 'What he meant to say, before embarking down a rather crude road of reference was... we thought you might like to make it into a home of your own. It's a lovely little cottage, I went to see it a few days ago. It needs a bit of decorating here and there but, well, we can help with that. It's somewhere you could find your feet so to speak, you know, as you start out as husband and wife.' She turned to look at Ted briefly, before continuing. 'I agree with what your dad said, Irene, about being in a home of your own, although not for the same reasons he alluded to. Men, honestly, they're all the same.'

Feeling the need to comment, but not wanting to get caught in the same suggestive trap Ted had fallen into, I smiled and looked to Irene.

'That sounds very generous. I'm not sure what to say, really. I don't want to speak for Irene but...'

Understanding my reticence, Irene interjected.

'That would be lovely, thank you, both of you. I don't know what else to say, neither of us do.'

I nodded, still overwhelmed by their generous offer.

Turning to her mother again, Irene grinned excitedly. 'There is one condition though. We can only accept if you promise to come and help me turn it into a proper home, like the one you and Dad have given me.'

Ted and Betty smiled at each other. They were both moved by their daughter's compliment, also the sincerity with which it was expressed. Momentarily, I felt jealous of the care and affection Irene had experienced growing up. Yes, Edith and I were loved, Mum had never left us in any doubt of that, but not in the same way as Irene. Within these four walls the love demonstrated towards her had been all-consuming; protecting her from any potential threats or concerns in her formative years. The love Edith and I had received from Mum had been equally protective, but designed rather to keep us safe from any unwarranted beatings Dad might hand out when he'd been drinking. Love is expressed in various ways, but the version I'd witnessed in Irene's home was the type I wanted more of, and to demonstrate to my own family, come the time.

'Thank you, Irene, and of course I would be thrilled to help you establish a home of your own.' Turning to me, Betty smiled reassuringly. 'But you needn't worry, Harry, I will only come when I'm invited, by both of you.'

I nodded my understanding. 'You and Mr Burrows have an open invitation to our home at any time, wherever we live. And thank you again for such a generous offer.'

Ted leant forward in his chair and nodded. 'Good, that's settled then. I'll arrange for the two of you to have a look at the cottage over the next few days.' He smiled. 'And, there's another little surprise we have for you as well.'

'Oh, Dad, what now? You've already been so generous. Honestly, I can't think of anything else we need.'

'Well I can, what about a honeymoon?'

I cleared my throat. 'We can't really afford a honeymoon as such. Mum said she and Edith would move in with our neighbours Edna and Frank for a couple of days to let us spend some time together, just the two of us but, apart from that we...'

Interrupting, he turned to me and smiled. 'Exactly. Now, I'm not saying that's not a kind thing to do, your mother offering to move out like that, because it is. But I'd also hope she wouldn't mind me saying that's not really a proper honeymoon, not in the real sense of the word anyway.' He rubbed the palms of his hands together and winked at Betty. 'I know we're paying for the wedding and all, but Betty and I haven't really bought the two of you a present as such, not really. So, what we've done is to book you into a hotel in Hastings for four nights. You can have a few days by the sea together. And before you ask, we've paid for your train tickets to get there as well. What do you say to that?'

Stunned by their continuing generosity I struggled to answer.

'I… I don't know what to say, Mr Burrows. I really don't.'

Waving away my faltering attempt at thanking him, he grinned. 'And that's another thing, lad. I've already said for you to call me Ted, so let's have no more of this Mr Burrows nonsense. My workers call me Mr Burrows, family call me Ted. And you're family, or as near as damn it, all right?'

'Thank you, Ted. As I say, that's so generous, I…'

It was Irene's turn to interrupt.

'Thank you from me as well. Thank you both. I love you so much. I have the best parents a daughter could ask for, and I'm about to marry the best man in the world, what more could a girl want?'

Ted laughed. 'She's setting a high bar for you, Harry, lad; I only hope you can live up to it.' He smiled at me warmly. 'Don't worry, son, I know you will.' Moving back in his chair, he gestured towards Betty. 'There's one final thing to say. Your mother and I have booked you into the hotel in Hastings for the night after the wedding reception. I'll come and collect you in the morning from the hotel here and take you both to the station in time to catch your train.'

Irene leapt to her feet, rushing over to hug her father.

'Thank you, Daddy.'

'Well, I must be in your good books. I haven't been called Daddy for a long time. But you're welcome, sweetheart, you deserve it.' Smiling across at me he added, 'You both do. You'll make a wonderful couple.'

Observing this display of affection reminded me once again how fortunate I'd been in winning the bet between Karl and I over which one of us could claim Irene for their own. How I would have loved to share this moment with him and to have had him be my best man, but it wasn't to be. Accepting I was unlikely to ever see Karl again, I resolved to let our relationship go. In future, I would hold it as no more than a joyful memory from a time gone by. Little did I know, following our wedding, how different my life with Irene was about to become and what a dramatic part Karl would play in our future together.

Chapter Fourteen

As we lay in each other's arms in our big hotel bed reflecting on the most incredible day and giggling at the fact we were now officially man and wife, I moved my head across the pillow and whispered in Irene's ear, 'I love you, Mrs Thompson, do you know that? I mean, really love you.'

'I do, and I really love you too. Never doubt that, Harry, not even on our dark days.'

'Dark days, what dark days?'

'Oh, I don't know. Maybe when we've had a disagreement or something horrible has happened. Horrible things do happen in life, and most people do disagree at some stage in their relationship.'

'We'll never argue about anything, except maybe over which one of us loves the other more.'

Pulling back slightly and raising her head from the pillow, Irene looked me in the eye.

'I'm being serious, Harry. You've told me how tough things were for you and Edith at times. Like when the two of you were never quite sure if your dad really did love you, especially when he was being violent. I just don't want that to happen to us.'

Pulling her into me again, I kissed the top of her head. 'I'll never treat you like my dad treated us. I'll never raise my hand to you, Irene, never.'

'I know you won't, and I wasn't saying you would. All I meant was, if we have a disagreement, like most people do, I don't want it to become any bigger than it is, or for either of us to doubt each other's love, that's all.'

Suitably admonished, I kissed her again, this time on the lips. 'Okay, I hear you. I promise never to stop loving you, or to doubt your love for me. Happy now?'

Snuggling into my arms, her breasts firm against my chest, she laughed. 'Yes, I'm happy. And you can make me happy all over again if you want, just like you did before.'

Whilst I recognised there were years of lovemaking before us to look forward to, I also knew that nothing would compare to these early experiences of mutual discovery. Every touch of Irene's fingers against my skin sent a shiver through me, a reaction I sensed was replicated in her as I took her in my arms once more and moved her body beneath mine.

As we lay, a few minutes later, luxuriating in the afterglow of our shared intimacy, Irene squeezed my hand. 'I hope we'll always be as happy as we are at this moment, Harry.'

As the soft mattress and Irene's body, warm against mine, encouraged kindly sleep, I whispered, 'Me too.'

We both woke early the next morning, the intoxication of being newly married still fresh in our minds. We were also excited at the prospect of spending the next few days together in Hastings. I watched as Irene drew back the curtains, the sun silhouetting her slim frame against the early morning light through her nightdress.

'Being August, the sea should be nice and warm. I haven't been swimming in the sea since I was a young girl. I was about twelve when we last went to the seaside for a proper holiday. What about you, Harry, when did you last go in the sea?'

I looked up, my cheeks flushing red with embarrassment. 'I've never been in the sea. In fact, I've never been to the seaside.'

Irene laughed. 'Really, is that true? Where did you go for a holiday when you were younger then?'

'Some of the dockers would take their families to the coast for a day out on the train, but we could never afford that. Any spare money in Dad's pocket went behind the bar in The Blue Anchor. The only time I remember going away was when we went to Mum's sister in Kent for a few days. We went there a couple of times when Edith and I were little. Mum and Dad seemed to work most of the time we were there though, picking fruit to pay for our train ticket home. It was nice though, being out of London and seeing trees and green fields all around instead of the shipyards.'

Walking back to the bed, Irene leant down and kissed me. 'I'm sorry. I never knew that, or that you'd never had a proper holiday. But don't you worry, I'll make it up to you over the next few days. We'll go swimming every day and build a sandcastle. We'll have such fun. You'll love it, I promise.'

Easing myself from the warm confines of our bed, I smiled. 'That sounds great. As long as I'm with you I'll be happy, whatever we do.'

Arranging our clothes for the day, we continued to chat; both of us feeling slightly embarrassed, having never looked at each other in the daylight before in a state of undress. Our conversation was interrupted by a knock at the door.

With both of us now dressed, Irene moved to open it. 'Come in.'

A young chambermaid stood in the doorway. She wore a long black dress with a starched white pinafore which was fastened by a large bow at the back. Her thick brown hair was held in place by a grip at the back of her head under a white mop cap. She smiled nervously.

'I'm sorry to bother you, what with you being newly married and the like, but your father telephoned the hotel a few minutes ago, madam, to say he would collect you in an hour to take you to the station as arranged. I was to say that if you wanted some breakfast, you should come down soon or it might be too late.' She grinned coyly. 'Or I could bring something to your room if you would prefer?'

Irene smiled. 'Thank you. We'll come downstairs in a minute. We can't have you running up and down looking after us. I'm sure you have plenty of other more important things to do.'

The young girl scratched the side of her head, slightly dislodging her mop cap which slipped a little to the side. 'Oh no, madam, it's no trouble, honest.'

I felt the need to join Irene in reassuring our willing assistant that all was well. 'Thank you again, but as my wife says, we'll be down shortly.'

Attempting a form of curtsey, the young girl took a step back and smiled nervously again. 'Very well, sir, I'll let the manager know.' And with that she was gone, closing the door behind her.

Irene looked at me and laughed. 'I've never been called madam before; I quite like it.'

'Same here, I've never been called sir either. Maybe you should call me that from now on, what with me being head of the house now.'

'And maybe you'd like to get divorced as well.'

Taking her in my arms, I kissed her on the side of the cheek. 'Okay, you win, I'll settle for Harry. Now come on, let's go down for something to eat. All that talk of breakfast has made me hungry.'

Returning my kiss, Irene moved to put the final touches to her hair. 'Me too. We can come back and collect our things afterwards.'

Having never eaten in a hotel before or seen so much cutlery laid out in front of me was a new and somewhat intimidating experience. I also struggled with the idea of being waited on. At home, as a child, it was a case of help yourself to whatever was on offer, which more than often wasn't a lot. Fortunately, Irene was well-seasoned in the art of hotel etiquette and guided me through the slightly nervy process.

'They must think I'm stupid,' I said, watching as the smartly dressed waiters glided effortlessly between tables tending to their patrons' needs. 'You probably think I am as well. Breakfast in our house was very different to this. A bit of bread and dripping and a cup of weak tea was pretty much a feast, but compared to this...'

Irene reached across the table and took my hand. 'I was unsure about what to do the first time I stayed in a hotel as well, but soon got the hang of it. And no, I don't think you're stupid. I think you're lovely, and I'm really happy to be married to you.' She laughed. 'Mind, don't get too used to this way of life. This is a treat, remember, as part of our honeymoon. This time next week and we'll both be back at work, having to pay our way again.' She laughed. 'You never know, it might be bread and dripping for us until I learn to cook properly.'

'I'd eat bread and dripping every day if it meant I could be with you.'

Placing her blue-patterned bone-china cup back in its matching saucer, she paused. 'Seriously, Harry, we will have to start saving our own money to buy the things we need, including food. We can't expect Mum and Dad to help out all the time.'

'I know, and we will. But wasn't it fantastic of your dad to suggest our taking on that cottage? What a great start for us. I know we could have stayed with them, or with Mum and Edith until we found somewhere of our own, but this is like a dream come true.' I looked at Irene and smiled. 'You're a dream come true, and I'm the luckiest man in the world.'

'Thank you, that's a lovely thing to say. And I think I'm pretty lucky to have you as well. Now eat your breakfast before it gets cold.'

Irene was correct in saying I would get used to being waited on. By the time I'd finished my eggs and bacon, washed down with a large pot of tea and some toast on the side, I felt entirely at home in my new surroundings.

'I could put up with this every day. A cooked breakfast with someone to serve it, and then clear the table and do the washing up as well; this is definitely the life for me.'

Laughing, Irene shook her head. 'Like I said, it might be bread and dripping next week.'

'No chance. I'll work hard to give us the best.'

Smiling again, she squeezed my hand. 'I know you will. I was only joking. When we get back from Hastings, we can start building that new life together. At least we both have jobs and that's a good start, especially now the country is at war. I'm pleased you're not away fighting, Harry; I couldn't bear to think of you not being here with me.'

Draining the last of the tea from my cup, I felt my heart thump in my chest. Now definitely wasn't the time to tell Irene of my decision to join the rest of the volunteers in the war effort. Equally, I recognised it wasn't a conversation I could avoid for long.

After finishing our breakfast and packing the last of our belongings, we waited in the hotel foyer for Ted to arrive. Being a passenger in his new car was another first for me and one I wasn't particularly keen to repeat, at least not with him behind the wheel. London's roads didn't appear the safest place to be, especially not at the speed we were travelling, and with horse-drawn carriages intermingling amongst the various other forms of transport. Ted insisted he wasn't driving fast and didn't share my concern that our lives might be in danger. Thankfully we arrived at the station in good time for our train and onward journey to Hastings.

Ted helped me load the luggage onto the train and wished us well as we climbed aboard. 'Have a lovely time, you two. We'll look forward to hearing all about it when you get back.'

As we settled into our seats, sitting opposite each other, I heard a man's voice shouting outside the carriage. 'All aboard.'

I glanced across to see a uniformed rail official waving a green flag above his head and placing a silver whistle to his lips. As he blew hard into the whistle the train lurched forward.

'We're on our way, Harry. Just think, in a few hours' time we'll be walking hand in hand by the sea.' The country's armed forces may have been fighting across Europe, but Irene had other things on her mind, and they certainly didn't include thoughts of a war raging just a few hundred miles away.

Leaning forward, I touched her knee. 'That sounds wonderful, Mrs Thompson.' I moved back in my seat as the train picked up speed and the station moved out of my range of vision.

Irene laughed. 'I wonder if I'll ever get used to being called Mrs Thompson.'

'You better do. I'm not planning on marrying anyone else.'

The train didn't appear to be carrying many passengers, at least not in our carriage. I decided this might be the time to broach the subject of my joining the army. Knowing she would object, I thought it better to talk about it in a public place so as to avoid any major disagreement on the first full day of our married life together. I looked at Irene and smiled. She looked so beautiful; her long blonde hair secured up and back beneath her hat. A tiny curl had come loose at the side and bounced from side to side in rhythm with the train as it rolled along the track. The last thing I wanted to do was to hurt her, but I also knew I had to tell her about my plans to join the war effort. The fighting had only been going for a couple of months, but it was clear, even at this early stage, that more men would be needed to join the conflict. This may not have been a war we had started but it was clear it was one we needed to win. Lost in my thoughts momentarily, I suddenly became aware of Irene staring at me.

'Are you all right, Harry? You look as though you have the troubles of the world on your shoulders.'

'Sorry. Yes, I'm fine,' I replied, convincing neither of us of any truth in the statement. I knew I had to come clean.

'Actually Irene, there is something I need to tell you. And I hope when I do that you won't be too angry with me.'

She laughed. 'Angry with you? Why should I be angry with you? Unless you are going to tell me that you're already married. Then I would be upset.'

I grimaced. This wasn't going to be easy, but it was a conversation I couldn't avoid.

Smiling hopefully at her, I drew a deep breath. 'Well, the good news is I'm not already married but... but the bad news is, I'm intending to sign up for the war effort when we get back.'

My words hung heavy in the air as she struggled to comprehend the enormity of what I'd just said.

'Sign up for the war effort? I don't understand what you mean.'

'I've been thinking about it for some time. And now that we're physically at war with Germany, I feel the need to do my bit by joining in the fight.'

I noticed tears fill her eyes as she struggled to respond. 'I still don't understand. Why do you need to fight? That's what our soldiers are doing already. Why do you have to be a part of that? You're not a soldier, you work for Mr Anderson. You're learning to be a baker. I don't understand what...'

Her voice trailed away as the reality of what I was proposing began to take hold. Leaning forward, I took her hand and rubbed it gently.

'I'm sorry, Irene, I should have told you before, but I was worried you might call the wedding off if I did. I couldn't stand the thought of losing you.'

Her mood switched from sadness to frustration as she bit back at me.

'But you don't mind if I lose you in some stupid war. That's all right, is it?'

'No, that's not what I'm saying. I just meant...'

Interrupting, she pulled her hand away. 'How could you be

so selfish, Harry, just thinking of what you want to do and not talking to me about it first.'

'But we are talking about it. Or at least I hope we are.'

'This isn't talking about it. It's you telling me what you've decided to do, and that you've been planning it for weeks. That isn't a discussion, it's a fait accompli.'

Feeling guilty and accepting I should have said something earlier, I attempted to apologise.

'I'm sorry, Irene, really I am. I just thought if I said anything it would worry you. You already had enough to think about, what with the wedding and all. Please... I really am sorry. Can you forgive me?'

Taking a new lace handkerchief from her sleeve and wiping her eyes, she looked directly at me.

'I'm not sure, if I'm honest. Oh, I can forgive you for wanting to fight for your country, but what I find harder to excuse is that you decided to keep it from me...'

Reaching for her hand again, I interjected. 'I didn't mean to keep it from you. I thought I was protecting you, or at least I was trying to. But I can see now I was wrong. I'm not sure what else I can say, except that I'll never do it again. I promise.'

Staring down as I stroked her hand in a physical attempt to placate her alongside my words of contrition, Irene sniffed back a tear and wiped her eyes again.

'If I asked you to reconsider your decision, would you?'

'I... I don't know how to answer that.'

'A simple yes would suffice.'

'But there is a war being fought, and our country is a part of that conflict. Soldiers from all sides are dying and...'

Pulling her hand away again, she interrupted. 'And you want to be one of them do you? You want to make me a widow less than a month after marrying me, is that what you're saying?'

'No, you know it isn't. You're not being fair.'

'And what's fair about you wanting to go off and fight, and maybe get yourself killed? How is that fair?'

'Even if I said yes to what you're asking, in a few weeks' time the army will probably come knocking at our door to get me to join up anyway. There are calls already for men of my age to consider doing the right thing. And we both know that means becoming a soldier and fighting. We *are* at war, Irene, and that won't go away by us choosing to ignore it. Eventually I'll have to go. I'm just hoping the sooner I, and others like me, sign up, the sooner the war will be over, and we can get on with the rest of our lives again, in peace. Please, Irene. I just want to do my part to protect you, and our families. Please say you understand?'

I moved back in my seat to allow her the space to reflect on my request for understanding. We sat in silence for a few minutes while she stared out of the window, tears running down her cheeks as she considered her response. Eventually, wiping her eyes, she turned to look at me again.

'I do understand your desire to protect us, Harry, really I do. I even admire you for wanting to fight as well. The thing that I am still struggling with, is that you kept it from me because you thought I might not agree, or that I wouldn't marry you if you said anything earlier. Perhaps that sounds silly.'

I shook my head in an effort to reassure her as she continued.

'I had a friend once, when I was younger, who also kept a secret from me about another girl we both knew. It meant I had a big argument with this other girl and accused her of something that hadn't happened, and all because my other friend had kept the truth from me. Just like you, she said she was trying to protect me. But what happened was, we broke off our friendship and never spoke again. I tried, once I found out the truth, to make up with her but it was too late, the damage was done. I swore there and then if anybody knowingly kept a secret from me again, or lied to me, no matter how well-intended, I would end that relationship. You might argue we were only children and that things change as we get older, with more important issues taking precedent in our lives. But I really liked that girl, and the hurt of losing her as a friend has stayed with me all these years. That same pain came to the surface again just a couple of years ago when I heard she'd died from pneumonia. I spoke to her mother who said Mildred, that was her name, had also never reconciled herself to losing me as a friend either. All those years apart, with both of us unhappy and missing each other, and all because of an unnecessary secret.' Taking a deep breath, Irene smiled, her lips pursed. 'So now do you see the damage a lie or a secret can inflict, Harry? I suppose you could argue I've kept my story about Mildred a secret from you. But her relationship with me has nothing to do with us or how we feel about each other. Or at least it hadn't, not until now.'

I reached out for her hand again. 'Except in a way it has. Much of the reason you're struggling with my not telling you about wanting to join the army is pretty much based on a confidence that was kept from you all those years ago and is still affecting your thinking today. The last few minutes of our conversation has demonstrated that.'

Forcing another smile, Irene nodded. 'Perhaps you're right. And if I am at fault, then I apologise.'

I moved across to sit beside her, kissing her lightly on the cheek.

'This isn't about blame or apologising to one another. This is about the two of us learning a very real lesson between us early on in our marriage. And that is, we must *never* keep secrets from each other again, either from our past or about our plans for the future. And we must definitely never lie to each other, no matter how much we might think it will protect the other from ill or harm. Agreed?'

After taking a moment to consider my proposal, Irene returned my kiss.

'Agreed. Although I'm still not happy about you wanting to join the army. We'll talk about that again. But for now, an agreement for no lies or secrets between us will do. Anyway, I've told you my secret now. I swore to myself I would never share that story with anyone but… well, now I have, and so it's out in the open. And in a way I actually feel better for sharing it with you. It's like a weight I've been carrying around with me all these years has been lifted.' She kissed me again, this time on the lips. 'And so I thank you for that.'

'My pleasure.' I laughed, relieved the earlier tension between us had eased. Even so, I knew we still had a difficult discussion to navigate regarding my desire to join the army.

The next few minutes were spent with both of us staring out of the window, contentedly observing the lush green countryside as it rushed by on our way to Hastings. However, the renewed good humour between us soon took a darker hue as Irene posed a question I couldn't ignore, especially considering our earlier exchange.

'Is there anything you haven't told me about your past, Harry? You know, some secret you've kept for years, like mine with Mildred?'

Lazily watching the fields pass by the window, I answered without thinking.

'Can't think of anything. You know about my childhood and the tough times Edith, Mum and I experienced with Dad. Apart from that, there's nothing much to tell.' I laughed again. 'And you know about that silly bet Karl and I had over asking you out. Thankfully that's already out in the open.'

'Ah yes, Karl. I bet you got into trouble at times.' Poking me in the ribs, she continued. 'Come on, there must be a secret or two there you haven't told me about. Something the two of you did that you regret or are a little bit ashamed of. I bet you both went scrumping for apples, that sort of thing. What is it they say, boys will be boys?'

As she spoke the blood ran cold in my veins. Baby Billy! Here was the darkest secret of all. How could I share that story with my new wife? Equally, how could I not? Irene and I had just taken a vow never to lie to each other or keep another secret from one another. And yet, I had also made a vow, taken an oath with Karl never to reveal what really happened that fateful day. I swallowed hard as my body trembled slightly. Sensing my reaction, Irene quizzed me again.

'There is something, isn't there? Come on, you have to say now, especially after everything I've just told you.' She laughed. 'No secrets or lies, remember.'

I took her hand and looked away, taking a moment to collect my thoughts. I knew the next few minutes would have a profound effect on our relationship. Shifting uncomfortably in my seat I took a deep breath.

'I... I don't know how to say this, or even where to start if I'm honest.'

I felt her squeeze my hand reassuringly. 'Gosh, it must be something awful. The colour has drained from your face.' Kissing me lightly on the lips she continued. 'If it's too terrible to speak about then tell me another day. We've already had one difficult conversation. I don't want to spoil our honeymoon.' Recognising her attempt to encourage me had done little to assuage my unease, she tried again. 'Come on, Harry, nothing can be that bad. I'm sorry I told you about Mildred and what happened between us. Of course, I don't want us to have any secrets from each other, but if this is going to upset you then, like I say, it can wait until another day.'

Much as I wanted to take her at her word and put what had happened to the back of my mind once more, another part of me recognised that unless I came clean, I would never be totally free to move on with the rest of our lives together. In truth, my greatest fear was not in making my confession but the lasting effect it would have on our relationship if I didn't. Might she decide she couldn't forgive what Karl and I had done and end our marriage? Would she demand I went back to the police and tell them the truth? If so, would that mean my going to prison for something I'd been party to as a child some eight or nine years previously? Suddenly, all of that counted for nothing; I had to be honest with her. This wasn't just a secret I was keeping from Irene, it was a part of my life I was truly ashamed of and needed to confess, as much for my own well-being as for anyone else's. Perhaps I had been able to keep it locked away in the recesses of my mind for all these years, but it clearly still bothered me, and now I was married I couldn't keep it a secret any longer, certainly not from my beautiful wife. I wasn't particularly religious but had meant the vows the two of us had taken just twenty-four hours earlier. I knew, if there was a God, I certainly wasn't honouring him or Irene by keeping this terrible secret from her. What is it the bible says? *'Confession is good for the soul.'* And, if an all-knowing God really did exist, he would already be cognisant of what I'd done. Keeping it from Irene would simply be compounding my transgression and the promise of transparency between us. This may not have been the moment I would have chosen to reveal what Karl and I had done, but there was no avoiding it now. I took another deep breath and smiled.

'Irene, I love you. Please never doubt that.'

'I don't, but you're scaring me now and I don't like it. In fact, whatever it is, I don't want to know. I...'

Interrupting, I squeezed her arm. 'I have to tell you. This whole conversation has made me realise you were right; we can't have any secrets from each other. How can we be honest over some areas of our lives and not others? I just hope when you've heard what I have to say, that you'll be able to find it in your heart to forgive me.'

A tear formed in her eye again as she shook her head. 'Please, Harry, don't...'

Interjecting, I took her hand again. 'Just listen, please.' I raised my hand to brush away the tear running down her cheek. 'Karl and I became blood brothers when we were younger. Our parents weren't happy about it. It was just a stupid thing we did as boys, but it created a sort of bond between us. We agreed it meant we could never betray the other one or lie to one another.' Attempting to lighten the mood, I grinned. 'A bit like us getting married, albeit a little bloodier and more dramatic.'

'You've already told me about the two of you becoming blood brothers, we've talked about that before.'

'I know, but I just wanted to give you a bit of context to help you better understand what I'm about to say next. When we were about twelve there was an accident in our road with a baby being killed in its pram. The pram ran down the slope and crashed into a milk cart and the horse pulling it.'

Irene nodded vigorously. 'I remember that. Everybody talked about it at the time. It really upset me to think of that little baby dying like that. I was only young myself, but I remember crying when I heard Mum and Dad talking about it.' Smiling, Irene looked at me. 'Is that what you wanted to tell me? Of course, I hadn't realised it had happened in your road. That must have been awful for you, and Karl. Did you both see the accident?' Moving closer, she kissed me on the cheek. 'Oh, Harry, how horrible for the two of you, I...'

Gesturing for her to stop, I interrupted. 'No, that's not it. It's about the accident itself.' Bringing to mind once more the terrible act Karl and I had committed, my voice faltered. 'It... it wasn't an accident. Karl and I did it. We were responsible for the baby dying.'

A stunned silence filled the carriage. Only the sound of the train trundling along the tracks interrupting our shattered thoughts as we both considered the enormity of what I had confessed to. In a way, I was as shocked as Irene by the words I'd just spoken. In the past, I'd always allowed Karl's insistence that it *had* been an accident, with neither of us intending any harm towards Billy, to hold sway in my feelings of culpability and associated guilt. But now, having declared so openly our responsibility for what happened, my own mind became as befuddled as Irene's must have been in hearing my confession for the first time. She was the first to break the silence.

'I don't understand. I thought it was the horse that killed the baby?'

'It was, but Karl and I were responsible for the pram being there.' I took another deep breath, exhaling slowly and deliberately. This wasn't going to be easy. 'We'd been playing football outside Mrs White's house. She was the baby's mum and lived a few doors up the road from us. She told us to go somewhere else as she didn't want us to wake Billy who was in his pram outside her front door. I apologised and said we'd go and play on the wasteland nearby, but Karl had a go at her. Apparently, she'd had a falling out with Karl's mum before about him playing near her house, and he must have got into trouble or been told off about it. Anyway, he started going on at her and arguing back.'

Pausing momentarily for breath, Irene interjected.

'I still don't understand. What's that got to do with you and Karl being responsible for the baby dying?'

'I'm coming to that. Eventually, I managed to pull Karl away with her voice still ringing in our ears about how she'd tell our mums what we'd been up to and with him shouting the odds back at her. Karl decided he didn't want to play football anymore, so we went to the docks to watch the ships coming in. After a while we both got bored and set off for home again. When we got near Mrs White's house, we noticed Billy's pram was still outside. It had a wooden wedge under the wheel to stop it moving. Karl said it would be fun to give the pram a gentle shove so it would roll down the slope a bit. We could then shout for Mrs White to come and see. The idea being, Karl would stop the pram from rolling away and Mrs White would think he was a hero and we'd be back in her good books. I said I wasn't keen, but Karl insisted. And, while I was still talking he moved the wooden block from under the wheel. I shouted for Mrs White to come as he nudged the pram forward. Only, Karl tripped over and by the time Mrs White arrived the pram was halfway down the slope, gathering speed towards the milk float. Karl and I looked on in horror as the pram crashed into the horse. The poor thing was terrified and reared up in the air before coming back down with its hooves onto the pram. Mrs White screamed, and all the neighbours came out to see what was going on. The poor milkman was beside himself and could only watch as Mrs White rushed forward to see what had happened to Billy, only by then it was too late.'

'And the two of you didn't say anything?'

'I think we were both in shock. And with everything else going on it was difficult to know what to say, or at least how to verbalise it. We were only children ourselves, remember.'

'What about later when you both got home? Didn't you say something then?'

'I wanted to but Karl said no. He reminded me that we'd taken this blood oath which meant not getting the other one into any trouble.'

I sensed an increasing tension in Irene's questioning. 'And that included lying about what had happened to that poor woman's baby, did it? Not owning up to what the two of you had done?'

'It wasn't like that.'

'What was it like then? Surely the police spoke to you at some point, if only to get your account of what had happened?'

'Yes, they did. But again, Karl said he was going to deny he'd done anything other than see the pram moving, and that we'd called out to Mrs White to come.'

'And you agreed to that?'

'Like I said, we had taken this oath not to tell on the other one. I know that sounds pathetic now, but we *were* only children. I think we just panicked; I know I did. And because of that I just went along with what Karl said. After a few days of telling the same story to our parents and the police, it didn't seem like a lie anymore. It began to feel like that's what actually happened, although we both knew it wasn't true. We were scared of going to borstal or prison as well.'

'So it was just easier to stick to your lie then?'

Recounting the story again after so many years did make our actions sound both heinous and cowardly. I had no real defence to offer for what we'd done.

'I don't know what to say, except, I'm sorry.'

It was clear Irene was stunned by what she'd heard and held little sympathy for me, or Karl.

'Sorry for what, Harry? Sorry that you did such a terrible thing, or sorry that your unforgivable actions have finally been exposed. Honestly, when I think of all the stories you've told me about how badly your father treated you when you were younger, only then to discover you and Karl had been equally cruel in your behaviour towards this poor woman and her family. Not only are you responsible for the death of her baby, but you are equally culpable in your denial of any responsibility for it happening.'

'I'm not denying anything. I've just confessed to what we did, and I *am* truly sorry for it. Telling you has been the hardest thing I've ever done.'

'Not quite, Harry. Surely the hardest thing would have been to admit it to Billy's mother, but you couldn't do that, could you? And why, because your friend Karl told you not to, and you'd rather listen to him than to your conscience.'

Irene shifted away from me nearer to the window. I moved to apologise again, but she interrupted.

'I don't think I want to talk to you anymore just now, Harry. I have a lot to think about. Maybe we both have.'

The rest of the journey was spent pretty much in silence, as was the first day of our stay in Hastings. The hotel itself was very grand, with a doorman at the entrance to welcome us. Ted had booked us a double room overlooking the sea. After registering, Irene spent much of the rest of that day sitting by our bedroom window looking at the view, not really wanting to engage with me. We didn't make love on that first night either. In fact, we did little more than say goodnight to each other before turning out the light. I was beginning to doubt the future of our relationship when, early the next morning, I felt Irene move closer to me in bed and take my hand.

'I'm sorry I've been distant, Harry, but I needed time to think; to work things through in my mind.'

With tears of relief filling my eyes I responded gently. 'I've tried to give you the space you wanted, but I must admit I've been scared about losing you. I'm so sorry, Irene, for everything.'

Squeezing my hand, she leant across and kissed me on the neck. 'You won't lose me, I love you. I just needed time to process what you told me.'

'And have you?'

'I think so. Like you said, you were only young boys, and obviously scared by what happened. It was more the horror of Mrs White losing her baby in such awful circumstances that shocked me. How would we respond if that happened to a baby of ours? How would that make us feel?'

'I know, you're right. The whole terrible event has haunted me for years. Telling you, difficult though that was, has at least brought me a little closer to finally accepting the reality of what the two of us did. The truth that bothers me most of all though is, I can never bring Billy back. Poor Mrs White has had to live every day since he died with the picture of her baby son crushed beneath those hooves rooted in her mind. How can anybody ever help her to overcome that?'

Moving closer, Irene placed her arm across my chest.

'We can talk about that later, and we will. For now, I want you to know I understand why you reacted as you did at the time. I still don't approve of what the two of you did or said, but I do believe it was an accident, and that neither of you intended to hurt Billy. You panicked. As for the rest of it, like I say, we can talk about that another day. Let's just leave it there for now.'

I felt a tear run down the side of my face onto the pillow beneath my head. It was a tear of both gratitude and guilt. Gratitude that, in part, Irene had forgiven me; guilt that it had taken so long for me to begin the process of confessing what Karl and I had done. There was still a long way to go, I knew that. At some point I would need to tell others the truth as well, but I'd made a start. I turned to Irene, pulling her close into me. As I moved my mouth towards hers, she whispered, 'Make love to me, Harry.' It was an invitation I was happy to accept. We'd struggled emotionally and physically with a number of issues in the short time we'd been married but, for now at least, we appeared to be back on an even keel. As our bodies melded into one, I thanked God once more for Irene and for the future we hoped to build together in the years ahead.

The rest of our stay in Hastings was spent in long walks along the promenade, enjoying the views and taking in the sea air. We would sometimes stop for an ice cream or pot of tea and cake before returning to our hotel in preparation for supper and the evening ahead. Following our meal we would sit and talk, making plans for the future before retiring to our bedroom and making love deep into the night.

As we wandered along the beach one day, allowing the sand to run between our toes before being washed away by the final ripples of an incoming wave, Irene brought up the subject of my joining the army.

'I know we haven't really talked about you wanting to join the fight against Germany since we've been here, Harry, but I have been thinking about it.'

'And?'

'And, much as I'm not keen for you to go, I also understand your desire to protect our families. I've been reading reports about the fighting in the newspapers. It appears you were right in saying more young men might have to be called up. So, it could be that you won't have choice in the end anyway. If you do go it probably means you won't be here for our first Christmas together as man and wife either. I'd already started planning for that, even though it is a while off yet.' Looking at me mournfully, her bottom lip quivering slightly, she continued. 'I'm just a bit scared at the thought of losing you so soon in our married life. I know that's me being selfish, but it's how I feel.'

'You won't be alone in that, Irene, and you're not being selfish. There'll be a lot of newly married couples, and others who are feeling the same way. But we can't let Germany win this war. If we do, where will it end?' Nudging her gently in the arm as we walked together, I grinned. 'Anyway, who said anything about losing me. I'll only go if the army promises I can come back. I'm certainly not ready to leave you yet.'

'If only that were true. But in war, I think we both know, there are no guarantees.'

Stepping forward and taking her in my arms I kissed her deeply before seeking to counter her fears once more.

'Remember we made that vow never to have any secrets from one another, and to always tell the truth? Well, I promise to come back, so will that do?'

Irene laughed before kicking the gentle surf towards me. 'Just remember, you'll have me to answer to if you don't.'

Lifting her into my arms, I took a few paces into the sea before lowering her feet into the water. 'Well at least I'm here to save you from drowning.'

Kicking out and splashing my clothes, she ran back to the beach. 'Idiot. Now look, you've got me all wet.'

Joining her on the sand and shaking the water from my own clothes, I retorted. 'What about me, I'll need to get changed now as well. Or?'

'Or what?'

'Or, we could go back to the hotel, and both take off our wet clothes and see what happens?'

'Is that all you can think about, Harry Thompson?'

'Oh, forgive me, I thought we were on our honeymoon. Isn't a man allowed to take pleasure in his wife then?'

Laughing, she turned and ran up the beach, shouting as she went. 'Only if he can catch her.'

Chapter Fifteen

Ted was waiting for us at the station when we arrived back in London.

'Have you had a good time?'

Feeling a little embarrassed but equally grateful for our few days away at his expense, I nodded. 'It's been lovely, thank you, Mr Burrows. I mean Ted.'

Laughing, he placed our bags on the back seat of his car. 'Still happy you tied the knot then?'

Irene smiled at me, pinching her father playfully on the arm. 'Dad, that's a terrible thing to say, Harry's a lovely man. Of course I'm happy to be Mrs Thompson.'

Winking at me, Ted nodded. 'I wasn't talking to you; I was addressing Harry. I've lived with you all your life, remember; I know what you're like.'

Settling herself next to our luggage, Irene leant forward and poked me in the back as I took my seat beside her dad. 'He's very happy as well, thank you very much. Aren't you, Harry?'

'If you say so, dear,' I muttered apologetically.

Poking me again, she retorted. 'Honestly, you men, you're all as bad as each other.'

Looking at the two of us, Ted smiled broadly. 'Maybe we are. Your mother's been saying that for years. But we also love you very much. Isn't that right, Harry?'

'I couldn't disagree with that, Ted, especially after the past few days. Irene is very precious to me.'

Closing the car door, he patted me on the back. 'Thank you, Harry, that means a lot.'

Although I'd travelled in Ted's car a few days earlier, I still felt nervous as he pulled into the road and away from the station. Sensing my unease, he changed the subject in an effort to reassure me he had everything under control.

'Your mother and I have prepared a little surprise for the two of you. *Your* mum and Edith have been a part of it as well, Harry.'

Irene was first to respond.

'A surprise? But you've done so much for us already.'

Feeling compelled to agree, I nodded. 'Irene's right, Ted. You've all been very kind.'

'That's nice of you to say, Harry, and you, love, but I think you'll both be happy to accept this as well. You know we talked about you both having the cottage?'

Nodding, we replied in unison. 'Yes.'

'Well, we didn't say anything before you went to Hastings, just in case, but Charlie and Helen managed to find somewhere else to live just before you two got married. As I say, we didn't mention it at the time because we didn't want to raise your hopes, but...'

Excitement getting the better of her, Irene interjected. 'But, what?'

'Calm down, lass, I'm just coming to that. The idea was, if we could get them moved out in time then we would have these past few days, while you've been away, to get some of the decorating done. Also, to get a bit of furniture in so you could move straight into your own home, rather than having to spend time with us, or with your mum, Harry.'

Irene was now bouncing enthusiastically up and down in her seat. 'Oh Daddy, is that the surprise? Are we really going to go to our own house, I...'

Laughing at his daughter's show of delight, Ted interrupted. 'Calm down, girl, or you'll break the springs in my car, jumping up and down like that.'

Not quite sure what to say, I let Irene pick up the conversation again. 'Sorry. But is it; is that the surprise?'

Nodding, Ted looked at me and raised his eyebrows. 'See what she's like, Harry? Honestly, lad, I feel sorry for you, I really do.' Turning his head momentarily to smile at his daughter, he continued. 'And yes, that is the surprise. You will get to sleep in your own bed tonight in your own house. And that's another little surprise for you both as well, a new bed. There'd not be much room in that single bed of yours, Irene, not for the two of you. Mind, it's not all sorted. We haven't been able to finish all the decorating, that will take a little while yet. But I've arranged for a couple of lads from the factory to come in and finish it over the next week or so.'

Feeling truly humbled I offered my own feeble words of gratitude. 'I don't know what to say, Ted. You and Betty have been so generous already, and now this. I, we, can only say thank you again.'

'It's not just us, Harry. Like I said earlier, your mum and Edith have done their bit as well. They've been at that cottage every day, cleaning through and making the place look special for you both. They deserve just as much credit as Betty and me, maybe more. We might have paid most of the bills, but your mum and Edith have been on their hands and knees scrubbing floors and tidying the place from morning till night, making it a proper little home for you both. You should be really proud of them, Harry, lad, I know I am. Things can't have been easy at home since your dad died.'

Feeling much more than simple pride for Mum and Edith, I nodded my agreement. I knew if I attempted to speak I'd break down, such was the feeling of love and gratitude I held for the two of them at that moment. Equally fulsome in her thanks,

Irene spoke up, tears filling her eyes.

'We are *so* grateful to all of you. And we say that from the bottom of our hearts, don't we, Harry?'

Biting my lip, I nodded again.

Sensing my discomfiture and not wanting to add to my embarrassment, Ted moved the conversation on.

'I'm taking you both to our house first though, for a cup of tea and a piece of cake. Your mum's made a fruit one especially, Irene. Florence and Edith will be there as well.' He laughed. 'I'm under orders. They want to hear all about your time in Hastings.' He grinned knowingly. 'Well, maybe not *all* about it.'

'Dad!'

'All right, but you know what I mean. And they want to go through every detail of the wedding again, just like they have been with me for the past few days. Oh, joy of joys.'

Turning to me, he grinned. 'You and I can talk about the lease for the cottage while they are all reliving the wedding day if you like, Harry. Maybe over a glass of port, rather than a cup of tea?'

Regaining my composure, I smiled. 'That sounds just the job, Ted, thank you. Good idea.'

The rest of the journey was spent talking about the work that had been carried out on the cottage and recounting a little of our time in Hastings.

It was good to see Mum and Edith again and to thank them personally for their part in readying the cottage for Irene and I. Also, to show my gratitude once again to Betty for all she and Ted had done for the two of us over the past few months. As suggested, Ted and I left the ladies to their wedding and honeymoon review while we discussed the legal agreements concerning the cottage. Still aware I had one more piece of information to reveal to our families, I waited until we were all together again in the sitting room before broaching the subject of my intention to sign up.

Lifting my cup, I proposed a toast. 'I know this isn't a glass of the wonderful champagne we had last weekend at our wedding, but it will serve just as well. Can I say, formally, on behalf of my wife and I, just how grateful we both are to each of you for the help, love, and support you've shown us over recent weeks.'

Nodding, Irene tapped the side of her cup with her spoon. 'Absolutely. Without all of you, Harry and I would have never had this wonderful start together, so thank you.'

A unified round of applause from our appreciative audience followed, with Ted standing to respond as it faded.

'That's very kind of you both to say that. But I think you'll find, and I believe I can speak for all of us here when I say this, that it is we who have received the greater gift in seeing the two of you become one. You make a lovely couple, and we are all very proud of you.'

Another short round of applause followed. Sensing this to be the moment for pronouncements, I got to my feet.

'Could I add one more thing? And I hope it won't come as too much of a shock when I say this.' I noticed a flash of concern on the faces opposite me. Seeking to reassure my captive audience, I smiled. 'I have already discussed this with Irene. At first, she was a little reticent about my proposal, but has come to accept it, as I hope each of you will do.' The air was still with expectancy. Nervously, I drew a deep breath before continuing. 'With England now formally at war, and recruits already being sought to defend our country and its freedom, I have decided to do my part and join the army.'

An audible gasp broke the silence, with Mum the first to respond.

'Oh, Harry, no. I've already lost your dad in the past year; I can't stand the thought of losing you as well. And what about Irene? You've hardly been married a week.'

Betty was quick to add to Mum's appeal for rationale in my thinking. 'Your mother's right, Harry.' Shaking her head, she turned to Irene. 'Tell me you haven't agreed to this idea, love? Like Florence says, you've only been wed a week. Do you really want to be a widow within a month?' She tugged at Ted's arm. 'Say something to him, Ted. Tell him no. Tell him he can't leave our Irene to get himself killed in some stupid war that'll probably be over soon anyway.'

I looked deep into Ted's eyes. I knew, ultimately, his response was the one that really mattered. Of course, I expected Mum and Betty to object, even Edith perhaps, but how Ted reacted would set the course for our family's journey for years to come. Would he understand, as a man, my decision to want to fight for our family and its future, or would he join the women in their cry for me to change my mind? I knew if it was the latter, I was risking more than just losing his respect. He might order Irene to move back home, perhaps claiming I'd lost my senses. Then where would our marriage be? I stood, rooted to the spot, unable to tell anything from his gaze, fixed squarely in my direction. After what seemed like an age, and shaking loose Betty's grip on his jacket, Ted rose from his chair and spoke the words I was desperate to hear.

'Good for you, lad. I only wish I could join you. I've always been fond of you, Harry, ever since our Irene set her heart on you. But now… well, now you have my respect as a man as well. Putting the needs and safety of others before your own is not a natural thing to do in this world. Most of us are selfish in life, no matter how hard we might argue to the contrary. But, putting your life on the line to defend more than just your own family; to defend the greater freedom for all, goes above and beyond, lad, and I take my hat off to you.'

Moving towards me, he offered his hand. 'I was proud to welcome you into our family last week, Harry, but that pride has just gone up tenfold.' Gripping my hand and shaking it firmly, he turned to Irene. 'You've bagged yourself a real man here, Irene, I hope you know that.'

I looked across to my beautiful wife, tears running down her cheeks as she replied, 'I do, Dad, I do. Although I can't help wishing he wasn't doing it all the same.'

Still holding my hand, Ted turned to face Mum and Edith. 'You have quite a son here, Florence. And you, Edith; as brothers go, you should be very proud of him.' Releasing my hand and moving towards Betty, who was sniffing into her handkerchief, he placed an arm around her shoulder. 'And so should you be, Betty, love. How many lads do we know who would give their lives for our daughter? Well, we've got one here, and he's married to her. We couldn't ask for more than that, could we? So, you can stop your crying and thank him for being the man he is, and that he cares not only for our Irene but for all of us here as well. Like I said, if I were a few years younger, I'd sign up as well, and be proud to stand shoulder to shoulder with him in sorting out those bloody Germans.'

If I was seeking more effusive support than I'd just received, I'd have struggled to find it. I felt my own eyes misting over as I took his hand again.

'Thank you, Ted, that means a lot, especially from you.'

Irene walked over and slipped her arm through mine. 'I'm proud of you too, Harry, you know that. I'm just a bit... well, you know.'

I pulled her into me, kissing her gently on the lips. 'I do, but if you think I won't be coming back to you, then you don't know me as well as I thought. I'm planning on spending a lifetime with you, Mrs Thompson, and our children, when they decide to come along.'

Mum and Betty smiled at each other, with Mum the first to speak. 'I'm still not sure about you signing on, but I'm definitely looking forward to being a grandma. I know Betty is as well.'

Wiping her eyes, Betty laughed. 'At least one of each would be nice.'

Irene pressed into me. 'Give us a chance, Mum, we only got married last week.'

Edith smiled. 'I quite fancy being an aunt as well. Then I can tell them the truth about their dad.'

We all laughed, with the conversation moving back to our time in Hastings once more. Irene and I thanked her parents again for the wonderful gift of those few days by the sea. It felt good to be together and share stories about the wedding and our honeymoon break, but Irene and I were also keen to get to the cottage and settle into our new home. We were pleased, therefore, when Ted suggested he take us, adding there would be plenty of other opportunities for family get-togethers in the days and weeks ahead.

'I think that's enough for one day, Irene and Harry look tired. They've had that long train journey, remember, as well as entertaining us for the past hour or so.' Turning to the two of us, he smiled. 'I should think they'd like to see their new home, especially after all the work you three ladies have put into it while they've been away.'

Squeezing my hand behind her back Irene spoke for the two of us. 'That would be lovely, Dad, if you're sure it's all right with you?'

'Of course it is. Now you say your goodbyes while I get your coats.' Turning to me as he left the room, he nodded. 'Let me know when you're looking to speak to the army recruitment team, Harry, and I'll come along with you if you'd like? I'm sure you can manage on your own but, as your father's not here to go with you, I just thought you might like some male company. I hope you don't think I'm interfering, lad, it's just...'

Sensing his discomfiture, I jumped in to save him further embarrassment.

'Thank you, Ted, that's kind. Let me think about it. I'll give it a few days or so to give Irene and I a chance to settle into the cottage. And I'll need to speak to Mr Anderson at the bakery as well. He's been really good to me of late, to both of us. I don't want to let him down any more than I have to. Although, I should think a lot of men will be leaving their jobs to sign on in the months to come.'

Irene and I said our goodbyes to Betty and Mum. Turning to Edith, I gave her a hug as we parted.

'Not sure if I've told you this lately, sis, but you're pretty special. You and I have come through quite a lot over the past few years, and I want you to know how much I've appreciated having you there beside me. And thanks for all you've done for Mum since Dad's been gone as well. It can't have been easy with me spending more and more time with Irene and less time being there for you.' Holding on to her, I kissed her lightly on the head. 'Anyway, I just wanted to say thanks for being the best sister a brother could have. And remember, you're welcome at our home anytime, with or without Mum. Irene loves you as much as I do.'

Looking up at me, her expression told me everything I needed to know.

'I love her too, Harry, and you. Like you say, we've come a long way, and I hope we have a few more adventures yet to come between us. And don't forget what I said about being an aunt, whenever you and Irene decide the time is right.'

I laughed. 'I'll put that at the top of our list of priorities then. I'm sure Irene will appreciate that thought as well.'

Leaning up to kiss me, she whispered in my ear, 'And I am proud of you for wanting to join up as well. Just make sure you do come home safely again though, for all of us.'

'Will do, sis. You look after yourself too.'

Climbing into Ted's car, Irene and I waved our goodbyes as he turned the engine on and set course for our new home.

'Remember, there's still some decorating and one or two odds and ends to sort out before you can call it your own. But hopefully, we've made a good start, at least to get you settled in.'

'It will be lovely, Dad, I'm sure. We couldn't have had a better start than the one you've given us.'

I settled back into my seat contemplating everything that had happened over the past ten days or so. I'd gone from being a baker's apprentice living with my mum and sister, to marrying Irene and moving into a home of our own all in the space of just over a week. And in the days to come I was intending to join the army and go to war. I may still have been a young man, but myriad responsibilities now sat on my shoulders that hadn't been there a few days earlier. For all that, I was determined to fulfil each of them to the best of my ability, especially when it came to honouring Irene and my commitment to her.

I'd seen the cottage briefly, once before, but with the wedding and everything else going on hadn't really given much more thought to it, certainly not from the viewpoint of Irene and I physically making it our home. On that initial visit it still wasn't clear when and if the previous tenants would actually be moving out. With that caveat in mind Irene and I hadn't wanted to assume anything more than it would be wonderful to live there, if it happened.

The cottage itself was set at the end of a large plot of land owned by Ted but never developed, apart from the area near to the factory itself. The three of us bounced up and down in our seats as we made our way along the rough unmade track leading away from the factory and down to the cottage. Much of the rest of the land on either side had been left fallow with grass and bushes filling the space. The cottage itself had a small garden area, front and back, that had been well cared for by the previous occupants. There were flowers and a couple of rose bushes set at the front, although with autumn approaching much of the earlier colourful summer display was beginning to go over. At the back was a small, grassed area with an apple tree. This was laden with fruit hanging from its branches. A length of rope was attached at one end to a branch and a large hook fixed to the cottage wall at the other. I presumed this acted as a washing line and tried to visualise my shirts hanging from it, blowing in the breeze. The building itself was of a rusty coloured brick with dark wooden frames surrounding the windows. Having not taken too much notice on my earlier visit, I was pleasantly surprised to see it in such good repair. I was fully aware that beggars can't be choosers and, like Irene, was more than grateful to be given the opportunity, so early in our marriage, to have a place to call our own. However, on early inspection, the cottage appeared to be better than anything we might have hoped for or expected. Standing in the front garden, Irene and I exchanged excited glances as Ted took a key from his pocket and moved to the front door.

'Charlie and Helen looked after the cottage well in their time here, so there wasn't a lot of building work to do as such, more general tidying up and a bit of decorating. Like I said, we've all put in a shift and have done quite a bit of that already. We've also put a few sticks of furniture in to get you started as I mentioned before.' Turning the key in the door, he smiled at me. 'Including that new double bed. Our Irene likes to wriggle around in bed, or at least she did when she was younger. Takes up twice as much space as any normal person does. You might have noticed that for yourself over the last few nights.'

Without waiting for my response, Irene interjected. 'Dad!'

'I'm sure we'll manage somehow, Ted,' I replied, winking at Irene.

Although described as small, the inside of the cottage appeared roomier than I remembered. The ceilings were a little higher than traditionally might have been expected, and the room sizes felt more generous as well. This was probably because there still wasn't a lot of furniture in place yet. The flooring was stone with a few rugs strewn here and there. Some of these had seen better days and were quite worn, but still provided a homely feel to the place. Downstairs comprised of a scullery and sitting room. The scullery contained a wood burning stove, a large Belfast sink with a solitary tap over it, and a pulley drier hanging from the ceiling over the stove. There was also a small table set against the wall next to the door. Sitting on the table was a food hamper filled with the basic essentials along with several treats, such as fruit, a small box of chocolates, and a bottle of wine.

'Oh Dad, this is so generous of you.'

'Not at all, you both have to eat. And you don't want to be shopping on the first day in your new home, do you?'

'But there's so much.'

'Take it up with your mother, I just did as I was told. Although, I did say we should keep the chocolates for ourselves.' He laughed. 'Now come on, let me show you the rest of the house.'

Leading the way, he moved next door to a modest sitting room. It was painted a light caramel colour, similar to the scullery. In the middle sat a small dining table with a chair placed at either end. There were two high-backed armchairs sitting opposite each other next to an open fireplace. Set between them on the floor was a dark-red rug. The armchairs were a rust colour with a red-and-green paisley design. The fireplace was built into the wall with a wide chimney extending up to the ceiling and beyond. Standing by the side of the chimney in the hearth were a pile of logs and a pair of tongs. I recognised the armchairs from one of the downstairs rooms at Ted's house.

'Ted, you've done it again. We can't accept those chairs, they're from your house. This really is...'

Smiling, he interrupted. 'Well, if you don't take them, you'll have nowhere to sit of an evening. And besides, Betty said they were getting a bit old-fashioned, and she thought it was time we had some new ones.' He grinned. 'Now, we all know she only said that so she can let you have them. Fashion has got nothing to do with it. Although, spending more of my money might. Anyway, her ladyship said you were to have them, so that's that.' He pointed to the window. 'She also said you were to have those curtains. They're from our spare bedroom. Your mum altered them to fit, Harry, so remember to say thank you the next time you speak to her.'

Irene leant across and kissed him. 'Thank you, Dad. It all looks lovely.'

Ted smiled and pointed to the wall. 'As you can see, most of the place is painted this colour. It may not be your choice, but it's clean and you can always change it to suit your own taste later.' Looking around he nodded. 'This will have to double as the dining room, although I'm sure that won't bother the two of you. I don't imagine you'll be having too many dinner parties over the next few months, so small and cosy should suit you fine.'

I was beginning to feel embarrassed about the surfeit of riches being bestowed upon us.

'Please don't apologise, Ted, this is fantastic. You really have been so generous, all of you.'

'Thank you for that, Harry, but I wasn't apologising, just being honest. Both Betty and Florence would happily give you their last pennies, and I applaud their generosity, if not their common sense. We all have to start somewhere, and this feels like a pretty good place for the two of you to begin your lives together. And it won't do either of you any harm to struggle a bit as well. Irene's mum and I started out with next to nothing. We've worked hard to get where we are today. And I know how tough things were in your house over the years as well, lad. Pulling together to get the things you want and need won't be a lesson that's been wasted on you in the past, I'm sure.'

'Not at all, but thanks anyway. We are one very blessed couple, aren't we, Irene?'

'Absolutely. And I agree with you, Dad. I want to make it *our* home, no matter how long it takes. If we can't afford something, then we'll go without until we can. There are a lot of young couples who won't get anywhere near the start you've given us. We'll be fine.'

'I'm pleased to hear you say that, love. Sometimes, I think your mother has forgotten what it was like when we first got married; having no money and struggling to pay our way. And neither of us had a family in a position to help the way we've been able to support the two of you either.' Looking at me, Ted pursed his lips. 'No offence meant, Harry. I know there was never much money in your house. I think your mum has done an amazing job, as well as being a brilliant mother to both you and Edith.'

I smiled. 'No offence taken. And you're right, she is pretty amazing.'

Irene turned to leave. 'Is it just the one room upstairs? I can't really remember. We didn't really look at it before, what with the other family still living here.'

'Yes, well, sort of. There's a bedroom and a box room, not much more than a large cupboard really. I'll show you.'

Walking out of the room Ted led the way to the end of the hallway and up a short flight of bare wooden stairs with Irene and I following behind. At the top we were faced with a narrow landing and a doorway set to the right and another to the left about halfway along. Ted stood to one side.

'You two go ahead, the bedroom is on the right. There's not a lot of room in there for three, certainly not with your bed, dressing table and the small wardrobe in there.'

As we entered the room, we both felt it had an aura about it. It felt special. Ted was right, there wasn't a lot of room, not with the bed and furniture in place, but Betty and Mum had made it look lovely. There was a multicoloured quilt covering the bed and the small bedside cabinet had a vase of freshly cut wild flowers on it. To the left was the small wardrobe. It was dark brown and had a mirror fixed in the centre panel of the door. There was a brown-and-green rug set between the wardrobe and the bed. Looking around the room, we warmed to it immediately, recognising it as the one room in the house where we could be ourselves with nobody else around. This is where we would come to feel safe and cut ourselves off from the rest of the world. This was the room where we would laugh, cry, make plans, be strong *and* vulnerable with each other, make love and, hopefully, create new life together.

I took a deep breath and, reaching for Irene's hand, whispered in her ear, 'I just want to close the door, take you in my arms and never leave this room again.'

'I feel that too. I love it.'

As we stood momentarily lost in thought, Ted's voice interrupted our musings.

'The box room is over here, unless the two of you are planning on staying in there for the rest of the day?'

I glanced at Irene and laughed. 'Coming.'

Ted was right, the door opposite provided access to little more than a small closet area, but Irene and I agreed any additional storage space was more than welcome.

Moving to her father, Irene took his arm and rubbed it. 'Thanks again, Dad, it's lovely, all of it. We couldn't have hoped for a better start.'

I nodded my agreement. 'I truly don't know how we can ever repay you for all of this.'

'No need to, lad. Like I've said already, it's our pleasure. You just take care of our Irene, that'll be payment enough for us.'

'You don't need to worry about that. Irene will always be my first priority.'

Nudging me in the ribs, she grinned. 'I'll remind you of that.'

Sensing this might be his cue to make a move, Ted turned for the stairs. 'Time I wasn't here. I'll leave you two alone now and give you a chance to settle in.'

Looking back over his shoulder as he led the way down the stairs, he continued. 'I forgot, there is one more room you need to know about, the toilet. It's just outside the back door. Your mother had me put a new seat on it. I didn't argue. Anyway, it's outside the back as I said, along with a tin bath hanging on the wall.'

I laughed. 'Thanks Ted, although I think we'd have found it soon enough.'

He smiled at me knowingly. 'Of course you would. Now, there's one more thing I need to say. I know you've only just got wed, but if you do happen to surface over the next few days, remember your mothers would like to see you both. Maybe you could invite them over for a cup of tea, they'd like that. You never know, young Edith might like to come as well.'

'Will do, Dad, it will be nice to welcome them into *our* home, won't it, Harry?'

'Of course.'

'If it were me, lad, I'd leave them to it. I've learnt over the years that when women get talking there's not a lot of room for the men in their lives to join in or feel the need to. I've never been one for nattering on about the latest fashion, or whatever else it is they go on about. Might be a better idea for you to go and have that chat with your boss at the bakery about your signing on.'

'Good idea, thanks.'

Reaching the front door, Ted turned and smiled warmly at us.

'Oh yes, and there's a box of candles on that kitchen table as well. Electricity is still new round here and it certainly hasn't reached this cottage yet.'

Irene smiled. 'Thanks, Dad, you've thought of everything.'

'Hopefully. Well, at least to get you started. There's a box of matches on the table as well.' He smiled and nodded approvingly. 'I hope you'll both be happy here, we all do. This is *your* home now, for as long as you like, although I'm sure, once a family comes along you'll be looking for somewhere with a bit more room like Charlie and Helen. But for now, just enjoy being here as husband and wife.' He laughed. 'If my memory serves me right, it took your mother and I a good year to get used to each other. And I still wonder at times if I'll ever truly understand her.' Leaning forward, he kissed Irene on the cheek. 'Be happy, love.'

'Thanks, Dad, I will.'

Turning to me and taking my hand, he continued. 'Always remember, lad, this is my daughter you're married to. If she ever comes home in tears, you'll have me to answer to, although I'm sure that's something I'll never need to remind you of.'

I smiled nervously. 'I hope so too.'

He laughed. 'I know. If anything, she'll be the one to make you cry. She's a headstrong lass once she gets a bee in her bonnet about something.'

'Thanks for that, Dad.'

'Anyway, just remember to ask your mothers and Edith round for that cup of tea over the next few days, otherwise it'll be me that'll wind up in tears from their complaining.'

'We will.'

I slipped my arm around Irene's waist as we watched Ted walk down the short pathway back to his car.

'Bye, Dad, love you.'

Waving back at us, he climbed into his seat and started the engine. 'Bye, speak to you soon.'

And with that he was gone, the engine spluttering as the car bounced around on the track once more as it moved away.

I stepped outside and extended my hand towards Irene.

'What are you doing?'

'I want you to come out here.'

'What for?'

'So I can carry you over the threshold. That's what men do with their wives, or so I've been told.'

Moving towards me, she grinned. 'Go on then, Mr Muscles, but don't blame me if you hurt your back.'

Sweeping her up in my arms, I carried her into the house. As I placed her on the ground, I let out a slight groan.

'There you are, I said you'd hurt yourself.'

I smiled suggestively. 'Oh, I'll be fine. I think I just need to lie down on our bed for a while. Perhaps you'd like to join me?'

Laughing, she took my hand. 'All right, but I don't want you putting any more strain on your back.'

I pulled her into me. 'It'll be fine. I think a bit of exercise might do it good.'

Chapter Sixteen

Apart from a short time spent familiarising ourselves with the house and garden, the rest of the day was spent mainly in our bedroom making love, eating chocolates, and drinking the wine we'd been gifted as a housewarming present. The following morning as we lay in bed we both agreed this decadent lifestyle would have to end, at least temporarily while we addressed some of the more mundane duties in life. We knew, if we didn't invite our mothers and Edith around soon, they would come knocking anyway. I also needed to speak with Mr Anderson about my decision to sign up for the army.

I watched as Irene drew back the curtains.

'God, you're beautiful.'

She turned and smiled. 'You're not bad yourself either.'

'Come back to bed and say that again.'

Laughing, she placed her dressing gown around her shoulders and moved to the bedroom door. 'I know what that means, even if we have only been married for a few days.'

'Well, you can't blame me for trying.'

'Maybe not, but nature is calling. I'll see you downstairs.'

'Okay, I'll get the stove lit and we can decide our priorities for the day.'

The next hour was spent washing, getting dressed, eating

breakfast, and planning our day. Irene said she would walk to the factory and speak with her dad about arranging to get Betty, Mum, and Edith over. We agreed I would also make time to speak with Mr Anderson about my intention to join the army. Hopefully, he might agree to keep my job open for me after the war. Irene and I refused to entertain the idea of my not making it back.

It felt strange going our separate ways as we left the cottage. We might have only been married for a short while, but we hadn't spent more than a few minutes apart during that time. Rubbing her back with my hand, I kissed Irene goodbye.

'I love you, Mrs Thompson.'

'You too. I hope things go well with Mr Anderson.'

'Thank your dad again for everything when you speak to him.'

'I will, but don't forget our mums, and Edith too. They've more than played their part in all of this.'

'We can thank them together when they come over for that cuppa. I'll see you later.'

I felt Irene grip my hand as I made to walk away.

'Harry, I know we've discussed you going to war, and that I wasn't very gracious about the decision, at least when you first talked about it. But I can't think many brides would relish the idea of their new husband going into battle. But never doubt I am proud of you, and of your desire to join in this fight.' She smiled. 'And to protect me, of course.'

Leaning forward, I kissed her again. 'I'd happily give my life to protect you.' Squeezing her hand, I smiled. 'I'll see you soon, I don't want to be late for Mr Anderson. I'm not sure what he's going to say about all of this.'

I had only been away less than two weeks, but it still felt strange walking into the bakery again. Everyone was pleased to see me though and wanted to hear all about the wedding, and how Irene and I had got on in Hastings. Holidays by the sea were a rarity for most of the families living in and around Canning Town, and so reports of hotel catering and sunny walks along a sandy beach were listened to with good-humoured envy. I'd made one or two proper friends in my time at the bakery and knew I would miss them in the weeks to come once I was on the front line. One of the other lads had already signed up to fight, and I hoped Mr Anderson would accept my desire to join him with good grace, although I recognised it would have a detrimental effect on his workforce. Thankfully, I needn't have worried as he was readily accepting of my proposal.

'Good for you, Harry. Although I must admit I'm a little surprised if I'm honest, what with you being newly wed and all. I thought you might be hoping for a bit more time at home before considering doing your bit for the war effort.'

I explained I'd wanted to sign on even before getting married, and how it had taken a few difficult conversations to convince Irene I was doing the right thing.

'Well, I can't say we won't miss you, lad, because we will. You're a good worker and a positive influence on some of the others here as well. Especially those who might not be as keen as you to put their heads down and get stuck in when we're busy. Yes, I'm definitely going to miss having you around. But you don't have to worry about your job. It'll still be here for you when you come back.'

'That's very kind of you, Mr Anderson and good to hear. I know Irene will appreciate that as well.'

'And that's another thing. You tell your Irene that she'll not go hungry while you're away either.' He laughed. 'At least not as far as bread and cakes are concerned. She can come here whenever she likes, and I'll make sure she's cared for. She won't go short; I promise you that.'

'I'm not sure what to say, except, thank you, I…'

Interjecting, he laughed again. 'No need to thank me, son. If anything, it's me that should be thanking you. Going off to war to beat those bloody Germans at their own game and protecting those of us left over here. No, it's us that owe you a debt of gratitude, and all the other brave lads who've signed on. You shoot one of those buggers for me, Harry. And remember when the fighting's over, there'll always be a job here for a war hero. Especially one as hard-working as you.'

We shook hands as I thanked him again for his support, and of his offer to keep an eye out for Irene. It was good to know there would always be bread on the table while I was away. Equally, I knew both our families would also make sure she didn't go without. Although Irene had now fully accepted my decision to join the army, we still hadn't agreed on a physical date for me to sign on. As I walked away from the bakery, further buoyed by Mr Anderson's support, I felt there was no time like the present, and so made my way to the recruitment centre.

Might as well strike while the iron's hot, I decided. The nearest recruiting office had been set up in a disused warehouse near to the docks, less than a mile away. This allowed men of all ages, within reason, to sign up without having to travel further afield or to the nearest army barracks which were situated some distance away. As I approached the centre, I noticed a large poster with an image of Field Marshal Lord Kitchener's face on it declaring, *Your Country Needs You*. I'd already seen smaller versions of this appeal displayed on local walls and outside Dad's former haunt, The Blue Anchor. Clearly, the increased drive to get new recruits to join the fighting was on. That said, it would be almost eighteen months before the choice to fight was made mandatory, following the introduction of conscription in January 1916. Even at this early stage in the conflict it was obvious to all, especially those in power, that more men were needed to take up arms against the German aggressor. As I approached the recruitment centre, I noticed a soldier dressed in full uniform standing by the entrance. Pausing to collect my thoughts, I smiled up at him. He looked at me from beneath the peak of his cap, the sun glinting brightly against his regimental badge set above it.

'Come to sign up, have you, son? We can do with all the lads we can get ready to take the King's shilling, I can tell you. The Germans are giving our boys a tough time of it just now. A few more like you though and we'll soon have them on the run.'

I suddenly became aware of the enormity of my decision to join the fight. This wasn't a story in a book, this was real. Much as I wanted to help, my earlier desire to take up arms appeared far less inviting than it had when saying goodbye to Irene a couple of hours earlier. Once I stepped through the door in front of me and signed those recruitment papers our lives would be changed forever. The next time I said goodbye to Irene and our families could possibly be the last. Was I really prepared to make my wife a widow after less than a fortnight of us being married? As I stood pondering the prospect of my beautiful Irene being left alone, the soldier's voice broke through my conflicted thoughts.

'I know what you're thinking, lad. Am I doing the right thing? What about my girl and my family? I'm right, aren't I?'

I nodded meekly.

'We all think that. But I'll tell you something else we think about an' all. If we don't fight now and they win, then what? They'll be over here, that's what. And then we'll be fighting the buggers on our streets, maybe even in our own homes. How are you going to protect your family then, eh, when the bloody Germans are marching up your road shooting everyone in sight? Is that what you want? Of course it ain't. So have your doubts, yeah, but don't entertain 'em for too long, or it might be too late.'

He was right of course. But even so, this was still a moment that would alter the course of our future together forever. Equally, I couldn't stand the thought of Irene, and our families thinking I was a coward because I hadn't signed up to do my bit to protect them. I looked up again and nodded. 'You're right. It's just a bit... well, you know.'

'Daunting. Yeah, I get that. But sometimes we have to consider the greater good. You're doing the right thing, lad. You're over nineteen, aren't you?'

I smiled. 'Yes. I've not long turned twenty.'

'There you go then. You get yourself in there and make your family proud.'

I nodded my understanding and pushed open the door. As I entered, I blinked for a moment, adjusting to the light. The brightness of the sun had given way to a darker hue altogether. There was little natural light in the warehouse apart from a couple of windows set opposite each other at either end of the building. Beyond that, additional lighting was provided by a series of bulbs connected to lengthy wire cables hanging from the ceiling over a series of desks. Each one had an army recruiting officer sat opposite a prospective volunteer similar to myself. To my left were a number of seats, most of which were filled with other young lads and men waiting to be interviewed. A sergeant carrying a clipboard approached me. He was a tough-looking man of around six feet with a broad chest. There were several service medals and insignia pinned to his tight-fitting khaki jacket.

'Come to sign on, lad?'

'I think so.'

'Think so? You know this is the local recruitment centre, don't you?'

I shook my head. 'Yes. I'm sorry, I wasn't sure what to expect. And yes again, I am here to sign up, if you'll have me?'

'We're happy to take anyone, so long as they're healthy and can carry a gun.' He smiled. 'And you look healthy enough to me.'

I laughed nervously. 'Thanks.'

Taking a pencil from the top left-hand pocket of his jacket he smiled again. 'What's your name, son?'

'Harry. Harry Thompson.'

Writing down my name, he continued. 'From around here are you?'

'Yes, I've just got married. We live up by the Burrows factory.'

'Ted Burrows do you mean?'

'Yes, that's right. Do you know him?'

'In a way. My lad worked for him for a while. He's on the docks now though. Good man, Ted Burrows. I told Tommy he should have stayed there, but he likes the fresh air and being outside. Said working in a factory wasn't for him. Mind, if this war goes on much longer, I'll have him here signing on with the rest of you lads. I've told him already; it'll make a man of him.' He looked at me and scratched the side of his head with the pencil. 'Just got married did you say?'

'Yes, to Ted Burrows's daughter, Irene.'

'Oh right, good for you. My missus told me she'd got wed, not that I was really interested.' He laughed. 'No offence, lad, I'm sure she's a lovely lass and all, it's just I'm not that fussed about weddings if you know what I mean, especially not with this war on.'

'No offence taken, Sergeant. But you're right, Irene is a lovely girl.'

'The reason I ask is because we're not actively looking to take married men at the moment. I mean we're happy for them to join if they want, but we're not saying they have to sign up, not yet anyway.'

'I know, but we've talked about it and it's something I feel I need to do. Like the soldier out the front said, if we don't take the fight to them, then before we know it they'll be over here, and then it'll be a different battle altogether.'

'He's not wrong there.' Searching his notes, he glanced at me again. 'Good on you then... Harry, was it you said?'

'Yes, that's right. Harry Thompson.'

Using his clipboard, he gesticulated towards the seating area. 'Find yourself a seat over there then, Harry, and someone will call you over in a few minutes.' He grinned. 'There'll be a brief medical as well but, like I say, you look healthy enough to me.'

'I was when I left home,' I replied, attempting to portray a confidence to match my conviction.

The sergeant nodded. 'It's been busy today, but that's a good thing. Like I keep saying, the more the merrier, and the quicker we can get this war over.'

Nodding my thanks and understanding I moved to the seating area. As I waited to be interviewed, I looked around the factory. I could hear people talking but was unable to fully decipher what was being said because of the high ceiling and open space which made the conversation echo slightly as it bounced around the room. After a while I heard my name called.

'Harry Thompson.'

I held my hand aloft and swallowed hard. This was it, there was no turning back now. The next hour passed by in a whirl as I dedicated my life to the greater good, agreeing to wear the khaki service uniform of the British army and do battle with the German forces currently wreaking havoc on the other side of the Channel.

As I made my way home, I thought about everything that had happened since I'd left the cottage earlier that morning. A few hours ago, I had been lying in bed with my beautiful wife planning our future together. A future that may have involved my going to war but had also included life beyond that. We'd talked about what we would do with the cottage, and how keen Irene was to establish the garden as her own. And although we had only just got married, we'd also considered what life might be like once children came along. We both wanted a family but were equally determined to wait until we felt settled as a couple and able to cope with the responsibilities of parenthood. Also, with the country at war, we didn't feel it right to bring another life into the world until it was a more settled place where their safety and well-being could be assured. All of that seemed a long way off as I wandered home contemplating the reality of having just signed up to take the King's shilling. I was no longer simply Harry Thompson, husband to Irene and potential father to our children; I was a military recruit who would soon be going away for basic training before heading off to Europe to fight in an increasingly bloody war. Whilst I felt a degree of excitement about becoming part of something greater than myself, the little boy inside me suddenly felt vulnerable and afraid.

Yes, I'd declared to Irene I would happily lay down my life for her, but that's easy to say when sitting in your kitchen enjoying a cup of tea together, with no immediate threat to life or limb. But now, I'd taken the very real step towards fulfilling that promise by swearing allegiance to King and country and agreeing to actually lay my life on the line. Would I be able to live up to those pledges and see them through to their dramatic, perhaps even final, conclusion? Only the days and weeks ahead would tell. For the first time, nerves outweighed my enthusiasm to do the right thing. I knew I couldn't share any of this with Irene. How could I? What would she say about these new-found concerns I was experiencing regarding having to take up arms, point a rifle at another human being and kill him? I wanted to run back to the recruitment centre and tell them I'd made a mistake but knew I couldn't. Somehow, I would have to discover the inner strength required to declare I *had* done the right thing. Embracing this new but inevitably flawed resolve, I took another deep breath and continued my journey home.

As I made my way up the short path leading to the cottage, my mind still racing with all that had happened that morning, a familiar voice interrupted my thoughts. It was Irene.

'Oh, you've decided to come home then. I thought you'd left me.'

I looked up and smiled. 'Sorry, I got a bit sidetracked.'

'Sidetracked? Did Mr Anderson ask you to work today then?' she countered, a broad grin spread across her face.

'No, I went to…'

Rubbing her hands together impatiently, she interrupted. 'I was only joking; you can tell me later. I've got some exciting news.'

I might have only been married a short while but knew already that when Irene had a bee in her bonnet about something everything else would have to wait.

I sighed. 'Come on then, what is it that's got you so excited?'

Encouraging me into the kitchen, Irene pointed towards the teapot sat beside two cups and saucers on the table.

I nodded my head and smiled.

'Oh lovely, you've made a cup of tea.'

She laughed. 'Well, yes, I have. I saw you coming across the field, but that's not what I wanted to tell you. It's Mum and Dad, you'll never guess what they've given us now.'

Embarrassed already by her parents' overt generosity towards us in the short time we'd been married, I was equally aware I shouldn't appear ungrateful for whatever new blessing they were about to bestow upon us. I smiled quizzically.

'I don't know, but you're clearly happy about it.'

'Their bone-china tea service. You know, the one you said you liked when you first came round for afternoon tea.'

Trying desperately to remember the specific occasion she was referring to, as well as the tea-set itself, I grinned. 'Oh yes, that tea service. How kind of them.'

Sensing a failed attempt on my behalf to recall the crockery she was referring to, along with the required enthusiasm over her announcement, she turned on me.

'You've forgotten, haven't you? It was the white one with the dark-blue edging and gold leaf pattern on it. You said you thought it was lovely.'

Vaguely remembering the occasion she was alluding to, I sought to extricate myself from the hole I had dug.

'I'm sorry, love, you took me by surprise.' I drew a breath.

'But, yes, I do remember it now. And yes, it was, is, lovely. But why are they giving it to us now?'

'It was my grandmother's, on Mum's side. I think she might have mentioned that before?'

I shrugged my shoulders. 'I'll be honest, in those early days I was more intent on making a good impression on your parents than I was about remembering whose teacup I was drinking out of.'

Irene smiled. 'All right, I forgive you. Maybe it was a little unfair to expect you to remember that, but it is still a very special gift. My grandma handed it down to Mum and Dad when Grandad Albert died. She said she didn't need such a large tea service anymore and that she wanted to see it used by her family, rather than being put away in a cupboard and forgotten about. When I spoke to Dad earlier, he told me Mum had said the same thing to him. She said they were the ones on their own now and that, as the next generation, it was only right the tea service should come to us, especially once we have children.'

I scratched my head. 'She may have a point about our having a family at some stage, but I can't imagine you or her being very happy about us serving our children their afternoon cuppa in a bone-china tea service, let alone one that's a family heirloom.'

'Well, obviously not. I'm not that stupid. But what about when people come to visit, or when the children grow up and bring their boyfriends and girlfriends home? Then we can entertain them the same way my parents did with you, and the way Granny and Grandad did when Mum took Dad home in their courting days.'

I laughed. 'Oh, so we're inheriting this beautiful tea service some twenty years before we actually need it, just in case.'

'Now you're being silly, and a bit horrid too. I thought you'd be pleased. Anyway, when you're a manager for Mr Anderson, and you bring him and his wife home for tea we can use it then.'

Taking Irene in my arms, I smiled. 'And I look forward to that day as well.' We fell silent momentarily in each other's embrace, quieting any potential for further tension between us. I whispered in her ear, 'I love you, Mrs Thompson, posh tea service and all.'

Pushing me away playfully, she countered, 'I'll remind you of that tomorrow. That's when Mum and Dad are coming for tea. I thought we might go across to your mum's later and invite her and Edith as well. I didn't have the time before.'

'Good idea. It would be nice to have them here as the first guests in our new home.'

Moving to the table, Irene began pouring our tea. 'That's true. How exciting. And we can use the new tea service as well. Dad said they'll bring it with them tomorrow. Now, I want to hear all about how you got on with Mr Anderson. Was he all right about you wanting to join the army?'

I swallowed hard. If the embarrassment of my forgetting her mum's tea service had felt uncomfortable, the next exchange between us was going to prove painful in the extreme.

Sitting down and taking a welcome sip of tea, I smiled.

'He was fine. In fact, if I'm honest, he was not only happy about me signing on but envious he couldn't do the same. And the best news is, he said my job will still be there when I come back. Isn't that kind of him?'

Reaching across the table to squeeze my hand, Irene countered, 'I should think so too. You've worked really hard at the bakery in the time you've been there.'

'That's as maybe. But I still think it's a generous thing to do.'

Smiling, she rubbed the back of my hand. 'I know, I was just teasing.'

Withdrawing her hand, she looked at me quizzically. 'That still doesn't explain why you've been away so long.'

Shifting awkwardly in my seat and taking another drink of tea, I nodded.

'Well, the thing is, I was so emboldened by Mr Anderson's support that I went straight round to the recruiting office and signed up there and then.'

An awkward silence followed as Irene reflected on what I'd just said. Her response a few moments later was slow and deliberate.

'I thought we'd agreed to go together, or at least to talk about it again first.'

Regretting my earlier decision and corresponding actions, I nodded meekly.

'I know, and I'm sorry, I just...'

Sitting upright, Irene cut short my apology.

'Sorry isn't good enough, Harry. We are talking about you going to war, to fight and, God forbid, maybe getting killed. And you decide on the back of an encouraging word from your employer that you should sign up straight away without further discussion with your wife.' Looking directly at me, her eyes brimming with tears, she continued. 'And the best you can say is sorry.'

I reached across to take her hand, but she quickly withdrew it from my grasp.

'I thought we'd had this conversation before, about talking things through and never going behind one another's back. And yet, when it comes to the biggest decision between us in the short time we've been married, you ignore any promise we might have made to each other and do what you want without any further thought or consideration towards me.'

'It's not like that, Irene, truly it's not. Yes, Mr Anderson encouraged me in wanting to join up; and yes, it confirmed to me it was the right thing to do. But you and I had already agreed that I would sign on. What we hadn't finalised was a physical date for me to do it.' I smiled apologetically. 'For not coming home to talk it through with you first, I apologise. You're right, I should have done that, I know, but I also thought you might try to dissuade me, and I didn't want us to fall out again about a decision we'd already made.'

'And so you decided the better way was to act first and present me with a fait accompli later, is that it?'

Frustrated with both myself and the repeated point she was making, I snapped back. 'That's not fair. I would never do anything without considering you first, you must know that. I love you.'

Still smarting, Irene shook her head. 'Well, you have a funny way of showing it.'

Accepting she was right and recognising the need to resolve our differences before the conversation moved to a darker level, I made another attempt to placate her.

'Irene, please, I do love you, more than you can ever know. And I'm not saying that to excuse what I've done. You're right when you say we agreed we would make all difficult decisions together. I haven't honoured that agreement on this occasion, not entirely, and for that I apologise again. But I didn't do it deliberately, and certainly not to hurt you. And I think, deep down, you know that. But I do have to do this. The thing I got wrong, and that I truly regret, is that I acted without consulting you again before putting pen to paper. And like I say, I am truly sorry for that.' Pausing momentarily, I reached for her hand once more and squeezed it. 'The truth is though, as we both know, I'd have to go sooner or later anyway, the recruiting sergeant told me as much earlier.'

I took a long drink from my cup and waited patiently for Irene's reply. Thankfully, my plea for understanding drew a positive response. Taking a deep breath and leaning forward she nodded.

'I forgive you.' She smiled. 'I do know you love me, but I was hurt; still am a little, if I'm honest.'

'And like I say I'm…'

'Waving away yet another attempt to apologise, she continued.

'Let's not argue anymore, what's done is done. As you say, at some point the decision might not have been ours to make anyway. Of course, I'm fearful about you going to war. You're my husband and I don't want to lose you so early in our marriage. But equally, I understand your reasons for wanting to go and am proud of you for that. Never doubt that, Harry, do you hear?'

I nodded meekly, grateful the earlier tension between us had eased.

'That said, there is one condition I have before you leave, and it's one I insist that you fulfil.'

Unsure of what she was about to say but recognising it was something I was unlikely to argue successfully against, I smiled inquisitively. 'And that is?'

'That you tell Billy's mother the truth about what you and Karl did.'

I felt my jaw drop. Whatever I had anticipated she might ask of me it hadn't been this.

'But what good will that do, especially after all these years? It will only cause her further pain. And don't forget she lost her husband just over a year ago with pneumonia. Hearing the truth about what Karl and I did on top of that will just bring all the hurt back again, only ten times worse, because now she'll have no one to share it with.' I looked directly into her eyes. 'Are you sure this is what you want, Irene? I really don't think it's a good idea.'

'I'm sorry, Harry, but I won't take no for an answer, not about this. As you say, Mrs White has been through hell and back over the past few years, but for her to go to her grave with her suspicions about what happened to Billy still unresolved would be a crime almost as great as the one you two boys carried out that day. I know it was Karl who physically moved the pram but, by your own admission, you were equally to blame.' Looking away momentarily before returning her gaze to me, she continued. 'I'm not particularly religious, Harry, but I have wondered at times, if there is a God, what he would say about what you and Karl did. Would he be forgiving, or would he be angry you hadn't told the truth? After all, one of the Ten Commandments says we shouldn't kill. And, much as it hurts me to say it, you and Karl *were* responsible for that little boy's death.'

Not really knowing how to respond, yet feeling an overwhelming sense of remorse about what Irene was alluding to, I stuttered my reply.

'I… I don't know what to say. I've never really thought about God being involved in all of this, or whether he truly exists. But, if he is real, then surely he wouldn't have allowed this war to start. And if he did, then he must have a lot more to worry about than some terrible mistake made all those years ago by two young boys? So no, I'm not prepared to add God's judgement to the list of things I've done that I feel guilty about, even if that particular event does still haunt me.'

'But that's the thing, Harry, by your own admission, even after all this time it *does* still bother you. Imagine if it were a child of ours, wouldn't you want to know the truth about what really happened?'

Trying to stay afloat in the sea of shame threatening to engulf me, I struck out. 'That's different!'

Equally determined not to accept my feeble rebuff, Irene snapped back. 'In what way? In what way would it be different if it were our baby?'

As I sat there, desperately searching for the words to quantify my rationale that things *would* be different if it were a child of our own, I realised Irene was right; there was no justification for what Karl and I had done that day. Stupid and immature we may have been, but that didn't lessen our guilt or culpability in causing the death of that innocent young boy. There was no point in my continuing to seek to defend the indefensible. I was guilty as charged, we both were, and it was time to make amends, or at least as best I could by admitting my guilt to Billy's mum. I looked at Irene.

'You're right. I think I'd just learned to accept the story Karl and I invented at the time; that the whole event had been some terrible accident. The truth is of course, if we hadn't moved the block from under the wheel, the pram would never have rolled down the slope, and Billy would still be alive today.'

'So you will speak to Mrs White and tell her the truth?'

'Yes. But what about our parents? I can't tell her and not them. They'd hear about it soon enough anyway.' I shook my head as the enormity of what I was agreeing to took hold. 'And, what about the police? I'll need to speak to them as well.'

Irene pursed her lips. 'I hadn't thought about the police.'

Leaning forward, I rubbed her arm. 'Well, you better think about them now. Either we tell everyone, or we tell no one, we can't have it both ways.'

'But what if the police charge you for what you did, and for lying to them? If that happens you could be wearing a prison uniform rather than an army one.' She shook her head. 'I wish I hadn't said anything now.'

I stroked her arm again. 'Well you did, and in a way I'm pleased. I've never been happy with what we said at the time, never really found peace in living with that lie.'

'So you're going to tell everyone then?'

I smiled. 'I thought it was me who'd argued to keep it a secret between us. Listening to you now, it sounds more like you're the one who doesn't want to say anything.'

'I don't want you to go to prison.'

'I don't think that's likely to happen. We were just two young boys. Yes, we did something incredibly stupid that had terrible consequences, but we certainly never intended to hurt Billy.'

I paused, allowing Irene to consider all we had discussed. Eventually, she broke the silence.

'When will you tell them?'

'Who, the police?'

'Anyone, everyone, I don't know. I just wish you'd never told me about any of it in the first place.'

'Let's not go down that road again. You were the one who said we shouldn't have any secrets between us, and now you're saying you wish I'd kept the biggest one of all from you. I can't win either way.'

'I know, and I'm sorry. Of course it's the right thing to do. I'm just scared of losing you.'

'But you're happy to let me go to war?'

'That's different. And anyway, you're the one who wanted to sign up, I never suggested you volunteer to join the army.'

'Fair point.' I smiled reassuringly. 'Listen, why don't we tell our families tomorrow when they come for tea and see what they have to say. Your father's a wise old bird, I bet he'll have an opinion on what we should do and how to go about it.'

'If you think that's right?' Laughing awkwardly, she added, 'I'm just glad we're married already. Dad might have called the whole thing off if he'd known all of this before.'

'I'm pleased as well. The thought of not having you in my life isn't worth thinking about.'

In that moment, agreeing to tell our families seemed the right thing to do. In reality, it proved to be one of the hardest things I had ever undertaken. Watching the expressions on their faces change from polite interest to ones of shock and disappointment left me feeling as disgusted by my actions as they clearly were. Only Irene's strength and support kept me going until the awful truth about what Karl and I had done had been fully revealed.

Mum was the first to speak following my confession.

'I'd have thought you'd heard enough lies from your dad over the years without you choosing to follow in his footsteps.'

Edith was quick to follow in her admonishment of our actions. 'I always thought Karl had some sort of hold over you. I was never sure about him.'

Betty, moving her chair a little closer to Irene, placed a comforting arm around her shoulder. 'We'll get through this, love. It'll be all right, you'll see.'

Ted was a little more forensic in his response.

'You say you were both around twelve when this happened?' I nodded. 'Yes.'

'Old enough to know better, but not yet an adult, at least not in the eyes of the law.'

'What do you mean?' Betty enquired, her arm still supporting Irene.

'The two of them were clearly responsible for what happened. Harry's confession confirms that, even if it was the other lad, Karl, who physically took the block of wood from under the pram's wheel. Equally, neither of them intended for things to end up as they did. Some might argue it was a mindless childish prank that went terribly wrong. Billy's mother had told the two of them off for playing football outside of her house and they decided to settle the score, no pun intended, by putting the wind up her, saying her son's pram was on the move. The tragic error of judgement the boys made was in giving the pram that fatal shove. It was stupid in the extreme. Harry's contrite confession pays testimony to that. But as far...'

Frustrated by what she was hearing, Betty interrupted. 'For goodness' sake, Ted, we know all that. It's what we do about it now that matters.'

Nodding politely, Ted smiled before continuing.

'If you'll let me finish, then you'll be in a better position to gauge what it is I'm suggesting.' He smiled again. 'As I said, Harry has admitted to what the two of them did. I have no reason to doubt what he has told us as being anything other than true, nor do I suspect, will the police. As young lads they panicked. And because of that, they concocted a story that would absolve them from any responsibility for the tragic consequences of their actions. It sounds from what I've heard that some, certainly Billy's mother, maybe even the police, questioned their explanation from the off. Equally, and without evidence to the contrary, they were unable to prove the boys were lying and so had to accept their story as fact. Scared children, knowing they are guilty of some misdemeanour, will often lie to escape a beating or other form of punishment. I can remember lying to my own father as a lad about something I'd done to avoid a whipping.'

Edith interjected. 'But in this case a baby died. And Harry had plenty of beatings from Dad when he was younger, so he knew what that felt like already.'

Ted waited for her to finish before responding. 'Thank you, Edith. Betty and I have got to know you and your mother well in the time Harry and Irene have been together, along with some of the difficult experiences each of you have encountered along the way. It can't have been easy for any of you at times.' Noticing Mum's discomfiture, Ted smiled at her reassuringly. 'Sorry, Florence, none of this is intended to embarrass you, I am simply making a case for Harry's response to what happened at the time.' Mum nodded her understanding as Ted continued. 'What I was going to say was, no matter how used to receiving the strap any young person might be, the thought of yet another beating would still be something to avoid. And if this included lying to escape such violent retribution then so be it. Again, I can identify with that truth from personal experience. The other thing we need to consider is the age difference between the boys. Admittedly, it wasn't a lot but, as Harry has told us, Karl liked to play the dominant partner in their relationship. He would often use that small differential in their ages to emphasise that point. Harry hasn't tried to hide his part in what happened to Billy, but it is obvious that Karl led from the front in making up the story they used in their defence. And, as we all know, once a lie has been established, the only way to defend it is by lying again.'

I appreciated Ted's support but still wasn't sure how it was going to help in my defence when speaking to Mrs White and the police.

'But that's the point, I don't want to lie about this anymore.'

'I know you don't, lad, and I admire you for that. Equally, I can understand why your mother and Edith are disappointed in what they've heard; but I would ask them, and Betty here, to consider how much gumption it took to tell the truth when you could have just left things how they were. I remember when you told me about your decision to join the army and how others, even within this family, encouraged you to think again. But you stuck to your guns, and that impressed me. You're a man of principal, Harry, and, like I say, I admire and respect that trait in you. And it's the same with this story about the White boy. You did a bloody stupid thing, unforgiveable in the eyes of many, but you want to make amends when it would have been easier to let sleeping dogs lie. And, much as it pains me to hear about your actions that day, I can't find fault in your determination to come clean about it now, especially when you're about to head off to war.'

Pausing, he looked at each of us in turn, acknowledging our desire to know where his evaluation of this discourse was headed.

'All right, so where are we?' Looking at Irene and I, he smiled. 'The next couple of weeks are not going to be easy for either of you.' Irene took my hand in an act of reassurance as Ted spoke again. 'But you've made a start by confessing to us as a family what you did, and that can't have been easy. I know our Irene has forgiven you, and you already know how I feel about you, lad. And, I trust, whatever their feelings at this moment, hopefully the rest of the family will come around to forgiving you as well.'

I watched as tears of love and gratitude ran down Irene's cheeks. 'Thank you, Dad.'

'No need to thank me, love, you're the strong one here. I'm just trying to support the two of you, best as I know how.' He looked at me again. 'The harder part in all of this, is going to be when you talk to Mrs White and the police. I can't speak for her, but I don't think for a minute she's going to give you an easy time of it or thank you for your honesty. I wouldn't look for any understanding or forgiveness from her, lad. But, as far as the police are concerned, I might be able to offer a bit of help there. I'm friendly with a couple of the senior officers locally and would be happy to have a word with them on your behalf if you'd like me to. Just to get some idea of where you stand as far as the law is concerned. My gut feeling is, with the two of you not much more than children yourself at the time, there's nothing they can really charge you with, certainly nothing intentional. What you and Karl did was awful and cost that little lad his life. You'll both have to live with that for the rest of your days. But did you mean for it to happen? I think any right-minded person knows the answer to that, no matter how terrible the consequences of your actions.' Pausing to draw breath, he shook his head. 'No, I don't think the police will be looking to charge either of you with any serious offence, although I'm sure they'll want another statement from you for their records. I think your greatest challenge is going to be in coming clean to Billy's mother. I don't envy you that. But she has a right to know and respond as she sees fit.' He shook his head. 'Be under no illusion though, son; as I've said already, this won't be easy, for either of you.'

A reflective silence fell on the room as we each considered Ted's summation of the situation. What he had said was true, wise, and supportive, and I was grateful for that. Equally, as he had intimated, the hardest part was yet to come. Not only in admitting to the police what Karl and I had done but, more especially, to Mrs White. It was not a conversation I was looking forward to but recognised it was one I couldn't put off for long.

Chapter Seventeen

I went to the police two days later. Ted had called one of his contacts and arranged an appointment for us to speak with an officer. Whilst he might have appreciated my honesty in coming forward, he was far less understanding about my having taken so long to do it. He agreed, after such a long period of time and with the two of us being so young when the tragedy occurred, it was unlikely any charges would be forthcoming. Also, with Karl no longer in the country, it would be nigh on impossible to even get a statement from him. He did consider charging me separately with lying to a police officer and of wasting police time but, after hearing I was about to go to war, decided the country would be better served with me fighting for its freedom than spending time locked in a cell. That said, he left me in no doubt how lucky I was that he wasn't in a position to throw the book at me for my shameful part in what had happened.

'Don't think you've got away with this, lad,' he said, staring at me across his highly polished dark wooden desk. 'You and your friend are still ultimately responsible for that young boy dying. It may have been an accident the way it happened, but Stan Potter went to his grave a couple of years back still feeling he was responsible in some way for the little lad's death. He said he had nightmares about his horse clattering down on that pram. Said he used to wake up hearing Joan's screams.' Shaking his head and grimacing, he pointed to the sergeant stripes on his arm. 'Before I got these, as a young constable speaking with Joan and Bert at their Billy's funeral, she always claimed you two boys knew more than you were letting on. Probably just as well the truth didn't come out at the time, or I swear she'd have swung for the two of you, accident or not.'

I had no defence but felt the need to share my personal feelings about what had transpired that day.

'I've had nightmares about it as well, Sergeant. I said to Karl at the time we should tell the truth but...'

'But you didn't. Oh, I know you're coming clean now, lad, and credit to you for doing that. But for some, your confession will have come too late.'

Not knowing how to respond apart from offering yet another apology, I was grateful for Ted's interjection.

'You're right in what you say, Sergeant, but this hasn't been easy for Harry either. Irene and the rest of the family have also told him what we think. He hasn't had an easy ride from any of us, you can be sure of that, and certainly not his mum and sister. But it was his choice to own up when he could have kept quiet, and none of us would have been any the wiser.'

The policeman looked at me again, pursing his lips. 'It's a funny thing a guilty conscience. You can run from it, but in the end, it'll always catch up with you. Is that what happened with you, Harry? Did your conscience catch up with you, or is there something deeper worrying you, lad?'

I shook my head. 'I don't know what you mean.'

'Oh, I think you do. You're about to go to war, right? About to face the full force of the German army and all it has to throw at you. So what if one of their bullets has your name on it, eh, and you come face to face with your maker? It'll be a bit late to confess then, won't it?'

Ted jumped in again. 'That's not fair. You've read the boy the riot act, so let's leave it at that, unless you *are* intending to charge him? Like you said, we'll all be better served with him fighting for his country than having him sit in your prison cell. And yes, he'll be fighting for his life, but he'll also be fighting for our freedom as well, Sergeant. Yours as well as mine. We shouldn't forget that either.'

I looked on nervously as the policeman got to his feet and dusted down his uniform. 'That's a fair point, sir, and well made.' Staring down at me, he forced a smile. 'You're a lucky lad to have Mr Burrows as your father-in-law, Harry, not everyone would have been as understanding and supportive as him. If my remarks were perceived as being overly vindictive, they weren't meant to be. The thing is, my Rose and I became close to Joan and Bert after what happened. Our lad was born about the same time as their Billy, and we often talked about how we'd have felt if it had been young Tim who'd been killed. I spent a bit of time with Bert last year just before he died, and he told me how he'd never got over losing his son. How it had affected him and Joan. He reckoned she changed that day and was never the same again after. Their relationship was never the same either. He said all the colour went out of their lives after Billy was killed. Not that there's much colour to be had around the docks, but you know what I mean. I suppose you coming here today and saying what really happened just brought everything back, and I boiled over a bit. Not very professional of me.'

Ted and I rose from our seats, with Ted the first to speak. 'We understand, don't we, Harry?'

'Yes. And I am truly sorry for my part in Billy's death, and for not coming forward earlier.'

Placing his chair under the table, the sergeant spoke again. 'Traditionally, it would be our job to go and speak to the parents about what you've told me today. But, under the circumstances, and with you leaving for army training in the next few days, I'm happy to let you speak to Joan directly. However, I'm going to insist on being there as well. She's been through enough already. If I'm there when you speak to her, she'll have the benefit of having a friendly face and the police in attendance at the same time.' Pausing, his expression took on a more authoritative look. 'That's not an option by the way. Either I come with you, or I go on my own and you'll need to make some other arrangement. Although, I doubt very much once she knows the truth whether she'll want to speak to you at all. Are we agreed?'

Offering my hand, I nodded. 'Of course. I know it won't be easy, and I'm certainly not expecting her to forgive me, but I do need to clear my conscience as you said. And no matter how hard it is for her to hear; I think she deserves to know the truth. Like I said, I'm only ashamed it has taken this long for me to gain the courage to speak up.'

'Perhaps you'd like to telephone me later this afternoon to confirm a suitable time for us to go,' he replied, shaking my hand firmly. 'I don't think any of us see any benefit in allowing things to drag on, especially with you going away soon.'

Holding out his hand, Ted replied, 'I'll call you if that's all right, Sergeant. Harry doesn't have ready access to a telephone, and I have one in my office.'

'Of course. I look forward to hearing from you.'

Walking away from the police station towards his car, Ted put his arm around my shoulder.

'Well, that's the worst part over.'

I looked at him quizzically. 'Really? I'm not sure about that. I've got to speak to Mrs White yet, and I'm certainly not relishing that conversation.'

'Of course, and you're right to say it won't be easy. But you've made a start and that's the important thing.'

'If you say so.'

As we took our seats in the car, Ted turned to me and smiled.

'I can see why our Irene thinks so much of you, Harry. You've got integrity, and that counts for a lot, especially in these uncertain times.'

Taking a deep breath, I nodded my appreciation at his comment.

I liked Ted. He was kind and generous, but also had a depth of character about him I admired. I could see why Irene loved and respected him so much. I felt proud to have been accepted so readily into their family. If only I could have spoken so openly with my own father, how different our relationship might have been. All young boys need a male role model to nurture and inspire them as they grow towards adulthood, and Ted was providing that support and encouragement in a way my own father never had.

'We'll stick by you, lad. You're part of the family now and that's what families do. Like we've already agreed, what you did was bloody stupid, but you're owning up to it and looking to set things straight. I can't criticise you for that, none of us can. Irene chose you because she saw something special in you, and from what I've seen and heard over the past few weeks I'm inclined to agree with her. Not everyone would have chosen the path you have, joining up and heading off to war, especially after only being married for a short while. I respect you for that. Honesty and bravery are rare traits these days, Harry, but you've proved you have them both, even if you have made a few mistakes along the way.'

I felt tears of gratitude sting my eyes. 'Thank you, Ted, that means a lot, especially coming from you.'

He grinned. 'Don't get too carried away with yourself, son. I might be proud of you for coming clean, but I'm certainly not impressed by what you did, even though you were only youngsters at the time.'

'I know, neither am I.'

As the car's engine shuddered into life, Ted gripped the steering wheel. 'Right, let's get you home before our Irene thinks they've locked the two of us up. Do you want me to come with you again when you speak to Billy's mother?'

'No thanks. Irene wants to be there, and I think I'd like that too. And of course, that police sergeant will be with us as well.'

'That's fine with me. You and Irene give me a day and a time you want to go, and I'll arrange it with the sergeant when I call him later.'

We sat in silence for much of the journey home, both lost in thought about our earlier conversation with the police and of the one still to come with Mrs White. As we pulled up outside the cottage, I invited Ted in for a cup of tea.

'No, you're all right, lad, I'll be off home. Betty will want to know how we got on, as no doubt will your Irene. I'll leave you to fill her in on that by yourself.'

He was right of course, with Irene quizzing me over every detail of our earlier exchange with the sergeant. We agreed we would ask Ted to arrange for us to speak with Mrs White a couple of days later. This proved opportune, with the army also contacting me to say I was due to leave for training at the weekend.

As we lay in bed that night, holding each other in a gentle embrace, I suddenly felt an overwhelming sense of fear wash over me.

'What's the matter, Harry, are you all right?' Irene asked, as a chill ran down my spine causing my body to shiver involuntarily.

'I'm okay, just going to miss you, that's all.'

Kissing my neck, she replied, 'I know. I feel the same way too.'

'It all made sense when I first said I wanted to join the army, but now, with you here in my arms, I'm not so sure. Have we done the right thing do you think?'

'Of course, I don't want to see you go but, as you said, if you hadn't volunteered they would probably come for you soon anyway. Dad thinks they'll be introducing conscription next if enough men don't come forward voluntarily. Hopefully it won't be for long though, and then we'll be together again, just you and me in our little home. That's what I hang on to anyway, as the alternative is too awful to consider. Promise me you'll come back, Harry.'

I laughed and pulled her into me. 'Why wouldn't I with this beautiful body waiting for me.'

Pushing back slightly, she looked me in the eye. 'I'm serious. I can't imagine my life without you.'

'I'm serious too, and not just about you having a beautiful body. I don't want to be out there fighting any longer than I have to, but if I don't go and do my bit, then what? The bloody Kaiser and his lot will just keep going until they've taken over the world.'

Snuggling back into me, she kissed my neck again. 'I know, you're right. I just… you know.'

'I do, and I promise I'll do my best not to get shot.'

'Don't even say that, it's too horrid to think about.' Slipping her hand down to my thigh she whispered in my ear, 'Let's change the subject.' The next few minutes were spent in silence, our bodies moving together, locked in a loving embrace as our passion reached a new intensity.

As we lay together in the afterglow of our lovemaking, I stored the memory of this precious time away in my mind to draw on in the weeks to come. I knew, once I was with my troop, the best I could hope for in the way of company would be my rifle and an army officer shouting orders at me.

Whilst I was apprehensive about joining up with the other recruits, my more immediate concern was for the meeting I'd arranged with Joan White. I knew it wasn't going to be an easy conversation but one I needed to have. I just prayed she would listen to what I had to say. As for gaining any semblance of forgiveness, certainly in the immediate future, I recognised that as a hope too far.

Lying in the dark listening to Irene's gentle breathing my concerns about the next few days abated a little. Yes, I had some very real issues to address, but I also had much to be thankful for. And no treasure could be greater than my beautiful wife resting peacefully beside me. I kissed her lightly on the forehead and allowed sleep to draw me into its equally tender embrace.

The two of us spent the next day preparing for my departure to join my troop. Whilst we kept busy and attempted to maintain a lightness in our conversation, the truth was we were both feeling the pressure, not only about my going away but also about our meeting with Mrs White.

The next day, Ted had arranged for the sergeant to meet us at Mum's house, a few doors down from Mrs White's. It was good to see Mum and Edith again and to fill them in on the detail of my leaving at the weekend. Mum, especially, found it hard to settle with the thought of me going to war.

Her eyes brimmed with tears as she took my hand. 'We're going to miss you, son, aren't we, Edith?'

Smiling, Edith joked, 'You might be, I can't wait to see the back of him, isn't that right, Irene? You and I can get up to all sorts once he's gone.'

Irene laughed. 'Oh yes, we'll be partying every night.'

I looked at the two of them and grinned. 'Nice to know who your friends are.'

Edith shook her head. 'You idiot, of course we'll miss you. And don't you worry about Irene, we'll look after her all right, won't we, Mum?'

Wiping away a tear with her handkerchief, Mum nodded. 'We certainly will. Between the two of us and Betty and Ted she'll want for nothing, especially company. You're welcome here anytime, day or night, but you know that already I hope?'

Irene smiled, emotion getting the better of her as the reality of my imminent departure took hold. 'I do, Florence, thank you.'

Mum moved across and rubbed her arm. 'Now you're married to our Harry, why don't you call me Mum? I look on you as another daughter in our family, and I know Edith thinks of you as a sister as well, don't you, love?'

'Absolutely. Although a bit of a crazy one for marrying my brother.'

Laughing, Irene agreed. 'You might be right there, Edith. And thank you, Florence... I mean, Mum.'

As we were talking there was a knock at the front door.

'I'll get it, it'll be the policeman. Ted said to meet us here.'

Opening the door, I was greeted by the sergeant, the silver buttons on his jacket glinting in the morning sun.

'Good morning, Harry.'

Before I could reply, a voice spoke out from behind me. It was Irene.

'Good morning. You must be Sergeant Taylor?'

'That's right. And presumably you're Mrs Thompson?'

'Correct. It's nice to meet you. Thank you for agreeing to come with us, I know...'

Shaking his head, the sergeant interrupted. 'No need to thank me, I'd already said I would be here. This is a serious matter, and with your husband's confession as to what actually happened that day, I would need to be there to hear what he and Joan have to say to one another anyway. Harry might have told you; my wife and I were on friendly terms with the Whites following their Billy's death. Our son was born about the same time.'

'Yes, he did mention that.'

Interjecting, he nodded in the direction of Mrs White's house. 'Well, if you're both ready.'

'I'll just get my coat,' I replied, moving back into the house. 'I'll get yours as well, Irene.'

'We're off now, Mum,' I said, entering the living room.

'I hope it's not too difficult.' Mum put her arm around Edith and smiled. 'We'll be thinking of you both.'

'Thanks, see you later.'

As I retraced my steps to the front door, I felt a nervous chill run through me. Had I done the right thing in owning up, or should I have stayed quiet as Karl had demanded? It was too late now, whatever my misgivings. I had opened a pandora's box and there was no closing it again. Irene and I followed the sergeant in silence as we made our way towards Mrs White's house. My feet felt like lead as I forced myself up the street.

Sensing my reticence, Irene took my hand and squeezed it. 'Don't worry, Harry, I'm here. You're doing the right thing. I know you feel guilty and scared, but it *was* an accident. Neither of you meant to hurt Billy. Just remember that.'

I forced a smile.

Turning to face us as we arrived outside Mrs White's house, the sergeant paused momentarily before speaking. His tone measured and authoritative.

'Right. Let me introduce ourselves as a party and then, presuming she's happy to hear what you have to say, I'll let you do the talking once we're inside. Take your time and don't rush. Remember, this will be the first time Joan will have heard any of this, or at least *this* version of what happened. You have to give her time to absorb it. God knows how she'll react, or what she'll say to you, but that's part of the reason I'm here. So don't be getting into an argument with her, do you hear?'

I hung my head in shame as the events of that fateful day came rushing back to haunt me. 'Argue with her. Why would I argue with her? All I want to do is say sorry.'

'Maybe argue was the wrong word, but you know what I mean.'

I nodded my understanding as he knocked on the faded brown wooden door. I took a sharp intake of breath as it opened, and Joan White's eyes met with mine. There was a look of sadness in her gaze. A lock of hair from the bun on top of her head had come loose and hung limply across her face. Pushing it to one side she acknowledged our presence with a nod of her head and waited for one of us to speak.

'Good morning, Joan.'

Forcing a smile, she turned to the sergeant.

'Morning, John.' Pausing to wipe her hands down the front of her grubby cream apron, she tilted her head towards Irene and I. 'I was expecting you, but you didn't mention anything about company. Certainly not him.' Looking directly at Irene, she continued. 'You must be Irene. I've seen you come and go from time to time. And Flo has mentioned you an' all. She said you're a nice lass, bright, with a bit about you.' Turning to fix her gaze on me once more, she continued. 'Mind, you can't be that bright if you've married him. He told you about my Billy did he, and what the two of them did? Like his dad this one, a bad lot beneath that smile of his. I feel sorry for Flo, always have, having to put up with Alf and his drinking for all those years, and then for her son to turn out to be trouble an' all.' Grinning sardonically at me, she continued. 'Still, I hear you've joined up, off to fight the Germans with the others. With any luck you'll run into that so-called friend of yours, and that'll be the last we'll see of the two of you. I just hope…'

Taking a step forward, Sergeant Taylor interrupted. 'Now calm yourself, Joan, the lad has come here to tell you something. Maybe you should let him speak before you say anything else.'

Pausing to draw breath, she looked at the officer again.

'If it's about my Billy, it'd better be the truth this time. I've never believed what they said in the past.'

Sergeant Taylor spoke again. 'Would it be better if we came inside? I'm sure you don't want all the neighbours hearing what he has to say.'

Stepping back, she gesticulated for us to enter. 'Probably best.'

As we moved into the house, she turned to Irene. 'I apologise for what I said just now. I'm sure you're a lovely girl, it's just…'

Interjecting, Irene smiled. 'No need to apologise, Mrs White. None of this can have been easy for you. And to lose your husband recently as well can only have added to your sorrow.'

The two of them walked together into the dining room with the sergeant and I following behind. As I moved through the parlour, I noticed a bundle of what appeared to be coloured rags on a small table. Pausing briefly to look again, I realised they were baby clothes. On top of them was a bible with the name *Billy* written across its red cover. Next to the clothes was a baby's rattle and a small note that read, *Forever in our hearts.* It was a shrine to Billy. It suddenly hit me how challenging the following conversation was going to be. Far from coming to terms with the death of her baby son, she was clearly holding on to so much more than just his memory. She might not be able to deny his passing, but she certainly hadn't fully accepted it. Would anything I was about to say help the healing process or would it simply add further anguish to her already broken heart? As I entered the dining room, I sent up a silent prayer asking God to bless what I was about to say and, more especially, that it would be received in the heartfelt way it was intended. I realised, this was no longer about appeasing my feelings of guilt, but more about bringing some closure to a woman who had spent years fighting a losing battle with her unmitigated grief.

Like most of the other houses in the dockland area, Mrs White's was in need of improvement and redecoration. But now, with her husband also gone and little money coming in, the chances of that happening were remote to say the least. The added years of pain at losing Billy were also reflected in the décor and general untidiness of the room. It felt unloved, reflecting the sadness that had filled the house for so many years. The brown striped wallpaper was peeling from the walls and the rug on the floor was threadbare to the point there were more holes in it than there was floor covering. There was a battered armchair by the fireplace. The stuffing in the armrest was hanging out and the seat was almost as frayed as the rug. The hearth was full of soot and clinker from a previous fire and looked as though it hadn't been cleaned for some time. There were holes in the curtains and the nets were stained yellow from the years of smoking by Bert White.

Embarrassed by how sad in appearance the house looked, Mrs White proffered an apology.

'Excuse the mess. I haven't been too well of late, and things have got on top of me a bit. You know what it's like.'

Irene leapt to her defence. 'Oh, please don't apologise, our house is just the same. I'm always telling Harry to clear up after himself, but he never does. And then after a few days I don't know where to start. Isn't that right, Harry?'

Acknowledging her attempt to alleviate Mrs White's discomfiture, I nodded my agreement.

'Absolutely.' I laughed. 'She nags at me all the time, and we've only been married a short while.'

Accepting we were trying to be kind, but also feeling patronised, her demeanour stiffened again.

'John says you've got something tell me?'

I took a step forward, distancing myself a little from Sergeant Taylor and Irene. This was *my* story, and I didn't want them to share any of the blame for what I was about to say, certainly not my precious wife.

'It's about what happened on the day Billy died.'

Leaning forward and taking a nervous breath, she grasped the back of a chair next to the dark stained dining table.

'And?'

I glanced at Irene and the sergeant before continuing. 'The truth is, we did start the pram rolling down the hill.' I noticed her grip tighten on the chair. 'Karl said we should get you back for shouting at us for playing football outside your house.

And before I knew it, he'd pulled the block clear of the wheel, telling me to shout to you that the pram was moving. He said he would grab it before it went too far. But he fell over, and the pram picked up speed, and... and, well, the rest of it you know.'

I swallowed hard and shook my head as an unmitigated sense of revulsion and guilt gripped my being. 'I am truly, truly sorry for what happened, and especially that we didn't admit to our part in it at the time. We were young and scared of what might happen to us.' I felt tears of remorse sting my eyes. 'Please, Mrs White, you must believe me. I am so sorry. Sorry that we lied, and sorry beyond words about what happened to Billy.'

I stared ahead as my words hung in the air before fully registering with her. As hate and tears filled her eyes she screamed. I had never heard a scream like it, not even from my mother at her most fearful during one of Dad's violent attacks. It came from deep within, displaying so much more than her obvious misery and pain. It was guttural and raw, exhibiting not only grief, but also her outrage and loathing for me, and for what Karl and I had done.

Letting go of the chair she lunged at me. 'I knew it. You killed my son and never had the guts to admit it. I'll sodding do for you now.'

As I put my hands up to protect myself, Sergeant Taylor stepped between us, placing his arms tightly around my would-be assailant.

'That's enough, Joan, stop it now. Take a breath.'

Shouting and sobbing at the same time, she continued her rant towards me, fighting to get free from the officer's grip.

'But he killed my Billy. You heard him. Arrest him. He should hang for what he and that German boy did.' Managing to release one of her arms, she reached out to slap me. 'Do you hear? You should hang for killing my boy, and even that's not punishment enough for what the two of you did. I hope when you get to France you get shot and die, Harry Thompson, and then your mother can know what it's like to lose a son. Do you hear me? I hope you get killed out there, I hope you die.'

Irene moved behind me and touched my back in an act of caring and reassurance. Grateful though I was for her support, all I could feel at that moment was an overwhelming sense of sorrow and shame. Not only for what Karl and I had done but, more especially, for this poor woman stood in front of me who we had allowed to flounder in such unutterable suffering and misery for so many years.

Unable to speak, I watched as she collapsed into Sergeant Taylor's arms, her sobbing loud and unrestrained. Turning to Irene and I, he motioned towards the door.

'I think it might be better if you two left. There's no point in you being here any longer. I'll stay with Joan. I've got your statement and will go through it with her when she's had a chance to calm down. If you stay here any longer now you've said your piece, it'll only upset her all over again. So, go on, be on your way. I'll call into your mother's when I leave.'

I considered apologising again but thought about what the sergeant had said. He was right. Any more wittering from me would only cause further grief. For now, Irene and I leaving appeared the best idea.

We both nodded our acceptance of his suggestion and left the room without speaking. As we made our way back through the parlour, I pointed towards the pile of baby clothes.

'Look at that, Irene. She's made a shrine to Billy. God, I feel awful.'

Squeezing my arm, she pushed me towards the door. 'There's nothing more you can say or do, Harry. You've told her the truth. All we can do now is pray that what you've said might bring her some sort of closure. Clearly, that won't be today, but maybe over time.'

As we stepped into the street another howl of grief resonated from the dining room.

'I just hope I haven't made things worse.'

Closing the front door behind us, Irene looked at me ruefully. 'I'm not sure things could get any worse for that poor lady.'

Taking Irene's hand, the two of us made our way back to Mum's in silence.

Chapter Eighteen

The next couple of days proved a strange mix of sadness and apprehension for all of us. Irene and I tried to avoid talking about our time with Mrs White, and in how she had reacted to my confession. Of course, we had to relay the story of what had happened to our families. Fortunately, they were all supportive and encouraged us not to focus on it any more than we needed to, especially with me leaving to join my troop in less than forty-eight hours.

Whilst I knew I had done the right thing in signing on, I still retained a feeling of regret at leaving Irene so soon after our marriage. Sensing my emotional unrest, and accepting we had both been a little distant over recent days, Irene attempted to reassure me all would be well as we sat at our kitchen table eating breakfast together on the morning of my departure.

'I'm sorry if things have felt a bit strained over the past few days, Harry. None of this has been easy for any of us. But I want you to know I'll be okay, and that you're not to worry about me. It's yourself you should be thinking about.'

'Thank you. I'm sorry too.' I smiled. 'But of course, I'll be thinking about you. As for me, I'll be fine. After all, I'll have the other lads and our troop commander to keep an eye on me.'

Irene laughed. 'And I'll have my parents, Edith, and your mum to look after me. I know which I'd prefer out of those two options.'

Looking at her over the rim of my teacup, I grinned. 'Fair point. Even so, I'll be thinking of you every day.'

Struggling to smile as tears filled her eyes, she said, 'And you don't think I'll be doing the same?'

I reached out towards her. 'Now come on, girl, we agreed no tears, remember?'

'Oh, don't worry, these are tears of joy, not sadness.'

Taking a piece of bread from her plate, I laughed. 'Thank you very much. Just for that you can go hungry.'

A brief silence followed as we gazed lovingly into each other's eyes. Breathing in deeply I caught the faint aroma of Irene's perfume.

'God, I'm going to miss you.'

Closing her eyes to conceal her tears and secure this moment in her memory, she whispered, 'I love you, Harry Thompson.'

'You too.'

Struggling to contain her emotions, Irene got to her feet.

'We better get a move on; Dad will be here soon.'

Acknowledging her attempt not to crumble completely, I pushed back my chair.

'You're right, I'll get my case.'

As I left the room there was a knock at the front door. It was Ted. Dressed in a long grey overcoat, matching trilby hat, and with his black leather shoes gleaming, he looked every inch the successful businessman.

'Good morning, Harry. I know I'm a few minutes early but, better safe than sorry.'

'Morning, Ted. Betty not with you?'

'I dropped her at your mother's. She's happy to walk to the dock with her and Edith. I wasn't sure how much room you might need in the car.'

I laughed. 'That's kind, but I've just got the one case, so we should be fine. Mind, if I'd have packed everything Irene suggested I take, there wouldn't have been room for any of us in the car. I had to remind her the army will be supplying my trousers, shirts, and socks for the foreseeable future.'

I felt a prod in my back.

'I heard that. Morning, Dad. Thanks for this.'

'My pleasure. Your mother still insisted it would have been better if you'd both stayed at ours last night, to save you rushing this morning. I tried to tell her, as gently as I could, that you'd probably both appreciate a last night on your own, what with you being newly married and all. She told me I had a mucky mind.'

I winked at him and smiled. 'That was very thoughtful of you, Ted.'

Blushing, Irene turned and walked towards the kitchen.

'I'll finish making your sandwiches while you bring your case down.'

'Sorry, lad, I didn't mean to embarrass her.'

'You didn't, but it's still early days and you are her dad after all.'

'Fair point. Now, is there anything I can put in the car for you while she's making those sandwiches?'

'No, you're fine. Do you want to come in while I get my case?'

'That's all right, I'll wait in the car. Give you both a bit more time together. It's going to be a tough day for our Irene. She'll have plenty of time to spend with us after you've gone. Anyway, it's a lovely day, so ten minutes sitting in the sun won't do me any harm, even if it is a bit chilly. I always think of mid-October as the start of winter. Take your time son, no hurry.'

I watched as he pulled on his brown leather driving gloves and headed back to the car. It had obviously been cleaned especially for the occasion with its black paintwork and chrome headlights glinting brightly in the morning sun.

Those next few minutes flew by as Irene and I gathered everything together ready to leave. I held open her powder-blue overcoat as she slipped her arms into the sleeves and placed a matching blue hat with fur trim on her head. They had been a gift from her parents as part of her wedding trousseau. I watched as she buttoned up the coat, thinking how beautiful she looked.

Catching my gaze, she stopped and looked at me quizzically.

'What is it? Why are you looking at me like that? Have I done something wrong?'

'Far from it. In fact, just the opposite. I was thinking how perfect you look. I'll carry this picture of you in mind every day while I'm away.'

Not wanting to give way to her emotions again, she tutted.

'Oh, stop it. There's nothing special about me, you're just being silly.'

Feeling tears sting the back of my eyes, I drew a breath. 'If only you knew just how precious you are to me.'

Stepping forward, I took her in my arms and pulled her close.

'This isn't goodbye. I'll be back before you know it. It's just for a while, until we sort those Germans out. Even so, I doubt I'll be home in time for Christmas.'

Kissing my neck, she leant up and whispered in my ear, 'There'll be other Christmases for us to enjoy. For now, just know I love you. Never forget that, Harry. Even on the toughest days, please know I'm carrying you in my heart and am praying for you.'

Pulling back to look her in the eye, I nodded. 'And I'll be praying for you too, every day until I hold you in my arms again.' I drew her back towards me and kissed her, my tongue reaching deep into her mouth to emphasise the passion I felt for her. Our bodies melded together in a loving and intimate farewell. For all our promises to each other that this parting would be brief, we both knew, in war, there are no guarantees. And whilst neither of us could countenance the thought of never seeing the other again, the possibility of it happening couldn't be entirely discounted. With one last kiss, I stepped back and smiled, slipping my coat on as I did so.

'Come on then, Mrs Thompson, we better be going, or your dad will wonder where we are.'

Chewing her lip to stop herself from crying, Irene took a handkerchief from her coat pocket and dabbed her eyes. 'I'm ready.' Holding a neatly folded pack of sandwiches out towards me, she grinned. 'And don't forget these. It might be the only proper food you get for the next few weeks.'

'I hope not. I won't be much good to the army fighting on an empty stomach, will I?'

Opening the door, I tucked the sandwiches under my arm and picked up the suitcase. 'Here we go then.'

Sensitive to our situation, Ted encouraged us to sit together in the back of the car, rather than have me in the front alongside him, as would normally be the case. We gratefully accepted his suggestion; quickly moving closer together to ward off the early morning autumnal chill.

It didn't take long to reach the meeting point at the docklands the army had designated for all new recruits to attend. Betty, Mum, and Edith were already there waiting for us. Betty was dressed in a full-length fur coat with matching hat and a pair of black leather gloves. Mum and Edith were equally well wrapped up, but not as stylishly as Betty. Mum had on her dark-brown winter's coat, which looked smart enough but had clearly seen a few years of wear already. She wore a light-brown woollen cloche hat, with a similar-coloured scarf and a pair of knitted green gloves. Edith also wore a cloche bucket-style hat which was dark blue and matched her winter's coat with its black velvet collar. I smiled at the memory of her getting this outfit a couple of years previously as part of her Christmas present. She was thrilled at the time, but today, as a young woman, was fully aware of her slightly less than fashionable appearance, especially when standing next to some of the other young women who had come to say goodbye to their brothers, boyfriends, and husbands.

There were several ships in dock, waiting to be unloaded or being prepared to sail. We could see them standing proud above the buildings and warehouses set around the dockyards themselves. Men were coming and going as they started or ended their shifts, depending on which end of the day they were working. All were dressed in the customary dark suit, waistcoat, and flat cap. I smiled inwardly, recalling how often I had witnessed my own father dressed this way as he left for a day's work at the shipyard. Those who could afford them also wore overcoats and woollen gloves, and most had scarves wrapped about their necks to keep out the immediate cold. Despite the sunshine there was a stiff and chilly breeze, causing families to huddle together as they waited for the army truck to arrive and transport us recruits to the training camp.

'Thanks for coming, Mum. And you, Edith.' Laughing, I added, 'I would have understood if you'd decided to stay at home.'

'Don't be daft,' Mum said, rubbing her hands together and shaking her head. 'What sort of mother would I be, letting my lad go off to war without wishing him a proper goodbye.'

'And what about you, Edith, are you here to wish me a proper goodbye as well?'

'Not really,' she said with a laugh. 'I'm just here to make sure you go.'

'Charming, I'm sure. I love you too.'

Irene stood back a little, next to Ted and Betty. I was aware she'd done this to give me time with Mum and Edith; also, to control her emotions better when the time to say goodbye finally arrived. We didn't have to wait long. A few minutes later a large army truck pulled up. It was open-topped with a tarpaulin sheet stretched over the metal stanchions on each side of the vehicle to act as cover and protect us from the elements. A cheery-looking sergeant with a clipboard tucked under his arm jumped out of the truck to greet us.

'Good morning, everyone. A good turnout I see. Now, you mums, dads, and families who've come to say goodbye to your men, don't you be worrying about them. Me and Lord Kitchener will be looking after them from today, and we'll treat them like our own.' A nervous laugh went up as he continued. 'So come on, you boys, let's be having you.' Moving to the back of the truck, he dropped down the tailgate and held his clipboard aloft. 'In a line here if you please so I can check your names on my list.'

Suddenly, it was happening, I was off to join the fight. There was no turning back now. I hugged Mum and Edith.

'Love you, Mum, and you, sis. Look after Mum for me. She'll need you more than ever with me away.'

Edith laughed. 'How do you think we've managed over the past few weeks since you and Irene have been married?'

'You know what I mean.'

She leant forward and kissed me. 'Of course. And don't you worry about us, we'll be fine. Love you, Harry.'

'You too.' I moved to hug Mum and felt her become stiff in my arms; not because she didn't want to be embraced but rather because her emotions were getting the better of her and she didn't want to let me down by crying.

'You take care, Harry, lad. We'll watch out for Irene; don't you worry about that.'

I kissed her on the cheek and felt her relax a little as she put her arms around me. 'Love you, Mum.'

'You too, son. I'm so proud of you, we all are.' Pulling back a little she looked me in the eye. 'You look after yourself, do you hear? And come back to us in one piece.' She smiled. 'I want to be a grandma, so you'll need to be here to help Irene with that one, all right?'

I laughed. 'Sounds pretty good to me.' Pulling her into me again, I whispered in her ear, 'Thanks for watching out for

Irene as well. I know Betty and Ted are here, and that she's their daughter, but she's got a soft spot for you and Edith.'

'And we love her as well.'

Kissing her again and rubbing her arm, I turned to face Irene and her parents. Ted put out his hand and smiled broadly.

'Take care, Harry, lad.' Glancing at Irene, he continued. 'We'll look out for this one, don't you worry about that.'

Shaking his hand firmly, I smiled. 'I know you will, Ted, and I'm grateful for that. And thanks again for everything you've done for us already. The wedding, the honeymoon in Hastings, and of course the cottage, it's more than we could have hoped for. Having somewhere to call our own so early on has been… well, fantastic. We couldn't have had a better start, and so much of that is down to you and Betty.'

'As I've said already, when Irene chose you, she chose well. Betty and I are proud to have you as part of the family, especially after your bravery in speaking up about that other matter. So you just go and do what you have to do and bring yourself back safe and sound.' Turning to look at Betty, he smiled. 'I heard what your mother said just now, and I think my Betty here wouldn't mind being a grandmother either, would you, love?'

Blushing slightly, she took my arm. 'That's up to Harry and Irene when the time is right. But yes, it would be nice. Goodbye, Harry, come back safely to us.'

'Thank you, Betty, I'll certainly try. And thank you too for all you've done in making Mum, Edith, and I such a welcome part of your family, it means a lot, especially to me.'

'We are all one family now, and happy to be so.'

I leant forward and kissed her on the cheek before turning to Irene. As I did so, the sergeant came up behind me.

'Come on, lad, the war'll be over if you take much longer saying your goodbyes.'

'Sorry, Sergeant, I'm just coming.'

'Well be quick, most of the others are already on board.'

I moved to take Irene in my arms for one last time. Pulling her tightly into me, I kissed her on the cheek, recognising this wasn't the time for anything more passionate. 'I love you, Irene Thompson, don't you forget that.'

Tears filled her eyes as she forced a smile. 'I love you so much, Harry, and...' Unable to finish her sentence she gave way to her emotions. Ted put his arm around her as the sergeant called out again.

'Last time of asking, son, let's be having you.'

I looked on as the tears ran down Irene's cheeks. Ted gestured towards the lorry.

'Go on, Harry, off you go. She'll be fine, we'll look after her.'

Overcome myself, I mouthed once more to Irene that I loved her and turned away before my own tears fell. The sergeant was stood by the lorry, clipboard in hand as I arrived.

'Oh, so you've decided to join us then, have you? Thompson, I'm presuming is it?'

'Yes Sergeant, Harry Thompson, and I'm sorry if I've held you up. It's just...'

Interjecting, he lifted my case and threw it on the back of the truck. 'I know, lad. It's not easy saying goodbye, unless it's to my old lady, and then I can't wait. She gives me more earache than a German bomb going off. Now, on you get.' He laughed. 'And don't be thinking I'll be lifting your case off at the other end for you either. It's only 'cause I'm a soft bugger that I'm helping you now. After today, you'll be carrying a lot more than a suitcase, and, like I say, there'll be no more help from me.'

Tucking the clipboard under his arm and giving me a hearty shove from behind I found myself elevated up on to the truck. With little light finding its way on board through the tarpaulin I peered through the gloom at the other faces sat around on the wooden bench seating. This was going to be a very different journey to the one I'd just enjoyed in Ted's car with Irene by my side. The sergeant closed the tailgate and made his way back to the cab at the front of the truck. We all gripped the seating or metal stanchions to balance ourselves as the engine burst into life and the truck leapt forward. Fortunately, being one of the last on board, I was sat near the opening at the back and was able to see Irene and the family for one last time as we pulled away. I shouted goodbye, but they couldn't hear me above the noise of the engine revving up as it changed gear and moved further down the road. I could just see Irene's head buried in Ted's shoulder. I felt an immediate pang of sorrow at having left her so upset. As I sat contemplating life without my beautiful wife, the man next to me nudged me in the ribs.

'She'll get over it. Mine didn't even come to say goodbye.' He laughed. 'Mind, she has just had twins a couple of weeks ago, so I suppose she's got that as an excuse. To be honest, I'm pleased to be away. The little bleeders cry all day and night. I ain't had a good night's kip since they arrived. You got any kids?'

'No. I've only been married a few weeks.'

'What, and you signed up for this war malarkey when you could be at home getting your end away?' He winked and slapped me on the back. 'I'd have had a few more months' home comforts if that'd been me, if you get my meaning?'

'She knew I was joining up before we got married.'

'And she let you go?' Laughing again, he continued. 'Sounds a bit odd to me, unless she's got some old boyfriend or other ready to jump in and keep the bed warm while you're away.'

Still struggling with having just said goodbye and knowing that being unfaithful would be the last thing on Irene's mind, I reacted.

'You keep your dirty thoughts to yourself. Irene and I love each other, and neither of us would want anyone else, so you can just shut up.'

'All right, mate, no need to get narky, I was only having a bit of fun. I didn't mean anything.' Recognising he might have gone too far, he apologised. 'Look, I'm sorry, okay? I guess it's a bit of a strange time for all of us, yeah? Like I say, I didn't mean anything by it.' Attempting to win me over, he offered his hand. 'My name's Arthur, Arthur Brown, but my friends call me Half Pint.'

Not sure if I was doing the right thing, but equally not wanting to fall out with anyone before we'd even arrived at the training camp, I took his hand and shook it.

'Harry Thompson.' I shook my head. 'I'm sure there's a simple answer but, Half Pint?'

He laughed. 'Yeah, I suppose it does sound odd. Like I said, my real name's Arthur Brown, but if you think about it, it sounds a bit like *half a brown*, get it? So, half a brown becomes half pint. And, seeing as I'm a bit on the short side an' all, Half Pint sounds about right.' Shaking my hand again, he grinned. 'Pleased to meet you, Harry. I think you and me are gonna get on.'

I wasn't so sure but smiled politely as I withdrew my hand.

Like most new recruits we were expecting a couple of months training before heading to the front. The bulk of this would be carried out in France near Étaples, a coastal fishing port around fifteen miles from Boulogne. This was also a base for the lads who were sick or had been wounded on the front. Here, they would either be patched up and sent back out to fight or, if their wounds were serious enough, sent back home to Blighty. Arriving in Étaples after only a couple of days' acclimatisation into army life was a real shock to the system and left none of us in any doubt as to what we'd signed up for. The base camp at Étaples could hold anything up to a hundred thousand soldiers at any one time. The hands-on physical training was carried out nearby, around the local sand-dunes known as The Bull Ring training camp. Conditions from the off were tough and we quickly learned we were not just here to bolster the numbers. We had entered a real hell-hole of a place that grew more horrific and challenging with every passing day. Soldiers were transported back from the front with appalling injuries caused by bullets, bayonetting, and shelling from the bigger guns. They also recounted equally chilling tales of the conditions they'd faced in the trenches and what we could expect when it came our turn to face the enemy.

Even at this early stage of the conflict, life expectancy in the heat of battle was little more than six weeks. And with winter just around the corner, life on the front line was becoming more uncomfortable by the day. Heavy rain would often fill the trenches and leave soldiers wading through mud up to their knees. Equally as bad were the latrines. These were little more than large holes dug in the ground with boards across them to support you when you squatted down. They were also subject to flooding on a fairly regular basis as well. One poor lad who'd been on sanitary duties when the rain came told us of his experience in attempting to keep the latrines in good condition for his troop. He described how, after fighting a losing battle against the rising water, he'd gone to report the problem to an officer and had been shot. Even with his arm ripped apart by gunfire he still considered himself lucky. He said another soldier standing next to him had lost the side of his face in the same barrage of bullets and had died on the spot.

For all Arthur had irritated me on the truck with his teasing about Irene, we soon formed an early bond of friendship during those first few weeks of training. His ready sense of humour, even on some of the toughest of days, helped lift the mood in our unit, and the name Half Pint was frequently on the lips of those seeking some encouragement or a funny story to raise their spirits. He would often instigate a sing-song amongst the lads as well with, 'When Irish Eyes Are Smiling' or 'You Made Me Love You' being amongst the favourites of the day. Another popular choice was, 'It's a Long Way to Tipperary'. Whilst many of us would dream of life at home and question our decision in joining up, Arthur would always offer up a joke or reason for us to be grateful for being where we were.

'I don't know what you blokes are moaning about,' he would say. 'You wouldn't be getting sausage, fried potatoes and bread and butter for your breakfast at home, would you? And all washed down with a nice cup of coffee or Rosie Lee. And, we don't have to wash up neither. I'll tell you what, I've never had it so good.'

'But our old ladies ain't threatening to blow our heads off like Fritz, are they, Half Pint?' one of the other lads would reply.

Arthur would laugh and shake his head. 'Well, you obviously ain't had an argy-bargy with my missus then, have you? Honest, a bullet in the head would be quicker and a lot less painful than what she puts me through when she gets going, I can tell you. If you stuck her up against the Kaiser, I reckon he'd surrender in five minutes. She'd soon sort him out.'

And so it would continue, until he'd convinced us that maybe life wasn't so bad in Étaples after all, despite many of the boys having to sleep in tents rather than huts. There always appeared a shortage of proper accommodation for us new recruits, especially when the wounded returned from the front. They would be allotted the huts and better facilities for obvious reasons but, with winter fast approaching, a tent, camp-bed, and blanket being your only defence against the wind and rain meant a decent night's sleep was often hard to come by. Even with your greatcoat thrown over you for added protection you'd still wake up feeling cold.

Whilst training in The Bull Ring was tough, nothing could have prepared us for life in the trenches themselves. I remember the day we headed out. We'd been told we were heading for the France-Belgium border to a place called Comines near Warneton, not that that meant much to us. Wherever it was, it sounded an awful long way from Irene and Canning Town.

It was now early December and the weather had taken a turn for the worse, with snow and a chill northerly wind blowing in our faces as we climbed aboard the transport that would take us to the front. Arthur, keen as ever to keep our spirits up, led another round of singing as we made our way out of Étaples. Unfortunately, the weather, coupled with our fears about what we were about to face, got the better of many of us, meaning he found precious few voices to accompany his cheery offering.

'You're a rum lot you are,' he joked; again, garnering little meaningful response from his less than enthusiastic audience.

Even the sergeant sensed our desire to be left alone with our thoughts as we journeyed towards the unknown.

'You're a good lad, Half Pint, but maybe button it for a while, eh?'

'Fair enough, sarge, I was only trying to put a smile on their ugly mugs.'

The next couple of hours were spent pretty much in silence as we made our way inexorably towards the front line. Only the throb of the lorry's engine, along with the increasing sound of gunfire and shelling broke through our thoughts as we endeavoured to focus on those we'd left behind at home. Even until a few days earlier, direct combat had still felt a distant threat; but now the fighting began to sound very close and very real. Looking out from the truck we could see the results of earlier battles all around. Trees, once standing tall and proud, now resembled little more than huge splinters poking out from the ground, their branches shattered and devoid of any life. And the earth in which they stood had become a quagmire of boggy terrain, soddened by the rain and snow. The whole area appeared to be from another world rather than the lush, vibrant countryside it had been just a few months earlier.

Wagons and handcarts lay on their sides, either blown apart by shelling or deserted because they had become stuck in the mud. Occasionally, a horse would be lying next to a wagon. They had either died from exhaustion or been shot to save them from further misery as they battled against the brown sludge which clung to their legs and hooves like glue. As our spirits began to sink at the horror of what we were witnessing, a scene came into view none of us were prepared for. Just a few yards away lay a group of dead soldiers. They were British and had clearly been shelled by heavy German artillery. There were body parts strewn across the ground; arms, legs, and heads, severed from their owners, twisted and contorted in the blood-spattered mud. Another group of soldiers were moving amongst the dead and mutilated, working to recover what they could as means of identification of the fallen.

We looked on in disbelief, none of us knowing what to say or how to respond to the carnage laid bare before us. The sergeant's voice broke through our befuddled thoughts.

'They gave their lives to protect their families and loved ones, same as we'll do, if and when the time comes. We may not have started this war, but we'll bloody well finish it. Do you hear me? And we'll sodding well win it an' all.'

A number of us raised our heads, nodding in a feeble attempt to demonstrate collective solidarity with what he was saying. Sensing our need to be convinced further, he tried again.

'You'll see worse in the days to come, lads. But remember, if you're here to witness it, it means you're still alive. And, as long as you're alive you can fight. Fight to save your mate stood beside you, fight to save yourself, and fight for the freedom of those we've left behind at home.' Pausing momentarily to look again at the field of death stretched out before us, he continued. 'I know it ain't pretty, boys, but take it in and let it act as the spur you need to keep yourself alive and going, and to fight against the bastards that did it.'

I sat upright, staring at the tableau of death and horror laid bare before me. My thoughts torn between agreeing with the sergeant's call to arms, and my greater desire to be holding Irene close to me in the safety of our home. Much as I craved the latter, I knew it couldn't happen. There was no going back. I had pledged myself to fighting for the greater good and, if only for the sake of those lying bloodied and torn apart in front of me, I had to see that commitment through.

After travelling for what seemed like an eternity, with the sights and sounds of war gaining in intensity and volume the nearer we got to the front, the lorry drew to a halt. Jumping out and opening the tailgate, the sergeant shouted up at us.

'All right, you lovely boys, let's be having you. Out you get, this is it. You've arrived at your new home for the next few weeks. Welcome to hell on earth. There's a couple of horse-drawn carriages that'll be able to take most of you the rest of the way.' He laughed. 'The rest of us'll be travelling courtesy of that other well-known nag and mode of transport, Shanks's pony.'

Arthur and I were included in the group that continued by foot. With the falling snow and thick mud wrapping itself around our boots and puttees, every step seemed to weigh us down.

'Bugger this eh, Harry. I can think of better ways to spend the day. We'll be too knackered to unpack our kit bags by the time we get there, let alone fight the bloody Germans.'

Laughing, I shook my head. 'You're not wrong there. I bet Irene's sat at home in front of the kitchen stove with a nice cup of tea in her hand deciding what to have for her tea.'

Grinning, he wiped the snow from his face. 'I'd be down The Sailor's Rest if I was at home with a nice pint in front of me; its frothy head running down the side of the glass where Bill had filled it to the top. Bloody lovely that. Nectar of the gods it is.'

As we entered the mud-filled trenches the sound and feel of war took on a new intensity. A corporal approached us as we clambered down the wooden ladder into the trench itself.

'Good to see you, boys, and your mates, we need reinforcements. We've taken a bit of a battering over the past few days.'

As he spoke a shell landed a few yards away, sending mud and debris flying into the air before crashing back down to earth and onto our helmets. The corporal shook his head. 'As you can see, the buggers are at it again. We were meant to be rushing them, but the captain says we'll leave it for today, keep our heads down and hope they run out of those bigger shells they're lobbing at us.'

Pulling a clod of earth from his collar, Arthur tilted his head to one side. 'Is it always like this?'

'Pretty much. But it does ease off a bit at night. Mind, then we send out lads to no man's land for a bit of a recce. You know, to have a look at how the barbed wire and other defences are holding up, and maybe dig a new trench if we've managed to take a bit of land from them, but that hasn't happened recently. They've been making most of the advances over the past few days.' Noticing our backpacks, he pointed towards the end of the trench. 'There's a rest area down there. You can drop your kit off and get a cuppa before the captain does his rounds. It'll be up to him what you and the others do after that. Like I say, it's good to have you here.' He laughed. 'Only hope you feel the same way in a few days' time. That's if we're all still here and haven't been blown to smithereens by Jerry.'

The next few days were indeed a steep learning curve for Arthur and me, along with the rest of the lads who'd travelled to the front with us. Three of our team didn't make it past the first full day, being shot with other members of the troop making a rush for the enemy lines the following morning. I'd never seen anything like it. The Germans had access to a large number of machine guns compared to the few available to our troops. And their superior firepower was obvious to all, as our lads went over the top that morning. The machine guns ripped through them like a knife through butter. Many of them didn't manage the first fifty yards before they were shot to ribbons by the hail of death being directed at them.

Living day in and day out in a mud- and water-filled hole was an experience in itself. Walking around bent over so as not to have your head shot off by some German sniper was something you got used to pretty quickly as well. The constant barrage of shelling, and never knowing if the next piece of shrapnel or bullet had your name on it, meant you were living on your nerves every waking hour. You got used to picking bits of debris out of your tea and food after a shell landed nearby, chucking earth and muck into the air. But the sight of one of your mates being stretchered back from the battlefield with half his head missing or an arm or a leg blown off half an hour after you'd been chatting with him over a cup of tea never got any easier.

I'd excelled at rifle skills during training and so was held back during these raids into enemy territory to provide sniper cover for our lads as they rushed forward. When the Germans showed themselves in preparation to mow our lads down, it was my job to take out as many as I could before they began firing. Trying to get a clean shot away from around a hundred yards or so in a smoke-filled battlefield while your own men zigzagged about trying to dodge the bullets and shells being thrown at them was never easy. I did take out a couple of their machine-gunners early on, and whilst it registered I was killing another soldier, I also knew I was saving the life of one or more of our own boys at the same time. I soon learned to absolve myself of any potential for guilt about taking another man's life. You understand pretty quickly, it's you or them, and that war's a dirty business with no real winners, at least not on the battlefield. It's just a bloodfest with each of the protagonists killing as many of the opposition as possible, until one side either gives in or runs out of bullets and bodies to throw into the fray. Politicians and heads of state traditionally decide the terms of victory or surrender, with the average soldier merely a pawn in the bloody game of chess their leaders are playing. All you can hope is that you're fighting for the right cause, and that God is on your side.

The worst day for me came a week after we'd arrived. Arthur and I had just finished breakfast when he got the nod to go out as a stretcher-bearer and help bring back one of our boys who had been shot. He'd gone out just before dawn to recce a particular machine-gun post Jerry had set up a couple of hundred yards away to our left. The idea being, if it was also a holding store for ammunition to use in some new offensive, we could launch a concerted attack on it before they could make their move. It seemed this lad had got himself caught up in some barbed wire a few yards out from our trench on his way back. A German sniper had spotted him and shot him. One of our officers had watched the whole event through his binoculars and could see the soldier was still alive. We needed to get him back before they saw him move and finished him off. Arthur might have been smaller than a lot of the blokes in our troop, but he was stocky and strong. It was decided that he and another lad would crawl to the fencing pulling the stretcher behind them. They would then untangle the soldier from the barbed wire and drag him back to our trench. I was chosen, along with another sniper, to position myself opposite the barbed wire and set up my rifle to provide cover for Arthur and his partner should the Germans fire on them during the rescue attempt.

Even with my greatcoat, scarf, and gloves as protection against the early morning winter chill, I still felt a bead of nervous sweat run from the inside of my helmet, down the side of my face and into the collar of my woollen khaki shirt as I settled into position, aiming my rifle towards the German line a couple of hundred yards away. I watched as Arthur and the other lad climbed the rough wooden ladder to the top of the trench, keeping themselves flat to the snow-covered ground.

'See you when you get back, Half Pint.'

'Yeah. Hopefully, we won't be long.' He laughed. 'You just make sure you shoot the right bloke with that gun of yours. I don't fancy a bullet up the jacksy from my mate, all right?'

'Now there's a thought,' I replied, tapping him on the boot as he cleared the trench.

I stared down the sight of my rifle, watching for any movement along the enemy line as the two men slithered through the frozen mud pulling the stretcher behind them. Winking at the other marksman next to me as the lads reached their wounded colleague, I took a deep and grateful breath. 'So far, so good,' I whispered. We looked on as they began to cut the wire trapping the young soldier just a few yards from safety. As the last piece of wiring holding him in place was removed, he fell to the ground. It was as Arthur moved to position him onto the stretcher that all hell broke loose around them. The Germans had obviously been aware of their actions and waited until the three of them were together before launching their assault. Knowing there would be snipers ready to fire the moment they raised their heads, they used a more brutal style of weapon in their attack, a mortar shell. In the early stages of this terrible war these crude but equally lethal weapons were still in their infancy. They would be loaded with a small bomb launched through the short, barrelled mortar by a propellant charge for distances up to a thousand yards. Not always entirely accurate once deployed, they were still guaranteed to cause maximum carnage. Exploding on impact, they would spew out their deadly contents over a concentrated area. The blast and accompanying shrapnel would rip through clothing, flesh, and bone, either killing or severely maiming all within close proximity. And so it was on this occasion.

The mortar landed within a few feet of our boys as they readied themselves for the return journey to the relative safety of our trench. As the smoke cleared, we could see all three were dead. Arthur, who was kneeling as the mortar landed, had been thrown back onto the barbed wire. Much of his head had been blown away and his left arm was hanging in shreds from his body. The other two lads lay motionless on the ground, their bodies equally badly maimed from the impact of the explosion.

In a moment of unmitigated rage at what I'd just witnessed I began to shoot indiscriminately towards the enemy line. As tears of shock, wretchedness and outrage filled my eyes I kept firing until I felt a hand press down onto my shoulder. It was the captain.

'That's enough, lad. No point in wasting ammunition. Better to save it until you can actually see the buggers.'

Having lost all sense of reason momentarily, I turned on him. 'That's my mate they've killed, and I'll fucking have the bastards for it.'

Placing a hand on my rifle and pulling it gently away, he responded with compassion and authority.

'And I'm happy to let you when the time is right. But that time isn't now, so I'm telling you again, stand down.' Pausing, he smiled sympathetically. 'Take a breath and walk away, son. Get yourself a cup of tea and ask the sergeant for a drop of medicine in it.'

I knew he was referring to the bottle of whisky the sergeant kept for occasions such as this; when a soldier had been badly wounded, or his nerves were shot by something he'd witnessed. I nodded my understanding.

'Yes, sir. Thank you, sir.'

The captain knew how close Arthur and I had grown. Also, how popular he was with the rest of our troop; always ready with a quip or playful jibe to lift our spirits when things were tough.

'He was a good soldier, as were the other lads. And the best way we can honour them is to stay strong and make sure we win this war.'

Forcing a smile, I turned to walk away. 'Yes, sir.'

The next few days witnessed a ferocious intensity in the fighting, with less than a few yards gained or lost on either side. This, despite the increasing and entirely disproportionate loss of human life. Although there was little opportunity to focus on anything other than fighting and survival, I did find time to think about Arthur and how quickly and deeply our relationship had grown. Obviously, much of this was down to the war itself, where friendships could be struck up and ended within a day. At least Arthur and I had enjoyed each other's company for a few weeks, and the memories of our time together would stay with me for the rest of my life, however long that might be.

Reflecting on our camaraderie reminded me of the other great friendship in my life. Although Karl and I had enjoyed many more adventures together over a far longer period than in my time spent with Arthur, our relationship had ended in equally dramatic fashion. I hadn't really thought about it before but, it suddenly occurred to me that far from being my friend, Karl was now my enemy, although on a personal level I certainly didn't consider him to be my foe. The more I thought about our relationship, certainly in the early days before the tragic death of baby Billy, the more I remembered what fun we'd had. I looked at my hand, still carrying the faint scar from the day we'd become blood brothers, declaring our undying loyalty towards one another. I hoped Karl was safe and hadn't been killed in this terrible conflict. I wondered if he'd even joined up to fight, or whether he'd stayed at home to care for his mum. The one thing I did know, and prayed would never happen, was for the two of us to face each other in battle. It was a horror I couldn't and wouldn't countenance.

About a week after Arthur died, and with my mood still dark from his passing, I received a welcome boost from home, a letter from Irene. It arrived in a bag of mail, delivered by another group of reinforcements sent out to bolster our numbers on the front.

I was on sniper duty and spent the whole day with Irene's letter burning a hole in my pocket, waiting to be read. My mind raced as I considered what she might have to say regarding life in our little cottage without me, and how things were with our families. I was also interested to know if she had received any of the letters I'd written to her, Mum, and Edith, as I hadn't heard from any of them for a few weeks.

When writing home, we rarely referred to friends and colleagues who'd been wounded or killed in the fighting. We didn't want to place that image in their heads, nor the thought that we might be the next to die. Much of what we talked about would be the food rations and how we missed proper home cooking or being able to wear something more comfortable than our itchy woollen uniforms. How we yearned for the simple things like putting on a pair of slippers, rather than having to live in our boots and puttees wrapped around our lower legs. These were usually sodden from the water that lay at the bottom of the trenches, meaning our feet were almost never properly dry. This caused some of the lads to develop trench foot which, during the winter months, would be exacerbated by the freezing conditions, adding frostbite to the growing list of medical complaints to be treated. Considering all we endured in those mud-filled ditches, it was amazing how a simple letter from home could help boost a chap's morale. It served as a reminder there was still some sanity left in the world, along with friends and family who were missing us and praying for our safe return. I'm sure our letters to them were received with equal enthusiasm, but I'm not certain they could ever truly appreciate just how much even a simple kiss marked at the bottom of a page meant to a soldier when all around him were death and destruction.

When, at last, it was my turn to take a break I dashed back to my bunk to grab a cup of tea and spend a few precious minutes studying the contents of Irene's letter.

It was good to hear she *had* been receiving my news, and that all was well at home. Everyone had asked her to pass on their love and good wishes. I read each sentence twice to fully absorb what she was saying, and to focus on the style and detail of her writing. Irene had a way with words, always grammatically correct and presented far neater than my own. As I looked down at the cream-coloured sheet of paper, I was reminded that just a short while ago it had been held by her. That thought alone brought me closer to my beautiful wife, along with the scent of her perfume hanging faintly in the air. Holding the paper close to my nose, I inhaled deeply and whispered, 'I miss you.' As I turned the page and took a drink from my cup, my heart skipped a beat as I read the words in front of me, declaring Irene was pregnant! I could hardly believe it and reread the line again to make sure there was no mistake. I was going to be a father.

Suddenly, I was lost to all that was going on around me; my mind focused entirely on the words leaping up to greet me with their joyous news from the letter gripped tightly in my hand. She said she had missed her monthly, but hadn't spoken to her parents, presuming, initially, this might be because she'd not been sleeping well due to her concerns about my welfare since leaving for the front. However, one morning she had been physically ill and felt she should mention it to her mother just in case she was coming down with some form of bug or sickness. She said Betty had suspected Irene might be pregnant after she'd explained her symptoms but suggested a visit to the doctor to be on the safe side. They went to see their family practitioner, Doctor Morrison, who, after a few tests and brief examination, was pleased to confirm Irene was indeed expecting our baby.

Tears filled my eyes as I read this section of the letter over again; Irene and I were to become parents. I wanted nothing more than to take her in my arms and tell her how much I loved her. I prayed the war would end immediately, allowing me to return home and be at the birth of my child as he or she entered the world. As I sat, lost in thought at the prospect of becoming a father, and in how much I wanted to be with Irene, the captain entered.

'How are you doing, Thompson? It's been a rough period these past few days, and I'm still aware of you losing your mate, Half Pint. He was a good man to have around. I know how close the two of you were. Are you feeling any better in yourself?'

I was struck by a sudden pang of guilt. Here I was overjoyed at hearing that Irene was pregnant, while Arthur's wife and family would be receiving the worst possible news, that he had been killed in action. Even so, I couldn't help but smile as I considered the prospect of becoming a father. Perhaps I was being selfish, but it wasn't intended. I looked up to face the captain.

'Yes, thank you, sir. Just had some good news from home.' I raised Irene's letter aloft. 'I'm going to have a baby.'

The captain laughed. 'Well, that'll be a first. I've seen some strange things out here over the past few months, but I've never had one of my lads pregnant before.'

Realising what I'd said, I smiled and shook my head. 'Sorry, sir. I meant my wife and I are going to have a baby. She's just told me in her letter.'

'I think I'd worked that out for myself, Thompson. Congratulations. Let that serve as an incentive for you to keep your head down and survive this lot. Then you can get yourself home and look to be a proper father to the little one. I've got a boy of my own, and I'm looking forward to seeing him again as soon as this fighting is over.' Stepping back to leave, he smiled once more. 'Congratulations again, Thompson. Give my best to your wife when you next write home.'

'I will do, sir. Thank you, sir.'

I watched as he walked away, my thoughts still torn between joy and sorrow as I considered how Arthur's family would be feeling at the news of his death. Attempting to reconcile the disparity in my thinking I decided, if we had a boy, I would ask Irene if we might name him after my friend. If she agreed, we could then tell Arthur's family in the hope it might offer them some small measure of comfort knowing we'd done it to honour his memory. Smiling to myself as I finished my tea, I read Irene's letter again.

Chapter Nineteen

As Christmas approached my thoughts turned increasingly to Irene and the discussion we'd had before I'd left about being apart for the yuletide festivities. It had been difficult enough to reconcile not being together so early on in our marriage but now, with her expecting our baby, the distance between us and my desire to be at home felt even greater. All the lads were missing their families and wrote home whenever they could, praying their letters would arrive in time for Christmas. With so many losses on both sides we had no way of knowing whether we would still be alive if and when they did get there. That said, we still felt a strange form of catharsis in knowing, even if the worst did happen, our wives, girlfriends, and families would know they had been uppermost in our thoughts when the end came.

With little more than a few hundred yards between us and the German lines, we could often hear them shouting at each other as, no doubt, they could us. It made the fighting feel even more senseless in a way, with each side seeking to gain control of a small patch of barren land, and with little more than a few yards being gained or lost each day. The human cost on both sides by comparison felt entirely out of all proportion. Often, white flags would be raised to allow opposing troops to venture out and retrieve the dead or wounded before another onslaught began. In the main these brief truces were respected by both sides, but could never be guaranteed, as had been the case with Arthur. Of course, we believed in good triumphing over evil, but the constant shelling and butchery began to tell in ways that would be difficult to describe to anyone not directly involved with such endless carnage. A number of the lads, especially the younger ones, began to lose their nerve after weeks holed up in a trench, being bombed and shot at for days on end. Some even made a run for it, not that there was anywhere to go; it was just they couldn't take any more. Once fear consumes your mind so completely you lose all sense of rationale and reason.

We had already heard of one young lad from the 1st Battalion of the Royal West Kents, Private Thomas Highgate, who had been executed for desertion a couple of months earlier. He was just nineteen and had been fighting at Mons when he lost his mind, brought on by the endless fighting and horrific living conditions. With nowhere to run he was soon returned to face his commanders who decided to make an example of the young recruit by having him shot in front of his comrades to deter the others from attempting a similar dereliction of duty. One of our boys was also shot for desertion after seeing his friend blown apart by a mortar. Terrified, he just threw down his rifle and ran. We were all ordered to attend the execution, presumably to teach us the same lesson as Private Highgate's troop. All it did for me was to make me question the sense in my having signed up in the first place. It also confirmed my determination to get home to Irene as soon as I could. We all stood to attention as they put a blindfold over the young soldier's eyes and tied him to a post. His body shook with fear as they pinned a card over his heart with a red mark on it. Asked if he had any last words before a volley of shots ended his short life; all he could utter was that he was sorry, and would someone tell his mum and dad he loved them.

Many of us went to bed that night hating our commanders as much as the Germans. Yes, we understood we were fighting a war, and that we were expected to kill the enemy, but to execute one of our own simply because he panicked in the face of unutterable horror was a step too far for most of us; it certainly was for me. In the few short weeks I'd been on the front, my view regarding war and its apparent total disregard for the sanctity of life had been challenged forever. I knew these thoughts and ideals were ones I could never openly share with Irene. Having vowed never to have secrets between us again, I was aware this was a pledge I would not be able to keep, not if I wanted to protect her from the brutal and unspeakable slaughter I'd witnessed in battle.

As Christmas arrived a seemingly bizarre event occurred. During one of the many treks into no man's land to retrieve the dead and injured, soldiers from both sides approached each other, shook hands, and talked with one another, as best as language differences would allow. Commanders from both camps met and agreed a short truce to commemorate the season. Almost immediately, opposing forces laid down their weapons and the air became hauntingly still. For the first time in as long as I could remember, and without the relentless barrage of gunfire and shelling, I heard the birdsong of a sparrow. With this brief respite in hostilities these hardy little birds made a brief return to the land that was traditionally considered their home. There was little prospect of them finding any food, with all vegetation, trees, and greenery absent from the wasteland laid bare before them. That said, their cheery call served as a catalyst to encourage both British and German soldiers to leave the questionable safety of their trenches. Men from both sides tentatively approached one another and began to embrace, sharing stories about home, loved ones, and how much they all wanted the war to end. Soldiers don't start wars, politicians do. All we do is follow orders. And if that means killing other human beings, no matter how costly or senseless that might appear, then so be it, at least in their eyes.

As the day went on, fires were lit, with food and drink being shared on both sides. It felt surreal to be exchanging refreshments, stories, and gifts with men who up until a few hours ago we had been seeking to wipe from the face of the earth. As we talked it became obvious that, apart from a few hotheads on both sides, most of us had no desire to be fighting, and wished we could be at home with our families. War, it appeared, made as little sense to the young German soldiers as it did to our boys.

As I wandered across the barren space between our two camps thinking about Irene and how much I wished we could be together, my thoughts were distracted by a voice I recognised. Turning to my left, I saw one of our lads talking with a young German soldier. They were sitting on the shattered remnants of a tree that had been blown apart during the fighting. The two of them were in animated conversation, with the German lad speaking in near perfect English. It was Karl. Shaking my head in disbelief, I stopped and stared at the two of them. Could it really be him, my best friend and blood brother who I hadn't seen since he and his mum had returned to Hamburg?

Struggling to believe it really was Karl, even though he was sat in front of me, I moved forward. As I approached, he became aware of my presence and looked up. With equal shock and surprise, he smiled.

'Harry?'

'Karl, it *is* you.'

The other soldier looked on, shaking his head. 'Do you two know each other?'

We both laughed, with me the first to respond. 'Do we? This is my best friend.'

Looking confused, he took a step back. 'Your best friend? But he's a German. I don't understand.'

'We grew up together in London when we were younger, before he went back to Germany.'

'And you're best friends?'

Getting to his feet, Karl nodded. 'We were, but it has been a while. And now the war is here, so things have changed. But it is good to see you, Harry.'

Shaking his head again, the soldier moved to leave. 'Still not sure I understand, but I'll leave you to it.'

Karl and I watched as he walked away before offering each other our hands. Not content with a simple handshake, I pulled Karl into me and hugged him. His reaction to my embrace was less effusive, but I presumed this to be from the shock of suddenly seeing me again. Whatever his response, it felt good to hold him and be in his company again.

'I can't believe it's actually you. I thought I'd never see you again; certainly not here. How are you?'

Releasing my hand, he indicated for me to sit next to him. 'I am well, although for how much longer if this war continues, I do not know. And you?'

I was excited at seeing my friend again but could tell he was struggling in our conversation which, at one time, would have felt natural and relaxed. Perhaps it was the war. I needed to know. 'I'm fine. Are you really okay, Karl? I feel like there's a distance between us.'

'We are at war, Harry, is that not a reason for some distance?'

'Our countries are at war, but you and I aren't. At least I hope not. I know we weren't getting along too well when you and your mum left, but I still like to think of you as my friend. That's not wrong, is it?'

'It is not wrong, I agree. But as you say, this was before Mama and I returned to Hamburg. We have not been friends for a while.'

It was true. Apart from me writing the occasional letter, Karl and I had not really kept in touch. Our friendship had become something of a faded memory; certainly, for him it appeared. I was grateful for this opportunity to renew our relationship, even if it was under the most unlikely of circumstances.

'And I'm sorry about that, I truly am. I did write a few times but never got a reply.'

'Yes, I received your letters, but never felt I wanted to answer them.' Pausing, he looked at me thoughtfully before continuing. 'We were very young when we met, Harry, but even then we were different. You were never as competitive as me, never as ambitious, perhaps? Remember, my father brought us to England to find new work after the strike in Germany. He was determined to make a good life for us, while your father settled for what he had, and for the drink he would buy with his wages. I didn't notice these differences in our families at first but, as we grew, I began to feel a prejudice against Papa and his work ethic. Your father used to complain that Papa was always given the better shifts, when really it was because he wanted the best for Mama and me. He wanted to work. Your father spent most of his time in the pub.'

Whilst I couldn't argue with what Karl was saying, it felt no less hurtful to hear it relayed in such stark terms, especially from him.

'I can't really disagree with that, at least the part about Dad. But why should that affect how you and I feel about each other? We never fell out over our family differences when we were small. I've wondered many times over the years what happened to cause the rift between us as we grew older.'

'I used to feel sorry for you, Harry. When you came to my home and Mama would feed you because you had little to eat in your own house. I thought she was being kind, but I have learned over time that it was because your mother was weak and should have stood up to your father or left him. Then maybe things would have been different for you and Edith.'

'That's not fair. Yes, I was grateful when your mum fed me, and yes, Edith and I often went hungry because Dad spent his money at The Blue Anchor, but I didn't come to your house for food. I came to your house because my friend lived there.'

'And I was happy to be your friend also, but as I got older, I could see that your father and the other men at the dock resented Papa. I thought perhaps they were jealous of him, but could never understand why. But then, when he was crushed by that pallet and nobody helped him, I realised it wasn't jealousy, it was prejudice. It was because he was German.'

'That's not true,' I countered, seeking to defend Dad and the others who had been there on the day, even though I knew Dad had never been a fan of Gustav's.

'I think it is, Harry. I don't remember many people asking us to stay when Mama and I decided to move back to Hamburg.'

'Mum did. She was always fond of you both, you know that.'

Nodding, he pursed his lips. 'Yes, that much is true. Your mother was a good woman but, like I say, she was weak.'

Irritated by his continued accusation about Mum's strength, and knowing how much she had suffered over the years when trying to protect Edith and I from the worst of Dad's drunken assaults, I got to my feet.

'That's the second time you've said that about Mum, and it's just not fair. She took more beatings from Dad than any woman deserved, especially when trying to protect Edith and me.'

'And as I also have said before, she should have left him.'

That I couldn't argue with. Edith and I had spoken many times as children about how we wished Mum had left. I also didn't want to fall out with Karl again. Conscious of this, I took my seat next to him once more, offering a conciliatory pat on the back as I did so.

'Sorry, mate, I didn't mean to have a go at you, but it really isn't fair to talk about Mum like that; not when I know how much she put up with to keep our family together. Anyway, right now, I'm more interested to know what happened to the two of us.' I pointed to the faint scar on my hand and laughed. 'We even became blood brothers to seal our friendship.'

Displaying his own faint scar and rubbing it with his finger, he nodded. 'These scars are much of the reason I lost faith in our friendship.' He smiled laconically at me. 'If you remember, we swore we would never lie to each other or betray one another when we cut ourselves.'

Not entirely sure where this conversation was headed, I nodded my agreement. 'I do.'

'And yet, you told Irene about our pact, and about what we had done with that baby; Billy, I think was his name. You told me that in one of your letters. And I'm still not convinced Irene chose you over me in the way you described when we made that bet about asking her out.'

'Well, she did.' I smiled. 'I can't help it if she found me better-looking than you.' Karl looked straight at me, without a flicker of response to my attempt at humour. Deciding not to engage in another disagreement, I continued.

'Anyway, I also made that same promise to Irene, never to have any secrets from each other. And what you and I did has always bothered me, blood brothers or not. I had to tell her, to tell someone, it was eating me up.'

Karl shook his head. 'You see, Harry, you are also like your mother; weak. We didn't kill that baby; it was an accident, but you have made it into something else.'

'An accident caused by us taking that wooden stop from under the wheel,' I retorted, unable to defend our actions any longer.

'Perhaps, but we agreed never to speak of it to anyone else, and you did. You broke the vow we had made together in blood. What sort of friend would do that?'

Frustrated, I snapped back, 'The sort of friend who doesn't want to lie, and cares about the truth.'

'Even if that truth damages more than just their friendship. What if Billy's mother found out that truth, as you call it? Would she be so ready to understand as I presume Irene was when you told her?'

Turning away, I looked to the ground, wishing we'd never started this conversation. I realised, if I *was* going to honour our agreement and be honest with each other I had to come clean about the other conversations I'd had before leaving for the front. Taking a deep breath and exhaling slowly, I raised my gaze to meet Karl's.

'I did tell her, and the police.'

'What do you mean? About what happened that day?'

'Yes. I spoke about it with Irene after I'd signed up to join the army. We… I, decided I couldn't come away leaving Mrs White not knowing the truth about what we'd done. But I also realised, if I did tell her the truth, I would need to speak to the police as well. If I didn't, there was every possibility she would tell them, and I would have to speak to them in the end anyway.'

A look of confusion spread across Karl's face. 'Are you saying you told his mother what we did? That we removed the block from under the wheel?'

'Yes. I spoke to the police first who said that as we were very young at the time, there wasn't much they could physically charge us with. They said I would have to carry the burden of guilt with me for the rest of my life but, as we were children when it happened, legally, it would prove difficult to make a case against us. We would probably have been too young to be sent to borstal. They also recognised we hadn't done it with any real intention of wanting to harm Billy. It was more as we'd told them in that first interview, a tragic accident that had gone terribly wrong, even if the circumstances differed from those in our initial account. They also said, as I'd just signed up, the country would be better served by me fighting than spending time behind bars for something I'd never intended to happen. Don't get me wrong, they read me the riot act, and insisted on being there when I spoke to Mrs White.'

Shaking his head, Karl continued to stare at me. 'I cannot believe you did this. Are you stupid?'

'No. In fact, difficult though it was to make my confession, I felt better for having done it. I've always regretted the events of that day, still do. But to speak it out, to confess my sin if you like, has had a cleansing effect on me. I may still carry the guilt for my part in what we did, but at least I don't have to keep that terrible secret anymore, if that makes sense?'

Karl took a packet of cigarettes from his pocket and, placing one between his lips, held the packet towards me.

'No thank you, I don't smoke.'

Lighting his cigarette and taking a long draw on it, he nodded. 'I didn't smoke either until I arrived here. It helps settle my nerves. Not fear you understand, I do not get scared. I just feel disturbed at times, and this is one of those occasions.' The ash on the end of his cigarette turned a bright orangey red as he sucked hard on it. 'I do not understand what you say about your feelings of guilt, Harry. I have never felt any guilt about what happened. It was an accident and that is all there is to it. Why should I feel guilty about it?'

'Because a baby died, and we were responsible.'

Taking the cigarette from his lips and gesticulating with it towards our surroundings, he said, 'And we both kill men every day in this hell-hole of a place; do you feel guilty about that as well?'

'That's different, this is war. Billy didn't deserve to die. He was just a defenceless baby.'

'So, what are you saying, that all these soldiers here *do* deserve to die?'

'No, of course not, but soldiers *do* get killed in war. Babies don't expect to die sleeping in their prams.'

'And there are men here, on both sides, who will never see their babies again because of this war. Will their wives and girlfriends find any more comfort in knowing their men died on a battlefield than in an accident at home? I think not, Harry.'

As he spoke a shudder ran through me as I recalled Irene's letter telling me I was to become a father. What if I were to be killed in the fighting? What greater comfort would she find in knowing my death had been caused by a German bullet or shell, as opposed to some terrible accident at home? Perhaps, her grief would be even more intense thinking of my body blown to pieces in a foreign field, with no opportunity to bury me or say goodbye. I was confused. Whilst I couldn't agree with Karl's argument that I'd done wrong in confessing my part in causing Billy's death, I also couldn't contend his assertion that Irene would be any less traumatised by my death on the battlefield. I watched as he finished his cigarette, saddened our friendship had deteriorated to such an extent. It appeared we were now opponents on all fronts. Suddenly a voice from behind broke the silence between us. It was Corporal Matthews from my troop.

'Come on, Thompson, we're gonna play football.'

I shook my head in disbelief. 'Football, here? It's a mudbath.'

'We've played in worse at home. Anyway, we're gonna clear the ground a bit. Both sides are up for it. The captain's been talking to his opposition, and they've agreed to a game. They're talking about a campfire later, singing some carols and having a few drinks. It'll be almost like Christmas at home. The only difference being, I won't be getting any earache from my missus. Come on, you like a game of football. Said you were pretty good before you came out here.'

Karl laughed as he watched the corporal walk away. 'Football. Our countries are at war, but we are to play football. Still, it is another chance for me to prove again I am better than you.'

'Perhaps, but at least if we're kicking a ball together it's better than trying to kill each other. I hate this bloody war.'

'Sometimes fighting is a necessary evil, if you are to win for a greater good.'

Whilst I still held a deep affection for Karl, I couldn't defend the obvious political inference he was alluding to. 'That depends whose side you're on.'

We held each other's gaze momentarily, realising no matter how close we'd been as boys, life and times had moved on; the world had changed and our relationship along with it. Could it be repaired; did we even want it to be? I wasn't sure but was relieved that for the next couple of hours we could step back in time and engage with each other once again as we had as young boys, on the football field.

It felt bizarre to be working with the German soldiers, dressed in their *feldgrau* uniforms alongside our boys clad in khaki, in clearing the ground along no man's land in preparation for a game of football. Both sides readily welcomed the opportunity to lay down their weapons and embrace a few hours' peace. Perhaps we weren't at home with our loved ones, but for this brief moment the unifying message of Christmas and all it embodied never felt more real to us. Karl and I worked together, laying out greatcoats from both sides at each end of the pitch to act as goalposts. We laughed as we attempted to outdo the other by placing our troops' coat at the top of the pile in an effort to display some early domination in the game. However, once we kicked off, Karl quickly reverted to his former self, tackling without quarter or respect for the opposition. One poor bloke on our side had to be taken off with a suspected dislocated shoulder after a particularly stiff challenge by Karl. This was witnessed by a couple of lads playing for us who sandwiched him between them in a tackle soon after, causing him to limp for the rest of the first half.

I smiled knowingly at him. This wasn't just the two of us having a kick-about on the wasteland at the top of our road, this was two opposing factions playing for more than just a bit of fun. That said, the spirit between both sides was open and, in the main, good-humoured. We had all had enough of the endless shelling and smell of cordite filling our lungs. We learnt later, similar games to ours had been played along the front between the Allies and the Germans. We also heard that several of the military hierarchy on both sides hadn't been impressed by these so-called 'Christmas truces', but for those of us doing battle in the trenches they came as a welcome relief.

The game itself ended in a three-all draw, with both teams happy to accept the result, despite the very real effort by each side to win. Soldiers from both camps trudged off the pitch slapping each other heartily on the back, laughing together as if they had just played a game at home. The difference here being that each player wore a military uniform declaring allegiance to their country and cause rather than their local team. Even so, for this brief period, all thoughts of war and fighting had been placed to one side. The rest of the afternoon was spent drinking and exchanging small gifts as a further sign of harmony between us. A varied assortment of bottles appeared, all downed with relish, along with a constant supply of jacket potatoes that were placed in braziers built alongside the trenches. As the light faded and snow began to fall again, both sides came together to sing carols. We may not have spoken the same language, but the tunes were familiar to all. Each side sang out lustily, as if hoping their voices would be carried across the land and sea to the ears of those they loved and missed the most.

During the evening, Karl and I spoke about our childhood again, and how our lives had changed since we'd last spent time together. I told him Irene and I were now married and that she was pregnant, but I could tell his mind was elsewhere. He was still struggling with my having spoken to the police and Mrs White about what happened to Billy. To me, it felt as if God had given us this opportunity to heal the wound between us. I desperately wanted to give him a hug, but recognised Karl felt differently. It upset me to think at some point in the next few hours we would become enemies once more; taking up arms against each other again, with this brief respite having passed without us having settled our differences. The more I struggled with these thoughts the harder it became for me to reconcile the rights and wrongs regarding this or any war. We were all young men who, for now, were laughing and drinking together; each of us desperate to be at home with the ones we loved. And yet, because of historical and political differences between our two countries, we would instead seek to obliterate one another from the face of the earth again in just a few hours' time.

Word went round that from seven o'clock the following morning hostilities would recommence between us. Men on both sides shook hands and exchanged last toasts together before returning to their opposing battle lines. I sought out Karl once more, determined to make a final effort to heal the rift between us. Taking him to one side, I offered my hand.

'It has been good to see you again my friend, despite the circumstances. And I call you friend because, for all our differences, both now and in the past, I am truly grateful for the time we spent together, and for the fun and memories we shared along the way. I never meant to betray you, Karl, or the oath we took, by sharing what we did with Irene and the others. If you think I was weak, then I am happy to accept that. But please, don't think I did it to hurt you, or to damage our relationship. Whatever you think of me now, I want you to know you were my dearest friend as a boy growing up. What we had together will stay with me for the rest of my life.'

Shaking my hand firmly and smiling, he nodded. 'I still can't agree that you did the right thing in telling what we did but, if it helps, I forgive you. I too have happy memories of being your friend when we were young, although, as I have said, they are coloured by what happened when my father was killed. Also, in how others reacted to his death. I cannot forgive how your father was, and in the things he said about Papa. Perhaps that is why I have found it hard to stay as your friend. But I am shaking your hand now, Harry, as a sign that you and I are not enemies, whatever happens in this war. Yes, you will be my friend again, I think. Who knows, if we both survive, maybe we can meet again and talk through all that has happened between us.'

My eyes misted over as I gripped his arm with my other hand. 'I would like that, Karl. I would like that very much. Please give my love to your mother next time you write to her. Tell her how grateful I am for all the times she cared for me.' I laughed. 'And fed me.'

Squeezing my hand in a genuine show of affection, he nodded again. 'I will, Harry. And you say hello to your mother and Edith from me. And to Irene of course. It will be interesting to think of you as a father. Maybe if we see each other again after the war I will meet your baby? That would be nice.'

Whilst we hadn't fully rebuilt our relationship, we had made a start. At least Karl was speaking to me again and had forgiven me for what he had seen as some form of betrayal. I felt safe in calling him a friend again, and hoped he would come to feel the same way once this awful war was over. We gripped each other's hands once more, grinning at one another affectionately.

'Goodbye, Harry.'

'Goodbye, Karl. I hope we…'

Withdrawing his hand and shaking his head, he interrupted. 'Let us not say anything more. Tomorrow we will fight again, but today we are not. Let that be enough.'

He was right of course. Neither of us could make promises we couldn't keep, at least not until the war was over. I took a breath and smiled as he turned to leave.

'Goodbye, my friend. I presume I can say that much?'

Returning my smile and waving, he moved away. 'Goodbye, friend.'

And with that he was gone. Tears filled my eyes as I watched him walk into the gloom across no man's land towards his trench. The snow was falling more heavily now in a stiffening breeze which caused me to shiver slightly as the chill winter air ran across my body. As Karl disappeared from view my body trembled again. This time the cause of the tremor was not due to the weather, but rather the veracity of what he had intimated a few moments earlier. *'Today we are friends, tomorrow we will be enemies again.'* Could it be true that young men on both sides who, just a few hours earlier, had been playing football together and sharing stories of home and mutual family concerns, would soon be seeking to annihilate one another again in the name of some supposed greater cause? It was a prospect I found hard to countenance as I turned and made my way slowly back to the confines of my mud-filled dugout.

Chapter Twenty

I slept badly that night, tossing and turning on my bunk, with thoughts of Karl and all we had shared earlier running through my head. It felt good to have found him again, even in the most unlikely and unwelcoming of surroundings. I felt a sense of personal closure in having been given the opportunity to tell him about my confession to all parties regarding the tragic death of baby Billy. Further, that he had forgiven me and was willing to call me his friend again. Yes, things were different now, we were different, but neither could deny the depth and intensity of our relationship as youngsters growing up together in Canning Town. They were special times. And, to the greater extent, I looked back on them with genuine affection. My hope, now we had cleared the air between us, was that Karl would be able to embrace our reunion with equal fondness. As I lay there mulling over all that had transpired between the two of us across the years, my thoughts turned to Irene. I offered up a silent prayer of thanks that she had chosen me rather than succumb to Karl's early advances. Life without my beautiful Irene seemed unimaginable when I considered all we had achieved in the short time we'd been together. And now, with a baby on the way, our future appeared assured. I couldn't wait to get home and tell her about my meeting with Karl. She, more than anyone, would understand how difficult our parting had been for me following his return to Hamburg.

Despite the early morning cold and damp I felt a warm glow settle within as I thanked God once more for Irene, our baby, and the return of my dearest friend into my life. Thoughts about how blessed I was were abruptly interrupted by the sound of a trumpet call, along with the voice of our sergeant major barking out for us to rise and shine.

'Come on, you idle lot, let's be having you. There's a war to be fought and Jerry won't be waiting around because you fancy another half hour in your pit.'

Suddenly, all reflections on events from the previous day, along with thoughts of Irene and home were dashed as the harsh reality of the imminent renewal of hostilities took precedence in my mind. As seven o'clock approached and dawn began to break, I looked across the stretch of land which, less than twenty-four hours earlier, had played host to a game of football. I smiled as I recalled how soldiers from both sides had exchanged yuletide wishes and token presents as a sign of peace and goodwill towards one another, depicting the real meaning of Christmas. But now, as I stared across the snow-covered patch of ground once more, with its barbed wire fencing and barriers back in place, the events from the day before felt like a distant memory. And one that was shattered entirely as seven o'clock arrived, along with the first mortar round fired from the German lines. It exploded just a few feet from our trench, sending earth and sheaths of red-hot shrapnel hurtling towards us.

'Heads down, men,' the captain shouted as we ducked in sync to avoid becoming the first casualties of the day. Within minutes bullets and shells were being exchanged across the divide once more as each side attempted to make up for lost time following the brief peace initiative of the day before. With the German mortars and larger shells finding their mark with increasing accuracy, it was decided a section of our troop would attempt to rush the other side. The hope being, to get close enough to toss a grenade at their mortar operators. We all knew it was little more than a suicide mission, with virtually no chance of success; but unless we tried, the superior firepower of the German artillery would eventually account for us all. Something had to be done, and there were plenty of hands went up when volunteers for the mission were requested. Most knew they might not survive, but the thought of saving their mates or the vague hope that, if only wounded, they might be sent home was enough to encourage them to step forward.

No sooner had the first group made their ascent up the rough wooden ladders than a machine gun from the other side rattled out its murderous cry, spitting out its deadly intent towards our boys. As a sniper it was my role to try and get a shot at the machine-gun operator and take him out. If successful, it would give our boys a better chance at making the crossing. But, with all the smoke and early morning mist swirling around it was nigh on impossible for me to see my target, let alone get a clear shot away. I needed to be closer. With the horrendous loss of life continuing above ground and some of our lads turning tail and jumping back into the trench, something had to be done, and quickly. The captain called me over.

'Listen, Thompson, if we throw everything we've got at them for a couple of minutes, do you think you could make it to that large crater fifty yards further up to the right? If you can get there you might get a better shot at that bastard who's blasting our lads into eternity on that bloody machine gun. If we don't take him out, the chances are they'll overrun us, especially with those mortars coming in. They've pretty much got our range now.'

A shudder of nervous energy and adrenaline ran through me. Much as I didn't want to expose myself to the fiery hell being rained down upon us, I equally knew the captain was right. Without taking out that machine-gun post we were pretty much doomed to destruction. Rubbing my sweat-soaked palms together, I nodded my understanding and agreed to the captain's proposal.

'Of course, sir. I'll give it a go.'

'Good lad. Get your rifle and some extra ammo. You never know, with any luck you might be able to take out one or two more of them while you're at it.'

'I'll do my best, sir.'

'Well done.' Holding his whistle aloft, he smiled. 'On my signal, all right?'

'Yes, sir.'

Grabbing an extra case of shells and checking the sights on my rifle, I hurried to the farthest ladder to the right at the end of the trench. Despite the cold, I could feel perspiration running from beneath my helmet and down the side of my face as I waited for the order to go. I watched as the captain organised the additional cover further down the dugout. Putting my rifle strap over my shoulder I placed a foot at the bottom rung of the ladder ready to make my ascent. One of the other Tommies reached out and touched my leg.

'Give that bugger what for, Harry. Fucking Germans. They played dirty yesterday and they're at it again today with that bloody machine gun of theirs.'

Forcing a smile as I waited for the signal to go, I nodded. 'I'll try, mate. You just make sure you cover my arse while I'm up there, otherwise we're all in the shit.'

'Be my pleasure,' he replied, waving his gun at me.

Looking back down the trench, I saw the captain put the whistle to his lips. Chewing on the leather strap of my helmet, I offered up a silent prayer that I might make it there and back in one piece.

Blowing hard on his whistle, the captain gesticulated for me to make my move. As I clambered up the makeshift wooden ladder I became aware of a thunderous explosion of noise as our boys threw everything we had at the German lines. In a moment of shocked surprise at the ferocity of our attack their firing eased for a few seconds. It was enough time for me to make it to the crater. Throwing myself into the snow-filled hollow I fell on my rifle, winding myself in the process. My brief curse at the sharp pain I felt to my ribs quickly turned to thanks as I realised I'd made it to my vantage point without being directly targeted or hit. The wet mud and snow soaked through my uniform as I lay for a moment regaining my breath and equilibrium. Having recovered their own composure following the brief blitzkrieg from our lads, the Germans began their lethal response. Gunfire and mortars rained down on our side of the barricades once more as their weapons spewed out their message of death. Having waited a few seconds to ascertain if any of the shelling was being directed towards me personally and realising it wasn't, I raised my head towards the rim of the crater. Although there was still a lot of smoke in the air, I had a much better line of sight to the machine-gun post and its operator. I reached for my binoculars to gain a clearer view of my intended target and of any additional assistance he might have that I would need to take out as well. There didn't appear to be any immediate support close by and so I turned my gaze directly towards the shooter himself. As he came into focus my heart missed a beat. It was Karl.

My worst nightmare was about to be realised. My dearest friend who I thought I'd lost, only to rediscover yesterday was, as he had intimated during our short reunion, once more my enemy. It was now a case of kill or be killed. I knew, without a shadow of doubt, following our conversation yesterday and from earlier exchanges during our childhood, Karl would never back down from a fight. And there could be no greater conflict than the one we were both currently engaged in. I also remembered the oath we had taken as young boys to protect one another, even if it cost us our own lives in doing so.

As I lay there battling my thoughts, along with the action I had agreed to take in order to save the lives of my comrades in arms, a loud whistle blew. I turned to see our lads pouring over the top once more in an effort to draw the fire and attention of the one German soldier I was supposed to kill; Karl. Tears began to mist my eyes as I brought my 303 up beside me. How could I end the life of my best friend, my blood brother; but how could I not if my troop was to have any chance of survival? As bullets flew on both sides a rogue mortar shell landed near to my foxhole, exploding just a few feet from my position, sending mud and shrapnel flying in all directions. My head spun as the impact from the blast took my breath away. I felt a loud reverberation in my ears from the proximity of the shell landing so close. I could see our lads falling under the relentless firing from Karl's machine gun. I had to act. I moved to draw my rifle into position, but my left arm didn't respond. I looked down to see I had taken a hit to the shoulder from a piece of shrapnel from the mortar. It was only now with my head clearing from the initial shock of the mortar exploding that I became aware of my injury. Blood was flowing freely from the wound and my arm hung limply at my side. Panic and pain ran through me in equal measure as I dragged my rifle into position with my right hand. I had to take the shot before I drifted into unconsciousness; a state which threatened to consume me at any moment as my head began to spin once more.

Taking a deep breath, I pointed the rifle directly at Karl and took aim along the sight. Pausing only to apologise, I squeezed the trigger. 'I'm so sorry.'

Instantly, the machine gun fell silent and a cheer from our lads went up as they rushed forward breaching the German defences. The sound of rifle fire and men on both sides yelling and screaming as they met their end or delivered it to another filled the air. I fell back into the crater, my job done, and my heart broken.

As I lay there thinking about Karl, my body shivered. I was cold and could feel my senses drifting away from me. Was this to be the end for me as well? A form of poetic justice perhaps. Having sworn an oath to defend each other so many years before, were our lives to end together here in a similar pact? I coughed and felt the taste of blood in my mouth. I didn't want to die in this godforsaken field. I'd promised Irene I'd return home safely. Breathing more slowly as the energy drained from me, I prayed. *'Please Lord, let me live. Let me hold Irene again, and our baby. Let him or her know their father.'*

As my vision dimmed and darkness drew in around me, I heard a voice.

'Bloody good shooting, Harry. You got the bugger. Just hang in there, mate, and we'll get you back to base.'

I felt arms raising me up. Whether they were human or celestial I didn't know, but a feeling of peace washed over me as I drifted into unconsciousness.